DANGEROUS MEN

FORTUNE CITY MAFIA
BOOK 1

EVELYN WARD

Copyright © 2025

All rights reserved.

No part of this book may be reproduced in any form or by any electronic or mechanical means, including information and retrieval systems, without written permission from the author, except for the use of brief quotations in a book review.

No AI use or training: Without in any way limiting the author's [and publisher's] exclusive rights under copyright, any use of this publication to "train" generative artificial intelligence (AI) technologies to generate text is expressly prohibited. The author reserves all rights to license uses of this work for generative AI training and development of machine learning language models.

Cover design by Igor Andrich @igorandrichdesign

Editing by Marilyn Haynes at MH Editorial Services

www.mheditorialservices.com @mheditorialservices

*Thus, I descended out of the first circle
Down to the second*

...

*Whereupon said I: "Master, who are those People,
whom the black air so castigates?"
"The first of those, of whom intelligence
Thou fain wouldst have," then said he unto me,
"The empress was of many languages.*

*To sensual vices she was so abandoned,
That lustful she made licit in her law,
To remove the blame to which she had been led."*

From Canto Five of the Inferno by Dante Alighieri

CONTENT WARNING

What you're about to read is a dark reverse harem mafia romance. That means this book is full of bad men doing bad things—*sometimes* to bad people. This book contains graphic sex scenes, violence, torture, murder, dub-con and one dark doctor with a voyeurism kink.

It also contains references to domestic violence and emotional abuse (not by any of the MMCs), stalking and harassment, voyeurism without consent, the death of a parent/parents (recurring theme throughout the series) and numerous references to infidelity.
The first two chapters contain a scene in which a character is drugged without her knowledge—no SA occurs.

We start you off light with this one, but please know: it will get darker from here.
Proceed with caution.

Author's note: while some elements of this book were inspired by real events, this is a work of fiction. Any character resemblance to persons living or dead is purely coincidental.

If you or someone you know is experiencing domestic violence, we urge you to contact the National Domestic Violence Hotline: 1-800-799-7233

To all the good girls reading this:
Don't be afraid, darling.
You can take it.

1

SYDNEY'S NIGHT

"Please tell me you're not thinking about Chase again."

I sink further in my seat, focusing all my energy on the drink in front of me and deliberately not meeting Jade's eyes. I don't need to look at her to know exactly how she looks right now, leaning back in her chair with her arms crossed and her lips set in a tight line. We've known each other for so many years now that her look of disapproval is permanently etched into my brain.

"The two of you broke up months ago," Jade reminds me. Her naturally black hair is dyed a bright bubblegum pink tonight and is tied back from her face in a messy bun. Out of the corner of my eye, I watch a strand of it fall forward, brushing against her cheek, and in the lights of the club, the color seems to glow. "And, in case you forgot, Sydney, he's a total *asshole.*"

"I promise you, I'm not thinking about Chase," I lie, taking a sip from my *fourth* martini of the night. The gin pools in my stomach with the rest of tonight's drinks, but I've lost the pleasantly warm buzz I had earlier. It's gone, just like my good mood. "And we don't need to keep talking about him. Honestly, I'm so bored just hearing his name come out of my mouth."

I paint a smile on my face, willing myself to believe what I'm saying is true, willing myself to stop thinking about him, even if just for one night.

"Syd..." Jade presses, and when I finally glance over at her, her dark brown eyes don't look disapproving at all. They look concerned.

Great. Now my stomach is full of both gin *and* guilt.

Jade knows me. Truly knows me in the way only a best friend can. And she knows me too well to believe me when I say I'm okay right now. I'm far from okay.

I slump in my seat even more, the weight of my mood dragging me down.

I was okay when the night started, though. I was doing *great.*

But that was before we ran into *them.*

I was only two martinis deep and enjoying a rare fun night out when I spotted Katie across the dance floor of the club. Not just Katie, either, but the whole college gang. Friends of mine, not Jade's. Friends I hadn't seen in months—not since the breakup.

It's my fault I haven't seen any of them, I know. After Chase and I fell apart, I cut myself off from the whole group, isolating myself from everyone but Jade. Jade, who was mine and mine alone. Jade, who was my port in any storm, my oldest and best friend. Katie and Sarah and all the rest of that group were my friends, sure, but they'd been Chase's friends, too. Hell, Katie's husband was practically his best friend, and had been for years.

Seeing them meant almost certainly seeing Chase. Something I wasn't ready for. Might never be ready for.

Every time I'd considered reaching out to them, and every time I weaseled my way out of yet another social gathering, I'd thought about that. Thought about the risk of us ending up at the same place at the same time. Thought about being in the same room with him after everything he'd put me through.

Call me pathetic, but I couldn't stomach the idea of running into Chase again. So that left me with only one logical option: cutting myself off from everyone completely. Ignoring every invite and every phone call from everyone who reached out.

Not that many of them did.

But when I saw them tonight and realized that the club was too loud and too busy for me to have to explain my sudden exodus from their lives, I'd wanted to go over there. I'd wanted to say hi to them, to hug them, to remind them I was still alive! Still here!

Still mattered!

I had just worked up the courage to do it when I spotted him. Chase. Chase and his new, very blonde, very preppy girlfriend.

It hit me then. The crushing realization that not only did Chase pick this girl over me, but apparently so had all my friends.

Was I so easily replaced? So easily tossed aside and discarded by all of them?

I'd held on so tight to what Chase and I had together, and it almost killed me. I'd wanted so badly to fit with someone, to be someone's other half. Over the course of our relationship, I molded myself to be the epitome of everything I thought he wanted. Everything I thought would make him happy. I was the perfect girlfriend. Day by day, minute by minute, I became an "us".

And it still wasn't enough.

No matter how much I bent, how much I changed, it was never enough. I became smaller and smaller until I didn't even recognize myself anymore...and he *still* found someone better.

Chase and I weren't good together, I try to remind myself. Nothing about it was good, and Jade doesn't even know half of what I put up with from him. She doesn't know how bad it got at the end. So why is it still so painful? I finally took off the rose-colored glasses I had pressed so tightly to my eyes, but I'm still crushed over losing the person I thought I'd be with forever.

I watched them all leave together, unable to summon the courage to walk over to them. My ex, his new girlfriend, and my old friends. As they filed out of the club, Chase finally looked across the crowded room and met my eyes.

And my heart shattered into pieces again. Not just for what he did to me. Not just for what he took from me. But for what we could have been if things had been different. For the life we could have had together.

For the person I could have been.

The light touch of Jade's fingers on my hand pulls me out of my thoughts and back to reality. I take a deep, calming breath and recite one of my favorite therapy mantras as I pull myself back into the present.

I am an ocean of calm.

It doesn't matter. It doesn't matter how destroyed I feel right now, it doesn't matter that my heart is breaking or that I'm still crushed from the breakup. I refuse to fall apart in the middle of this club. I refuse to let him take another thing away from me.

It was my idea for the two of us to blow off some steam

tonight and have a little fun. Jade and I have been working nonstop at our shared business, and between that and my breakup, I feel like we haven't had an opportunity to truly let loose in a while.

We need this. *I* need this.

"I promise, I'm okay," I insist, squeezing Jade's hand. The fake pep in my voice is almost convincing enough to be believable. "Come on, we look too good to be sitting here all night. I want to dance!"

It's obvious the change in my tone isn't genuine, but Jade still lets me pull her up from the table and into the crowd of dancing bodies, laughing as I tug her along. If there's one thing that I can always convince Jade to do, it's show off her gorgeous self and her killer dance moves.

I've always loved to dance. To lose myself in the music, to surrender to the flow of the beat. As we sway to the upbeat tempo, I feel myself come alive—a flower finally in bloom.

Fuck Chase. Fuck my fake friends. Fuck everything but this moment, right now.

I let the music take me away, swaying my hips and moving to the rhythm. I can feel my little red dress clinging tight to every inch of me in the heat of the club, but I don't even care. This is the feeling I needed. I lost myself in my relationship with Chase—my self-esteem crumbling until there was barely anything left—and in the process, I lost this. The joy of just existing in my own skin. It's been too long since I truly felt like *myself.*

Moving to the music, I lose myself in the flow of the song and in the night's energy. With a bright laugh, Jade wraps her arms around my shoulders and pulls me in for a hug.

That's when I feel it.

The hairs on the back of my neck stand on end, my spine tingling with the sensation that someone is watching me. I step away from Jade, my eyes scanning the room. Maybe I'm just being paranoid after my run-in with Chase, but I swear something in the air just shifted. I can feel someone's heavy gaze on me, but when I look around the club, I can't see anyone. The lights are too dim, the crowd too thick.

But this feeling? It's magnetic. A pull toward something unknown and dangerous, like I'm standing on the edge of a cliff, wondering what it would feel like to jump.

I touch the back of my neck, frowning as my eyes search the dark corners of the club.

This is ridiculous. What I'm feeling is nothing more than a few too many drinks, an overactive imagination, or a mix of the two. My mind must be playing tricks on me. You can't actually *feel* someone staring, can you? That's insane.

Still, the sensation lingers, like the ghost of a touch.

Unable to shake the feeling, I signal to Jade that I need a break, pointing toward the bar. She nods enthusiastically, falling into step beside me as we make our way off the dance floor, toward the quieter side of the club where the music isn't so deafening.

By the time we order our fifth round of drinks and stumble back to a table, I'm sweaty, emotional, and bordering on very drunk. And right on cue—as if they have a sixth sense for intoxicated women—two very eager men approach our table. From the sleazy smiles on their faces, and the way they quickly lean into our personal space, it's easy to guess what they're interested in.

"Gay!" Jade shouts at the men without even blinking.

That stops them in their tracks. The two men look at one another, frowning. "What?" nondescript man number one says. "No! We're not—"

"*Gay*," Jade interrupts, pointing at herself. "Very, extremely, vagina-loving *gay* woman here. Move along and please do not interact with or startle the lesbian." She says it without an ounce of volume control or restraint. I hide my laughter behind my hand as the men look back and forth between the two of us, distressed. Jade takes a loud slurp of her drink as she watches them.

When they finally regain their composure, both men shift their full attention to me. Maybe they've accepted that their efforts are lost on Jade. More likely, they just think I'm the weaker target.

"How about you?" man number two asks, leaning an elbow on our table, his grin wide and too eager. "Can I buy you a drink?"

I raise my martini to eye level, wiggling it at him. "I've actually got one already, but thanks."

And here we go. There's something that happens in the male brain that translates "no" to "try again, please." Instead of leaving us alone and crawling back under the bridge they came from, both men sit down at our table, clearly willing to press the issue. Even if I were in the right mindset to meet someone—which I'm decidedly not—this isn't the approach.

"Come on, sexy. One more?" He smiles at me, adding a wink for good measure.

Gug.

"I'm truly uninterested," I say, more firmly this time.

"Don't be like that. It'll be fun. A drink, maybe some dancing?" He shifts closer, until his legs are pressed against me, ignoring the way I tense at the contact. His hand reaches out and touches mine, his fingers trailing over the lip of my drink. "I saw you out there dancing, you know. You looked so hot." He whispers the last part into my ear, like it's a gift. Like all my life, I'd been waiting for a gremlin to spot me from across the room and breathe hot, stale breath onto my neck.

His words conjure the memory of how I'd felt on the dance

floor, under that enticing touch of someone's gaze, but I don't think these were the eyes I felt on me. Nothing about this man is reminiscent of the dark, magnetic pull I'd felt before.

Misinterpreting my silence as an open invitation to something more, he lifts his hand to stroke my hair, fingers playing with my brown curls.

That's the last straw.

Jerking away from him, I gulp down the second half of my drink and stand up to leave. Jade instantly follows my lead, rolling her eyes at both men as she stands and grabs her leather jacket. Usually, I would never give up a table to avoid a slimy guy—or even two—but I think this is the universe telling me that tonight is a wrap. Between seeing Chase and the creepy progression of this interaction, it's time to pack up and move on.

When I turn to leave, though, the guy next to me stands up too, blocking my path. I feel a rush of anger at his audacity, but I force myself to push it away.

I'm not that angry girl anymore, I remind myself, stifling my rage.

I am an ocean of calm.

I move to pivot around him, but he reaches out to grab my wrist, pulling me closer until we're chest to chest. "Fucking bitch," he spits at me. "Do you have any idea who I am?"

Jade stares daggers at the guy as she tugs me toward the exit, murmuring, "Come on, Syd, they're not worth it. Let's just go." The opinions of these men mean nothing to her, and I can tell she's hit her limit of liquor and drama for the night. Gin has always made Jade adorably lethargic and calm.

Unfortunately, it has a very different effect on me.

I like to think of myself as a docile person. A *good* person. But I guess a few too many drinks and a couple of entitled assholes are all it takes to unleash my violent side.

"Excuse the fuck out of me?" I yell, pulling my hand away.

Now that I'm standing—as unsteady as it may be—it's obvious I have a couple inches of height on him, even without my heels. And I'll be damned if I'll let this gremlin of a man speak to me like this or put his hands on me. Reaching out, I snatch his glass of cheap whiskey off the table. He realizes what I'm about to do just a split second too late, mouth gaping like a fish right before I throw the drink in his face. When he recoils, sputtering and wiping liquid from his eyes, it gives me plenty of time to grab his friend's drink and toss that one in his face, too.

I'm pulling back my hand to deliver a well-deserved slap to his whiskey-drenched cheek, blinded by my rage, when Jade grabs me by the arm.

"That's enough of that!" She laughs, tugging me away. "Come on, Syd, time to go!"

The fog of my anger clears enough for me to realize she's right. A swift exit is probably for the best. Both men are shouting now, and people around the club are turning to stare at us, drawn to the uproar. I let Jade drag me away, stumbling after her as we push through the crowd toward the emergency exit.

It's a fight to get through the throng of people, and—distracted—I slam face-first into someone's chest. For a split second, my world narrows to the scent of expensive cologne and a deliciously well-toned body. Then another yank from Jade pulls me away.

The shouts behind us grow louder, angrier, but the second we hit the emergency exit and stumble into the back alley, the door slamming shut behind us, the noise cuts off, and the world turns quiet.

Safe.

We hit the pavement laughing and take off running like we're being chased. My adrenaline is dizzyingly high, and neither of us slows down until we're two blocks away from the club. When we finally stop, we're panting, breathless, giggling messes.

"That was amazing!" Jade throws back her head to whoop.

I laugh, wiping sweat from my forehead. It's the height of summer, and the suffocating heat enveloping Fortune City tonight isn't any better than the heat of the packed club we just left. The air is still as the dead, without even the promise of a breeze to cool us down. It makes the world feel strangely distant and hazy. I stumble, a little unsteady on my feet.

Maybe that last drink was one too many.

"You were ready to slap that guy," Jade says, still laughing. But she doesn't sound like she's admonishing me. She sounds *proud*. "Oh God, Sydney, you haven't acted like that since... since... since we were kids!"

I stop walking, swaying on shaky, gin-addled legs. On any other night, being reminded of the angry person I used to be would hurt. Those memories are too sharp, too brittle, and when they cut, they cut deep. But tonight, instead of shame spiraling over the violent girl I used to be, I revel in it.

It felt good to stand up for myself like that, didn't it? No—better than good. It felt *great*.

Jade stumbles over a crack in the sidewalk, giggling as she catches herself against a parking meter. It's clear from the way she leans against it for balance that she's only a few minutes away from slipping into the bad place—that point where the liquor takes over completely and it's lights out. Time to officially call it a night.

My Jade loves to drink, but she's a tiny, stubborn thing, and the combination usually lands her in trouble. My apartment is only a few blocks away, but Jade lives further out in the central district, and there's no way I'm letting her walk home in this condition.

"Okay, let's get you home, little miss drunky-drunk," I say, digging in my bag for my phone to call her a ride.

"Syd, I can get myself home," Jade insists, her words slurred. "It's not that far. I'll grab a share bike."

"Jade, my love, my best friend, my *everything*"—okay, maybe I'm a little too drunk, too, because I'm slurring just as badly as she is—"I'm not letting you bike home alone. We're getting you a lift. And that is final."

"I hate when you make sense." Jade pouts dramatically before throwing her hands up in surrender, almost tipping over in the process. "Fine! Order me a car. But you better text me the second you get home, okay?"

According to the app, there's a ride available right around the corner. I've barely finished entering her address and setting the pickup location when the car pulls up to whisk her away.

I tuck Jade safely into the backseat—mildly concerned that the driver, Edward, according to the app, looks like he hasn't finished puberty, let alone earned his license—and shut the door.

"Love you!" Jade yells drunkenly from the backseat, face pressed against the window, her words misting the glass.

"To the moon and back!" I yell right back at her, waving as the car pulls away.

The air feels a little cooler as I start my walk home, and the streetlights are unusually bright against the dark night sky. I blink at them, drunkenly, trying to focus. But they keep moving. And they're getting brighter by the second, shining like little suns.

Huh. Isn't that *pretty*?

I had fun tonight, but I'm grateful the night is nearly over. Soon, I'll be passed out in my comfortable bed. I'm looking forward to it, craving it, as I stumble down the sidewalk.

Naturally, this is when I realize something is wrong. Something is very wrong.

My legs feel unnaturally heavy, and time seems to twist and slow. The bright lights around me dim, and then fade to black, and the last thing I see is the sidewalk rising to meet me as I fall.

Shit.

2

ALEC'S NIGHT

Magnetic.

That's the only way to describe her. Even when I try to look away, this woman's presence pulls me back. I'm hypnotized by her—the way she moves, the way her hips sway in perfect time with the thumping club music. It's been a while since I've bothered picking up a beautiful woman for a night of casual fun. Maybe tonight I'll indulge.

A little fun could be exactly what I need.

I'm only at this miserable club tonight to close this business deal, but she caught my eye the second she made her way onto the dance floor with her friend. A perfect temptation, with those long chestnut curls cascading down her back, golden skin glowing under the flashing lights, and that tight red dress clinging to every curve of her body.

A few more sways of those sinful hips and her dress might ride up just enough to see exactly what I'm looking for...

As if sensing my eyes on her, she stills. Her hand brushes the nape of her neck, and her gaze scans the crowd, searching.

But she doesn't see me, hidden in the shadows of the second-floor balcony, watching her every move.

What would she be like, I wonder, if I got her alone? If I had her all to myself?

I'm eager to find out.

With one last cautious glance around the club, my mystery woman takes her friend's arm, and they weave through the crowd toward the bar. I track her movements, my eyes drinking in every curve, imagining how they'd feel underneath me. Under my tongue.

"So ... we've got a deal?" Tony asks, dragging me back to the present. He pushes the contract toward me over the dark surface of the table between us. Reluctantly, I turn my attention back to him. The woman in red can wait.

Tony Delmano. What a pathetic excuse for a man. How he scraped together even a fraction of power in this city is beyond me. If my brothers and I didn't need the shipment of weapons he's currently selling, I'd be tempted to leave right now and join that little seductress downstairs, deal be damned.

But expansion requires firepower. And firepower requires working with Tony.

"As long as the shipment is on time, we've got a deal," I tell him, pushing the contract back to him without sparing it a glance. "But I don't sign this sort of paperwork. You should know that."

As if a man of my social standing in Fortune City would be caught dead signing an illegal weapons deal.

Tony balks as he takes the contract back, shuffling the papers nervously. "Of course, of course. Sorry, man." I turn in my seat, dismissing him as my eyes drift back toward the dance floor, but he keeps talking. "Hey, while you're here..."

My jaw tightens, and I turn back to him, letting the full weight of my stare settle on him until he shifts in his seat.

Tony wets his lips before he speaks. "You know, business at The Pink Panther has been going well…"

The Pink Panther? My brows furrow. It takes me a moment to recall that particular property and even longer to remember that Tony here manages it, in addition to the club we're currently meeting in. The Pink Panther is so inconsequential it's beneath my notice, nothing but a seedy strip club that was shut down twice for health code violations before my brothers and I purchased it.

I keep staring at Tony until he swallows hard, losing his nerve.

"And?" I ask, quirking a dark brow.

He stutters, speaking more to the tabletop than to me. "And…I was thinking maybe… maybe business would be even better if the, uh… if the girls could do more than just dance, if you know what I mean?"

Obviously, I know what he means. Tony has all the subtlety of a brick to the head.

"Like that other place you run, The Second Circle," Tony continues, listing one of the more lucrative hotels in the Sterling empire. *My* empire. "You've got a good operation there. I was thinking we could do something similar with the Panther, you know? Have the dancers give customers more than just lap dances in the backroom. Hire some working girls."

"Sex workers," I correct, drumming my fingers on the table. My patience is growing thin, and I already know where he's going with this. He needs to get there quickly.

"Sure, sure. Sex workers." Tony waves the term away like it doesn't matter. "You know. Some real classy bitches."

I wonder what Francesca would say if she heard this overgrown boy masquerading as a man calling her employees *bitches*. One look from the madam who manages The Second Circle would probably be enough to make Tony wet himself.

"And who did you have in mind to manage them?" I ask, humoring him.

Tony looks confused. "Well... me, obviously."

Obviously.

I lean over the table toward him, and he earns a few points for not visibly flinching. He does fidget, though, his hands nervously touching the papers in front of him.

"I don't let men manage the sex workers who work for me," I tell him, cutting right to the chase. "They do a shitty job of it, and they only think with their dicks."

Tony opens his mouth to argue, but I cut him off.

"You're lucky I even let you keep running that dump you call a strip club." I stand then, pushing my chair back and straightening the cuffs of my suit jacket. Tony's eyes dart to the gun on my hip before I twitch my jacket over it to cover it. "Stay in your lane, Tony. And if you bring this up to me again, it won't be me or Ashton you'll be speaking with. It'll be one of my other brothers."

I watch the blood drain from his face, leaving him pale beneath his cheap facial tattoos. The businessmen of this city are right to be frightened of Ashton and me.

But they're downright terrified of Sebastian and Viper.

"Are we done here?" I ask, buttoning my jacket. It's not really a question, and he knows it. I am *telling* him that our business has concluded for the night.

"All good, yeah. We're all good here," he says, nerves betraying him as he stumbles over the words.

This is par for the course when doing business with lower-level thugs who think they're important. Who think their ideas are worth anything at all to me. They talk a big game, with big dreams, until they realize they are woefully outmatched and outgunned.

Make them fear you. That had been the first of Dante's

lessons when we'd gone to work for him. *Make them fear you even more than they fear death. That's how you take a city. That's how you build an empire.*

My eyes go back to the first floor of the club, and I feel an unexpected rush of relief when I spot her again, seated at a table with her pink-haired friend. My woman in red.

There's still a chance to end this night right.

As I watch, though, two of Tony's peons approach, sliding into the open chairs at their table. It's obvious even at this distance that the women aren't interested, but Tony's men seem to have trouble taking the hint. She shifts away, distancing herself, but one of them keeps encroaching on her, moving into her personal space.

He moves closer to talk to her, and as he does, his hand hovers over her drink for a heartbeat too long. Then, with a practiced flick of his fingers while she's distracted, he slips something inside.

"You've got to be *fucking* kidding me," I snarl.

That bastard is trying to drug someone. In my club. In *my* fucking club.

I storm away from the table, leaving a confused and sputtering Tony in my wake. Fury drives me down the stairs to the first floor, straight through the crowd, muscling people aside.

I couldn't give a shit about the drugs in my city. I know for a fact Tony runs harder stuff than liquor out of this miserable place, and as long as I get my cut, I keep out of his business.

But drugging a woman? That's not business—it's pathetic. And those two may as well have signed their death warrants for attempting it. Not in my city. Not in my clubs. Not ever.

I'm close enough to see them when she suddenly stands, and before I can shout out a warning, she turns to leave.

Good, I think. *Get the fuck away from him. Now.*

But then he grabs her. His hand clamps around her wrist,

yanking her back. If I were closer, I wouldn't hesitate—I would have already broken his hand, or maybe worse. Hell, I wouldn't even think twice about putting my gun to his temple and blowing his brains out right in the middle of this club, fuck the consequences.

A lesson clearly needed.

But I'm not close enough. Not yet.

Instead, her voice cuts through the music—sharp, furious, shaking with rage—and then she does something I don't expect. She throws not one, but two drinks directly into his face.

It stops me in my tracks, a shocked laugh breaking free before I can catch it.

Who is this woman?

That fire, that fight—I wasn't expecting it.

Reading people is something I'm good at. Fuck, it's something I'm *great* at. Of the four of us, only Sebastian is better at understanding people and anticipating what they'll do next.

It's always been a point of pride with me that I'm ten steps ahead of everyone. But this woman—this little seductress—she's a surprise. Something wild. Something unexpected.

I'm standing there, still grinning in shock, when they come barreling through the crowd toward me. For a fraction of a second, her body collides with mine, and her curves press against me in a fleeting, electrifying moment...

And then she's gone, she and her friend vanishing into the crowd, racing toward the back door.

Tony's two peons are now hysterically shouting for the waitstaff to call 911, claiming assault. With one last glance at the emergency exit as it closes, I shove my way toward them and their whining.

When I reach them, my gaze drops to the table, and my stomach sinks.

Next to the two drinks she threw, her glass is empty. She

drank it. The whole damn thing, including whatever this bastard slipped inside.

I wasn't fast enough.

Drawn by the commotion, Tony and the bouncer covering the front door appear in the crowd, looking pissed as they make their way over to us.

I intercept them first, my voice low and hard as I speak to the bouncer. "Take those two to the back, away from the crowd," I say, jerking my chin toward Tony's men. "Hold them there until I say otherwise."

At the very least, I want those two fired. But a much darker part of me wants to send them straight to Viper. He has a special talent for keeping guests alive and screaming for days before he finally lets death have them.

The bouncer glances at Tony, who nods quickly. "Do what he says."

Knowing Tony will hold them until I get back, I leave them there, ignoring the increasingly frantic arguing from Tony's peons as they're escorted away. I follow the path the two women took through the crowd, the image of that empty glass stuck in my mind.

They couldn't have gone far, I think, as I shove the back door open and step into the night.

Only to be greeted by an empty alley.

Shit. No sign of them.

I stand there, scanning the darkness for any trace of them, frustration building under my skin. Why am I doing this? I don't know this woman. I owe her nothing, and God knows I'm not the hero in this story. She's probably fine. She's with her friend, right? She probably threw the drink in his face with the others; she probably didn't even drink it.

But what if she did?

Fuck.

Grinding my teeth together, I pick a direction and make my way out of the alley and to the next block. The streets are dead, the hour late enough that most people are out drinking or at home in bed. But I don't see them anywhere.

Out of the corner of my eye, I spot my town car parked against the curb, my driver Earl perched on the front bumper with a well-worn paperback in his hands. He looks, frowning. "Mister Sterling, sir? Everything okay?"

"Did you see two women go by?" I ask, still looking around for any sign of where they may have gone. "One with pink hair and a leather jacket, and one in a red dress?"

To my relief, he nods. "Yes, sir. They went off that way."

I take off in the direction he gestures, scanning every alley for a glimpse of them.

Then I see it.

A shape on the ground ahead sprawled across the sidewalk. My pulse quickens, and I break into a run when I recognize the red of her dress.

It's her.

Her purse lies spilled open on the ground next to her, with her wallet and phone beside it. But nothing appears to be missing.

She's unconscious, crumpled on the pavement. I crouch beside her, checking for any visible injuries. There's a scratch on her elbow and a nasty scrape on her knee, but otherwise, she looks unharmed.

Where the fuck is her friend?

Scowling, I shove her things back into her bag and scoop her into my arms, letting her head sag against my shoulder. Her hair smells like coconut. I take a deep breath, savoring it, as I carry her back to my waiting car.

I run into Earl first. I had no idea he was following me. The older man is a little winded when he stops, startled by the unconscious woman in my arms. "What happened?" he asks.

"I think she was drugged." The words come out with a sharp edge of panic.

Earl steps closer, placing a steady hand on her forehead. Then he takes her wrist to check her pulse. He might not have a full medical degree like Sebastian, but he served his time as a medic overseas, and he knows his shit. Nestled in my arms, she murmurs something as he touches her, her words muffled, and a possessive surge flares in me. I have to fight not to pull her away from his touch.

Earl lowers her arm carefully. The heavy look in his eyes is all the confirmation I need.

What if I hadn't gone after her? What if someone else had found her like this?

Something dark and violent rises inside me at the thought. I think I'll give those men waiting in Tony's backroom to Viper after all.

She stirs in my arms, her face pressing into my chest, breath warm against my shirt. I should call someone. I should get her to a hospital. My fingers flex around her, and I open my mouth, ready to order Earl to call Sebastian and get him down here to examine her.

But something stops me.

Some fucked-up, possessive part of me doesn't want him here. I want to be the one to save her, I realize. For once in my life, I want to be the hero.

"Bring the car around," I say instead. "We need to get her home."

Earl doesn't question why I'm bothering to help her. He nods once before taking off and is back with the car in barely any time at all.

I open the door and set her down gently in the spacious back seat before circling to the other side to climb in beside her.

As we pull away from the curb, she stirs again, a soft sound escaping her lips.

"Hey," I say quietly, leaning closer. "You doing okay, Red?"

She doesn't answer. My gaze drifts over her face, taking in every detail before dropping lower to where she's almost spilling out of the top of her dress. It's difficult to pull my eyes away.

"Where to, boss?" Earl's voice cuts through the silence from the front seat.

Where indeed? I open her bag and pick through her belongings until I find her driver's license.

Sydney Sinclair. In her ID photo, she's smiling. Happy.

She lives just a few blocks away, and after giving Earl the address, I lean back against the leather seats, trying to calm my thoughts. It doesn't take long for us to pull up outside her apartment. The building is some sort of café, but when Earl drives around to the other side, there are two apartments taking up the second floor, accessible only from the back.

I find her keys inside her purse, gather her things together, and help her out of the car. She can stand and walk with a little prompting, but whatever they gave her, mixed with whatever she was drinking, has her pliant and unaware of her surroundings.

I don't believe in God, but I thank whatever deity, real or fictitious, out there that let me be the first to find her. Fortune City might be a hell of a lot better off since my brothers and I took over here, but it's still not a safe place for a beautiful woman like her to be alone and unconscious.

I guide her up the stairs to her door, unlocking it to let us inside. Her place smells like her—like coconuts and new books.

It reminds me of the library they used to take us to when we were kids, on the brief occasions we left the orphanage. I have the sudden urge to see her home with the lights on. I want to experience it the way she sees it every day.

When I close the door behind us, she guides me to the bedroom, my hand on the small of her back to steady her. I lay her gently down on her bed, taking off her shoes and pulling a sheet over her.

Standing next to her bed, I hesitate, suddenly wanting to lie down next to her. The desire to do it is so strong I almost give in.

I grind my teeth together and push that temptation aside, heading to the kitchen to get her some water instead. She'll need that. I spot a clean kitchen towel and run it under some cold water. She'll need that, too.

When I make my way back to the bedroom and place the water on her nightstand, her chest is rising and falling steadily, and I assume she must be asleep. I sit down on the bed next to her and lay the cold compress against her forehead. I have to brush some of her wild curls away to get it to lay flat, and after I do, I can't help but trace the curves of her face, bringing my fingers down her cheek, to her chin, and lower to her throat.

Her eyes are open, I realize.

Her gaze is glassy as she stares up at me. She doesn't pull away from my touch, doesn't look frightened. She just looks up at me with those gorgeous brown eyes, like she has all the trust in the world in me. Like I'm someone who deserves that trust.

It's enough to make me jerk my hand away. I need to leave. I shouldn't be here. I shouldn't have touched her. She's vulnerable, drugged, and I'm no better than the scum waiting for me at Tony's club if I let myself cross that line.

Before I can second-guess myself, I stand and move away

from her, walking quickly to her front door. I let it close behind me and lean against the door frame to take a deep, steadying breath, my heart beating too fast.

What the fuck is happening to me?

3

TWO WEEKS LATER

SYDNEY

THE BUZZ OF MY PHONE AGAINST THE COUNTER IS unfathomably loud in the quiet of our shop. I wince, pausing in the middle of restocking the bakery case, as Jade leans over to read the screen. I already know whose name she'll see there, even before her face darkens.

"Sydney... why is *Chase* messaging you?" Jade asks.

Unfazed by her anger, my cell phone vibrates again, happily buzzing on the counter. Jade's eyes narrow as she glares at it. For a second, I think she might pick it up and throw it.

She's definitely considering it.

"I don't even know," I grumble, standing and removing my thin, plastic, food-safe gloves. I take a moment to appreciate my work. The bakery case is, once again, picture perfect, stocked full of Jade's incredible creations and beautiful baked goods. I wish organizing my life were half this easy. "He just keeps messaging me. I haven't even bothered responding to him. It's not like we have anything to talk about."

Not anymore, at least. Chase saw to *that* when he cheated on me, effectively ending our relationship. Though, I'm embarrassed to admit, I had still been responding to his occasional messages after our breakup. It wasn't until I saw him and his new girlfriend at the club together two weeks ago that I finally gained some self-respect and stopped engaging with him.

Apparently, my sudden silence was enough to convince him we needed desperately to talk. He's been blowing up my phone ever since.

Thinking about that night at the club makes me feel uneasy, and not just because I saw Chase. I can only remember bits and pieces of what happened that night before waking up in my bed fully dressed, with a phone full of anxious messages from Jade wondering if I'd made it home okay. It's rare for me to get that drunk, and even more rare that I'll black out entirely. And I'd felt horrible for days afterward, like my body was hell bent on punishing me for drinking too many martinis.

All in all, the night had been a disaster.

Another peppy buzz from my phone makes me groan, but before I can reach for it, Jade snatches it from the counter.

"I'm blocking his number," she says with a finality in her tone I wish I could match. Her fingers race over the screen as she unlocks my phone and navigates to my contact list. "He's just trying to weasel his way back in your life, Syd, and I'll be damned if I'll sit back quietly and let him do it. Not on my watch!"

I snort but make no move to stop her. "I really doubt that's what he's trying to do."

After all, he was with *her* now, wasn't he? Caroline. Even thinking her name makes me feel ill. I know I shouldn't hate her for it, believe me, I do. *He* was the one in a relationship. He was the one who cheated; *he* was the one who broke my heart.

The selfish, manipulative little—

I stop and take a deep breath, counting to ten in my mind, willing the anger to recede.

I am not a slave to my negative emotions, I tell myself. *I am in control of my own thoughts and actions.*

I am an ocean of calm.

"Done!" Jade declares, tossing my phone on the counter. It hits with enough force to make me wince. "His number is officially blocked. Honestly, Sydney, he's not worth this stress. The man had a *Captain Jack Sparrow* tattoo, for fuck's sake. You can do so much better than that."

I chuckle, shaking my head. Jade has *always* thought I could do better than every guy I've ever dated. I guess that's the role of a best friend, isn't it? To want you to have the best of everything. To believe you deserve it. I know that's how I feel about her. Even before we started this business together—when the idea of co-owning a bookstore and café was just a fantasy—I knew I'd do anything to make her life better.

And, sure, that also included plenty of times when I didn't approve of *her* girlfriends. Because Jade? For all her skills and business acumen? Oh boy, does Jade sure know how to pick the crazy ones.

"Oh! Did I tell you?" Jade smiles at me, raising an eyebrow. "Mr. Tall, Dark, and Handsome is back."

She gestures toward one of our café's small wooden tables, and I can't help but look. Tall, dark, and handsome is an accurate description of our newest regular, but it barely scratches the surface of the man sitting there. With short, ink-black hair, a sharp, chiseled jaw, and smooth, dark skin, he's nothing short of mouthwatering.

There's something else about him, though. Another reason I can't stop staring, even when I know I should. I'm not sure if it's just his size—the man looks like he could bench press our bakery case and not break a sweat—or just the confidence he exudes, but he feels... intense, in the best possible way. And strangely familiar. Since the first time he came in, I felt like I knew him, somehow, but just couldn't place him. That's impossible, though. There's no way I could ever forget meeting a man like *that*.

Oblivious to our stares, Mr. Tall, Dark, and Handsome lifts his *Book Boutique and Bakery* mug and takes a sip of coffee, eyes locked on the newspaper he's reading. He's been coming by the store almost every evening for the past couple of weeks like clockwork, ordering coffee and a pastry, and staying until nearly close. Whatever he does for a living must pay well. He's always in a suit, and even from here I can tell it's not something that came off the rack. It's perfectly tailored to his body, and that sort of look only comes from something designer and expensive.

"I think he has a crush on you," Jade says with a smile.

"Oh, please!" I laugh, but just imagining it makes me giddy. A guy like that? What woman wouldn't want to believe he was attracted to her?

"Why else would he be coming by here every day, Syd?" Jade presses.

I shoot Jade a saccharine sweet smile. "To visit your delicious café, of course," I say, fluttering my lashes at her.

Jade rolls her eyes.

There's truth to what she's saying, though. While we have a few loyal regulars who help keep us in business, it's unusual for a customer to frequent our shop as often as Mr. Tall, Dark, and Handsome. Our regulars usually come by once or twice a week, not every single day.

With his next swig of coffee, he drains his mug. He hesitates, frowning at it, before setting it carefully back on the table.

Jade shoots me a significant look.

Go, she mouths, shooing me with her hands.

I glare at her.

She glares right back.

Fine.

It's not like I had anything else to do right now, anyway. Abandoning Jade to her station by the espresso maker, I make my way across the café and over to his table. And, sure, maybe my heart is beating a little faster than usual, but what can I say? The man is a snack.

"I can take that for you, if you're all finished," I offer when I reach his table, gesturing to his empty mug.

The man looks up. His eyes are a deep brown, darker than I'd expected. So dark they're almost black.

"That would be lovely. Thank you," he says, his voice deep and melodious.

"No problem at all." I smile, reaching for his cup.

He continues to stare at me as I take it, and I hesitate, suddenly wanting this interaction to last a little longer.

"I'm Alec, by the way," he says, folding his newspaper carefully and holding out a hand for me to shake.

"Sydney," I introduce myself. His hand is so big it engulfs mine completely, and he holds on for a second longer than necessary before letting me go.

"Are you the owner?" Alec asks, gesturing around the store.

"Co-owner," I tell him. "Jade and I—that's Jade, behind the counter there, with the pink hair—we own it together. She runs the café, and I—" I gesture toward the rest of our shop. *My* shop. "I run the bookstore."

It might seem impressive, but trust me, it's not. Sure, the bookstore takes up most of our square footage, but it's Jade's coffee and pastries that bring in most of our profits. That's why we designed the place the way we did—with her café front and center at the entrance, and the rows and rows of books spiraling out from there. We even included little reading nooks around my portion of the store, with tables and comfortable chairs, so our customers can have a nice place to sit and enjoy their drinks while they read.

Alec stares around at the bookstore as though seeing it for the first time. And now that I stop to think about it, I've only ever seen him here, at the front of our shop, enjoying the café. Maybe he's not much of a reader?

"It's a beautiful store," he tells me, in that lovely velvet voice.

"Thank you." I smile at him, feeling proud. "I think so, too."

I was doing something, wasn't I? It's so easy to get lost in those dark eyes...

Right. His mug. That I'm still holding. Like an idiot.

"Well... I'll just take this to be washed," I say, turning to leave with a small laugh.

I'm halfway to the counter when he responds.

"Lovely to meet you, Sydney," he says. I want so desperately to turn back around, to see if he's watching me.

From the look of pure glee on Jade's face, he is.

"*Shut up*," I hiss at her, shoving the coffee mug in her direction and glaring at her ear-to-ear grin.

"Love you," Jade coos in a singsong voice to me.

"To the moon and back," I answer, finishing the phrase we've said to each other since we were kids.

———

I LOVE BOOKS. THEY'VE BEEN MY MUCH-NEEDED ESCAPE since I was a child, a way for me to explore the world and all it offers without ever leaving the house. There's nothing better to me than leaving behind the worries and pain of the real world and letting myself get lost in a different life. A better life.

And I love that now I get to share those books with others. Love that I made a career of it.

"Thanks for choosing the Book Boutique!" I say cheerfully, as I slip a bookmark and receipt under the book's cover and hand it back to my customer with a smile. "And have a great evening!"

They wish me the same, waving as they head toward the exit. My smile is genuine, and my mood is bright as I turn to give my full attention to the next customer in line.

"Hi there! Did you find everything you were—"

The rest of the words get jumbled in my brain as I lose myself in a pair of dark eyes, and I simply...stop talking.

"I found everything I was looking for, yes," Alec answers me. The slight curve to his lips could be the start of a smile. It softens him, makes his stark features even more handsome. A little less intimidating.

Internally cringing at my moment of awkwardness, I mumble something like "glad to hear it," and take the three books from his outstretched hands, setting them on the counter to ring them up. It's a funny coincidence, but all three are books I love, and I recognize them as books I know are currently on display in our Staff Picks section at the back of the store. The first two are recent popular literary fiction pieces, both nominated for several awards, but the third...

I pause as I'm ringing up the third book.

The cover is a nondescript red, decorated with a knife and roses, and even without reading the title, I recognize it immediately. The Prince's Knife.

"If... If you don't mind me asking," I say, voice as nonchalant as I can manage, "what made you pick this one?"

Alec's brow furrows as he frowns.

"I saw it on your recommendation display," he tells me in a measured tone. His eyes narrow slightly. "You've read it?"

At my nod, his frown deepens.

"Did you not enjoy it?" he probes.

"Oh no," I answer quickly. "I enjoyed it *a lot*, actually."

"Then... Is there a problem?"

Oh no, there's no problem here. Except that the book he's picked is the first in a fantasy romance series, and despite the rather misleading cover, it's... well...

It's smut. Borderline erotica.

Almost a third of the chapters in this book contain—on page—steamy sex scenes, and I can't imagine how Alec is going to react when he finds that out.

"No problem at all," I say, giving him my best customer service smile and taking his credit card. I slip a bookmark advertising our store between the pages before handing all three books back to him. "I hope you enjoy it as much as I did."

4

ALEC

CRYPTIC.

I replay my conversation with her again and again in my head as my town car takes me home, Earl singing tonelessly in the front seat, loud enough I can hear him through the privacy screen. My finger strokes the red cover of my new book as we reach the compound gates and the car stops, waiting for security to clear us for entry.

Yes. Cryptic describes Sydney nicely.

She's a mystery. One I can't seem to get out of my head, not since that first moment I spotted her at Tony's club. My woman in red.

It wasn't hard to figure out where she worked with her name and the right connections. It would have been even easier if I'd enlisted Sebastian's help, but my own sources were enough to get me the information I needed quickly. I made myself stop by her store the evening after I'd found her passed out, just to assure myself that she was okay. That she'd recovered.

I'm not sure what drove me to come back the next evening.

Or the next. And now I can't seem to stop myself from going back to her shop, day after day, trying to tease her apart. Trying to pinpoint exactly why I can't stop thinking about her.

At least the men who drugged her drink were punished for it. Or so Viper tells me. I didn't share with him what they'd done, or why I wanted them dead. Just like Viper didn't share with me all the horrible things he did to them before he turned them into carrion.

When Earl pulls to a stop and opens the car door for me, I slip the books under my suit jacket, out of sight. I have time to read a little tonight, don't I?

The answer, it seems, is *no*, since there's already a problem waiting for me when I make my way through the house and into my home office.

Ashton looks up at me from where he's sprawled on the couch, his feet on the armrest, when I enter. The cleaning bills I have to deal with because of him are getting out of hand.

"Hey," he greets me, sitting up. He runs his fingers through his sandy blond hair and frowns at the clock on the wall. "I thought your meeting with the board ended at four. Where have you been all night?"

"Out," I snap. I maneuver the books I'm holding under my suit jacket subtly, sliding them onto my desk and covering them with a stack of papers to keep them hidden from sight. Ashton doesn't seem to notice. "Don't you have a fight tonight?"

Officially, Ashton retired from professional MMA fighting three years ago, when he formally accepted a position with my company. But it doesn't stop him from setting up a new match every few months, drawing up hype and a massive crowd of people willing to pay top dollar to watch him in the ring. And, since I own the casinos that host these Fight Nights, I have no problem cashing in on his continued popularity.

Crowds will pay big money to watch a man who looks like

Ashton beat the shit out of someone. Something about his movie-star good looks and his boyish smile really gets them going.

Ashton just shrugs. "I had Jacob cancel it and put someone else in the ring for tonight. We have a problem, boss."

Great.

A muscle in my jaw tics as I sit, leaning back in my leather office chair to stare my brother down.

"What problem?" I ask, my voice dark.

"The payments from Golden Rings were short this month," Ashton tells me, nervously bouncing his knee. I know immediately he's not talking about front-of-house payments, the ones we report to stockholders and our board of advisors. He's talking about the sorts of deals that go on under the table, the ones that aren't exactly legal. "So, I sent Sebastian to go check it out..."

Of course he did. Sebastian handles all our accounts, legal or otherwise. I wait patiently for Ashton to continue.

"And my instinct was right. Giovanni, that fucker, has been keeping a cut for himself. When Seb confronted one of his thugs, he said it was protection money that Giovanni's been paying to someone else."

My eyebrows raise in surprise.

"Protection money?" I ask. Now that's interesting. That sounds like someone is trying to hustle in on our turf. On *my* turf. "Who's he paying it to?"

"We don't know yet," Ashton says. "The guy Doc questioned didn't say."

"Because he didn't know, or because he wouldn't talk?"

Ashton gives me a long look, and I retract the question. If Sebastian couldn't get it out of him, then the guy clearly didn't have the information. There's less than a handful of people on Earth who could hold up to Seb's interrogations and not talk.

And no one on Earth who could hold up to our other brother.

"Send Viper to have a chat with Giovanni," I tell Ashton. He pales, but nods. "And figure out who can take over at Golden Rings quickly. I don't need the board sniffing around if I don't have a replacement who won't run the damn thing into the ground."

We can't afford to have one of our top casinos out of commission, even for a few days, without attracting the board's attention. It'd be best if we could just slot a new player in to run it the second Giovanni is out of the picture.

And once Viper gets him, well...

There won't be enough of Giovanni left to fill a bucket, let alone run a casino.

"I'll let Doc and Viper know," Ashton confirms, coming to his feet.

"Good. Thanks," I tell him as he heads toward the exit. "And close the door behind you."

Ashton sarcastically salutes me, and the second the door shuts behind him, I reach out for the book that made Sydney hesitate, the one with the red cover. Maybe I have time to solve one mystery tonight.

Settling back in my chair, I open it and start to read.

5

SYDNEY

For the first time in years, I catch myself humming as I work. A silly piece of music, probably nothing more than an advertisement jingle I heard on TV, but humming nonetheless. A moment of joy, just for me.

Jade was right. Blocking Chase really was the best thing for me and my mental health. Without the low-level anxiety of knowing another message from him could disrupt my day, I've been in a better mood this last week than I have in months.

I should have blocked him right after we ended things, if I'm being honest with myself. But it just felt so... final. I've never been great at no-contact endings with anyone, let alone someone who had been such a huge part of my life for so many years. But the sinking feeling I'd get in the pit of my stomach every time my phone would buzz is suddenly gone, and with it a huge weight I didn't even realize I was carrying.

I'm feeling lighter than air as I set to work putting up the publisher's display for the third book in The Prince's Knife series. Sure, we can't technically put any copies out until the book's official release date, but we *can* start building hype among the book's fanbase by advertising it. Instead of the newest book (still nestled safely in an unopened box in our stockroom), I fill the display with copies of the other books in the series, as well as a few of the author's back catalogue and lesser-known works.

Satisfied, I step back a few paces to judge the full display. It looks good, but I can't help but think it still needs something extra to really make it pop. Maybe some of the fantasy-themed shirts and bookmarks we keep near the back register?

I chew my bottom lip and gaze around at the other displays, considering what to add.

That's when I spot him.

Lounging in an armchair sandwiched between our Science Fiction and Fantasy sections is Alec. He looks perfectly in his element sitting there, one ankle resting on his knee and a book in his hand, looking for all the world like he's been there for hours.

My heart skips a beat when I notice the book he's holding.

He's reading The Prince's Knife.

As if sensing my gaze, Alec looks up, and we lock eyes. It's too late to pretend I wasn't looking at him and too late to duck into one of the other aisles and hide. So, a little embarrassed, I raise my hand and wave.

A slow smile creeps over his face. He waves back briefly before gesturing me over.

My feet carry me over to him before I can even stop to think if it's a good idea or not.

"Sydney," Alec greets me, closing his book. I glance down at how far he is through it, morbidly curious, and see he's almost at the end. Great. No chance in hell he doesn't know exactly what sort of book it is by now. "I thought I might have come on your day off. I didn't see you up front."

"Oh, no." I laugh. "I hardly ever take a day off. It's too

much work for just Jade or me to handle on our own. And we're the only employees right now."

I reach up to touch my brown curls nervously.

"Are you... enjoying it?" I ask, motioning to the book in his hands. I ask it automatically, like commenting on the weather, and only when Alec smirks, his eyebrows raising, do I realize how suggestive it sounds. "I only mean, it's not, uh... not for everyone. This sort of book."

His smile only grows.

"I am enjoying it. Very much, actually," he tells me. "I like the political intrigue. And the overarching themes about the inevitability of corruption that comes with power."

I take a step closer to him, excited.

"Yes!" I agree animatedly. "This author does a great job of making you question whether it's better to submit to a corrupt but stable system or to overthrow it and risk chaos."

I'm so glad to hear Alec is enjoying the plot. And, sure, maybe it *is* a little smutty, but fantasy romance at least tends to be pretty plot centric. Why can't a book be good *and* have a few sexy scenes now and then?

"What's your favorite part so far?" I ask excitedly. For me, it's the twist—the *I can't believe it* moment when you find out a character you thought was dead has been alive this whole time, living under a different name.

"Oh, that's easy." Alec taps the book lightly against his leg. "The forest scene where Malachi orders Pheadra to get on her knees and beg for his cum."

My head empties.

I'm vaguely aware that my mouth is open as Alec watches me. I close it, only to open it again.

"Oh," I manage to say, mouth suddenly dry. My heart is beating unusually fast. I know the scene he's talking about, and while it was undeniably sexy and I enjoyed it, nothing at all prepared me for hearing those words come from this man's mouth.

But... that's something a man like him would do, isn't it? Alec looks like the type who would take charge like that, who would force a girl to her knees and make her say dirty, filthy things to him. Make her beg for him, make her lose all control...

Heat pools between my legs at the thought.

"I've made you uncomfortable," Alec says, sounding concerned. He sets his book aside and stands, his full attention on me.

"No, not... not uncomfortable," I admit. I turn away, worried the blush of my cheeks will give away exactly what I was thinking. "I just... was surprised, is all. You caught me off guard."

"I'm sorry," he says, reaching out to touch my upper arm gently. "That wasn't my intention, Sydney. I didn't think about how my answer would affect you, or how inappropriate it was. I just answered."

Oh, I don't think this man has any idea just how much his answer *affected* me. I think I need a cold shower.

"You're fine," I insist. "Honestly, I—"

He hasn't let go of my arm. I glance between where he's touching me and his face. Those dark, gorgeous eyes.

"I..." I lick my lips.

My service bell rings, the sound a little too shrill, announcing that I have a customer waiting. I step back, breaking the spell between us, and Alec lets his hand fall back to his side, almost reluctantly.

"Customer," I explain with a sheepish grin, motioning toward the back of the store, where my register awaits. "I have to go."

I can feel Alec's eyes watching me as I leave, the force of his gaze so strong it's almost physical.

6

ASHTON

"He's in there," Sebastian tells me. "The little bookshop on the corner."

I stare across the street at the building he's gesturing toward, my fingers tapping nervously against my thigh. When Sebastian asked me to meet him here, to show me what Alec had been up to...

Well, this wasn't what I expected.

"You're sure?" I press. "He's been getting off work and coming... here?"

"Positive," Sebastian answers, straightening his horn-rimmed glasses, face deliberately blank. He's worn the same style of glasses since we were kids, and on anyone else, they might look old-fashioned. Uptight. Sebastian manages to make them look timeless. He crosses his arms over his chest and shrugs, casually. "He's been in there every night this week, according to his credit card charges. I even checked his phone's location, to be sure."

"And he's not... meeting anyone?" I ask.

Sebastian glances at me over the rim of his glasses, a flicker of annoyance in his blue eyes. For someone as closed off as him, the gesture is practically the equivalent of flipping me off and calling me an asshole. "Like who?" he asks, the skepticism sharp in his tone.

"Like..." I wave my hands through the air, searching for an explanation. "Like a rival cartel, or a fucking FBI informant, or something. I don't know. Anything that would explain why he's so closed off lately and spending so much time in a... in a fucking bookstore!"

"Let me be sure I understand this. You'd rather believe our brother is working behind our backs with the FBI than believe he's spending time somewhere without telling you?" When my only answer is a glare, Sebastian continues, "I've been watching him come and go after work for the last two days. I haven't seen anything—or anyone—suspicious. He's not meeting anyone."

"So then, what? Why is he spending so much time here?"

Leaning back against his motorcycle, Sebastian pauses to consider his words, the breeze ruffling his dark hair. I wait. My fingers drum impatiently on my leg, my muscles twitching to move.

"I think it's a woman," he says finally.

Now that throws me.

"Bullshit," I snap, glaring at him.

Sebastian shrugs. Nodding toward the store, he says, "There's a woman I've seen a few times through the window. Looks like she works there."

"And?" I press.

"And she's attractive." Sebastian straightens his glasses again. He lets my irritation roll right off him when he answers, like he doesn't even notice. The prick. "Brunette. Good figure. She looks like his usual type."

"And he would be keeping this from me, why exactly?"

The corner of his lip twitches upward just a fraction.

"Maybe this time Sterling doesn't want to share his toys with you, Ashton. Ever think of that?"

"Fuck you," I say, but there's no heat to it. I run a hand over my face, rubbing at the stubble on my jaw. "We don't always share. He knows that."

Sebastian's snort is all the answer I need to know he doesn't believe me.

And since he's kind of being an asshole, I decide to repay him in kind. What else is a big brother for?

"Plus, I never heard you complaining," I tease, grinning at him and elbowing him in the side. "Tell me, Doc, how often are you watching when he and I bring home a girl to play with, huh? Do you ever consider just... joining in?"

Sebastian doesn't answer. Picking up his helmet, he slides it on as he disengages the kickstand on his motorcycle. That's all the warning he gives me to get out of the way before he straddles the bike and takes off, leaving me to wait for a car on my own.

Fucking prick.

7

SYDNEY

I was livid the day I caught Chase cheating. Angrier than I'd been in years. Angry enough the sheer force of it had scared me.

I'd been suspicious of the new girl he was working with ever since I'd seen them together at one of his work events a few months before. We'd been chatting happily with his boss when Chase had excused himself to grab us more drinks. When twenty minutes had gone by and he still hadn't come back with my Prosecco, I went to look for him.

I knew. The moment I saw them together, somehow, I just *knew*. Maybe it was the way he was standing at the bar, his face mere inches from hers, chatting and laughing. Maybe it was the way she was slowly stroking his arm. It wasn't the way you would touch a coworker. It was intimate. Sexual.

But I didn't want to cause a scene. I *never* wanted to cause a scene. I wanted to be good. Calm. So, instead of confronting them, instead of walking over and demanding why the hell she was touching my boyfriend like that, I simply...wandered back into the party, a sick, dizzy feeling starting in my head and working its way down to my belly.

When Chase finally found me, almost half an hour later, I had gone through enough of my deep breathing exercises and therapy mantras that I'd finally calmed down to the point where I could almost convince myself to let it go.

But I didn't. I knew I shouldn't have said anything to him about it; I knew he would just get defensive. But I couldn't help myself.

"Who's the blonde?" I asked him icily when he finally handed me my drink.

"Who? *Caroline?* We just work together, babe." He said it so dismissively, waving the mention of her away like it was nothing at all.

"You guys seemed close, is all. You certainly have *chemistry.*" I was seething as I said it, the words coming out caustic.

Chase didn't even acknowledge that I had said anything at all. And he never brought her up again.

But, months later, when I walked in on them fucking on our couch—the couch I had inherited from my *grandmother* and brought to his apartment, the couch we watched movies together on, cuddled together on—this was the moment he pointed to. The moment he claimed absolved him of all of it. After Caroline had grabbed her clothing and run out the door and I was sobbing on the floor of our apartment, Chase had leaned over me, lifted my chin, and told me, "It didn't mean anything, babe. I don't even find her that attractive. It's just...you kept going on and on about how we have *chemistry.* And it just...it made me look at her differently."

And then he said the words that broke me. Truly broke me. "Really, this is your fault, you know," he'd told me. "I never would have even considered it if you hadn't put the idea in my head."

Even remembering it makes me sick with rage. Makes me want to break something. Makes me want to—

"Earth to Syd!" Jade's hand appears in front of my face, waving. "Hello? You still in there?"

I blink, pulling myself out of my thoughts and back to reality. The anger I was feeling dissipates into nothing, leaving me feeling oddly shaky and empty in its absence.

Shit. I must have zoned out. What were we talking about? I glance down at the tickets next to the register and remember, my stomach sinking. *Oh, right.* The charity event.

"No. That's not happening," I say decisively. Well... semi-decisively. There's a little decisiveness in there, I swear. I push the tickets back toward her.

Jade's eyes are big as a kitten's as she stares at me. "Oh, come *on.* Please?"

I draw a deep breath. Jade's hair is purple today, a startling change from the pink, but like all the fashion colors she chooses, it suits her somehow. I used to think there was a method to her madness, an emotional explanation behind every color Jade picked when dying her hair.

Now? Now I suspect she just gets bored and grabs whatever bottle of hair dye she finds first, to hell with any logic or reason.

"You have been looking forward to this for *months,* Sydney," Jade whines. "You can't just not go!"

I frown at the tickets. Expensive tickets. Printed on expensive paper. The calligraphy is handwritten, not printed. Everything about them screams wealth and class. "Yeah, I *was* looking forward to it. But that was... before," I finish.

Before. It feels like my life is now permanently divided into two parts: *before,* when I was still with Chase, and *now.* When I'm alone.

"You have two tickets!" Jade presses, tapping them with a

fingernail. She's painted them purple too, I notice, to match her new hair. "I'll even go with you if you need company! But you can't let that dress go to waste, Sydney. It would be a *crime.* And I will call the police. I swear I will."

She's not wrong. The dress I picked out for the annual Sterling Charity Banquet is extraordinary. And there's no way I could return it now, so long after buying it and with no idea what happened to the receipt. It would be a waste of money to just let it sit in my closet, forever unworn.

When I first picked up two tickets to the charity banquet almost half a year ago, I was so excited to go I could hardly think of anything else. It sounded like a dream, like something out of a fairytale or one of my romance books. Chase and I, all dressed up and fancy, rubbing elbows with Fortune City's elite.

Sure, the tickets had been *way* too expensive, and the dress had a price tag that almost made me faint when I first saw it, but it was all for charity! And the idea of going there together, of dancing with my boyfriend? It sounded magical. Special.

He'd laughed at me.

I came home so excited that day, giddy to surprise him with a night just for us. Not with our friends, not arguing in our apartment, not in tears. Just one magical night to go back to how things were when we first met. Maybe this would be the thing to fix us. Maybe this would remind him I was supposed to be the love of his life. He would hold me close, press a kiss to my forehead, and we'd dance the night away. Hopelessly, deliriously in love.

But instead, he'd laughed at me.

He said it "wasn't his thing," and that was that. Discussion over. I hid the dress in my closet and haven't felt excited about it since.

I groan, putting my face in my hands and pushing the memories away.

"You *have* to go, Sydney," Jade insists. And I know she won't give up until I agree.

"Fine. I'll go," I mutter into my hands. I feel Jade break out her victory dance next to me but refuse to dignify it by looking. Even though her victory dances are glorious. The stuff of legends, really. "But only if you come with me!"

"Yes!" Jade squeals. "Oh, I'm going to meet a rich sugar momma, just you wait. This time next week, I'll be retired on a private beach in Fiji."

"And leave me here, to run this place all on my own?" I lower my hands to glower at her. "You wouldn't *dare*."

"The heart wants what it wants, Sydney. What can I say?" Jade lifts her shoulder in a casual shrug. "You wouldn't stand in the way of me and true love, would you?"

"I would if it means I have to handle all of our bookkeeping myself," I grumble. Jade throws back her head to laugh. Out of the corner of my eye, I see someone approaching the shop counter, book in hand, but I can't resist getting in one extra jab. "You're immediately making me rethink attending this stupid thing. You know that, don't you?"

"Attending what stupid thing?" a velvety voice asks.

I glance over at the customer, instantly recognizing the wide shoulders, the dark, perfectly styled hair. Mr. Tall, Dark, and Handsome himself.

"Hello again, Sydney," Alec says with a smile. I shiver. I wonder if he says my name that way on purpose, in an octave just slightly lower than he says everything else. It sends heat through my veins every time I hear it.

"Good evening, Alec," I greet him, swallowing all my naughty thoughts and giving him a work-appropriate smile. Jade saunters away after shooting me a conspicuous wink, leaving me all alone with him. "Did you find everything okay?"

"I did," he tells me. "But you haven't answered my question. What event are you attending?"

"Just a charity banquet thing," I answer, glaring at Jade's retreating back. *Traitor.* I turn back to give him my least flirtatious smile. Nothing but professional. "For the Sterling Children's Foundation. They have one every year. Have you heard of it?"

His lips twitch. "I've heard of it." There's a subtle amusement in his tone that makes me think it was a dumb question to ask him.

It probably was a dumb question. Of course he's heard of it. I mean, just look at the man's suit. He's exactly the sort of person who attends charity banquets and silent auctions and... and ballroom dances, I imagine.

I bite back a sigh and hold out my hand to take his book. When he passes it to me, I can't help but smile, any embarrassment at my social faux pas dissipating into the ether.

It's the second book in The Prince's Knife trilogy.

"You've already started it!" I laugh, noting the bookmark lodged in the pages about a quarter of the way through.

"I did," Alec confesses, almost sheepishly, sliding his hands into his pockets. "I couldn't resist. I hope that's all right, to read a little before purchasing it."

"Of course," I assure him. I often encourage customers to read the first few chapters of a book before they buy it. I'd much rather they leave with something they will read and enjoy than end up with a book that's just going to sit on their shelf for years gathering dust. I scan the book at the register and reach out to take his credit card. "Are you enjoying it?"

When I glance up, Alec's face says it all. My stomach falls.

"You're... not enjoying it," I interpret.

His frown deepens.

"No, I *am*," he says, choosing his words carefully. "I'm just... concerned."

"Oh?" I hand back his book with the receipt tucked inside the front cover. "Concerned about what?"

"I enjoyed the romance in the first book. Quite a bit. I liked Malachi and Phaedra's dynamic. It was... electric."

I nod enthusiastically. His words from before, about his favorite scene, jump into my head, and I force myself not to dwell on them.

"But..." Alec taps the new book, frowning. "Now there's this other man."

"Zayden," I supply.

"Zayden," Alec confirms, frowning at the book in his hand like it somehow offended him. "And he and Phaedra are becoming close."

"Oh!" I laugh. "I see. You don't want her to lose what she has with Malachi, right?" When he nods, I smile reassuringly. "Don't worry. This is a why choose series."

Alec stares back at me blankly.

"I have no idea what that means," he admits.

"It means the main character can have more than one love interest without giving up any of them," I explain. The trope has become so popular lately, I've had this conversation at least three times just this week. It's a concept I'm getting good at explaining. "*Why choose*, as in... why choose between the two of them, when you can have both?"

Alec still looks confused, so I continue, "You are picking up on the chemistry between her and Zayden. There's obviously romantic tension there, but that doesn't mean she's giving up on Malachi. They both offer her different things, right? Zayden is safe, and he makes her laugh. Malachi would burn the world down for her. She isn't going to pick one over the other, if that's what you're worried about happening. She's going to be with both of them."

Alec blinks slowly. There's something unreadable in his gaze as he stares at me. Something unexpectedly dark.

Oh dear. I feel a blush creep over my cheeks. He probably thinks I'm some sort of pervert now.

"So—and I want to make sure I'm understanding this, Sydney—you're saying Phaedra can be with Malachi, and also be with—"

"Zayden," I finish, nodding. "Yes."

His face is still unreadable as he regards me. "I didn't know that was a thing in these books," he admits, voice husky.

"Some of them," I say. "Certainly not all. It's more accepted in certain genres."

"And is this common in the books that *you* enjoy, Sydney?"

His gaze is so focused, so dark, and I know I've ruined it. He, officially, thinks I'm some sort of deviant. Great.

"Well, I read a lot of books," I tell him, noncommittally, fighting the urge to fidget. I'm not going to admit to him that... yes, actually. It has quickly become one of my favorite tropes. The idea of being shared between two men? Or maybe even... more?

It's thrilling in a way I can't quite explain. Sinful and selfish, sure, but *thrilling*. And there's a part of me—a small part, sure, it's there—that wants to know what that would be like. That wants to experience that outside of the pages of a book.

"I see." Alec licks his bottom lip. "Thank you, Sydney. That was... very informative."

"Anytime," I answer, my voice a little small.

Informative. Yeah.

He definitely thinks I'm a pervert now.

8

ASHTON

I could have sworn Sebastian said she was a brunette.

The woman behind the counter is cute, sure, but...

That's definitely some *bright* purple hair she's sporting, isn't it? But I haven't seen another woman working here so far, so just in case, I give her my biggest, sweetest smile. The smile that's dropped a thousand panties. The smile that's practically an invitation to sit on my face and stay there as long as they want.

"I'll have a chocolate chip blended ice coffee," I tell the woman behind the counter. "Extra pump of syrup. The biggest size you've got."

I watch her make the drink, careful not to stare too intently or in a way that might make her uncomfortable. Honestly, Sebastian must be going crazy, because she doesn't really look like Alec's usual type at all. And, yeah, she's gorgeous, in an alternative punk rocker kind of way, but I can't imagine she's the woman he's been coming here to see every day. She's just not very... him.

Not very *us*.

When she hands me the drink, I slip a twenty in the tip jar, just in case I'm wrong and she is the girl Alec is spending time with. Hell, even if I'm right, it always pays to overtip when you can afford it. And we can definitely afford it. The pretty grin she gives me as I saunter away with my treat is well worth the cash.

I take a big gulp of the sugary drink as I wander through the rest of the shop, stopping now and then to check out some books and make it look like I'm a real, honest-to-goodness bibliophile just popping in to sample the wares. Nothing suspicious here, folks. Just your regular run-of-the-mill bookworm.

The place is cute. Every aisle is clean and tidy, with fun displays on the ends advertising new releases and highlighting local authors. Some even have merchandise for the store itself, and I stop to admire a collection of *Book Boutique and Bakery* mugs and tote bags, grinning at the logo. There are a few different styles, some featuring adorable cartoon baked goods, with massive, animated eyes.

Cute.

I slurp more of my drink noisily through the straw and wander down another aisle. I still haven't seen any other employees. Maybe Sebastian was wrong. Maybe there is a girl Alec has been coming here to see, but she's a customer. Maybe—

"What the fuck do you think you're doing?" a familiar voice stops me.

I grin. Busted.

"Shopping for books," I answer, not turning around to acknowledge Alec at all. I pull a book from the shelf at random and make a show of reading the blurb on the back before putting it back where it came from. "What does it look like I'm doing?"

"Cut the shit, Ashton," Alec snaps.

I turn around, my free hand and iced drink raised in surrender. *Okay*, I smile, *you caught me.*

"Look," I admit. "Doc noticed you'd been spending a lot of time here. We just wanted to figure out why, that's all. No harm, no foul."

"And Sebastian didn't think to *ask me?*" he asks through gritted teeth.

"You and I both know Doc is more of a watcher, not an asker." I chuckle. "And you're not exactly the most approachable guy lately, boss. Even with us."

Exhibit fucking A, he looks like he might shatter a tooth with how hard his jaw is clenched.

"We're giving you your space, okay?" I tell him. "As you requested."

"This is not giving me my space," Alec argues.

"Well, this is about the best we can do." I laugh, moving down the aisle and toward the next section, turning to talk to him over my shoulder. "You know us, boss, we're just as big of control freaks as you are, so if you think—"

I slam into someone, not looking where I'm going. My drink spills, the cup crushing against my chest and splashing ice-cold coffee over the front of my shirt.

I barely even notice.

For the first time in my life, I'm left completely speechless, as I stare down into the most delicious pair of brown eyes I've ever seen. Chocolate eyes. Sweet as a chocolate chip blended iced coffee with an extra pump of syrup. Wild brown curls, and the cutest little nose that's ever existed. Now this woman...this is our—I mean *his*—type.

"Shit!" The woman in front of me yelps. She's holding a huge cardboard box against her chest, and I'm relieved to see that none of my drink spilled onto her. As if catching herself, she readjusts her features and looks up at me. "I'm so sorry, I didn't see you, and—" She gasps, twisting the box away to see the mess of ice and sugar running down my shirt. "Your shirt! Oh, no!"

Her face crumbles, and I nearly trip over myself trying to reassure her.

"Completely my fault," I say, because truthfully, it was. Of course she couldn't see over that massive box, and I'm the dickhead not looking where I'm going, just barreling into everything, as usual. "Are you—are you all right?"

She ignores the question entirely, staring at the mess running down my front.

"That shirt is going to be ruined. That will never come out." She lets out a deep breath. "I'm so sorry about that, I—"

The shirt. The shirt is upsetting her. That's fixable. Not stopping to think, I thrust what's left of my drink behind me toward Alec, and pull my shirt off, turning it inside out and balling it up to make sure I don't accidentally drip on anything.

"There we go," I tell her. "All better, see?"

"I don't think that... oh." Her eyes go straight to my abs. She swallows, gaze trailing up my chest, and slowly back down to the waistline of my jeans. "*Oh.*"

Christ, she's adorable. I've never been so thankful for 5 AM workouts with my trainer in all my life. A blush creeps over her cheeks, staining them a delightfully naughty pink.

This girl could be the death of me.

"Let me take that from you," Alec says, stepping around me and reaching for the box she's carrying.

"Oh. Oh no, that's all right. I'm—" But he's already taking it, tossing my drink in the trash in the process. Asshole. What a waste. There was still plenty left. Eh, easy come, easy go, I guess. I toss my ruined shirt into the bin right after it.

"Are you sure you're all right?" I ask as Alec sets the box down on the shop floor and starts to open it for her.

"Uh-huh," she answers, hooded eyes locked on my chest. The tip of her tongue comes out to wet her lips. "Never better."

Naughty girl.

I reach out, touching her chin and angling her head up until she makes eye contact with me. God, those eyes of hers. So fucking sweet.

"Are you okay?" I repeat.

She clears her throat. "Yes," she finally answers. "I'm... I'm fine, thank you."

"Is this the final book in The Prince's Knife series?" Alec asks. He sounds excited, eager even, and I shoot him a surprised look. Since when does he even read?

"What? Oh! Oh, yes! We got them in a few weeks ago, but I can finally start putting them out for sale after we close," she answers him.

"Would you put one aside for me, Sydney?" he asks her.

Sydney. I nearly groan. The name suits her. Sinfully sweet Sydney. Yeah, I like that.

Curious, I reach for a book, lifting it out of the box. There's a dragon on the cover, and that's cool, I fuck with dragons.

"One for me, too," I tell her, reading the back. A lot of complicated names, here.

"It's the third in a series," our naughty girl—*Sydney*—objects, as I flip through the pages. "You should read the other two first. They aren't stand-alone books."

"Nah, it's chill." I watch action flicks out of order all the time. What's the difference? "I'll figure it out. So, does she ride the dragons, or hunt the dragons? What's the story there because I love—"

I stop, eyes widening as they flick over the page.

This scene has nothing at all to do with dragons.

"I need that back. I'm not supposed to let anyone have them until after midnight," Sydney says, a little firmly, reaching out to take the book from me. But I pivot away from her, holding it up higher until she can't reach.

Because this?

I could fuck with this.

"Is she..." I swallow, flipping the page. "Is she fucking three guys at once here?"

Alec's eyes snap up.

"*Three?*" he asks. "What do you mean, *three?* Who's the third?"

"How should I know? There's a Zayden... Malachi, and some guy named..." I try to pronounce the word, mouthing it before I say it. "Damascus?"

Sydney gasps, a hand flying up to cover her mouth.

"No!" she squeals, the words muffled from her fingers. "The *prince?*"

"Wow, he is *hung*," I mutter, flipping to the next page. "Is she... holy shit, there is a lot of double penetration happening here. I don't think this position is even physically possible, but I guess if you had a railing, you could..."

"That's enough," Alec says, shooting to his feet and yanking the book out of my hands. My cock twitches in disappointment. It was just getting good. "First of all," he snaps at me, "no fucking spoilers. And second of all, she told you no one is supposed to read it until midnight. You're going to get her in trouble."

He hands the book back to her, and she clutches it to her chest, looking stunned.

"Sydney, please excuse him. This is my... coworker, Ashton."

Coworker? Okay, *ouch*, we're practically brothers. But, fine, I get it.

"You can call me Ash," I tell her.

"It's nice to meet you, Ash," she says, sounding a little dazed.

"I am sorry about that, Sydney," I tell her, grinning and rubbing at the back of my neck. "I got a little caught up in the, uh, story."

I wink, and the way she blushes in return is sweeter than any iced coffee with extra syrup I've ever had.

"It's okay," she assures me. "But I, uh... I really need you to put on a shirt. It's café policy. All customers have to...you know, wear clothing."

She sets the book back in the box and looks around, eyes landing on the display of *The Book Boutique* merchandise.

"What size are you?" she asks, walking over to the display and kneeling in front of it. I watch as she pulls out a stack of simple white shirts with their store logo.

"XXL," I tell her with a smug smile. Next to me, Alec rolls his eyes, but so what? It's true.

Sydney frowns, selecting a shirt from the pile and standing up. "I'm so sorry, the biggest size we have is a large. Will this work?"

She hands it to me, and I grin. There's a muffin on the front of it, with big sparkly eyes. I pull it on over my head, yanking on the fabric to cover my stomach.

It's useless. The shirt doesn't reach my belt, and the sleeves are so tight around my arms I feel like I'm going to burst through the seams. I'm one hard flex away from ripping the entire thing into pieces. But the way her eyes linger on my body, the tip of her pink tongue coming out to wet her lips again, has me grinning.

"It's perfect," I tell her.

And for the first time, I don't give a fuck whether Alec wants to share.

Because I won't be able to stay away from this one.

9

SEBASTIAN

I'm surrounded by idiots.

"Can you take that stupid thing off?" I ask, glancing over at where Ashton is lounging on the couch, taking up the whole damn thing all on his own. As usual. "It's an eyesore."

Ashton just shakes his head with a laugh, running a hand over the front of his new shirt. The words printed on the front are stretched so tight across his chest they're not even legible. A grotesque cartoon *something* above them looks like it was flattened by a truck.

"No way, it was a gift from our girl," he says, grinning like an idiot. "I might never take it off."

"Excuse you?" Alec says, pivoting in his office chair to stare him down. "Since when is she '*our* girl'?"

His tone is openly hostile, but he's not fooling either of us. For whatever fucked-up reason this is what he's always preferred. What *both of them* have always preferred. One woman shared between the two of them. Whatever possessive streak he has with this new one is hardly going to change that.

"Since I saw her and fell head over heels in love!"

Ashton groans, rubbing his face. "And come on, you can't tell me she isn't down for it. With that stuff she likes to read? Fuck, I bet she's thinking about it right now, imagining all the things the two of us could do to her. All the ways we could take her..."

Fucking idiots.

"*Focus*," I snap. "Viper will be here any minute, and she's not going to be anyone's girl if he finds out about her, right? So, cover it up or *take it off*."

Grumbling, Ashton finally does as he's told.

Smart move. Our final brother isn't exactly right in the head, and if Alec and Ashton are the type to fixate on something, it's nothing, *nothing*, compared to how obsessive Viper can get.

They'll want to keep him as far from her as possible until they're finished with her and have moved on.

Right on schedule, a few seconds after Ashton pulls on a massive hoodie to cover his ridiculous shirt, the door flies open, and in he walks. Murder on two legs. Almost as big as Ashton, hair cut right to the scalp to showcase all his scars, Viper stalks into the room.

Viper was never quite right, even back at the orphanage where we all grew up together. He was always a little too violent, a little too close to having a full-on meltdown over nothing at all.

Years of working for the East Coast mafia in Empire City with us under Dante just made him worse. Far, far worse. And now the creature that stands before us isn't so much a man as he is a loaded fucking gun. Thank God we're the ones with our finger on the trigger.

Viper doesn't say anything. He enters with a grin, showing too many teeth, and walks right up to Alec's desk before dropping something heavy on top of it.

Giovanni's decapitated head lands on the wood with a wet thud.

"Jesus fucking Christ," Ashton swears, standing up from the couch and turning away from it. He grips his hair in his hands, bending forward at the waist, and I wonder briefly if he's going to be sick. For all his fighting, for all the violence he's endured and inflicted, Ashton never really developed a taste for blood.

Not like some of us.

Alec barely reacts. He stares into Giovanni's cloudy gaze for a long moment before looking up at Viper.

"Did you get a name?" he asks.

Viper laughs, slow and soft at first, letting it build until he's practically hysterical.

"I got a name!" he squeals. Reaching into his pocket, he pulls out a voice recorder.

A guttural scream fills the room when Viper presses play on the device, and this time, even Alec flinches. Ashton swears again, voice low and nearly inaudible over the sounds of the recording. I don't move, don't even blink.

I've seen Viper's work up close and personal so many times it doesn't even faze me anymore.

"Please!" the man on the recording shrieks. "Oh God, please, I'll give you anything."

"This is the best part," Viper assures us, smiling. His eyes are wild and black, like a shark's. The sound of loud buzzing whirs to life on the recording, and the screaming intensifies. I shoot Viper a glare, recognizing the sound of a bone saw.

My bone saw.

"I cleaned it. Don't worry, Doc," he assures me with a wink.

Idiots, every single one of them.

"Viper, is all this really necessary—" Alec begins, reaching for the recording device. Viper just laughs, holding up a finger for him to wait.

The screaming goes on for another ten seconds. Long enough that I'm sure, this time, Ashton is going to be sick.

And then...

"*DANTE!*" Giovanni's disembodied voice screams from the recording. "Oh God, he said his name was Dante. That he knows you from way back. Please, I beg you—"

The recording stops.

"*Dante!*" Viper coos, throwing his arms wide in excitement. "Told you I got a name! And what a fucking name it is!"

But Alec isn't looking at him anymore. And Ashton isn't looking for the waste bin.

They're both staring at me.

The symptoms of a panic attack are remarkably similar to a cardiac event. So much so that patients often confuse the two. A racing heart and tightness bordering on pain in the chest. Sweating. Numbness or tingling in the hands and arms. A sense that you are, at this very moment, about to die.

I don't let any of it show on my face as my brothers watch me.

"He's lying," I hear myself in a voice completely devoid of emotion. Inside, I want to fucking scream. "Dante is dead."

Even as I say it, a sickening voice inside me asks, *But what if he's not?*

What if you fucked up?

The look on my brothers' faces makes me wonder if they're thinking the same thing.

"It's a trick," I hear myself say. "We've been actively encroaching on his old territory over this last year. Someone is trying to scare us away, that's all. Trying to make us think he's back."

It's smart. Something I would do. Dante was the face of

organized crime on the East Coast for decades before I put a bullet in him. He was feared. Untouchable.

The perfect phantom for someone to use if they wanted to scare us.

We had hoped that the mess we'd left Dante's organization in had hobbled any loyalists that bastard still had. Hoped it was over. And when Alec started taking over Dante's territory in Empire City piece by piece over the last year with no pushback, it felt like those hopes might be proven true. That we could finally reclaim the kingdom that should have been ours. Alec as the heir apparent, back to take his throne.

Turns out I'm a fucking idiot, too.

"You think this is a takeover?" Alec asks me carefully. "Someone making a play for our organization?"

I shake my head.

"I think... I think someone is testing the waters," I say, willing myself to believe it. "They're trying to see if we're as strong as everyone says we are. Trying to see if we can be scared away. A first strike. They'll be looking for any blind spots and how to exploit them next."

"Well," Alec says, coming to his feet. The head on his desk stares up at him blindly. "Let's make sure they don't find any, shall we?"

10

VIPER

The man in our wet lab today is a bleeder.

I set my knife down and consider some of my other instruments, laid out on the table before me like a feast. Bleeders don't last long if you don't use them right. I click my tongue, frowning down at the collection I had originally picked out for tonight. No. No, these won't do at all.

My cell phone rings, Schubert's Ave Maria filling the room, soulful notes hitting the tile walls and echoing back at me.

"Just a second," I say to the man strapped to the table. His sobs are wet and loud and discordant with the music, two disparate songs layered over one another. "I have to take this."

For once, I'm glad Sebastian isn't down here with me. I reach for the phone, and my fingers smear blood all over the glass when I swipe the screen to answer. That prick always makes me wear gloves.

And isn't it so much better when you can get your hands dirty?

"Morning, boss," I say into the speaker. I have to speak

loudly, over the bleeder's crying. I lean against the table, smiling down at the phone even though he can't see me.

"It's seven at night, Viper," Alec informs me.

Eh. Six in one hand, half a dozen in the other. Time means nothing down here in the lab. The real world and its rules don't exist here.

I pluck a ball hammer from the table and consider it, twisting it in the light. The man strapped to the table whimpers.

Nah.

"Found out anything yet?" Alec asks.

"Nope," I say, popping the *P* and setting the hammer down. Besides being our wet lab's current occupant, the man on my table is also co-owner of a brothel just south of Empire City, in a shitty little city called Seneca. And back in the day, this fucker used to be nice and cozy with our old boss, Dante.

Cozy enough he might know exactly who's impersonating him. Who's stupid enough to use that fucker's name to scare us.

And if that's true, and this little bleeder knows who might be behind the curtain? I'll find out, one way or another tonight. And if it's not? Well... at least I have something to keep me entertained for a few hours, right?

The best things in life are free and bloody, after all.

"Nothing yet," I say. "But I'll keep looking. You checking up on me?"

Alec snorts a laugh.

"Hardly," he says. "Just calling to remind you that we'll be out tonight. All of us."

Oh, right. The *fancy* thing. The reason Doc isn't down here with me, rolling his eyes and reminding me to put on a pair of gloves. The reason we aren't getting our hands dirty together.

"But I want you to call if you have any updates for me. Understand?"

"You got it, boss," I sing into the phone, though I'm ninety percent sure he's already hung up. I pick up the phone from the table and slide it into my pocket, ignoring the blood still smeared on the screen.

Sighing, I run my fingers over the instruments on my table, waiting for the right one to speak to me. When my hand hovers over the ice pick, I feel that familiar tug.

Bingo.

Picking it up, I turn back to my guest and grin.

"Sorry for the interruption. Now...where were we?"

11

SYDNEY

I AM A SEDUCTRESS. I AM A SIREN, BORN OF DESIRE and sin.

I am sex incarnate.

At least, that's how I feel tonight. In this dress, with my makeup done and my hair perfectly styled, I feel beautiful. Really, truly *beautiful*.

But even more, I feel powerful.

Sure, my dress is a little low-cut, showing off a bit more cleavage than I would usually flaunt. And, yes, the slit up the side runs so high it practically hits the top of my thigh. But that just adds to how sexy I feel tonight. The way the midnight blue fabric sparkles like stars, slowly morphing into a shining silver hem, makes this dress a work of art. It's the most beautiful piece of clothing I've ever owned.

I never want to take it off. I might spend the rest of my life in this dress, shopping in it, doing chores in it, sleeping in it, the works.

Even food tastes better when you're dressed like this. Or maybe that's just a testament to the incredible catering they hired for the Sterling Children's Foundation Annual Charity Banquet.

As they clear our plates away at the end of an outstanding meal, I'm pleasantly full, and only half listening to the keynote speaker as he winds down.

"And of course, none of this would be possible without the wonderful work of our biggest benefactor, Mr. Mason Sterling. Everyone, please give him a round of applause."

Someone stands as we all clap, but our cheaper-ticket table is so far from the stage I can barely make out anything other than dark skin and hair. Plus, I'm admittedly a little distracted.

Jade hasn't yet found a sugar momma to take her to Fiji, sadly. But she has attracted the attention of one of the wait staff.

"You should go talk to her," I whisper, nudging Jade as I say it.

"And leave you here all alone? Hardly." Jade huffs, leaning her elbow on the table. Her purple hair has faded to a soft lavender, and it's a perfect color match to the full-length satin dress she chose to wear. Despite her objections, her eyes flick to the far wall as she says it, to where the cute blonde keeps glancing at her and blushing.

"Oh, please." I roll my eyes. The speaker finishes detailing exactly how much money this event has raised for underprivileged children in Fortune City, and we all clap politely again. "Just go talk to her, Jade. I'll be fine. I want to check out the orchestra and the ballroom, anyway. Maybe grab a drink. Who knows? Maybe I'll find someone to *canoodle* with, too."

I wiggle my eyebrows at her, and Jade smirks. A flurry of movement around the room tells me the speeches must have finally finished. The people around us have come to their feet and are filtering out of the elegant dining room, toward the live music and the ballroom. I nudge Jade again.

"Nope." Jade scrunches her nose and shakes her head. "Not going to happen. I dragged you here. I'm sure as hell not abandoning you now."

"Jade, it's fine! Really. Go and talk to her." This time, we both glance over, catching the blonde watching us. She tucks her hair nervously behind her ear and looks away.

I can tell she's wavering by the way Jade's foot taps incessantly against the table leg. Jade can't resist a pretty face for long.

"I'm going to get a drink," I announce, pushing my chair back and standing. "And maybe spend some time in the garden until some lonely old millionaire takes pity on me and asks me to dance. And *you* are going to talk to her."

Jade throws her hands up in surrender.

"Fine!" she says. "But I'm coming to find you in thirty minutes, okay? So don't let anyone sweep you off to their yacht before then."

"I make absolutely no promises," I say, running my hands over the fabric of my dress, luxuriating in the feel under my touch. I glide away from the table, but not before shooting her a wink. "Love you," I sing, grinning over my shoulder as I navigate my way through the tables.

"To the moon and back!" Jade calls after me, loud enough to turn a few heads.

By the time I make my way out of the dining room and into the ballroom—stopping along the way to marvel at how beautiful and perfectly decorated everything is—I'm one of the last people out of the dining area, and the line to the bar is atrociously long. It stretches along the far wall, easily fifty people deep.

Fine. My drink can wait a little. To the garden, it is!

Already several couples have taken to the massive dance floor, waltzing close to one another, swaying to the rhythm of the live orchestra. I give the dancers plenty of space, keeping to the sides of the room as I make my way toward the open doors that lead to the garden.

Maybe my little joke about someone asking me to dance wasn't that unrealistic after all. I notice a few heads turning my way as I walk. Just for fun, I swing my hips a little more than necessary, loving the feeling of my dress's high slit and the way the fabric moves around my legs.

I am sex. I am beauty. I am—

A voice calls out my name, and I freeze, a cold chill running over me.

Oh no.

"Sydney?"

Oh no, oh no.

I know that voice.

Pasting a smile on my face to hide my panic, I turn, counting to ten in my head as I do so. *Think happy thoughts, Sydney.*

I inhale peace and exhale worry, I say to myself, not believing a single damn word.

I am an ocean of calm.

"Chase," I greet my ex-boyfriend as he approaches. Scratch that, my ex-boyfriend *and* his new girlfriend. My stomach sinks as I recognize the woman at his side, his arm wrapped around her waist.

Of course he's here. After I'd begged him to come, and he'd still said no. After I'd bought both our tickets with my own money, after he'd made me feel so guilty for expecting even the slightest amount of courtesy from him by wanting one special night. One night for me. Of course, after all of that, he shows up here.

With her.

And just like that, my dream night has become a nightmare.

He even dressed up, something he'd consistently failed to do when we were together. I recognize his suit as the same one he wore to his uncle's wedding two years ago, and though it's a little tight around the middle, it still fits. And he looks good. He's always been handsome, with his boy-next-door looks and charm, always been the sort of man to turn heads.

That was part of the problem.

Caroline gives me a shy smile, an unreadable expression on her perfectly contoured face. I wonder if she's as uncomfortable seeing me as I am seeing her. Her dress flows down her body in mirror opposition to mine, high-necked with a low back, golden hued and sleek.

She looks good, too. Really good.

I hate her a little for it.

"You got a haircut," I say to Chase, stupidly, regretting the words the moment they are out of my mouth.

"Uh, yeah," he laughs, touching the tips of his short hair. "A few since we broke up, actually."

His gaze rolls over my dress.

"That's quite a look," he says. If he thinks my outfit is too provocative—the neckline too low or the slit up the side too bold—at least he doesn't say it out loud. In fact, the way his eyes linger on my cleavage makes me think he approves. Caroline makes a sound, clearing her throat to draw Chase's attention back to her.

"Thanks," I say reflexively. I eye the exit to the garden, glancing back over my shoulder. "Well, I should get going. I need to find my date." The lie rolls off my tongue with surprising ease.

I say it to be cruel, wanting to hurt him. He doesn't need to know I'm here with Jade, and I want him to think that maybe I have someone else too. Make them realize they aren't the only ones that have moved on, even if it is a lie. But Chase doesn't react. He doesn't even look at me.

Acting like he wasn't even listening, he plants a delicate kiss on Caroline's bare shoulder, making her blush. My insides twist.

God, I'm pathetic.

Why am I standing here entertaining this? Why can't I just walk away? My fists clench at my side, and just as I'm about to turn and leave, Chase finally glances back at me.

"Hey, listen, I've been wanting to talk to you, but you, uh... you haven't returned any of my messages lately." He says it so casually, like he doesn't even care. Like he wasn't messaging me constantly, day after day, without pause.

Does your girlfriend know how much you've been messaging me? I wonder.

"I blocked your number," I say, the words tumbling from my lips before I can stop them.

That gets his attention, at least.

"I see." His face hardens. He hadn't expected that. Chase never dealt well with not being in control of a situation. The hand on Caroline's hip tightens visibly, and she winces. "Well, I guess that explains it, then."

I almost feel sorry for her, seeing that look of pain. I remember this. I remember the times when his anger got the better of him... when his touches were anything but gentle.

I remember what it was like to be afraid of him.

"Why were you messaging me, anyway?" I ask Chase, tearing my eyes away from where he's touching her. "I thought we—"

"I was only messaging you because I was being *nice*," he says, cutting me off. Always cutting me off. "Caroline is thinking about moving in with me, and we're just not comfortable having your stuff around anymore. I wanted to return the last of your things."

With those words, a flicker of surprise appears in Caroline's bright blue eyes, and she looks decidedly uncomfortable. Did she ask him to reach out to me, I wonder, or is this the first she's hearing of it?

He did that to me, too. Made decisions without me. Made inferences without my input and treated them like they were fact and not just his opinions.

"But if that's how you're going to act, I have no problem just tossing it all in the trash where it belongs," Chase finishes. His lip twists up into a hostile sneer, and I don't doubt for a second that he'd do exactly that.

I shake my head, frustrated tears welling in my eyes. Of course, he would ruin this night for me. Of *course*. I don't want to cry in front of them. I can't let them have this power over me. I can't keep letting him get to me like this. I can't keep letting him *win*.

But I don't know how to get out of this situation. As always, he's taken away all of my fight, all of my will.

Just walk away! a voice inside me screams. *Tell him to fuck off and walk away!*

But I can't.

"I guess I can stop by and pick them up," I say, resigned and just hoping for this interaction to end. Defeated by him once again.

"Great," Chase says, a cruel edge to his voice. "Well, maybe you can stop being dramatic and unblock my number so we can talk like adults. You can be so difficult when you—"

"Ah, *there* you are," a deep resonant voice interrupts, speaking over him. Someone touches me, taking my hand in theirs and wrapping a thick arm around my waist, mirroring the couple in front of us. "I lost you for a moment there, Red."

I blink in surprise as I stare up into the face of Mr. Tall, Dark, and Handsome himself.

Alec.

Now this? This is a man who was born to wear a tuxedo. The one he's in right now looks crafted just for him, hugging every delicious muscle in his body. He looks perfectly in his element here, like he was made for this ballroom. Or like it was made for him.

I stare up at this handsome creature, speechless, my mouth partially open in shock. Dark eyes locked on mine, Alec brings my hand up to his face, and places a soft kiss on my knuckles, sending a flutter of excitement through my body.

"Alec? What are you—"

"And who is this?" Alec interrupts me, pulling me close enough that we're standing hip to hip, my body pressed flush against his.

Oh. Right. For a moment, I'd forgotten all about him. *Them.* Caroline's eyes are tracking Alec up and down, her mouth agape. She looks genuinely stunned. And while I know Alec is attractive—possibly the most attractive man I've ever seen, if we're not including his muscular friend Ash—her reaction is still over-the-top.

"Babe, why don't you go grab us some more drinks," Chase urges, pushing Caroline away without looking at her.

Chase's posture has stiffened, and for the first time tonight, I know I have his full attention. A muscle in his jaw tightens as he stares at Alec's hand now resting casually on my hip. Caroline is clearly put off by the request, but she takes a deep breath, schooling her features. Not wanting to start a fight with Chase she's sure to lose. I remember that feeling vividly. Without another word, she walks away, glancing back at us over her shoulder a few times before she reaches the line to the bar.

"Chase," my ex introduces himself, holding out his hand for Alec to shake. I've never seen him so obviously jealous of another man. It makes me feel strangely powerful. "I'm Sydney's... *was* Sydney's fiancé," Chase finishes, awkwardly.

"Ah, well, better luck next time," Alec purrs, his fingers tightening on me in a gentle squeeze. Chase's eyes track the motion, and his scowl deepens.

"And you are...?" Chase prompts, hand still outstretched, waiting.

Finally letting me go long enough to take Chase's hand, Alec smiles widely.

"Mason Sterling," he introduces himself. My heart skips a beat. "How kind of you to come to my little charity event this evening."

12

SYDNEY

Mason Sterling.

Mason.

Sterling.

Whatever Chase and Alec are saying to one another now is lost to me. I can't hear a single word of it over the sudden rush of blood to my ears.

There's absolutely no way I heard him correctly.

Because there's no way that Alec—my bookstore Alec—is actually Mason Sterling, the multi-millionaire owner of every hotel and casino in Fortune City, who swept into town just a few years ago and suddenly seemed to own everyone and everything. The Mason Sterling who founded the Sterling Children's Foundation. The Mason Sterling who is responsible for this entire charity dinner.

Caroline's reaction to him makes a lot more sense now.

"Well, thank you so much for keeping my date company," Alec—or, rather, Mason—says, his voice pulling me from my stupor. "Come, Sydney, darling. You owe me a dance. A genuine pleasure to meet you, Chad."

"Chase," Chase corrects through gritted teeth as Caroline wanders back and delicately presses a beer to his palm. He doesn't even look at her as he takes it.

The dismissive gesture Alec gives him as he pulls me to the dance floor makes it clear he doesn't care either way.

I'm speechless. Numb, and barely aware of what's happening, as Alec pulls me to face him, taking one of my hands in his and sliding his other around my waist.

"He's still watching." Alec drops his head to whisper the words in my ear. "Let's give him a show, shall we?"

The orchestra strikes up a song, and then we're moving, Alec taking the lead and my feet mindlessly following as he leads me through a waltz.

Mason Sterling.

"You told me your name was Alec," I manage to say. The words sound flat.

"And it is," he assures me. He moves with an impossible grace, pulling me along with him, leading me effortlessly through the dance. "My full name is Mason Alexander Sterling. But I've always gone by Alec to my friends and family."

"I see," I murmur. It's a lie, I don't see at all. I can't reconcile the nebulous idea of Mason Sterling, millionaire businessman rumored to be involved in numerous illegal activities, with the Alec I've been lusting after these last few weeks. The Alec I've been fantasizing about. Sure, I knew he must have been well off, but...

We spin, moving across the dance floor with an ease that people stop to watch. I can feel eyes on us from all around the room. It's not just Chase who can't look away.

"I hope I didn't offend you by stepping in," Alec says. His hands shift where he's holding me, and I realize how closely he's pressed against me. How good his hands feel on my body, and how effectively he's leading me through the steps of this waltz.

And I've never ballroom danced a day in my life.

"With Chase?" I ask, tilting my head up to look at him.

He nods.

"You looked... upset," Alec explains, jaw tightening. "I thought you might need some backup."

"You didn't offend me at all," I tell him honestly. "Surprised me, though."

"Surprised you?" he asks.

"I didn't even know you would be here," I admit. "The Alec you, I mean. Not the Sterling you."

I can feel the laugh as it rumbles in Alec's chest.

"Were you hoping to see me, Sydney?" he asks in a husky voice. That voice. It does terrible things to me, instantly making me melt. "Hoping to find me here?"

"Maybe," I answer, a little breathless.

His hand moves to the small of my back, pressing me to him harder than necessary, as he leans down to whisper near my ear.

"Be honest, darling. Were you hoping I'd swoop in and save you?"

"No," I answer, with more bite than I feel. "I don't need someone to save me. Not even from him."

"Good," he tells me, voice turning dark. "Because I'm not a savior, Sydney."

He's close enough I can feel his next words warm my skin. "But if you gave me a chance, I would happily get on my knees for you and make you see God."

The music stops. For a moment, I think it's just that my hearing is gone, all the blood rushing out of my head. But no. The song has finished, the orchestra coming to a natural pause.

I can barely focus on the room around me. Did I just hallucinate? Did this man really just say those words to me?

My mind is completely blank except for one treacherous thought: There's nothing I want more in this world right now than for Alec—Mason Alexander Sterling—to get on his knees for me.

Other dancers are applauding the orchestra, but I'm frozen in place as Alec runs his hand down my side until he reaches the high slit in my dress. His fingers slip below the fabric, caressing my thigh.

"I love this dress you're wearing. It's so beautiful," he says, voice breathy. "But you have no idea how much I want to tear it off of you."

My breath hitches. I'm so turned on I'm shaking, hyper-aware of every part of me that's pressed against him.

"I..." I open my mouth, but nothing more comes out.

Before I can pull myself together, before I can even get my breathing calm or figure out what to say to him, I feel a hand on my shoulder, and I turn.

It's Ashton. Alec's coworker. The mouthwateringly muscular coworker...

"Mind if I cut in?" he asks with a bright grin. He's not asking me, I realize. He's asking Alec.

A brief flicker of irritation cuts across Alec's face, but he inclines his head and steps back, gesturing for Ashton to proceed. And just like that, I'm moving again, the orchestra striking up a new song, Ashton pulling me close for an entirely new dance.

13

ASHTON

God, she's adorable. Her dance with Alec has left her all hot and bothered, and though she's trying her best to hide it, she's completely failing.

Sweet girl. She'll learn soon enough that she doesn't need to hide anything from us. She couldn't, even if she wanted to.

But, because I can be a bit of an asshole and I love to stir the pot, I smile and let my fingers stroke the small of her back as I ask, "Are you feeling okay? You look a little flushed."

Flushed is an understatement. Whatever Alec said to her, she's a mess. Her lips are parted and ruby red, and her cheeks are glowing.

It's so fucking adorable.

"I'm fine," she assures me, giving me a shaky smile. "Just... It's a little warm in here, don't you think?"

I chuckle in answer.

She lets me lead in our dance, and though I'm not nearly as practiced as Alec, I manage to not embarrass us.

I think.

"Did you know?" she asks me suddenly, and when I frown

down at her, her lips thin and she shakes her head. "Of course you knew. What a stupid question. You work with him, don't you? I'm the only one who didn't know."

"Know what?" I ask, puzzled.

"He told me his name was *Alec*," she says in a tight voice. There's an unexpected edge to it.

"His name *is* Alec," I tell her, confused. I glance around to look for him. "What do you mean, he—"

I stop mid-sentence, a smile creeping over my face.

"Wait, you didn't know who he was?" I ask, voice teasing. "You really had no idea?"

"None," she confirms, sounding more than a little irritated.

I laugh, shaking my head at the glare she shoots me. "Sorry, Babygirl, I just... I assumed you knew. I mean... *everyone* knows Mason Sterling. He's been on the cover of nearly every magazine in the city. And, yeah, of course I knew. I'm his CMO."

Before she can ask, I quickly add, "Chief marketing officer. Don't ask me too much about the job, though. I'm terrible at it. We have a whole team to do the actual work. I'm just a pretty face."

I give her a wink, but it's not ego making me say it, it's just a fact. I've been there with Alec for most of those magazine shoots. Hell, I've even made a few covers, all on my own.

Not to brag or anything, but I've been named Fortune City's most eligible bachelor for two years in a row.

Now the blush on her face isn't from dirty thoughts. It's from embarrassment.

My smile falters.

"Hey," I stop moving, surprising her and a few of the couples dancing around us. Some of them glare at us as they pass. "Are you really upset?"

Sydney looks away and chews her lip.

"I don't know," she says.

It's a lie. An obvious one. She's holding herself back, and I don't like that. I want all of her, not just pieces.

"You can be honest with me, Babygirl," I say. "About anything. And if you're upset, I want to know. So I can fix it."

This time, she meets my eyes. She considers me for a few seconds, like she's weighing her next words carefully.

"I am upset," she finally admits. "It feels like he lied to me, even if he didn't actually... lie about anything. He misled me. Deliberately. And I don't know if I can trust someone who does that."

I nod quickly, eager for her to continue.

"And it makes me feel...stupid, I guess, that I didn't know." She huffs, crinkling her nose. "Plus, he's been coming to my shop every day, and buying books, and talking with me, and I just don't understand *why*. I didn't understand why *before*, and now, with this?" She gestures around the room, looking flustered.

"He likes you," I say. I mean, it's obvious, isn't it? "He comes by the store because he wants to see you."

Snorting a laugh, she rolls her eyes. "Yeah, right. Because I'm so amazing, and special and—"

"Stop." I reach up and cup her face in my hands, eyes boring into hers because I *can't*. I can't listen to her finish that sentence. "You are amazing, Sydney. Never think you're anything less. You're *perfect*."

She pulls back from me, out of my touch, looking stunned. "What?"

"You're *perfect*," I repeat. And I need her to know I mean it. "You want to know why he goes by your shop every day? It's to see you. Because he's half in love with you already. He's *smitten*. And that's not a word I've ever used to describe Alec before."

I'm not lying. Sure, he's dated women before, but the obsession is new. The way he's acting about her is new. She *is* special, and he recognizes it too.

Sydney shakes her head, looking incredulous. "But he doesn't even know me. *You* don't even know me, Ash. Neither of you do."

I clear my throat. "He probably knows more than you think." Not wanting her to dwell on that, or what surveillance he might have on her already, I add, "But if you think he doesn't know who you are, you can let him get to know you. If that's something *you* want. But don't tell me you're not amazing, because you *are*. I asked you to be honest with me. And that includes being honest with yourself."

"I just..." Sydney sighs, looking down at herself and shaking her head. "I don't know what someone like him could possibly see in me."

"Maybe ask him," I suggest. "I'm sure he's dying to tell you."

She frowns at me, considering. Then her gaze catches on something over my shoulder, and she steps away from me. Whatever she was thinking vanishes from her face, like she pulled on a mask.

"Excuse me, I... that's my friend," Sydney says, pointing. "I have to go."

Stay, I want to tell her. But I just stand there, like an idiot, while she walks away.

14

It's a relief to see Jade waiting for me across the ballroom, and I welcome the opportunity to excuse myself from dancing with Ash. I'm shaken after my conversation with him.

Shaken and *confused.*

Because the way Ash had touched me? The things he'd said about me? It made it sound like Alec wasn't the only one who was smitten.

But that couldn't be real, could it? What were the odds of one drop-dead gorgeous man wanting to pursue me, let alone two?

"Who," Jade asks, staring at me with wild eyes and a huge grin as I approach her, "was *that?*"

I glance back over my shoulder at them. Ash has joined Alec, chatting with him as they both wait in line for the bar. When he sees me looking, he waves at us, grinning.

"That's... Ashton," I tell Jade, squirming a little. "He's, uh. He's Alec's chief marketing officer."

Jade blinks.

"And Alec needs a marketing officer because...?" she asks.

"Because he's... Mason Alexander Sterling. I guess," I finish, twisting my hands together. "From, you know..." I wave my hand around the room we're in. "*This*. The Sterling hotels. And the, uh, casinos."

When I look at her, Jade looks like her eyes are going to pop out of her head.

"Shut up!" she squeals a little too loudly. A few people turn, frowning. She lowers her voice to hiss it again. "*Shut up!*"

I'm as stunned as she is.

"You know, I thought he looked familiar! Well, I was coming to see if you wanted to head home." Jade shakes her head and laughs. "But if you think for one second that I'm going to let you leave *now*, with both of those men practically drooling over you? You're out of your mind."

"Wait, what happened with..." I stop when I spot the cute blonde caterer standing a few feet away, waiting patiently. She gives me a hesitant but friendly grin.

"Oh, yeah." Jade smiles. "That's why I wanted to offer you a ride. Vanessa just finished her shift for the night, and—"

I slap Jade playfully on the arm, and she laughs.

"Vanessa!" I tease. "Tell me about *Vanessa!*"

"Well, Vanessa is a vegan," Jade says, forming the words carefully and refusing to meet my eyes.

I reel back.

"Jade, you love meat," I tell her, keeping my voice low so Vanessa can't overhear. "You once told me you would marry bacon—the *concept* of bacon—if they ever made that legal."

"And I stand by that," Jade says, face serious. "But... you know. I can pretend not to be a soulless carnivore for a little while, right?"

"At least you'll be *eating vegan* tonight." I barely manage to keep a straight face as I say it.

Jade smacks my arm. "Oh, Syd, that was *terrible*, really it was." She laughs. "But very funny. God, I'm so happy to have you back."

Something twists unpleasantly in my chest.

"What do you mean, have me back?" I ask. I force a laugh. "Where did I go?"

"Nowhere! It's just..." Jade hesitates. "Look, it's not your fault, but... But when you met Chase, it was like you just disappeared, a little. You were already having such a hard time after your parents, and then...when you met him, it's like you vanished even more. Like a part of you was just lost."

I don't know what to say to that, so I keep quiet. I felt the same way, but I had no idea that anyone else could see it, too. I didn't realize that I had changed that noticeably.

Jade exhales loudly and says, "I just mean... I missed you. It feels like you're really coming back to life lately. And I love that. I love *you*."

I know she means it, too. Jade has seen me through everything since childhood. She was there for me after my parents died, and later when I lost my grandmother. And she was there holding my hand after every fight with Chase. She knows me better than anyone.

I should have known I could never hide anything from her.

"It's good to be back," I tell her. And I mean it. But before she can get mushy on me again, I shoo her toward her date. "Now go! Take *Vanessa* home. I'm fine here."

Jade looks unsure. "You're sure? If you want me to stick around, I can tell her to leave without me."

"I mean it, go!" I glance back at the bar, where Alec and Ashton are both watching me. "I'm ... I'm interested to see what happens here. With them."

"Girl, *same*," Jade says with a chuckle. "Okay, well... if you're sure?"

I have to physically push Jade toward her waiting date,

laughing as I do so. She waves her fingers at me as the two of them disappear into the crowd.

"Love you," she calls over her shoulder.

"To the moon and back!" I answer, waving.

"Was that your ride?" Ash's voice asks from behind me.

The closeness of his voice makes me jump.

When I turn to look up at him, he's grinning at me, bright blue eyes sparkling. It's hard not to stare at him. It should be illegal for someone to be this good-looking.

"It was, yeah," I admit. I work very hard to keep my voice sounding neutral. Nonchalant. "But it's fine. I can always catch a taxi later."

Ash's grin widens. "Of course you can! Come on. Alec snagged us all a table."

He steers me through the crowd with a hand on my shoulder to where Alec is waiting with drinks. When we reach the table, Alec hands me a long-stemmed champagne glass, the bubbling liquid inside a strange shade of pink.

"Champagne with pomegranate juice," he informs me, seeing my confusion. "For a little extra taste. One of our signature drinks for the evening. I thought you might like to try it."

I take a sip, the bubbles tickling my lips, and instantly I'm in love.

"It's delicious," I tell him with a smile. "What's it called?"

Alec smirks. "Hades' Bargain."

Ash excuses himself to use the restroom, leaving Alec and me on our own. I sip at my champagne, trying not to blush at the intense way Alec is watching me. Trying not to think about the things he said to me before Ash interrupted us.

"Did you enjoy your dance?" Alec asks.

I pause before I answer, searching his face for any sign of anger at seeing me dance with another man. But I see nothing there. No jealousy, no irritation. He seems genuinely curious.

"I did," I answer honestly. "But... don't tell him, but you're a better dancer."

Alec's lips curve into a smile.

"I have a lot more practice," he assures me. "Ashton rarely attends these events, actually. He made an exception tonight. After he found out you were planning to come."

I take an extra-large gulp of my drink, ducking my head to hide my smile.

"I never thanked you earlier," I say. "For stepping in with my ex, I mean. Even if I didn't need saving, it was nice."

Alec taps his finger absently on the glass in his hand, nodding.

"Do you want to tell me about him?" he asks.

"I don't think I ever want to talk about him again for the rest of my life," I answer, and I'm rewarded with a chuckle. "But... we dated. For a little over three years."

"He called himself your fiancé," Alec presses. I don't miss the dark undercurrent in his voice. Like the idea that I could have been engaged is personally offensive to him.

I let out a long breath. "Well, that's news to me. He never officially asked me to marry him... I think he was going to, eventually. That's kind of what it was like with him towards the end. I was planning the rest of my life, building a business and a career, but to him it was just... an eventuality. Never something he had to put any effort into."

Alec is watching me closely, and even though I know I should stop, I can't. The words just spill out of me.

"I think I was holding on to how we felt for each other in the beginning. When things were nice and fun. And then, after we broke up, I realized I never stopped to question if he was actually any good for me. If I even *liked* being with him."

"Why did you break up?" Alec asks in a gentle voice.

The memory sends a wave of nausea through me.

"He cheated on me," I mutter. The words hang in the air, an embarrassment, and just for something to do, I swallow the rest of my champagne, twirling the empty glass by its stem in my fingers. "Had been cheating on me for a while, but... I finally found out, I guess. You sort of met her, the blonde he was with. Anyway, I found out, and that was that."

It wasn't, though. And knowing that makes the nausea in my stomach grow.

Because I didn't really end it, not then. I tried to make it work, even after what he'd done to me. I tried so damn hard.

It took two months after I found them together for it to finally sink in that this life I thought I'd been building with him —this future I thought we had—was just a lie. One stupid lie I'd deluded myself into believing.

He never stopped seeing her, either. He just stopped trying to hide it.

I'm pulled away from my thoughts when Alec takes my hand in his.

"It's not your fault," he says softly. "What he did to you? That's not your fault."

I swallow hard and can't meet his eyes.

"Believing him wasn't your fault," he insists. "Do you understand that, Sydney?"

I wish I could. But that's the problem, isn't it? Even after all this time, I don't believe it. Logically, I know I shouldn't be embarrassed that he fooled me. But emotionally?

"Hey, what did I miss?" Ash asks, coming through the crowd. He sets my empty glass on the table so he can take my hand, frowning. "Everything okay?"

"What's his last name?" Alec asks, ignoring Ash entirely. His thumb is stroking the back of my hand in a smooth, calming gesture that's leaving me a little breathless.

"Uh... Levine." I answer. "Chase Levine."

"Ashton, tomorrow morning I want you to find out where Chase Levine works," Alec says, voice low. "And buy the company."

"You... what?" I ask, stupefied.

"Sure thing," Ash answers, like it's a completely normal request. "Anything else?"

"Yes. I want you to fire him."

"Wait, that's not... that's really not necessary." I laugh, looking between the two of them, not sure if they're joking or not.

They are joking, aren't they?

"Oh, I think it's very necessary," Alec says. "I don't want anyone who is stupid enough to do that to you working at one of my companies."

"But you... you don't even own his company," I protest weakly.

"Actually..." Ash chuckles. He's so close I can feel his chest move when he talks. "I'm willing to bet he does. We own most of the businesses in Fortune City."

Oh.

"You don't have to do that for me," I protest.

"Okay, then. What can he do?" Ash asks. "We want to make you feel better, Sydney. Will you ... let us make you feel better?"

His hand slips around my waist as he says it, and the circuitry in my brain must be misfiring, because I swear Alec glances down, taking notice of Ash's arm around me, and doesn't object.

In fact, Alec slides closer, letting go of my hand to reach up and cup my face.

"Tell me what we can do," Alec whispers, "to make you feel better."

"I..."

I glance around, because surely someone will notice what's happening and break this spell. The city's richest man is looking like he might kiss me, his thumb stroking my cheek, while his business partner's fingers trail up my waist, drawing goosebumps over my skin.

But our table is out of the way, half hidden behind a sign for the Sterling Children's Foundation, and I realize that unless someone were specifically looking for us, they wouldn't notice at all.

"I'd like to kiss you, Sydney," Alec says in a husky voice. He tilts my head back, thumb curving down my face and over my bottom lip. I feel his touch throughout my entire body, in every nerve. And I want more. "Will you let me kiss you?"

My heart is beating so fast. Too fast. Behind me, Ash takes a sip from his drink and then sets it back on the table, moving so he's standing directly behind me, his hands on my hips. I squirm reflexively against him.

Alec is still waiting for my answer, a smile playing on his lips.

Not trusting my voice, I nod.

"Good girl," Alec praises, lowering his mouth to mine.

The words send a jolt through me, startling enough to elicit a gasp, but Alec's mouth is already swallowing it. He pushes me back, just a fraction, and Ash is right there, my back pressing hard against his chest, and his fingers gripping my hips.

I don't have time to think about Ash, though. Don't have time to appreciate how good the muscular plane of his stomach feels against me, or even think about what that hard bulge pressing against my back might be, because the moment I open my mouth for Alec, every thought disappears from my head.

Kissing Alec is like no kiss I've ever had.

He groans, his tongue playing with mine, fingers threading

through my hair. I'm drowning in his kiss, body going liquid, and thank God Ash is there to hold me up.

I never want this kiss to end. I whimper, my hands sliding over the front of his tux, and Alec groans in response, his kiss turning ravenous. Just when I think it can't get any better, Ash's hand moves up my side, his fingers brushing lightly against the bottom curve of my breast.

"That's it, Babygirl," he purrs in my ear. "Just let us take care of you tonight. Let us make it all better."

Alec breaks the kiss, licking and biting down my jaw and to my neck, and I arch back against Ash to give him more access, because this? This is exactly what I've always wanted, sandwiched between them, Ash's hands cupping my breast through the thin material of my dress, thumb stroking my nipple, Alec's leg vibrating against my thigh, and—

Hang on.

Vibrating?

"Fuck," Alec snarls, stopping all that delicious teasing and biting on my neck and pulling away from me. He's breathless as he pulls a phone out of his pocket.

Phone. Right. Well, that explains the vibration.

"I'm so sorry, Sydney, I have to take this," he says.

I nod, a little short of breath, as he answers the call.

"What?" Alec snaps, and I flinch, pitying whoever is on the other end of that call. Someone responds, and Alec's eye twitches.

"What do you mean, the deal *didn't go through?*" he snarls.

More explanation on the other end. Alec's eyes flick up to Ash's, and he gives a quick nod.

Still pressed against my back, Ash sighs, long and sad. His hands return to my waist.

"Give us five minutes," Alec says to the person on the other end of the phone before ending the call.

"Viper?" Ash asks.

Alec shakes his head, lips tight.

"Just some contract issue in Seneca. They won't clear the permits in time for us to break ground on the new building, and now it's looking like the whole thing might be fucked. Sydney, I am so sorry to do this, but Ash and I need to make a quick phone call," Alec says to me.

My heart drops.

Of course they do. I knew this was too good to be true.

"I understand," I say. I reach for my champagne glass, forgetting it's empty. I hesitate, suddenly holding a glass with nothing inside it.

"Babygirl." Ash puts a finger beneath my chin, angling my face toward him. "We wouldn't be doing this if it weren't an emergency. Fifteen minutes, that's all it will take. Promise me you won't leave until we get back?"

He looks so damn sincere. Staring into his bright blue eyes, I can't help but believe him.

"Okay," I say, wetting my lips with my tongue. Hell, if there's a chance of another kiss like that? I can wait a little.

"Fifteen minutes," Ash promises.

"Ten," Alec amends. He stoops down, pressing a warm kiss to my cheek. "And Ashton is right. Only an emergency would pull us away from you right now, and this... this is an emergency."

"Enjoy the party," Ash tells me as they walk away. "We'll be right back, I swear."

And then they're gone.

And it's just me...

And the throbbing ache they've left between my legs.

———

I hate whiskey. Always have.

And I'm pretty sure that's what Alec was drinking, because sure enough, when I gulp down the contents of the drink he left behind, I absolutely *hate it*.

Ash's drink is next, and I think it must have been a double, because it takes me a while to finish the whole thing. But I can't just stand here at this table, all by myself, thinking about what just happened without drinking, so...

Bottoms up!

By the time there's nothing but ice left in Ash's glass, I start to wonder if I really do hate whiskey after all. The last two sips weren't so bad. In fact, every sip went down easier than the last.

Went down.

I hiccup a giggle.

What am I even doing here?

What were *they* doing?

That kiss. It felt so natural to be between the two of them, with Ash's hands and Alec's mouth on me.

I'd wanted it.

I'd wanted *them. Both* of them.

But that sort of thing only happens in books, right? And sure, I love those scenes in my novels, absolutely devouring any romance between a heroine and more than one guy, but in real life?

In real life, I am much, much less adventurous.

I'd floated the idea of a threesome with Chase just once. He'd been excited and more than willing to try... until he realized I was talking about two *men*, not two women.

Then he'd soured on the idea completely.

"That's not how real men work," he'd told me, when I'd mentioned how common it was in some of my romance books. "No guy would ever be okay with sharing a woman he loved. We're just not wired that way."

But you'd share me with a woman? I'd wanted to ask, confused by the hypocrisy of it. I'd kept my mouth shut, though. And I'd accepted his words as fact until now.

But Alec hadn't seemed to mind at all that Ash's hands were all over my body. And Ash?

Squirming, I let myself think more in depth about that delicious hard length I'd felt pressing against my back. Ash had seemed very excited by what Alec was doing to me.

But this can't be real life. There's just no chance that these two men—these hugely successful, gorgeous men—want a woman like me. I couldn't even keep one man satisfied enough to not stray. Why would I think I could keep them interested? Of course they had a sudden emergency.

Oldest trick in the book, right?

With the whiskey and embarrassment running through my system, the room is feeling a little too hot. I scoop an ice cube out of Ash's glass and run it along my neck to cool down, but it's not enough.

I need some fresh air.

The room tilts when I go to move, and I reach out and grab the table to steady myself. Oh wow. Maybe I'm a bit drunker than I thought. Cold air, that's the ticket. That will fix me right up.

I wobble my way forward, through the crowd. My cheeks feel warm and flushed, and I just know the fresh air is going to feel amazing.

I make it about halfway when I stupidly step into the path of a dancing couple. I jump out of their way just in time, but my heel catches the hem of my dress. I stumble, and my foot hits the ground wrong, my ankle twists, and—

Sharp pain shoots up my leg, and suddenly I'm falling, my heart leaping into my throat as I prepare to hit the ground.

But I don't.

Someone catches me.

A long-fingered hand grabs my elbow as an arm encircles my waist, steadying me. Instead of finding myself face to face with the floor, I'm pulled up against a muscular chest wrapped in a dark suit. Black jacket over a black dress shirt. He smells like citrus and cedarwood, subtle and clean.

"Are you all right?" a deep voice asks. He's so tall I have to crane my neck up to see him, the words "yes" and "thank you" forming on the tip of my tongue.

When I see my rescuer, though, the words die before they make it past my lips. Black hair and a sharp, angular face, with icy blue eyes framed by thick, dark glasses...

He's breathtaking.

15

Those fucking idiots.

Sydney is shaky when Alec and Ashton leave her, legs still trembling from their attention, and even from my spot several tables away, I know exactly what she's going to do before she does it.

And... there she goes. I watch, amused by her predictability, as she reaches for Alec's abandoned drink and takes a sip. She pulls a face, clearly unable to appreciate the taste of top shelf scotch, but a few seconds later she gulps down the entire thing.

Morons. All of them. My brothers for leaving her on her own, and this girl for indiscriminately drinking that much hard liquor that quickly.

From my table, I had a perfect view of their little escapades with her. It didn't take them long to make their move, and it was an admittedly flawless execution by the two of them. The way she'd just melted back against Ashton, letting him run his hands all over her while Alec tongued her mouth...

Fuck, I'd loved seeing that. And though this table is nearly as hidden as theirs, it's not hidden enough for me to enjoy myself properly.

I'd wanted to, though. Seeing Ash roll her nipples through the fabric of her dress and seeing the way she'd reacted to it, I'd wanted to reach into my pants and stroke myself so badly. The way she had rocked back against him had me wondering what it would be like to have that sweet, plump ass rubbing against me.

Ash knows I like to watch. Hell, Alec probably knows, too, but he's never brought it up before. I don't think it's a coincidence that he angled the girl just enough to give me a show, before...

Fuck. She's moving.

I'm so lost in the memory that I almost miss it when she leaves their table and starts across the dance floor.

I make my way toward her without thinking, abandoning my table and moving across the room, eyes glued on her. Alec would kill me if I let her out of my sight.

Their whiskey has clearly left her a little tipsy. There's a noticeable sway to the way she's walking, and—

Fuck.

She almost collides with a dancer and slips, arms flailing as she struggles to stay upright.

She's going to fall.

I don't hesitate. Shoving another couple out of my way, I close the distance between us just as she loses her balance, barely reaching her in time to catch her. She lets out a soft sound of surprise as I catch her elbow, wrapping my arm around her waist and steadying her against my chest.

Great. Just fucking great. This girl is already more trouble than she's worth. Hot? Sure. But an absolute headache? Looks like it.

"Are you all right?" I ask her. Her heart rate is so fast I can feel it beating like a drum against me.

She looks up at me then, tilting her head back and opening her mouth to answer... but something flickers across her face, and she closes her mouth without a word. She just stares at me with big doe eyes, speechless.

Terrific. She's clumsy and an idiot. I tighten my grip. I'd expected a bit more from someone who graduated summa cum laude from Fortune City University. What a scathing indictment of our local education system, if she's among the best of it.

More than a few heads have turned to watch us, and while it's not a surprise that I've drawn attention with my little rescue, I fucking hate it. I can't stand being watched like this, can't stand the looks and the whispers from the surrounding crowd.

"Can you stand?" I ask. She's leaning her full weight on me, balanced on one foot.

Gingerly, she tries putting weight on her right foot, but the instant it touches the floor, she whimpers, burying her face into my chest and shaking her head.

"It hurts," she complains. Her breath is warm against the fabric of my shirt.

Great. Just great.

"Hold on to me," I tell her, briefly releasing my grip on her. "And don't struggle."

"Wait, why would I stru—" She lets out a high-pitched shriek when I hook my arm behind her knees and scoop her into my arms.

"Put me down, put me down, put me down!" Her voice is shrill, panicked. Instead of relaxing in my arms like I'd expected, the girl clutches the front of my jacket, holding on for dear life.

"I need to get you somewhere where I can check your

injury," I say through clenched teeth. "And I *told you not to struggle.*"

I'm not going to stand here in this crowd, being watched, for one more second. Especially now that her hysterics are drawing even more attention. I'm aware of every eye on me, watching us.

"Where were you going?" I ask. When she just stares at me with that same panicked expression, I try again. "Before you tripped. Where were you going?"

Her grip on my jacket loosens when she answers. "Outside. Th-the garden."

The garden. I glance over at the double doors that lead outside. That seems as good a place as any to take her now. I carry her through the party and away from all those prying, invasive eyes.

Outside, the garden is mercifully unoccupied, and—just as I'd hoped—there's a stone bench just the right size, nestled in the shadows, well out of the way and almost hidden. Perfect.

"I'm going to set you down, so I can check your ankle," I tell her. She isn't holding on as tightly, but she's so stiff in my arms it's hard not to be a little insulted.

As I set her down on the bench, and she finally loosens her grip on me, I mentally review everything I've learned about Sydney Sinclair over the last few days.

It's not that I don't trust my brothers. I absolutely fucking don't, but that's not the point. Their liaisons with women are usually over so fast I don't even bother looking into most of the ones they bring home. But this one? With both of them focusing on her so completely, and spending so much time around her, there was no way I wasn't going to look into her background.

Sure, from the outside she might seem like just an unas-suming little bookstore owner, harmless and brainless as a gnat, but you never know for sure until you look deeper. My misplaced trust almost cost us everything once, and I sure as fuck won't ever let that happen again. So while my brothers might be too stupid and too distracted by a nice pair of tits to help themselves, it's my job to know better. For all of us.

Luckily, their newest toy is no one we need to worry about. She's a nobody. A commoner with no red flags in her background whatsoever. The only interesting thing I learned about her was that her parents died when she was sixteen, leaving her an orphan, just like the rest of us. An interesting shared experience. But unlike the four of us, *she* didn't get sent into the broken and fucked up foster system of Fortune City. Oh no. She had a loving grandmother who took her in and, from what I can tell, she's lived a mundane and uneventful life ever since.

I hate her a little for that. For how safe she must have been, while the rest of us suffered.

Loved.

I hate her even more for how helpless she is. Weak. None of my research prepared me for what a fragile little thing this girl was going to be. If I'd known I'd be spending the evening rescuing a damsel in distress who couldn't even walk across a room without causing a scene, I would have stayed at home with Viper, where I belong.

Goddamn those fucking idiots. Goddamn this fucking girl.

When I kneel in front of her, she shifts a little on the bench, and the slit in her dress parts even further, falling open to reveal the entirety of her left leg from ankle to thigh. I refuse to let myself look too long.

"Oh God, that was so embarrassing," she mutters, covering her face with her hands. "I can't believe I just tripped in front of everyone like that. Do you think anyone saw?"

"I think *everyone* saw." I slide the fabric of her dress a little further aside to get a better look at her ankle.

Her fingers part, and she stares at me in horror before dropping her hands to her lap. "That-that's not comforting! You're supposed to say *no!*"

I glance up, slowly raising an eyebrow at her. "I'm supposed to lie?" I ask.

The only answer I get is a scowl. She crosses her arms under her breasts, glaring out into the dark of the garden. Terrific. I pull at the buckle of her left high heel. "Maybe if you wore shoes you could actually walk in, this wouldn't have happened," I mutter.

That earns me an irritated huff, at least.

"Why is it always the handsome ones that treat people like this," she mutters to herself as she starts to shift away from me. "Going around just manhandling people."

My fingers pause in the middle of unbuckling her shoe, and for a moment, I feel my carefully curated mask slip. Handsome? No. Ashton is the handsome one. We might share some of our mother's features, sure, but most people don't look past him to bother seeing me. He and Alec are the handsome ones, the ones women flock to.

The ones who get noticed.

"And why is it always the pretty ones that are absolute brats?" I retort, removing her shoe and setting it aside. When I start to remove the other one, she recoils.

"Careful!" she whines. "Oh God, I think it's broken."

This girl and her *whining*. I remove her right shoe with slow, deliberate care, and hold her gaze as I wrap my fingers around her ankle. "Does this hurt?" I ask, giving it a squeeze.

She sucks in a sharp breath and shuts her eyes. "Ow, ow, ow! *Yes!* Obviously!"

I let her ankle go. It's a struggle not to roll my eyes. "Then it's not broken."

"What do you mean?" she asks in a high-pitched, indignant voice. "I told you that *hurt*."

"And if it were broken, you would be screaming right now," I explain, giving her a deadpan look over the frames of my glasses.

Her lip curls, and I don't miss the flare of anger that crosses her face. "And who made you the expert on broken bones?"

"Empire University, when they signed my medical degree." I reach into the pocket of my slacks and pull out a single-dose packet of pain relievers. This girl's lucky I even bothered to bring any tonight, lucky I planned ahead for the almost inevitable headache this evening was sure to bring me. I hold the packet out for her between two fingers. "Here. Take these."

She stares at it like I just offered her a vial of poison.

"It's acetaminophen. An analgesic," I explain. At her continued confusion, I add, "It's *Tylenol*. Take it."

She hesitates a moment longer, and with an irritated sigh, I rip it open myself and grab her hand, tapping both pills out of the packet and into her palm.

Her skin is soft under my touch. I let my thumb slide over the pulse of her wrist just once, savoring the feeling of it.

"Can you swallow?" I ask her, letting my touch linger on her skin, my voice deliberately neutral.

Now that gets me a reaction. Her face flushes with color, and the pulse under my thumb jumps. "Excuse me?"

My, my, what a filthy mind you have. I fight back a smile, years of practice making it easy to keep a perfectly straight face as I say, feigning complete innocence, "The pills. Can you swallow them dry, or do you need some water?"

She snaps her mouth shut, but the color in her cheeks doesn't fade. If anything, her blush grows, like she's embarrassed for where her mind went.

"No, I... it's fine." When I let her wrist go, she raises her hand to her mouth, tipping the pills inside.

Watching the bob of her delicate throat as she swallows feels a little too intimate. I look away, glancing back over my shoulder at the party. It won't be long now until my brothers come looking for her...

And there he is. Almost immediately, I spot Alec through the crowd, moving frantically through the ballroom as he searches for his little pet. His eyes catch mine through the open doors, and he practically bolts toward us.

"What the hell happened?" he demands.

This close to her, I can feel it when she tenses, pulling away from his anger. That won't do.

"She needs ice for her ankle," I tell Alec, snapping my fingers. "Now."

Mason Alexander Sterling is not a man used to taking orders, and it shows. But after staring at me in stunned shock for a handful of seconds, he swallows his pride and nods. He gives the girl one last lingering look, from the top of her head to her bare feet, like he's convincing himself she's all right, before heading back inside.

"I want to check your vitals, to make sure you're okay," I say after he leaves. I'm kneeling between her open legs right now, and acutely aware of how close I am to her. My cock, already slightly erect from just the sight of her bare leg and the memory of her writhing between my brothers, twitches at the thought of touching her more.

I wait for her nod of consent before I shift forward, pressing my fingers to her neck to take her pulse. My other hand rests lightly against her hip.

She is pretty, I'll give her that. Soft. Sweet and innocent.

My brothers have the worst fucking taste sometimes.

After a few seconds of feeling the beat of her pulse beneath my fingers, I shift my hand to grip her chin. "Look at me. I need to check your pupils."

I don't need to check anything. She's fine, blood pressure and pulse seemingly normal. But I hold her face for a few more seconds, staring into her eyes. I wonder what they see in her that has them so fucking obsessed. Her lips part under my gaze, and her breathing quickens. A lingering remnant of arousal from her time with Alec and Ashton, no doubt.

Speak of the fucking devil...

"Here," Alec says, appearing at her side and sitting down on the bench next to her. He hands me a bag of ice wrapped in a bar towel and then turns his full attention to her, his voice softening as he brushes her hair away from her face. "What happened?"

I stare at the bag of ice in my hands. I guess it's my job to tend to her then? *Their* fucking toy?

Biting back the choice words I have for Alec, I shift back and set her foot in my lap, laying the ice over her ankle. This time, she doesn't flinch. She barely seems to notice.

"I'm fine," she tells Alec. So much for the "woe is me, my ankle is broken" bit. "I just..."

Shame steals the words from her.

"She twisted her ankle," I inform Alec. I adjust the ice on her leg to get a better look at it, but there's no visible swelling. I'd bet money the injury was minor, an overstretched tendon at the most, but no actual tearing. "Maybe if her *dates* hadn't left her on her own with only scotch..."

"What does she need?" Alec asks, ignoring the barb. His arm wraps around her middle protectively, pulling her close to his side. Fuck, he's got it bad for her, hasn't he? He's already in overprotective alpha mode, like he could somehow keep her safe from the world. From *our* world.

He can't even keep her safe from her own clumsy self.

I sit back on my ankles and reach up to straighten my glasses.

"Rest," I advise him, standing. I brush my hands against my slacks, subtly rearranging myself to hide my erection. "You should take her somewhere with fewer people. Somewhere quiet. Let her rest a little. She should be fine once the pain medication kicks in."

I give Alec a significant look. I just gave him and Ashton the perfect excuse to get her all alone. You're fucking welcome.

And Alec, proving he might not be a complete imbecile after all, jumps at the opportunity to take it.

"You heard the doctor," he says, helping the girl to her feet. She stands gingerly, still not putting weight on her right foot. "Let's get you somewhere to rest, shall we?"

"She needs to keep weight off of it," I warn him, gesturing to her leg. "Until the pain is gone."

I hand her the bag of ice, and as she takes it from me, she gifts me with a small, shy smile.

"Wrap your arms around my neck," Alec tells her, stealing that smile away for himself. She complies easily, relaxing against him and interlacing her fingers behind his neck as he lifts her into his arms.

Funny, she wasn't nearly as compliant with me. *Manhandled*, I think were her words.

"Your shoes," I remind her, scooping them up. I hold them out to her, dangling them from my fingers. Alec takes them from me without so much as a thank you, murmuring assurances to her as he carries her off and back toward the party, my role in her rescue completely forgotten.

Yeah. I grit my teeth. That's all the thanks I get.

As usual.

16

SYDNEY

"I've got you, darling. You're okay."

I don't feel okay as Alec tries to soothe me, carrying me back inside. I feel like an idiot. How *embarrassing*, tripping all over myself like that in the middle of a party. I almost wish I'd gone home with Jade. I almost wish I hadn't come at all.

At least that doctor had been there to catch me. Even if he had been a bit abrasive. Abrasive, cold, and... positively gorgeous.

My thighs clench at the memory of him, of those elegant hands touching me. God, was every man at this party pulled right out of my dirtiest fantasies? What kind of party was this?

I need to get home and have a cold shower. Or some alone time with a spicy book.

"I think I'm okay, now," I tell Alec. The pain in my ankle is nearly gone. I give it a twist to be sure, drawing a little circle with my foot. Guess the snarky doctor was right after all. Definitely not broken. "You could put me down if I'm too heavy."

"You aren't heavy in the slightest," Alec assures me. "And Doc said to stay *off* of it."

I can't exactly argue with that. It's just... extra embarrassing to be carried through a party. Though Alec is doing a great job of keeping to the wall, where there aren't many people. Barely anyone seems to notice us at all as we pass through the celebrations.

"I have a room here," Alec tells me, ushering past the crowds and down a quiet hallway, well away from the sounds of the party. It's cooler back here, the air-conditioning pebbling my skin. For a moment, I let myself just *feel.* I let myself enjoy the sensation of his suit against my cheek, the smell of his cologne. "Would it be all right if I take you there to rest?"

"Oh... you don't need to do that. I can just grab a cab and head home." I don't want to go, though. But I feel oddly ashamed. I feel like I should apologize for the inconvenience I'm causing.

Why is that, I wonder? Why do I feel the need to apologize for something I had no control over? Something my body did? Why do so many women feel the need to apologize for simply living?

"I don't want you to go," Alec protests. His voice is firm, and it warms something in my chest to hear him say it. "Please, Sydney. Just take a minute to rest, and then we can decide what you want to do from there."

Burying my face against this chest to hide my smile, I nod.

"Okay, yeah, I'd like that," I say. It would be nice to go somewhere quiet for a minute. To get away from all the chaos of the party. To... maybe spend some time with him. "Thank you."

"Of course," Alec tells me. He carries me toward a set of elevators, and—to my surprise—there's a familiar figure in a tux leaning against the wall, waiting for us.

"Whoa, what happened? Is she all right?" Ashton asks, looking between Alec and me, brow furrowed with concern.

"She sprained her ankle. Doc says she needs to go somewhere quiet and keep off it," Alec grunts. "Can you get the doors?"

Nodding, Ashton pulls a card from his pocket and touches it to a sensor near the elevators. They chime a moment later—a cheerful electronic tone—and when the doors open, Alec carries me inside.

Ashton steps in behind us.

I don't have time to consider the implications of that until the doors shut and Ashton presses the button for the penthouse floor.

Right. Of course. When he said he had a room here, I should have assumed... he meant a hotel room.

And now I'm alone. In this tiny elevator. With both of them. Going to his hotel room. My cheeks heat, a nervous flutter of excitement rolling through my stomach.

I shift a little, wriggling in Alec's arms, my thoughts preoccupied by the two of them. Ash is leaning against the wall of the elevator, looking impossibly relaxed and almost offensively handsome. And Alec...

Alec's arms feel so good wrapped around me like this. Almost as good as his mouth had felt before, when we...

I gulp nervously.

"I love this dress," Ash says suddenly. He straightens and steps toward us, running a finger up the slit of my dress and sliding it under the fabric. It's so reminiscent of the way Alec had touched me earlier. A small noise escapes me—half gasp, and half whimper.

Alec's hands tighten on me.

"Do that again," he demands.

"Do... what again?" I ask.

Ash's fingers creep below my dress, inching high enough to

brush against the hem of my panties, almost deliberately. I bite my lip and whimper.

"*That.*" Alec turns his face to stare down at me. There's a naked hunger in his eyes as he meets my gaze. "Make that sound for us again, darling. That beautiful fucking sound."

He's going to kiss me again, isn't he? Alec shifts his face a little lower, and my eyes flutter shut in anticipation.

The elevator stops too suddenly, the cheerful ding alerting us all that we've reached the penthouse. A warm flush creeps up my neck.

I swear Ash is smirking, and there's a smug look on his face when Alec carries me inside...and into a penthouse unlike anything I've ever seen before.

"Wow." I lift my head from Alec's chest to look around the room we've entered, completely stunned.

"Do you like it?" Alec asks, sounding genuinely interested in my reaction.

Like it? I love it. The penthouse suite is massive, a kitchen bar to the left of us, a California king bed tucked away in an open bedroom to the right, and floor-to-ceiling windows directly in front of us. The city lights sparkle like stars below us, stretching as far as I can see. My eyes linger for a moment on the bedroom, caught by the giant wall-sized mirror by the bed, and when the implications of that mirror's placement hit me, I glance away quickly. I don't want to think too much about why Alec would want a mirror reflecting his bed.

Alec carries me to the kitchen bar and sets me on the counter, letting my legs dangle. The ice pack the doctor gave me is dripping, condensation soaking the towel, wetting my dress. I give my ankle another experimental twist and then set the melting bag of ice on the counter next to me.

"I'm so sorry we had to leave you alone like that, Babygirl,"

Ash says, coming up to stand next to me, leaning against the counter. He wraps his arms around my hips, turning my upper body toward him and pulling me into a hug.

"Oh!" I gasp, surprised. I've never been much of a hugger. But his arms are so warm and gentle around me. I let myself relax against him, craning my neck to look at him. "It's fine, really. Did you take care of what you needed to do?"

"We did, yeah," Ash says. "But you don't need to worry about any of that."

He smiles at me, such a warm and honest smile, and then lowers his head to kiss me. Ash's lips are so soft and sweet against mine. Soft, and... completely unexpected.

Alec is right there, standing just inside the room, watching us, and I'm a little shocked at the suddenness of it all. Too shocked to really kiss him back.

Sensing my hesitation, Ash pulls away. He frowns at me, looking worried.

"Are you sure you're okay?" he asks, stroking my arm. "What's wrong? Is it your ankle?"

"No, no, I... I'm fine," I stutter, my body tense in his arms.

Alec moves forward just as Ash drops his arms from me and steps back, rubbing the back of his neck and looking self-conscious. The mood in the room has shifted, and panic brews in my chest.

I've screwed it up. Whatever this is, whatever it could have been, I've screwed it up before it even started. It shouldn't surprise me. I can barely remember the last time I was with anyone but Chase in... that way. I dated a bit before him, but nothing worth remembering, and certainly nothing like *this*. And even though I've started to come alive again these last few months, I've never been very confident sexually. It's no surprise I'm making a fool of myself. Of course I'm here, in a hotel room with two of the most beautiful men I've ever encountered, and so stuck in my head that I'm completely frozen.

I don't even know how to behave in a situation with *one* guy, and I definitely don't know how to manage *this*. Whatever *this* is. I've ruined it, haven't I? Before I can open my mouth and even start to explain the mess going on inside my head, Alec breaks the silence.

"Sydney, look at me. Did Ashton kissing you upset you?" His hand reaches out to caress my shoulder.

I glance over in time to see Ash's face crumble.

"No!" I rush to assure him. "No, not at all, it's just... earlier it was you who was kissing me, and..." I stumble with how to word it, feeling like an idiot. "I just want to understand what the dynamic here is. I don't... I don't understand what's happening."

I'm still not sure why it's *me* here with them. Me. When they could have anyone. Either of them.

Alec's other hand grips my arm, and he steps between my legs, pulling me forward until I'm sitting on the very edge of the counter.

"Did you like me kissing you, Sydney?" he asks. His voice has such a sexual purr to it I can't help but wriggle, hearing it.

I nod slowly.

"Use your words," he orders, fingers gripping my arm a little tighter. "I want to hear you say it."

"I loved it," I answer quickly.

The raw hunger in Alec's eyes grows, a slow smile spreading on his face.

"I loved it too," he admits. "And did you like it when Ash was touching you?"

I turn my head slightly to look over at Ash, but Alec captures my face in his hand, forcing my attention back on him.

"Ashton is a big boy," Alec tells me, voice stern. "He can handle rejection. If you didn't like it, you can tell me. But you need to be honest with us."

I swallow.

"I liked it a lot," I admit.

Alec nods, like that's the answer he expected.

"Would you like it if he kissed you again? And this time I could be the one to touch you..." He lowers his voice, every word a dark delight. "You have no idea how much I want to touch you."

"Yes," I whisper. "Yes, I want that. Please."

Ash steps forward, and there's another hand on my face as he tilts me away from Alec and leans down to capture my mouth again. This time I relax into the kiss, letting myself enjoy it. I moan softly, wanting so much more, but Ash takes his time with me, kissing me slowly, his lips a soft promise against mine for ages before his tongue slides into my mouth.

"You taste like scotch," Ash teases, pulling away a fraction of an inch, his breath soft on my lips. "Did you finish our drinks, naughty girl?"

I gasp as Alec's hand moves under the slit in my dress.

"Answer him, Sydney," Alec orders, fingers teasing the skin of my thigh.

"Yes." My voice comes out as a soft whimper.

"'Yes,' you finished our drinks?" Ash asks, hand drifting up to rub my nipple through the fabric of my dress. "Or 'yes,' you're our naughty girl?"

Oh, God.

I can't answer. I moan, writhing on the edge of the counter, wanting more.

"You like that?" Alec asks, as his hand curls over my bare thigh and squeezes tightly. "Because tonight you're all ours, darling. Our naughty girl."

His hand slips further up my dress, and he nudges my legs further apart to press against me, stealing my attention away from Ash to kiss me.

This time, it's so completely natural to feel Ash's hands roll over my body as Alec kisses me. I moan into Alec's mouth, pressing against him. Absently, I hear the slow pull of a zipper coming undone and realize it's my dress. Cool air touches my back as Ash eases the dress off my shoulders. Without missing a beat, his tongue still dancing with mine, Alec lifts me, pulling my dress down past my hips and letting it fall to the floor.

"Spread your legs for me, darling," Alec murmurs against my lips. Then he's trailing hot kisses down my neck and even further. Down my chest and stomach...

And dropping gracefully to his knees before me, hands on my thighs, spreading me open.

There are no words to describe it. No words to explain the thrill I feel seeing Mason Alexander Sterling kneel before me, his dark eyes gazing up into mine.

"Fuck, you're so gorgeous," Ash says, almost in awe, watching me. His hands make quick work of his bow tie and buttoned shirt, and when he tosses them aside, revealing a perfectly sculpted chest and stomach, my mouth waters.

No, I hadn't misremembered how perfectly toned he was from the brief glances I got when he was shirtless in my shop. I bite my lip, taking in the sight of him. His body looks like someone carved it from stone.

Between my legs, Alec kisses the inside of my thigh, before dragging his tongue higher.

And higher.

"Wait." Ash is staring into the bedroom, a distant look on his face. His eyes are locked on the mirror.

"I don't want to *wait*," Alec snaps. His hands are already reaching for my panties, the last item of clothing I have on. And his tongue is so, so close to where I need it, his breath a warm tease against my skin. "I've waited long enough for this."

"I want her on the bed," Ash says with a boyish smirk. "For the view."

Alec narrows his eyes, shooting Ash a glare from between my thighs. But after a moment, he nods.

17

SEBASTIAN

I could kill Ashton.

Or maybe buy him a new Lamborghini. I can't decide.

I lick my lips, watching through the two-way glass mirror as they carry Sydney to the bed, setting her up perfectly in my eye line. Putting on a show just for me.

It shouldn't surprise me that Ashton knows I'm here. He set this system up, after all, and God knows the fucker loves to show off.

But with the way he's been acting about this one, this new way he's been coveting her, I figured he might want to keep her to himself for a bit.

Well... keep her to himself and Sterling, at least.

It's Alec who lays the girl on the bed, after giving the mirror a significant and obviously irritated look. I smile, knowing he can't see me, and raise my middle finger.

Fuck you too, boss.

Ashton climbs onto the bed, laying down next to her and tilting her head to the side so he can kiss her neck. He smirks at the mirror.

"Look at you, naughty girl," he purrs, lifting her head until she's staring at her own reflection. Her breath hitches, a delicious blush staining her cheeks. "Look how *perfect* you are."

Her eyes are staring directly into mine through the two-way glass, and my cock jerks violently in my pants at the sight. Fuck, she has pretty eyes, doesn't she?

Alec lays down over her, kissing down her body until she's practically vibrating with excitement. He pauses at her panties, fingers teasing at the edges of the fabric.

"Please," she whimpers, writhing beneath him.

"Please, what?" Alec asks, continuing to tease her.

"*Anything*," she gasps.

Ashton was wrong to call her a naughty girl. She's dirty. Absolutely filthy.

I grip myself through my slacks, my cock so hard it aches, and admire the filthy girl as Alec delivers a single kiss to her pussy, through the thin fabric of her panties.

Even that light sensation is enough to have her arching off the bed with a gasp.

Filthy, filthy girl.

While Alec teases her, Ashton's hands come up to play with her perfect tits. She reaches for him, her hands inching towards his belt, but Ashton stops her.

"No, Babygirl, tonight is all you," he promises with a smirk. "Just let us take care of you, okay?"

Her face when he says that—like she doesn't know whether to be disappointed or excited—is exquisite.

Finally, Alec pulls her panties off, tossing them aside, and Ashton once again comes through for me, reaching down to peel her thighs apart, giving me a perfect view.

Fuck. My cock twitches in my hand, already painfully close to coming.

"Look how beautiful you are," Ashton praises. And she is.

So wet and perfect and ready for them already. Her pussy glistens in the light, deliciously wet. My hands are shaking as I unzip myself, pulling my cock out of my pants to stroke it.

Alec groans as he lowers himself to her slit, tongue sliding over every perfect inch of her. He grips her by the hips, holding her still while he devours her.

I can't see him work, not from this angle, but I can see her response to it, and Alec must be a fucking savant at eating pussy from the way she's reacting. Or maybe she's just never had good head before.

The entire time Alec feasts on her, Ashton plays with her breasts, kissing her neck and whispering to her. Whatever he's saying to her is working. She moans, writhing under their attention.

I want to be in there, in the room, I realize. Fuck, I want to be the one between her legs, tasting her. My cock agrees, twitching hard the moment the thought comes into my head. I slide my hand over myself, pausing to rub my thumb over the piercing at the head of my dick.

Normally, this is what I prefer—watching it all happen. But right now? I need to touch her. I need to be the one tasting her.

Ashton feels the same way.

"Let me have a taste," he says, sliding down the bed. Alec grumbles but moves aside, giving him room, and then Ashton is the one buried between her legs, making her gasp. She grips the bed sheets tightly as he works her with his tongue.

"She tastes so fucking *good*," Ashton groans, angling her legs open wider, pinning them to either side of him on the bed.

"Times up. Move," snaps Alec, and Ashton reluctantly obeys, giving her one last lap of his tongue. But Alec doesn't go back to licking her. He slides a finger up her thigh before running it over her pussy.

"Look at you, darling," he purrs. "So soaked for us."

He slips a finger inside her, curving his hand to rub a thumb against the hood of her clit.

"Is she tight, boss?" Ashton asks, breathlessly.

"So fucking tight," Alec growls out between clenched teeth. "We're going to have to stretch you out, darling, if you're ever going to take the two of us."

Sydney's eyes go wide, and I groan at the mental image his words summon. Alec and Ashton are huge—hell, all four of us are—and the idea of them stretching her open is almost enough to make me blow my load right now.

How would she take them, I wonder? One of them stretching her sweet pussy, while she sucks the other? Or maybe one in her ass, both of them fucking her hard, filling each hole?

Alec adds another finger, and Sydney arches off the bed.

"Too much," she gasps, gripping the sheets with both hands.

"Oh no, darling, you can take it," Alec tells her, lifting her thigh to fuck her even deeper. It gives me a perfect view of his fingers fucking her, his thumb working her clit. "Your pussy is begging for more, isn't it? I think this greedy little cunt can take three."

She looks like she's on the verge of falling apart already, writhing and panting on the bed.

"She'll have to," Ashton agrees, his eyes glued on her. "If you want to take us, Babygirl, you're going to need to fit a lot more than that. Do you trust us?"

She shouldn't. She should run screaming from all of us, but she doesn't know that yet. Doesn't know what perverted things they have in store. Doesn't know how dangerous we really are.

She nods, eyes full of trust and locked on Ashton.

Stupid, naïve girl.

He nods down to Alec. "Stretch her open."

"My fucking pleasure," Alec growls, moving his hand. He lowers his head down, sucking at her clit, and Sydney bows off the bed.

He adds the third finger slowly, tongue working her the entire time, until it's buried in that tight pussy. Both she and I are gasping for breath, right on the verge of breaking.

"You're going to come for us now," Ashton is telling her, fingers toying with her nipples. "You're going to come all over Alec's hand and tongue, and you're going to imagine that's his cock buried in you. Can you do that for us?"

Alec's hand is working fast, fingers blurring as they fuck in and out of her tight little hole. I'm barely hanging on, right on the edge, but I refuse to finish until she does. I need to see it, need to see our filthy girl break for them.

"Imagine it, naughty girl," Ashton murmurs. "Let it go, and imagine being stretched out by him, filled with his hard—"

Sydney is a screamer.

She arches off the bed with a gasping scream, body going rigid.

"That's it. Fuck yes," Ashton urges. "Give it to us. We want it all."

Whatever he says next is lost to me as I join her, coming so hard my knees buckle, and I almost fall. I throw out my hand to catch myself, the two-way glass shuddering with the impact, but I'm too lost in my pleasure to care. I come hard, jets of it hitting against the glass, my eyes locked on Sydney as she comes apart.

18

SYDNEY

I RISE TO CONSCIOUSNESS SLOWLY, AND THE FIRST THING I'm aware of is movement. The world is gliding around me, a gentle, familiar motion. I can hear the hum of an engine.

I'm in a car.

I stir, trying to sit up.

"Hey there, darling. Are you awake?"

I glance up to find Alec sitting next to me, my body nestled safely under his arm and my head resting on his chest. The last thing I can remember was falling asleep curled against him just like this, in the massive bed in his penthouse.

Nude.

I blink down at myself. Oh, thank God, I'm wearing clothing. Somehow, my dress and shoes are back on me, and I might believe that what happened was just a wonderful dream if it weren't for the deliciously satisfied ache between my legs.

"I'm awake," I tell Alec, rubbing my eyes and sitting up a little more. "Where are we going?"

"We're taking you home."

The words come from Ash. It's not just Alec I'm nestled up

next to, I realize, turning to look. Ash is on my other side, smiling down at me, his huge hand resting on my thigh.

"I argued against it, for the record," Ash tells me, grinning. "I wanted to keep you all night."

Alec releases a long breath.

"She likes to get to work early," he explains, giving my shoulder a soft squeeze as he says it. I don't know how he knows that, but it's true, and the idea that he knows me better than I thought makes me a little giddy. "And if I were to let you stay over, this bastard"—he directs that at Ash, who grins without a hint of shame—"was sure to keep you in bed tomorrow morning for as long as possible."

"He's right," Ash agrees cheerfully.

"I thought you'd rather sleep in your own bed, above your shop," Alec continues. "But..." He looks down at me, and the raw lust in his eyes leaves me a little breathless. "If I'm wrong, tell me now. We can turn the car around and go back."

As tempting as that sounds... I shake my head. He's right. I have my routine, and I'd like to keep it.

"Home it is," Alec says, giving me another gentle squeeze with his hand. "And rest. It's already late."

"I'm so sorry for falling asleep," I say, fighting back a yawn. "After..."

Ash just chuckles.

"You have nothing to be sorry for," Alec assures me. There's a smug, satisfied look on his face as he says it. "I'm glad you fell asleep. It means I did my job right."

And *how*. My pussy aches from the attention he gave me, more sore than I'm used to feeling after fooling around. But God, it was so good.

I lean back against him, sighing and relaxing into his body.

But something's off. I stiffen when I realize it and shift in my seat.

"Something wrong?" Alec asks.

"I, uh..." There's no delicate way to phrase this. I open and close my mouth a few times before I summon the courage to say it. "I think whoever dressed me forgot my underwear."

"What, these?" Ash asks. I turn my head toward him just as he takes them out of his suit pocket, running the fabric between his fingers. "No, these are *mine* now." He raises them to his mouth, tongue sneaking out between his lips to lick where they're still wet.

It shouldn't be such a turn-on, but it is. My legs squeeze together as I watch him slide them back into his pocket.

"That's to keep me satisfied until we do this again," he tells me with a wink.

"Again?" I ask, voice a little weak.

The car rolls to a stop. We're here, in front of the dark building that houses my store and my little apartment.

"Yes, sweetheart. Again," Alec says, leaning over me to open the car door. "That is, if you'll have us?"

His dark eyes are so intense as he says it. Hungry.

Oh, I'll have them, I decide.

I'll have them in every way I can.

But I just nod, and Ash steps out of the car, offering me his hand to help me exit.

"Until next time," he says sweetly to me, pressing a kiss to my cheek. The stubble of his cheek smells faintly of whiskey, and a little of me, and the combination makes me feel dizzy.

It's only much later, as I'm falling asleep, that it occurs to me I never told them where I lived.

19

ALEC

EARL KEEPS THE CAR IDLING BY THE CURB UNTIL SYDNEY disappears into her apartment, safely home. Both Ashton and I watch, eyes locked on her door, until the car moves and we lose sight of it.

"*Fuck*," Ashton groans. He takes Sydney's panties back out of his pocket and presses them to his lips, chasing the taste of her. I don't need to. I can still taste her on my lips.

But I want more.

"Let's take her out tomorrow," Ashton says, slipping her panties back into his pocket and grinning. "What do you think she likes? The carnival is coming to town soon, right? Think she'd enjoy that?"

He's practically bouncing in his seat with excitement. I can't help the smile that spreads across my face, imagining Sydney at a carnival. Sydney licking cotton candy from her fingertips. Sydney tasting like sugar and sin when I steal kisses from her in the shadows between the carnival booths.

Tonight went well. Better than planned. But she's not ours, not yet.

"Don't get ahead of yourself," I warn Ashton, leaning back to relax against the supple leather of the car's interior. I take my phone out of my pocket, looking at it for the first time in hours. "We need to be careful. If we rush into this, we risk scaring her off."

"Nah, fuck that." Ashton laughs. But he pauses then, turning serious. "You're going to have to tell her, you know. About—"

The words die on his tongue when he notices I'm no longer listening.

3 missed calls.

I pull up the call log on my phone and my pulse ratchets.

"What is it? What happened?" Ashton asks, sensing the change in my demeanor.

I shake my head to silence him and press the screen to call back the number. I switch the phone to speaker mode so Ashton can hear.

When Viper answers the call, there's no sound at first except the rush of running water in the background.

"About fucking time," he says finally.

"What happened?" I ask. A rage bordering on panic colors my voice.

"Well..." There's a snap on the other end of the phone as bone breaks. No screams follow it. "Dante might not be as dead as we'd thought."

Next to me in the car, Ashton looks ashen.

"What the fuck does that mean, Viper?"

Another crack of bone, eclipsed by a low laugh. "Let's just say the reports of his death have been greatly exaggerated."

"Sebastian shot him," I manage to say through gritted teeth. "Twice. And he's the best marksman of the four of us."

"On a *target*," Viper emphasizes. The sound of water cuts

off abruptly. "This was his first kill with a gun. You know that. His *only* kill with a gun."

"And he fucked it up, didn't he?" Ashton snarls next to me. He threads his hands through his hair and groans. "God*damnit*, Doc!"

I still don't believe it. Can't believe it.

"We were *there*. All four of us. And we searched every hospital record in the region," I remind them both. "For *months*. He never turned up in any emergency room."

"Never turned up in any morgue either," Viper hums from the phone.

Fuck. *Fuck.*

"You sure about this?" I ask.

"Nope." Viper cackles on the other end of the line, and something lands with a loud, wet *splat*. "*He* seemed pretty sure, though. Hadn't seen the big man himself, but rumor among the old guard is he's back and he's *pissed*. Didn't have an address for him, didn't even have a phone number. But he had a location."

I'm gripping my phone so hard it's a wonder I haven't cracked the screen.

"Where?" I demand.

"Empire City," Viper coos through the phone. "His old turf."

His *old* turf. Our new turf.

I don't bother saying goodbye before hanging up the phone. I'm singularly focused as I message my personal assistant, instructing him to get me a plane ticket and ensure my hotel room is clean and waiting.

Looks like I'm going to Empire City.

20

SYDNEY

The Boss: Good morning

I READ THE TEXT AGAIN AS I BRUSH MY TEETH, FROWNING at my phone. I don't recognize the number, and I certainly don't remember saving it. But it's in my contacts as The Boss.

I haven't had a boss since I worked in retail during college. And somehow, I doubt my old manager is messaging me to see if I'll cover a shift at the local high-end lingerie store.

Curious, I open the text thread. There are no other messages from this number. Just a single text at 5:30 this morning, wishing me a good morning.

Before I can decide to ignore it, another comes in.

The Boss: Are you sore?

I look away from the message for a moment to spit my toothpaste in the sink and rinse.

Who is this?

The phone comes with me back into my bedroom as I pick out my clothing for the day. The weather is still warm, and I'm itching to wear one of my sundresses, but they're buried somewhere in the back of my closet, boxed up and forgotten in a storage bin.

I can't remember the last time I wore one, or why I stopped. But I've always felt so wonderfully free in a sundress. Alive and uninhibited.

I think it's time I started wearing them again.

> The Boss: Guess. And I asked you a
> question, Sydney. I expect you to give me an
> answer.

I think I have a pretty good idea who it is, based on the bossy tone alone. My only question is how Ash and Alec managed to get into my phone to enter their contact information. But I shrug that question aside and coyly ask.

> Why would I be sore?

The answer comes almost instantly.

> The Boss. Because I felt how hard you came
> on my fingers last night, darling. And I felt
> how much having three inside you stretched
> you. Now answer the question.

Yep. That answers that. I grin as I type my response.

> A little sore. Not… bad. A good sore.

> The Boss: That's my good girl.

I bite down on my bottom lip, not understanding how two simple words could get me so worked up. Reluctantly, I put the phone down and pull on a simple T-shirt and jeans, trying to focus on getting ready for my day.

I don't check my phone again until I've gone downstairs, greeted Jade, and started drinking my morning latte. I have a new text message already, but this time, the sender has an actual name saved.

Ashton: Good morning, babygirl!

His message makes my skin heat and my heart flutter, but I swallow those feelings down and don't text him back right away. They're both coming on a little strong, and even though I loved what we did last night, this morning I'm not sure how to feel about it. In the bright light of a new day, thinking back on our night together, I feel conflicted.

Because I'm not that girl.

I'm not the girl who goes to fancy parties and gets too drunk. I don't pull attention. I'm perfectly plain, always. Practically invisible. I'm certainly not the girl who finds herself flirting with not one, but *two* gorgeous men.

And I'm not the girl who lets someone bring her to a screaming orgasm after just a few hours of flirting. Definitely not.

I waited a full three weeks after our first date before I slept with Chase. That felt like an appropriate (and, according to Jade, downright *pious*) amount of time. I'd felt good about that decision, happy with it.

Later, I overheard him joking with his friends that he couldn't believe how easy it was, how quickly I gave it up. He thought he'd have to put in more work, he'd said. I learned my lesson quickly after that. While we were together, I perfected the skill of being coquettish, but *never* easy. It didn't take me long to realize Chase enjoyed the hunt. He wanted me to be available, but never *too* available. Eager, but never wanting it too much. And I was good at it. I was *perfect*.

I knew exactly how to be just what he wanted.

And now one evening filled with a few compliments and I'm naked in their bed? Willing to be *shared* by two men? It's like everything I ever learned about sex went flying out the window—along with my sanity, apparently. I'm officially everything that Chase accused me of when he'd get in one of his "moods"—a slut, an easy woman, a whore...

Not to mention, Alec and Ash are both reasonably famous, at least here in Fortune City. And I'm just not made for the spotlight. I need some time to adjust to the idea of being with both of them. Some time to think hard about whether that is even something I want.

Satisfied that I'm making the mature, rational decision—despite my body practically begging for more of whatever they'd do to me—I put my thoughts of them both aside and throw myself into my work for the day. I spend most of the morning putting up our displays for the new month. I like to set up end caps for any new releases and refresh our Staff Picks every few weeks. Though, truthfully, Jade's books rarely change, so it's mostly just shuffling hers around and picking out a fresh batch for mine.

The store hosts a book club on the second Friday of every month, so I spend a few hours finalizing the orders for that, to make sure everyone's books for the next month arrive on time. I might be too busy to participate, but I love The Book Boutique's book club and all its members. They always put in extra effort to support the shop, each member ordering a copy of their monthly books here at our store instead of online. Our book club has become something I rely on, both emotionally and financially. And I do what I can to make sure they know that and feel appreciated.

And that appreciation includes giving them a sizable discount on their orders, of course.

It's late in the afternoon, and I've managed to distract myself from the unanswered text messages waiting in my phone when I hear Jade's voice from the front.

"Hey, uh, Syd?" Jade calls to me from across the store. Her voice sounds oddly strained. "Could you come here for a second?"

Uh oh. Whatever has Jade sounding like that *can't* be good.

"Coming," I call back, haphazardly shoving the rest of my books onto the Staff Picks display. I can organize them better before we close, if I have time. I keep my eyes peeled as I make my way through the shop, but I don't see anything that qualifies as an emergency. And nothing appears to be on fire when I get to the café where Jade is standing, waiting for me. All good signs.

"What's up?" I ask her, frowning.

Jade certainly doesn't look like there's an emergency. She looks amused.

Hell, she looks downright smug.

"You have some visitors," she tells me with a smile, pouring milk into a frothing pitcher, prepping to steam it.

"Visitors? Where?" I glance around the shop. There's a short line of customers waiting to place their drink order at the café, but nothing unexpected for this time of day. I certainly don't recognize anyone in line. My eyes travel over the few tables that are occupied, not seeing anyone who she could...

Oh *crap*.

"So, there's three of them now, huh?" Jade asks, arching an eyebrow at me. "When did that happen?"

The table Alec normally sits at is full.

Seated there are Alec, Ash ... and the doctor from last night.

"Come on, girl, dish. Who's the new one?" Jade asks, hungry for gossip. "Because I swear, if one more gorgeous man comes in here looking for you, I'm going to think you're dabbling in witchcraft."

"I have no idea who he is," I tell her honestly. "I mean, I met him, but I don't... I don't know him."

From their table, Ash looks up and catches me staring. He grins and waves excitedly at me, gesturing at me to join them.

"I'll be right back," I mumble to Jade.

"Have fun!" she calls after me, laughing, as I make my way toward them.

Ash watches me approach, eager as a puppy looking at a fresh new toy.

"Hey, Babygirl," he says. He gives me a smile that makes my stomach flutter, wide enough to flash his perfectly white teeth at me. "We were just talking about you!"

The dark-haired doctor gives him a stony look over the rim of his glasses. Alec is chatting on the phone with someone, politely turned away, and while Ash looks happy as a lark to see me, the doctor looks just as cold as he did last night.

"Hi, Ash," I say cautiously. I look over at the doctor and give him a polite smile, offering my hand. "I'm sorry. I don't think we ever officially met. I'm Sydney."

As soon as the words are out of my mouth, I wish I could take them back. He glances at my hand but makes no move to shake it. I let it fall awkwardly to my side.

"Sebastian," he introduces himself. His eyes are a piercing sky blue, and colder than ice as they scrutinize me. "How are you feeling today? Any... soreness?"

A blush creeps over my cheeks, the phrasing of his question reminiscent of Alec's message this morning.

Are you sore?

"I—" I stammer. Next to him, Ash grins, rubbing the stubble on his chin.

"Your ankle," Sebastian clarifies. I could almost convince myself I see a measure of concern in his eyes, but the rest of his face is so blank it's unnerving. He clicks his tongue. "You look flushed this morning. Have you had any other symptoms? Any dizziness or nausea?"

"Uh, no." I brush a strand of hair behind my ear. "I feel fine. And my ankle is... fine."

I'd almost forgotten I'd hurt it. There's no pain at all this morning.

"I could give you a proper examination, if you'd like," he offers. The way he says the words is entirely neutral, but heat creeps up the back of my neck, as though he'd suggested something dirty.

"She said she's fine, Seb," Alec snaps, disconnecting from his phone conversation and joining the conversation. He slips the phone into his pocket, pinning the doctor with a look.

"Don't let Doc get to you. He worries too much," Ash says, eyes twinkling with amusement. It feels like a joke I'm not in on, and I don't get the sense that the other man at the table is worried at all. I glance at him and look quickly away. Annoyed. He seems *annoyed.*

Ash gets to his feet, coming to stand next to me. He's a giant of a man, and though he should feel intimidating, somehow he doesn't. There's something comforting about his presence, and his size just adds to that. He's like a giant teddy bear. "But... you would tell us if you weren't feeling tiptop, right, Babygirl? If you were dizzy or—"

"Sore?" Alec provides in a soft growl, his dark gaze burning into mine.

My quick intake of breath is a little too loud.

"See? I *told* you she's flushed." Sebastian stands and walks around the table, shouldering Ash out of the way with a glare, and turning me to face him. His hand is cold against my skin. I blink up at him, looking past his glasses and straight into the coldest eyes I've ever seen.

"Did I call you handsome?" I ask breathlessly, the tipsy memory leaping into my consciousness, pulled there by those eyes. "Last night, I mean."

Sebastian's jaw tightens. His mask of indifference shifts just a little, and something more than irritation flashes across his face.

"You did," he confirms.

"Oh." My blush grows. Great. Way to objectify a man I'd never even spoken to before. A professional just doing his job. No wonder he's abrupt with me. "I'm sorry. That was inappropriate. I—"

"You should stop apologizing so much," he dismisses me. "It dilutes the effect when you don't mean it." His fingers move to my neck, pressing against my pulse. I fight a sudden urge to lean into it, a flash of unexpected heat racing through me. I swallow.

"So... Sebastian. Seb."

"Sebastian is fine," he says.

"Seb." I get a perverse thrill at the way a muscle in his jaw flexes when I say it, a small line forming between his brows. "How, uh... how do you know Alec and Ashton?" I ask.

The question seems to throw him, his eyes flicking briefly to mine before they dart away again.

"We work together," he says, simply. Then his hand is gone, and he's stepping back away from me a little too quickly and walking back to his seat. "You're fine. Your pulse is stable," he adds, almost as an afterthought.

Ash laughs, shoulders shaking with the force of it, as Sebastian sits down and pulls out a laptop from the bag at his feet. He sets it up on the table in front of him, completely detaching himself from the conversation.

"Thanks. I guess," I murmur.

With his eyes fixed on the screen, fingers moving rapidly as he types, Sebastian doesn't give me a second thought. I frown, feeling suddenly unwelcome. "Well...I should get back to work."

"Don't let us keep you," Alec says softly. The tone is polite, but when I look into his eyes, there's a dark hunger there. He leans back in the chair, crossing one ankle over his knee, gaze boring into me.

I wonder what he must think of me. What he must think of the woman who was so easily lured into his bed. I feel uncomfortable in my skin suddenly.

"Good to, um, see you all. Again, I mean." I finish.

I'm less than three steps away when I hear Sebastian's voice. "You're scaring her away, you know." And then, a heartbeat later, "She's a bad match for you, anyway. Too weak. *Fragile.*"

I keep walking, but my hands clench at my sides. *Asshole.*

Ash groans slightly behind me, like he's stretching.

"Like you know anything about women, Doc," he says.

———

THEY STAY UNTIL CLOSE.

I catch myself watching them while I work, nervously making my way up to the café section of our shop every few minutes to check and see if they're still there.

They are, all three of them, all seated around the same table, chatting quietly amongst themselves. At least they're supporting the store. Every time I sneak a glance, their little table is full of drinks and food from the café. I make a mental note to ask Jade if they're tipping well.

I don't speak to any of them again until just before we lock the doors for the night. We're getting ready to shoo the last of our customers toward the door when Alec comes up to the register, a stack of hardcover books in hand.

I hate to admit it, but I have appreciated the extra income he's been bringing to our store. But now that we've fooled around, it feels a little too transactional. Like I'm being bought.

I'm acutely aware of his gaze as I ring up his purchases and swipe his credit card. But I have no idea what to say to him. I keep quiet and keep my eyes on the register.

For better or for worse, he breaks the silence first.

"I have to go out of town for a few days," Alec says. God, that voice. Every word he says is like fire in my veins, and I can't help my reaction. I chew my lower lip, remembering all the dirty things he'd said to me in that voice last night. Remembering how much I'd liked it. "There's a ...work problem in Empire City that requires my presence."

"Oh?" I ask, trying to sound neutral. Play it cool, Sydney. "Well, I hope you make some time to enjoy yourself while you're there."

Alec's amused look makes it clear I'm failing in my effort to appear nonchalant.

"I would love to take you out when I get back, Sydney," he tells me. His eyes trace my lips as he says it. "If you would like that, too."

"Just you?" I ask. I want the words to have a little bite to them, but I'm still a little shocked at how snappy I sound. How *bitchy.* I look away quickly, but I don't miss the slight smile that curves up Alec's face, the quirk of his eyebrow.

"Just me," he confirms. "I can bring Ashton, if you'd prefer the two of us. I don't mind sharing. But I'd like to have you all to myself, at least for one night."

I don't mind sharing. The words send an unexpected thrill through me. But I fight through it.

It's a shame. They should have listened to Sebastian, even though I hate to admit it. He was right. They *are* scaring me away.

"Listen," I say, toying mindlessly with the thermal paper that feeds into our receipt printer. "I... had a lot of fun with you and Ash last night."

"So did I."

The desire in his voice is so thick it's almost a physical presence between us. I tremble a little, hearing it.

"But..." I sigh, forcing myself to meet his gaze. "That's not me, Alec. I don't usually do that sort of thing."

"Neither do I," Alec admits.

I blink. Then cock my head to one side, letting my skepticism show.

"I don't believe you," I tell him, narrowing my eyes. There was no way. The way the two of them handled me, the way they moved together like that? That was practiced. That was... that was almost *planned.*

Shit, was it planned?

"Oh, I've slept with plenty of women, Sydney," Alec says. His tone makes it clear he's not bragging, just stating a fact. "Ashton and I both. And yes, often together. But last night?" God, those eyes again, looking at me like he can see straight through my clothes and is picturing exactly how I look naked. "Last night was more than just that. Don't you agree?"

I shake my head, willing my treacherous body to listen to

reason. I want to believe him. But I'm not an idiot. I'm not the sort of girl who's going to be so easily persuaded into falling head over heels in love with a man I just met. Especially after he just admitted that this is a regular occurrence for him.

No wonder he's fine with sharing. Maybe that's what's normal for them.

But it's not *my* normal.

"I think we should slow down," I say, putting a surety into the words I don't exactly feel. "I'm not ready to just... just jump into bed with you, Alec. More than we already did, I mean. Until yesterday, I didn't even know who you really were. What your *real name* was."

"Then we can slow down," Alec says immediately. "If that's what you need."

I'm so shocked by his quick surrender, I stumble over my next words.

"I... what?" I ask.

"If you need time, if you need some space, that's fine with me. I can respect that," Alec says. He reaches out to take my hand, giving it a gentle squeeze. "I can take it slow. I can match whatever pace you need, Sydney. I'm happy to wait for as long as it takes until you're comfortable."

I must still look skeptical because he smirks, his dark eyes sparkling. "I'm not expecting you to jump into bed with me, darling. I'd like to take you out on a date, that's all. A proper date, with just me. Give me a chance to earn your trust and get to know you. That's all I'm asking for."

A real, proper date.

With Mason Alexander Sterling.

"I, uh..." My heart is beating too fast. I can't seem to get my thoughts in order, can't seem to remember why that would be such a bad idea. "Yeah. Okay. I would like that, I think."

His fingers stroke my hand as he smiles. "And I'd like to

continue messaging you while I'm out of town. Would that be okay?"

Still stunned, I nod.

"Perfect." The words come out in a purr. "Well, until then, darling."

I can feel his touch on my skin well after he leaves. And I think, for just a second, that maybe moving fast isn't such a bad thing after all.

21

SEBASTIAN

"Earl gray tea," I tell the girl with faded purple hair behind the counter, my eyes fixed on the café's board of specials. "With a quarter inch room for cream. And an egg white and cheese croissant sandwich."

The nametag pinned to her apron this morning tells me her name is Jade—she/her pronouns—but even without the pin, I'm fully aware of who she is. A sizable portion of my work for our organization is research. My specialty is knowing exactly how to find out everything there is to know about a person. Including all the skeletons buried in their backyard.

Metaphorical and literal.

After the digging I did yesterday, I know more than I could ever need to know about Jade. Born to Korean immigrants, with only one sibling—a brother, currently studying computer sciences on the other side of the country—she's an open book to me. After the dossier I compiled on her, I could tell you Jade's credit score, past sexual history, and what she likely had for breakfast this morning.

(A single strawberry pop tart, straight from the package, if I were a betting man.)

I pay for my drink and wait until she's turned away, focused on making it for me, before I slip a stack of twenties into the café's tip jar. After combing through their store's financial records and tax returns last night, I'm all too aware of the razor-thin profit margin they're operating with. Even with Alec coming here and trying to buy out the bookstore practically every evening. And while I would *love* to not be wasting my time in this godforsaken place, it won't hurt my wallet to be a little generous.

"One earl gray," Jade announces, turning and setting it on the counter in front of me, "for the big spender."

Her eyes flick to the tip jar and back to me, an easy smile forming on her face. *Fuck.* I clench my jaw tight as I take my drink, not meeting her eyes. Of course she saw. It shouldn't surprise me that a barista keeps an eagle eye on her tip jar in a city like this. The last thing I want today is attention.

No. The *second* to last thing I want today is attention. The *last* thing I want is to be spending my time stuck here babysitting some inane woman my brothers are inexplicably obsessed with. Especially with the possibility that Dante is out there, somewhere.

Alive.

"Your sandwich will be ready in just a few minutes," Jade tells me, and even though I'm not looking, I can tell from her voice she's still smiling at me. "I'll have it brought over to you, if you'd like?"

I give a small nod in answer and make my way over to one of the tables set up around the café. High-quality furniture at least, albeit a little small for someone of my height. I make myself as comfortable as I can—which isn't very—before setting my laptop up and booting up my proxy software, settling in for another long workday in the most uncomfortable environment possible. Don't get me wrong, this place is cozy. *Cute.* But I prefer my desk, chair, and multiple monitor set-up in my office with the air conditioning on high and the smiles on zero.

I work best without distractions. And this place is full of distractions.

Speaking of... I've barely finished setting up when my phone flashes with a message.

> Sterling: I want updates. Anything that
> happens to her.

I roll my eyes and go to swipe the notification away. The screen flashes again almost immediately.

> Ashton: How's our girl today?

Our girl. Fucking idiots, both of them. I had hoped that after the charity banquet, they would have moved on to their next shiny new toy, but no. Apparently, this one is here to stay —at least for the next few days. I swipe Ashton's message away and flip my phone over for good measure, happy to leave them both waiting.

No distractions.

Maybe once they actually fuck her, they can get over this new obsession of theirs. Sure, my brothers can get a little fixated from time to time—It's what makes Alec a successful businessman, and what makes Ashton a great fighter—but fixating on a woman like this? That's new. And irritating as all hell.

I'm half tempted to just leave. The only reason I'm even here is because Alec is out of town and wants eyes on his new *pet*, and Ashton is stuck in meetings covering for him all day.

Otherwise, they'd both be here, sitting together at this cramped little table.

And I'd be home where I belong.

I shift a little in my seat, uncomfortable with the lie. Okay, so maybe I would be here even if Alec hadn't insisted. I'm a little curious about her, myself. Curious about why *she*, out of all their playthings, has them acting like this.

She's no one special, as far as I can tell.

My fingers go still on my laptop keys as I catch sight of someone approaching my table, plate in hand. Even in my peripheral vision, I can tell it's not the colorful barista with the subpar credit score and junk food addiction.

It's her. The girl.

"Be careful, it's still hot," she tells me with a polite smile, setting the plate down next to my laptop. She's dressed in a blue sundress today, and she fills it out well. Well enough that I'm reminded of what she looked like wearing nothing at all.

I manage a curt nod that could be interpreted as a thank you without looking up from my work, hoping she'll take the hint and leave me alone. She doesn't. She hesitates, instead, twisting her fingers together and hovering next to my table.

"I never thanked you," she says. She pushes a lock of her hair behind her ear, nervously. "For helping me at the party, I mean, when I twisted my ankle. So...thanks."

I keep my eyes on my screen. "It was no problem," I tell her. "Any physician would have done the same."

"It's funny seeing you here alone," she adds conversationally. "Without Ash and Alec, I mean."

I say nothing. On my laptop, I flip through the dossiers of potential suspects I've managed to curate over the last twenty-four hours. A who's-who list of organized crime fuck ups who might be stupid or vengeful enough to come after us, all while pretending to be the big man himself. Dante.

I still don't want to believe he's back. Occam's razor dictates that the simplest explanation is usually the truth, but I can't seem to logic out which would be the simplest explanation here. That Dante is alive, somehow, and managed to stay under our radar for this long, biding his time? Or that someone with an axe to grind and at least some knowledge of his organization is trying to fuck with us?

"Nice, I mean," she corrects, fidgeting. "It's nice seeing you here."

The desperation to be seen as likable and *pleasant* coming off this girl is so thick it's almost nauseating. She wants me to like her. She wants to impress me.

It's enough to make me want to vomit.

I flick through the dossiers, ignoring her. Steven Aster, a mid-level thug we'd worked with under Dante for years, would be a likely candidate... if he weren't currently in jail for an ill-conceived Ponzi scheme that is almost embarrassingly childish in its planning. Who thinks they can get rich selling *vitamins*, of all things? I move him from the maybe column to the unlikely column.

As the seconds tick by, I can feel her staring at me, and I can tell she's waiting for me to engage in this unnecessary conversation. Fine.

"Sterling and Ashton would be here if they could," I assure her. I flick through more profiles. Marcellus Koll, deceased as of last year, also goes in the unlikely pile. "Sterling is already in Empire City, and Ashton is picking up his slack at our main office. But since I can do my work from anywhere?" I wave my hand, indicating that her little shop falls under the broad category of *anywhere*. "I'm making do."

To my surprise, she laughs.

"You can work from anywhere, huh? I don't know, *Doc*, I'm not sure that's how medicine works."

Her tone is teasing enough to make me glance over at her. Her smile is more genuine now. Warmer.

"I have a medical degree, but I don't have my own practice," I clarify. "I used to be Ashton's personal physician, back when he was still making a living fighting."

I know I've said something wrong when she reels back in surprise, blinking those doe eyes at me. "Ash used to fight? Like... professionally?"

Fuck, she doesn't know anything about them at all, does she?

"Mixed martial arts." This conversation has already gone on longer than I would have liked, and I have more important things to occupy my attention. Luther Almay, incarcerated for murder and currently on death row in a different state, also joins the others in the unlikely pile. "He still does it, occasionally, but it's... rare now. Now that he's retired, I make myself useful in other ways. I'm Sterling's accountant. I run the books for all his businesses."

It's only partially true. I run the books, sure, but I also run security for our compound. I keep us safe—all four of us.

"They just think it's funny to call me Doc," I add. There's a hint of bitterness in my tone, but she doesn't notice.

"You're a doctor turned accountant, then. That's... unusual." She leans her hip against the table and watches me closely, like this conversation is oh-so interesting to her. "Do you like it? Doing their accounting?"

Annika. My heart stutters when I reach her dossier, and I hesitate with where to sort her. I've never known where to sort her. I flip to a different dossier instead—deciding to leave her for last—and distracted, I nod.

"Ashton loves the limelight," I say. There are fewer than ten profiles left, and I'm quickly running out of suspects. "And

Sterling was born to boss everyone around. Viper and I, we prefer working in the shadows. It suits us."

"Who's Viper?" she asks, curious.

Fuck.

I grind my teeth together and minimize my research, furious at myself for the slip-up. *This* is why I hate talking to people. *This* is why I don't want to waste my time making small talk. I keep my voice just as calm and casual as before as I answer her. "He's the last of our little gang. We're a bit like brothers, the four of us."

"Oh." Sydney twists her hands together again, nervously. When I glance up to watch her, her eyes are full of questions I'd rather leave unanswered. "When will I get to meet him?"

Never, if she wants to live to see another day in her happy little world. She's lucky he's away, following up on a business deal gone wrong in Seneca, where Alec has been pushing out our territory. Far, far away from this fragile girl and her *cute* little shop.

"Ask Sterling," I say.

She shifts a little, from foot to foot, and I finally can't stand it any longer. Her hovering is making me anxious, and it's impossible for me to concentrate like this.

"Leave or sit," I tell her. "Your choice, but pick *one.*"

I want to take it back immediately when she slides into the chair next to me, smoothing the skirt of her sundress over her legs. Great. Just great.

"Can you answer something for me?" she asks, watching me, hands still nervously smoothing her clothing. "Honestly, I mean."

Probably not.

"Maybe," I say.

"Are you here to watch me?" she asks.

Now that? That's a surprising question. I look away from

my laptop and lean back in my chair, crossing my arms over my chest and finally giving her my full attention.

I can almost see the attraction. She's beautiful. Sexy, in an effortless girl-next-door kind of way. The image of her on that bed, back arched, is burned into my memory.

"Yes," I answer truthfully.

"Did they ask you to do that? Alec and Ash, I mean?"

I don't answer that one. Obviously, they did. Why on earth would I be here wasting my time otherwise?

"Does that bother you?" I ask her instead, tilting my head to the side as I say it. "That they want to keep an eye on you?"

She shrugs, idly drawing patterns on the table's surface with her finger.

"I'm not sure yet," she tells me. She pulls her bottom lip between her teeth as she considers it. "I barely know them, and they're having me watched? Doesn't that seem a bit...intense?"

I snort a laugh but don't respond. "Intense" barely scratches the surface of the two of them.

But my reaction does something to her. She grins at me like she finally broke through my façade, like that one little sound means we're becoming *friendly*.

We're not.

"I like Alec," she tells me, gifting the words to me like I'm her confidant. She smiles a little more when she admits it. "He's...sweet. Really sweet."

I straighten my glasses, expression neutral. I can't imagine anyone calling Alec *sweet*, but I'm not about to shatter whatever twisted fantasy she's concocted about my idiot brothers.

"And Ash is, well... Ash." She shrugs like that explains enough. And maybe it does. I nod without thinking. "But I don't know if all of this is...right for me."

Good. Maybe she's smarter than I initially gave her credit for, if she's figuring that out all on her own.

This girl isn't strong enough to survive one day in our world. It'll be better for everyone if she stays right here, in her *cute* little store, and my brothers go back to doing what they do best. To what *we* do best.

Because now is the worst time possible for them to be distracted like this.

"You seemed comfortable enough with them before," I tell her, lifting one shoulder in a shrug. I say it without thinking, remembering how easily she had come for them while I watched, and to cover, I quickly add, "Seemed like flirting with two rich men came quite easily to you."

She flinches at that. A direct hit. "I'm not...it wasn't *easy*," she insists. There's a flare of anger in her eyes when she says it, and that flash of emotion beneath her perfectly curated nice-girl persona is intriguing. "And I don't care that they're *rich*. I didn't even know who they were!"

I don't say anything, letting my silence speak for itself. *Methinks the lady doth protest too much.* Her obvious sensitivity to what I said makes me think I've hit the right nerve. Maybe that's her game. Just another gold digger trying to get her claws into Alec's fortune.

How boring. How utterly plebeian.

"I didn't do anything wrong," she adds defensively when I don't react, rapping her fingertip hard against the table for emphasis.

"If you're not doing anything wrong—if all of this is perfectly fine and normal—then why are you here complaining to me about it?" I press. I know I'm probably being an asshole, but I really can't bring myself to care. If my attitude is enough to scare her away, then what would Viper do?

Send her screaming. That's what.

"I wasn't trying to complain," she responds haughtily. "Listen, you obviously know them. And you're acting like this is normal. But it's *not*. It's not normal to send someone to watch over the woman you're... I don't know, the woman you're *courting*."

I raise an eyebrow. "Courting?" I repeat in a mocking tone. "I think you're getting a little ahead of yourself, don't you?"

That curious flash of anger, quickly repressed again. Tragic. It might be the only interesting thing about her I've seen so far.

She takes a deep breath through her nose, closing her eyes as she does it. When she opens them again, that spark of anger is gone, and the dull, boring girl is back.

"I'm just scared," she admits, hugging herself as she says it. "Scared of losing myself in someone else, I guess. Being with them feels like being pulled into a riptide. And I worry I might not resurface this time."

She looks at me, then, as though remembering who she's speaking to. "But why would you care? You're obviously *extremely* busy with...whatever the hell a *doctor accountant* does."

This time, she almost pulls a real laugh from me. My lips twitch up a fraction.

"If you're so worried about that, why not just walk away?" I ask. *Make it easier on me*, I want to say. Get out before I have to waste any more of my time here.

"Not that it's *any* of your business, but I just got out of a bad relationship, okay? And Alec makes me feel...good." She exhales slowly, and I get the impression she's speaking more to herself now than to me. "And maybe I need that right now. Maybe after the shit he put me through, I deserve to feel good."

"'He' being your ex," I say. Not a question, just a statement. "Chase Levine."

Sydney frowns, brows furrowing as she turns back to me.

"How do you know his name?" she asks, eyeing me suspiciously.

Fuck.

Lie or truth? I consider the consequences of both before deciding. "I just finished reviewing his employment contract this morning. And started drafting his termination notice, on Sterling's orders."

Sydney's face goes blank.

Huh. I guess I should have lied.

"Alec was serious about that?" she asks, voice cold.

I stay quiet, watching her.

Her eyes narrow. That fire is back, raging in her gaze as her lip lifts in an angry sneer.

"This isn't his fight. And it's *definitely* not *yours*," she seethes. "If Alec fires him, I'm canceling our date," she tells me, a surprising amount of steel in her voice. "Tell him that."

"I'll be sure to pass along the message," I say, just the barest hint of amusement creeping into my voice.

She stands up, pushing her chair back too hard. She looks ready to storm off, but before she does, her eyes focus on the sandwich she'd brought me, forgotten on the table.

"Here," she says, picking it up and thrusting it toward my chest. "It's gone cold. *Enjoy.*"

22

SYDNEY

I'm exhausted by the time we lock up the shop for the night. Emotionally and physically spent.

Sebastian—the asshole doctor with a tongue like a sharp knife—stays until nearly close, packing up and calmly slipping out the door without a word to either Jade or me just minutes before we lock up. I spent my day trying to avoid him, keeping to the bookstore and out of the café, not wanting to waste any more time on him.

He's nothing at all like Alec or Ash. He's a rude prick, and I'll be quite happy if I never have to speak to him again.

When I'd brought him his order, I'd thought we could at least be friendly. Get to know one another. Ha. Fat chance of that, now, after the way he spoke to me. The way he looked at me, like I was something disgusting stuck to the bottom of his shoe. Like my very existence was an inconvenience to him.

Asshole.

I don't care that Alec asked him to be here. He has no right inserting himself into my business. I don't appreciate him keeping tabs on me. And I really don't appreciate that, even though he's shown me nothing but disdain, I kept finding reasons to creep close enough to spy on him. Whatever Ashton and Alec have awakened in me needs to calm down, because there's no reason whatsoever that I should be drooling over a man who is that much of a dick.

Even if he is tall. And handsome. Smart. He has nice hands, too, and—

I slam the cash drawer on my register a little too hard after I finish counting it for the night, furious at myself for even thinking about him, and Jade looks over her shoulder at me, frowning.

"Everything all right there, Syd?" she asks, flipping our *open* sign to *closed.* The store's lock clicks as she engages it.

"I'm fine," I lie. "It's just... You know," I wave my hand in the air, "*men.*"

Jade laughs. "Why do you think I have nothing to do with them? No one needs that sort of stress in their life."

"A shame I'm so tragically heterosexual." I sigh.

"That is a real shame," Jade agrees, nodding. Then she grins, snapping her fingers. "What you need is a girls' night. Tonight. With pizza and ice cream and estrogen and crying. That'll clear you right up. Get all that nasty *male* right out of your system!"

"That...sounds perfect, actually." I smile at her. "My place?"

"I'll even let you pick the movie," Jade answers.

———

Two hours later, we're upstairs in my apartment, cuddled up on my massive couch and surrounded by junk food and pizza, all while Alicia Silverstone gives an impeccable performance as Cher in the 1995 cinematic masterpiece, Clueless.

What can I say? I'm a sucker for the classics.

"So." Jade sets her plate of pizza aside and gives me a Cheshire Cat-style grin. "Sydney. My sweetest and most bestest friend in the whole entire world…"

"I don't like where this is going," I say around a mouthful of pepperoni pizza, narrowing my eyes suspiciously at her.

"It's time to spill the beans. I want details. Lurid and smut-filled details. All of them."

I swallow my bite of pizza, reaching for my glass of wine and not meeting her eyes as I say, "Jade, my love, I don't have any idea what you're talking about."

"Nope, we're not doing the whole demure and cutesy thing," Jade says, waving her hand as though batting my words away. "When I left you at the charity banquet, you had not one, but *two* of the most gorgeous men I've ever seen in my life hanging all over you. And now there's a *third* one—"

"Do not speak to me about that man," I interrupt, glaring at her. "He's an asshole, and I won't even have his name uttered in this apartment."

"A hot asshole," Jade corrects. And when I refuse to acknowledge the truth of that statement, she adds, "Who spent the entire day staring at you, by the way."

"Because he's a weird stalker," I insist. I leave out the part where I spent most of the day staring at him, too.

Jade shakes her head with a laugh. "Never mind him, then. Forget the sexy stalker who shall remain nameless. You still owe me details, Sydney. I want to hear *everything*. What happened between you and Mr. Tall, Dark, and Handsome, anyway?"

On the TV, forgotten in the background, Cher huffs dramatically and insists *I totally paused!*

I know Jade won't let it go until she gets what she wants, and secretly, I've been dying to tell her, anyway.

"Well..." I pick at my pizza, tearing off bits of crust and not meeting her eyes. "After you left, we uh... we ended up in the penthouse... and we"—I gesture vaguely—"well... you know."

"If you can't say 'we had sex,' you lose your privileges of having it, Sydney. That's my one rule. You know that."

Jade has a lot of "one rules"—enough to fill a book—but they're all good rules to follow. Never book a flight the day before a holiday. Always stock up on candy the day after Halloween. Super glue can be used in lieu of surgical stitches in a pinch, but don't you dare try that with duct tape. Those sorts of things.

"We didn't actually have sex," I admit to her. "Not technically, anyway. But we... fooled around."

"That's still sex," Jade corrects. "But I'll ignore that, because it's about damn time you and Tall, Dark, and Handsome did *something* other than mentally undressing each other in front of me." From the grin on her face, you'd think she was the one who ended up with a millionaire between her thighs. "How'd the other one take it? The blond one, who looks like he belongs on a movie set?"

I clear my throat, eyes locked on my pizza.

"Well, actually... he was there, too."

When I glance up, the look on Jade's face is almost better than what Ash and Alec and I did together. Jaw hanging open, eyes comically wide, Jade stares at me in shock.

"You *didn't!*" she gasps.

I grin. "Well, I sort of did, yeah."

Jade squeals, clapping her hands together. "Oh, Sydney! I am just... I'm just..." I think she might cry. "I'm *so proud of you!*"

I duck my head, hiding my face behind my hair and grinning.

"Did you enjoy it?" she asks.

"I loved it," I admit. I squirm a little in my seat even thinking about it. "Every second of it. They were very... attentive."

"So does this mean the three of you are..." Jade pauses, considering how to say it. "An item? A throuple?"

"No!" I answer too quickly, before even giving it much thought. "At least... I don't know, actually. Alec asked me out, and I said yes, so... Maybe? Is that...weird?"

"Sydney, my love, my best friend in the whole wide world, my *everything*," she says. "I have been running in queer spaces long enough to know that polyamory isn't *anything weird*. It's not even that uncommon."

I raise an eyebrow at her. There's no way that could be true, right?

"Honestly, it's about time you straights caught up," Jade tells me. "You're always like... ten years behind everything. It's embarrassing for you all."

"Have you ever tried it?" I ask. "Dating multiple people, I mean?"

Jade pulls a face. "Never. Sadly, I am simply too much woman for most people to handle. Even as a group." She stares into space, sighing dramatically. "It's my curse, really."

I giggle.

"Listen..." Jade turns serious. "I'm happy for you, really I am, but... are you sure about this? Not the multiple partners thing," she adds quickly. "But with him, I mean. Mason Sterling."

My plate is now full of shredded bits of crust. I brush crumbs from my fingers and pick up a new slice of pizza. "What do you mean?"

Jade shifts uncomfortably. "Look… I know you missed a lot when you left for college. When we were growing up, there were so many blue laws, gambling was still illegal, and—"

I swallow my bite of pizza. "And what?" I ask. The college I attended might have only been an hour from the city, but it could have easily been one hundred, considering how cut off I was from local events. It had been a shock when I'd moved back to see how much the city had changed in just four short years. How unrecognizable it was from the place I grew up.

"And then… suddenly, those laws started disappearing. Sterling hotels started being built all over the city," Jade tells me. "Out of nowhere. And, a few months later, the mayor is out after a huge scandal, the entire city council has been replaced, and—"

"There's no way you're saying what I think you're saying, Jade."

"—and overnight gambling is legal again," Jade continues, speaking over me. "And before the end of the year, there are *three* Sterling casinos inside the city limits, like they'd known. And just like that, Fortune City is the gambling capital of the country."

I frown. "What does any of this have to do with Alec?"

But I already know the answer.

"Sydney…" Jade pulls a face. "Look, I might not have recognized him when he was coming around the shop, but… even I know the rumors about Mason Sterling. And his… organization."

My heart sinks a little. Because she's right. I know the rumors too.

For all his charity work, for all his donations to various causes to help uplift the city, the Sterling name isn't one tossed around lightly in our city. It carries weight.

It makes people afraid.

"There's no way those rumors are true," I insist. "There's no way Alec is—"

"—the face of organized crime in Fortune City?" Jade finishes.

I wince.

After I'd graduated college and started paying more attention to local politics, I was shocked by the transformations that my city had gone through. Most of it for the better, sure, but... There was no escaping the rumors surrounding the sudden changes. The abruptness of it all. Politicians flipping their opposition to gambling entirely, and those who were staunchly against it...

Simply disappearing. Some resigned in disgrace from scandal after scandal hitting the news, but others just... vanished.

"He's a nice guy, Jade," I insist. "You've met him! He's not some mafia crime boss."

"People can be more than one thing, Syd." But when my face falls, Jade backtracks. "Look, I don't think I fully believe the rumors, either. I mean... for some of this stuff to be true, he'd have to have the entire police department *and* the city government on his payroll, right?"

I nod, a bit reluctantly.

"And that stuff only happens in movies. Or in poorly written novels by authors who have no idea how the mafia works."

"Hey, those authors do a lot of painstaking research," I protest.

"I'm just worried about you," Jade finishes. "You're my best friend, Sydney, and if I just stood by and let you get hurt again—"

I flinch, and Jade abruptly stops mid-sentence.

"What do you mean again?" I ask, dread creeping through

my veins as I stare at my plate. She doesn't know, does she? There's no way she...she could know.

Jade swallows.

"You don't talk about it, Syd, but I think.... I think things between Chase and you were a lot worse than you've let on. He wasn't just a callous dick. I think it's time to admit that he was emotionally abusive to you."

I say nothing. And my silence speaks more than words ever could. I fidget with the food on my plate, not meeting her eyes.

"He made you feel small. He made you feel *less*." I can hear the anger creeping into Jade's voice as she speaks. "And I... I should have done something, you know? I should have helped. Because you're not small, Sydney; you're *wonderful,* and you never, ever deserved to be treated like that."

I look up at her, then, a swell of emotions thick in my throat.

"I feel like I failed you by letting him get away with that for so long," Jade admits. She stares at the TV screen, like she can't bring herself to look me in the eye. "Like I should have done more."

I take her hand. "You never failed me," I tell her.

"Well, I *feel* like I did. And I feel like if I let you get involved with a mafia boss, without at least making you stop and consider the consequences, that might be a best friend failure, too," Jade explains.

"He's not a mafia boss!" I protest, laughing.

"Even if he is," Jade tells me with a straight face, reaching out to snatch a piece of crust from my plate and tossing it in her mouth, "at least he's a hot mafia boss."

As if! Cher declares from the TV.

23

ALEC

THIS TRIP IS A NIGHTMARE.

The windows of the sterile meeting room I'm in overlook Empire City's east midtown, a picturesque view that I can't appreciate. My head throbs from one of the worst headaches of my life, made worse by the dull artificial light beaming down from the ceiling. I've been stuck in this spot since seven this morning, working diligently through lunch, and now the sun is setting behind the skyscrapers.

And in all that time we've discovered fuck all.

I've been listening to Dave—one of the men who manages our new Empire City clubs—walk me through the money we're currently losing in our underground business dealings here. The contracts that keep falling through with little to no explanation. The money that is mysteriously disappearing, sliver by sliver, as our earnings trickle their way up to me. It's not nearly enough to put a dent in our operations here, but it's just enough to not go unnoticed. And over and over we keep hearing the same thing. Employee after employee admitting that they've started paying protection money to someone calling themselves Dante.

And that money is coming out of our cut.

I roll my shoulders, trying to work out some of the tension creeping into my muscles. Someone is encroaching on our turf. Someone is working against us.

But no one has produced a shred of evidence that would convince me this is the real Dante, back from the dead.

The whole thing makes me nervous, and I'm never nervous.

I'm lucky to have my brothers by my side, but in situations like this, the pressure sits with me alone, weighing me down. I'm the one always in control, the one who keeps things organized and moving forward. I don't have the luxury of going off the rails like the others do.

Ashton flits about, flirting and fucking and fighting, and never taking anything in his life seriously. I love him—he's family—but he's an unfocused mess when he's left to his own devices. I couldn't ask for a better right-hand man, but without direct instructions, Ashton would never manage to accomplish anything on his own.

His brother Sebastian sits behind an emotional fortress that grows more impenetrable by the day. He's as stoic as I am, but he's so disconnected from his feelings that I don't think stress even registers for him anymore. I get it—it makes sense after what he's been through—but nothing ever seems to touch him. Cold and emotionless as the numbers and research he spends his days staring at.

And Viper, well...Viper is simply Viper.

We all have our demons. Viper rose above his when he was still a kid and became something even demons should be afraid of.

Which means figuring out who's behind this minor turf war and what to do about it falls to me. Today has been full of strategy meetings trying to do just that, but it's not enough. I need to understand who it is that's trying to turn our connections against us, and why they're using Dante's name to do it.

We might own this territory now, but someone is slowly cutting us off from some of our low-level connections. Someone is trying to undermine us.

But the way they're going after us is little more than a nuisance, and Dante would know that. If he were alive and wanted to hurt us, he'd go over something bigger. Something we actually care about...

"Sir...?" Dave asks, cautiously. At my irritated scowl, he falls silent.

I've mentally checked out from this meeting, but these guys aren't giving me any information that I don't already know. Anger is slowly taking me over.

I hate wasting time.

I hate being in Empire City.

And more than anything right now, I hate not having my delicious Sydney quivering underneath my tongue.

Over the years, there have been a few women in my life who stayed long enough that what we had could be considered a relationship. But it was always casual. They knew when I called them it would be for a night or two of fucking, but that was all. Pleasurable, but transactional.

But with Sydney? My woman in red? I can't get enough of her. I want her surrounding me in every way possible. I want her hair wrapped around my fist and to feel her panting in my ear, sure, but I also want to wake up with her in my arms. I want to take care of her.

Protect her.

And right now, I want to hear her screaming my name, begging me for *more*.

Slow, I remind myself. *She wants to take it slow.*

I sigh heavily, wishing I weren't needed here. Wishing I were back with her.

Sebastian, that fucker, has ignored every message I've sent asking about her over the last few days. Though, that's not unexpected. I trust him to tell me if something were wrong, and that's enough. Silence from him means there's nothing to report and no reason to worry.

Still, I can't help but wonder what she's doing right now.

"Everything you've given me is next to useless," I say. There's enough of an edge to my voice that it makes Dave flinch. "Did you at least get the surveillance pictures I asked for?"

The one thing Sebastian did send to me today was a short list of suspects to keep an eye out for. I had them sent to our security department, making sure they combed the security footage available from our clubs to pinpoint if any of them were showing up to cause trouble.

"Uh...yes, sir. Of course, sir." Dave shuffles with the papers in front of him before pulling them out. "We got those pictures back this morning, but there was nothing new in them. There's no one matching Dante's description, but we pulled some of our regulars, and there was only one potential match to your list —" He stills as I rip the pictures out of his hand. My breath catches.

Fuck.

Of all the names on Sebastian's list, this is the one I least expected.

"Annika," I mutter, fighting to keep my face blank.

There's no denying it's her. The camera caught her full, upturned face, her eyes fixed on the lens as though she was staring right at me.

I refuse to show any sort of reaction in front of these people. I need them to respect me. Fear me. I've worked to curate a very specific image of myself. But I can't help myself as I process this new information. There's no amount of control that could keep me from reacting to seeing her.

Now it makes sense.

Because there is one obvious person who knew enough about Dante's organization to come after us. One person loyal enough to that asshole that they might have actually cared when we wiped him off the face of the Earth.

But we'd left her alone. And over the years, she dropped off our radar completely. Out of sight, out of mind. Isn't that exactly where she did her best work? Annika excelled at being a ghost. At pulling strings behind the scenes.

She looks good, I admit as I stare down at the picture. She always did. Statuesque, beautiful, with flawless pale skin. Her white-blonde hair is shorter now, cut in an abrupt bob just below her ears. If I didn't know that this woman was made of pure evil...

Annika loves a long game. She's methodical and ruthless. The sort of woman who knows exactly how to break people down and doesn't care how long it takes. And she'd know nothing would unnerve us more than the hint that Dante might still be in play. Might still be alive.

This information changes everything. And now I'm left with the impossible task of relaying this to my brothers. How do I bring up a ghost that we've agreed to never mention again?

How do I break this little piece of information to Sebastian?

"Everyone out," I command with a finality in my voice no one would dare argue with.

They pack up and head for the doors without a word. But I know they're still waiting outside in the next room, staying close by so I can call them back in here if I need them.

I sit frozen in that spot as the minutes tick by, watching the sun as it disappears over the horizon and darkness creeps over the city.

My city.

Annika was always loyal to Dante, but so were we all at one point. We made a mistake thinking she would join us in breaking away from him. *Trusting* her was a mistake.

Under all her charm and beauty, there's no moral compass at all. Just like her father.

I release a heavy breath. Annika's return is a problem I won't be able to solve in one night. And as much as I hate the idea of uprooting our peaceful dynamic, if she is back and hell-bent on revenge, I need to let my brothers know. All of them.

Because if Sebastian finds out from someone else, it'll cause an even bigger issue. And an unstable Sebastian is the last thing we need right now.

But what do I need?

My thoughts stray back to a specific little temptress. Maybe I could use a bit of a distraction to help work through this issue. Yeah...that's exactly what I need right now.

With a smile growing on my face, I take out my phone and snap a picture.

24

SYDNEY

My phone chimes just as I've finished drying my hair and slipped into my favorite oversized sleep shirt, ready to curl up under the covers for the night.

It's Alec.

The Boss: I miss you.

The smile that reading those words evokes threatens to take over my whole face. I've been missing him these last few days, too.

Still, I set my phone down and don't respond, crawling into bed instead and trying to get comfortable. I consider reading my book—I still haven't had time to get past the first page in the final book in my favorite trilogy—but I know there's no chance I could get any reading done tonight. I'm too distracted right now.

I can't stop thinking about the night of the charity banquet. I've never been with anyone so focused on my needs and my pleasure. I feel a little selfish thinking back about it. Guilty that neither one of them had, well... *finished.* But when I'd tried to touch him, Ashton had stopped me, wanting the night to be about me.

I kind of loved that, loved that my pleasure had been the focus. It was certainly a first for me.

My phone chimes again, and, curious, I reach for it. This time it's an image. For a brief second, my stomach sinks, a sense of dread creeping into my chest. Is Alec the sort of guy to send a dick pic out of the blue? God, I hope not...

Even if, secretly, a part of me maybe, possibly, might be curious about it...

I breathe a sigh of relief when I open the image and am not accosted by unwanted genitalia. It's a city skyline at night, seen from a tall building.

And it's beautiful.

> The Boss: I'd love to show you Empire City sometime.

I grin, fingers typing out a response.

> I'd like that.

> The Boss: How was your day, darling?

> Good.

I pause after sending it, considering.

> Sebastian was in the store all day again.

Three dots appear.

> The Boss: Do you want me to ask him to leave?

I think about it a bit before responding. Do I? Sure, he was a dick to me the first day he showed up, but he kept to himself all day today. And Jade won't shut up about how much he's tipping her and complimenting her food.

No

I type out my next message, hoping I won't regret it.

It's fine. He's not bothering me.

The Boss: Tell me if he does, darling.

I chew my lip and hesitate before sending the next message, typing it out and erasing it a few times before I finally settle on the right phrasing. I've always avoided conflict, especially in relationships. Somehow, it's so much easier to stand up to Sebastian than Alec. But I need to say it.

Can you do me a favor? Please don't actually fire Chase.

There's barely any pause at all before he answers.

The Boss: Anything for you. And doc already passed along your message.

Satisfied, I set my phone aside, ready to sleep. I roll over. A thousand thoughts race through my head. I roll back. I can't seem to get comfortable.

In my head, I can hear Alec's voice. Between my legs, I can feel his tongue.

Groaning in frustration, I flop onto my back and kick my feet. And then, surprising myself, I reach for my phone and type out a message.

I can't sleep.

And before he can even respond, before I can second-guess myself, I send another.

I can't stop thinking about the way you touched me the other night.

Three dots appear and disappear.

Silence.

Maybe that was too bold? My heart sinks a little. I did just tell him I wanted to take it slow. Maybe I shouldn't have...

My phone vibrates violently in my hand, the screen lighting up with an incoming call from The Boss.

Hesitantly, I answer.

"Hi," I say.

"Hi." Alec's voice is a growl. I hear a door click closed, followed by the thud of a lock. "I needed to get somewhere private," he tells me.

Oh. I wriggle under my covers.

"Tell me why you can't sleep, darling," Alec says. He has this way of speaking sometimes where he demands rather than asks. I think I like it.

"I... I'm lonely," I say in a voice barely above a whisper.

"I can help with that, Sydney," he says in a dark purr. "Would you like me to help?"

My thighs clench together.

"How?" I ask, a little breathless.

"Can you turn on your video for me? I want to see you."

I do, switching to video calling. A moment later, it connects, and I can see him, sitting in a dark room, lounging in a chair with his shirt partially unbuttoned.

"Hi," I say, nervously.

Alec smirks.

"Is there somewhere you can put your phone down so I can still see you? I want your hands free for this," he says.

I nod, a little nervous, and set my phone on the table beside my bed, angling it so he can see almost all of me, including the tops of my bare legs.

His jaw tightens.

"What are you wearing under that shirt?" he asks in a gravelly voice.

"Just my underwear," I tell him.

He swears in a low voice, running a hand over his face and hair. And that small moment of him losing his composure makes me feel strangely powerful.

"Show me," Alec demands.

My hands are shaking a little as I peel the shirt up over my hips, spreading my legs just a bit to show him. I'm wearing a pair of bikini cut panties, not the sexiest underwear by any stretch of the imagination, but the way his eyes devour me makes me feel like I'm the sexiest thing he's ever seen.

"Fuck, you're gorgeous," he breathes. His hand goes up to his own shirt, unbuttoning it further. Bit by bit, he reveals that toned chest, and by the time his shirt is fully open, I'm practically drooling.

"Take off your shirt for me, darling," he says. "I want to see you. All of you."

I wriggle out of it, tossing it aside.

"Panties, too."

I hesitate, my fingers pausing on the waistband of my underwear. I've never done this before, and I've only had phone sex once, years and years ago. Suddenly, I'm nervous, too conscious of how I must look right now.

"*Now*, Sydney," Alec snaps. "I don't like having to ask twice."

The command in his voice sends a surge of heat through

me, and I obey, pulling my underwear down my legs and kicking them off.

"Lay back, darling," Alec says. I hear a zipper, and glance at my phone to see him opening his pants. "Let me see all of you."

I lay back against my pillow, arching my back.

"Good girl," he praises, voice breathy. "You're such a good girl for me, aren't you? Are you wet for me, darling?"

I nod, biting my lip.

"Show me."

Slowly, I slide my hand down my body, over my stomach. I let my legs fall open as I reach down, gliding a finger over myself. Just that tiny bit of friction is enough to make me gasp, my nerves overly sensitive.

"That's it," Alec's voice is guttural. "Fuck, I wish I could taste you right now."

I glance at my phone, working myself with my fingertips, and—

Holy. *Fuck.*

Alec's cock is out, jutting from his open pants, and I've never seen anything so beautiful in my life. He's huge, intimidatingly so, and as his fingers trail over his hard length, I think back to the party, to him stretching me open with three fingers. He and Ash were right. It wasn't enough, not nearly enough, to prepare me to take all of *that.*

"You look so fucking beautiful, Sydney," he breathes, gripping himself.

"I was just thinking the same thing about you," I admit, with a small smile.

He smirks.

"Yeah? Do you like this, darling?" Alec squeezes the base of himself as he asks it, and his cock jerks in response. A bead of precum glistens on the tip, sparkling in the low light.

I nod, biting my lip. I do, I do like it.

"Show me," he tells me. "Let me see how much you like it."

Knowing what he wants, I let my thighs drift open a little more, using my fingers to show him exactly how much I like the view.

"Fuck, I love watching you touch yourself, sweetheart," he says. His hand moves over himself, quickening. "Do you have a toy nearby? I want to see you fill that greedy little cunt."

A toy? My pulse quickens.

I don't. I owned a bullet vibrator years ago, but Chase guilted me into getting rid of it. He said it made him feel like I didn't trust him to get me off properly. Only sluts use toys, he'd told me.

Funny, now that I think about it. That vibrator did a much better job than he ever managed to. Maybe he was right to be a little jealous.

I shake my head in answer to Alec's question, and the hand touching himself pauses.

"No toys?" he asks.

Swallowing, I tell him. "No. I uh... I don't own any."

"Use your fingers," he says, starting to stroke himself again.

I do, sliding a finger down from my clit and easing it inside. It's not enough, not nearly enough, when I'm watching him stroke himself. I need more. I need *that* inside me.

"If I buy some toys for you, would you use them?" he asks.

I moan, my finger sliding in and out of me, and nod. I think I'd agree to anything right now.

"Two fingers, darling."

I slip another finger inside me.

"I want to know you're taken care of when I'm not there," he says. "I want to know that pussy is satisfied."

"Yes," I gasp, my fingers moving faster.

"You're going to take this," he tells me, gripping his cock harder, so there's no question whatsoever what he's referring to.

"You're going to take every inch of me, you understand that? I want you ready for it. I want you to know what you're in for."

"Oh God," I gasp. I'm already getting close. Who knew dirty talk was my thing?

"I'm your god tonight. Three fingers, darling. I know you're close, I can see it. Be a good girl for me. Give that pussy what it wants."

I've never been so wet in all my life, but it's still a stretch to get the third finger in.

Alec praises me the whole time, stroking himself.

My hips raise off the bed as I fuck myself for him. If I could see myself, I'd probably be mortified at how I look, but right now, at this moment, my entire world has narrowed to Alec's body and the pressure building between my legs.

"My sweet, sweet Sydney, you're right on the edge, aren't you?" Alec asks, eyes boring into me. "I want to see you fall apart. Show me. Show me how you make yourself come."

His words put me right over that edge, and I shatter, arching back and crying out as I come undone.

"That's it, that's it. *Fuck.* You're such a good girl for me. Such a good... fucking... girl..." He groans, and even in my ecstasy I'm aware of him finishing with me, his cock jerking in his hand as he shoots his release onto his chest.

We're quiet for several seconds after as we catch our breath, stars dancing in my vision. I feel incredible. The muscles in my legs are shaking.

I look over at my screen and suck in a breath.

Alec's chest is coated in his own cum, and it glistens in the light as his chest rises and falls. His hand is on his still hard cock, stroking it slowly, leisurely. He's staring at me as though enraptured, making no move to clean himself. And something about him sitting there, covered in his own pleasure, is so primal and raw my pussy clenches.

"That was perfect," Alec tells me, sounding amazed. "And just what I needed tonight."

I nod in agreement, not trusting myself to speak.

"You should get some sleep, sweetheart. It's late."

"It's later where you are," I tease.

He just laughs.

"Sleep. Can I message you tomorrow?"

I grin. I love the way he asks, like he's checking in on me every step of the way. Suddenly, it seems impossible that I'd ever doubted whether he could slow down for me. Hasn't he shown me, time and time again, that he's willing to respect my boundaries?

"I'd like that," I tell him.

"Good. Sleep well, darling."

I imagine I'll be awake late into the night, replaying our session together in my head, but I don't. The second I put my head on the pillow, I'm out. I drift off almost instantly, into a deep and dreamless sleep.

25

"Sydney Sinclair?"

I look up from the register, frowning at the petite woman standing in the doorway of our shop. She doesn't look like a customer, and she's wearing a delivery uniform, a large, flat silver box clutched in her hands.

"That's me," I tell her, handing my waiting customer their books and change.

The woman grins, holding out the box.

"This is for you," she says. "From a Mr. Sterling. I've been instructed to say he hopes it helps you sleep."

Warily, I take the box from her. She's gone and out the door before I can even think to tip her, her high ponytail bouncing as she disappears down the street.

"Ooooo!" Jade coos, watching as I set the box on the counter. "What is it?"

"I'm not sure," I tell her, laughing.

The box is surprisingly heavy, and even the packaging feels expensive. Silver satin, tied with a matching bow.

There's a card on the top, and I open it.

Until we see each other again, it says. It's simply signed *Alec*.

"Open it, open it!" Jade chants excitedly.

I glance around. Business is slow right now, with only a few customers peppered around the store. A few customers and Sebastian, set up at his usual table, typing away. He doesn't seem to notice Jade and me at all, his attention focused entirely on his work.

Grinning, I untie the ribbon, setting it aside so I can lift the lid off the top. I can't imagine what could be inside. The box is way too big for jewelry, and maybe a little too flat for flowers. A dress, maybe? To wear on our date when he gets back into town?

When I finally lift the lid, I pause, staring into the box, confused.

The interior of the box is a darker gray velvet, and inside is... is...

"Are those sex toys?" Jade squeals loudly, managing to sound both shocked and impressed.

The sound of Sebastian's typing falters, just for a second, and I see him glance up at us from the table he's occupied these last four days, eyebrows raised.

"I... think so?" I whisper back.

Thank God there are no customers nearby to see this. I reach into the box to touch one of them. The box is *full* of so many different things, including a pair of leather wrist cuffs, several varieties of vibrators, and...

I gulp, pulling my hand back. There's a wide selection of different, uhhh, *sizes*, in the box, and while a few seem manageable, there are at least two that are *way* too big to be for what I think they're for.

"Sydney!" Jade shrieks, slapping my shoulder playfully.

"Girl, you have been holding out on me. Who knew you were such a toy hound?"

"I didn't... I didn't ask him for this," I try to explain, stammering.

Jade laughs, plucking an item from the box and... yeah, that's undeniably an eggplant-colored butt plug she's waving around, isn't it? I try to snatch it away from her, but she completely ignores me, scrutinizing the toy in her hand. "High quality stuff, too. You know, I knew this guy was a keeper. Look at all of this! He *really* wants to keep you happy, doesn't he?"

When she sets the toy back in the box, I close the lid over it all quickly, hiding my smile as I duck down to stash it away under the counter.

"Now *that's* a man. Jeez, can you imagine Chase giving you something like this?" she asks with a bright laugh.

I shake my head, chuckling. "God no. Are you kidding? That man was jealous of my tiny little bullet vibrator. He'd throw a fit if he saw *half* of these."

A look of pain flashes over Jade's face, quickly replaced by anger.

"Well, fuck him," she says, curling her lip. "It's every woman's right to enjoy herself. No *real man* would ever be jealous of a toy. Toys are teammates, not competition."

"She's right," a low voice says from the bakery counter.

I look up to see Sebastian's looming form at the café register and wince, mortified. Of course, he overheard everything.

"What can I get for you?" Jade asks him, grinning. She gives him a lewd wink. "It's on the house for a man who appreciates a woman's pleasure."

Sebastian's lip quirks slightly at the corners, the ghost of a smile. It's the closest I have ever seen him to showing an emotion that isn't some flavor of irritation.

"Earl gray, with room," he tells her. "But I'm happy to pay for it."

Jade shrugs, moving away to start on his drink. "It's your money, big spender."

"Did you ... uh, know about this?" I ask, gesturing vaguely toward the box.

Sebastian straightens his glasses and shakes his head. "No. I ... noticed a rather substantial purchase come through Sterling's personal account this morning, but I didn't recognize the company."

I don't know if that's a relief or not. Somehow, the idea of cold, emotionless Sebastian helping pick out sex toys makes my skin feel a little too warm.

When Jade hands him his drink, taking his money and putting it directly into the tip jar, bypassing the register completely, he adds, "But I approve. Your friend is right."

Jade smirks at me in victory.

"A real man wants his partner to be pleasured. In every way possible," he says, staring down at his drink instead of either of us. The words make my blood heat a little more. Even more so when he finally looks up and locks eyes with me.

"But if you can't handle that sort of attention," he says in a voice colder than ice, "you should let him know. And he can find someone who *can.*"

Then he leaves, heading back to his table without another word. It's like he can't help himself. He says something so hot I almost find myself attracted to him, and then he ruins it all by insulting me in the same breath.

I glare at his back, seething.

Turning back to Jade, I throw my hands up to signal *see what he's like?*

"I can't tell if I love or hate that little freak." Jade laughs, shaking her head.

Hate, I decide. Definitely hate.

————

"Love you!" Jade calls in a singsong voice, waving her fingers at me before she turns and disappears around the corner, heading home.

"To the moon and back!" I answer, struggling to wave back with the giant gift box from Alec in one hand and my keys in the other. I'm forced to juggle the box a little in order to fit the keys in the lock and close up the store, but finally I manage, relaxing at the heavy sound of the lock sliding into place.

Safe and sound.

The entrance to my apartment is only accessible by a staircase hidden around the back of our shop, half concealed by a small garden I keep back there, and a handful of tall trees. Technically, the building houses two duplexes, both with exterior doors side by side at the top of the stairwell, but in the whole time I've lived here, Dorothy, our landlord, has never bothered to rent the other one.

In fact, before my breakup with Chase, Dorothy had never bothered renting either of these apartments. Not that I'm complaining about the absence of another tenant. There's a certain freedom that comes with never having any neighbors. I like knowing I can watch bad reality television as loudly as I want, without bothering anyone.

I'm so distracted trying to carry the box without dropping it as I navigate the stairs, I don't even notice Ash standing in front of my apartment door, leaning against the wall, until I'm at the top step.

"Hey," he says, grinning at me. He lifts his hand, showing off a white plastic bag full of takeout containers. "You hungry?"

My stomach growls loudly in answer.

"Starving," I admit, a little sheepishly. I rarely have time to eat at work, save for shoving a few of Jade's pastries in my mouth when we're not busy. Normally, I wait until we close to finally eat, devouring a massive dinner in front of the TV right before I head to bed.

So what if it's not the healthiest thing in the world? Few of the best things in life are.

Ash's grin widens. "Good. I got enough for both of us. But, if you're tired and would rather eat alone, I can take mine to go. No pressure."

I shake my head. Even out of the tux, he's stunning. In his T-shirt and jeans, sandy blond hair ruffled and unkempt, Ashton somehow looks like he stepped right off the runway. And despite his size and his fighter's body, he manages to look boyish. Sweet.

It's the smile, I'm sure. Ash has a smile that shines like a star.

"No, it's fine. I'd love the company." I say it automatically to be polite, but am pleasantly surprised to realize it's true. I'm excited to see him and excited to eat a meal with another person. Especially someone as fun and affable as Ash. "Let me just get the door, and—"

"Here, let me help," Ash says, stepping closer and lifting the box out of my hands. The relief in my arms is instantaneous, and I thank him, moving up the door to unlock it and let us in.

I don't have a lot of visitors other than Jade, of course, but thankfully, I'm a neat person by nature. I wave Ash inside, closing the door behind him and turning on the lights.

He whistles, staring around. "Wow. This is—"

"It's small, I know," I say, talking over him. And, well, it is. The apartment is only a one-bedroom—two, if you count the tiny workspace I use mostly for storage. The living room is nice and spacious, though, with plenty of room for my old comfortable couch. Plus, there's a claw-foot tub in the bathroom that's big enough to lie down in, so honestly, it's the best place I've ever lived.

"I was going to say it's 'gorgeous,'" Ash laughs, shooting me a wink. "It's very... you."

I frown, looking around. It's very me? What does that mean? And why does he say it like it's a compliment?

My place is neat, but not exactly *decorated*. My personal library has expanded beyond my one giant bookcase and spread to cover every open surface. There wasn't much to do living with my grandmother, so books became my favorite escape, and I can't bear to let any of my favorites go—even the ones that are almost falling apart from being read so many times. I don't have art on my walls, preferring them bare. Which means my only real decorations are the collections of pillows and blankets I have scattered around the place, piled on the couch, and in the armchair in the corner where I like to read.

Cozy is what I would call it. Jade once described my style as librarian chic.

"Have a seat," I tell him, motioning toward the couch and the coffee table. "You can just move the blankets if they're in your way. I'll get us some plates."

Yeah, I eat on the couch. Sue me. I like to be comfortable.

When I return with a stack of plates and a bottle of wine, Ash has already made himself right at home. I've always thought my giant couch could seat a small party, but Ash has managed to take up more space than I thought possible for one person. He sits with his legs spread wide and arms draped over the back of the seats on either side of him.

"I *love* this couch," he says. "Top tier comfort levels, right here."

I laugh, setting the plates in front of him.

"Oh! I forgot the wine glasses," I realize, straightening and turning toward the kitchen again. "Let me just—"

"No, please, sit," Ash says, standing up. "I'll get some. Where do you keep them?"

I'm so stunned by the offer, I answer without thought, "Uh, above the sink, in the cupboard on the right."

Ash returns with two wine glasses and some napkins, making quick work of the containers and dishing out a full plate of food.

I'm surprised when he hands it to me.

"Ladies first," he says with a grin.

It smells delicious. Giving him a small grin in return, I take it from him and dig in.

"So, what's in the box?" Ash asks, after a few minutes of eating in silence. He nods towards the gift from Alec, sitting next to the couch.

"Oh." My cheeks heat, and I try to play it off by leaning over to take a drink of wine. "It's, uh... just a gift. From Alec."

Ash looks amused. "He sent you a gift?" he asks, smiling. "Sly dog. What did he get you?"

"It's nothing, really. You know, just... a gift."

"That's so intriguingly vague, Sydney. You know I have to open it now," Ash says.

"No, really, it's—"

Too late. Ash sets his now-empty plate down on the table and pulls the box into his lap, tipping the lid off.

If having Jade see what was in there embarrassed me, it's nothing compared to the mortification of watching Ash as he peers down into the box.

"Huh," he says, both eyebrows raised and face unreadable.

"I think it's a joke," I tell him quickly, reaching for the lid to cover it up again. "An inside joke between the two of us."

"The only joke is the idiot didn't think to include any lube," Ash says, straight-faced.

Oh.

My fingers pause mere inches from the lid. I look back into the box. I guess he didn't, did he?

"Maybe that was on purpose," Ash says, voice dropping an octave. "He knows first-hand how soaked you can get with the right motivation."

My thighs squeeze together, a flash of heat going through me.

"Have you tried any of these yet?" Ash asks, looking over at me. God, his eyes are so intense suddenly. When he looks me over, gaze slowly moving down my body and then back up, I almost feel like he's touching me.

I shake my head.

"It... it just came this morning. I'm not in the business of getting myself off at work. Think that would be a whole different type of job," I say, laughing. I surprise myself when I say it. I never make sexual jokes. Chase always said they made a woman sound cheap.

Ash grins and turns his attention back to the box. After a few more seconds of staring into it, he sets it aside, next to him on the couch, and I breathe a small, shaky sigh of relief.

But no.

"We're going to need room for this," he says in a husky voice, stacking the empty takeout containers and grabbing his plate. "Have you finished eating?"

I look down at my forgotten plate, clenched in my hands. It's empty.

"Uh... yes," I say.

He hesitates. "You're sure? There's plenty more. And I can wait."

I don't think he can. Ash looks ready to explode. But he patiently stands there while I consider it.

Finally, I shake my head, and he takes my plate, carrying it to the kitchen. I hear the tap turn on, followed by the sound of him rinsing our dishes and placing them in the dishwasher. A few seconds later, I can hear him putting the leftovers into my fridge.

When he emerges, I shrink back on the couch, slightly unnerved by the intensity in his gaze.

"Do you want to tell me why Alec sent these to you?" he asks, setting the box on the table in front of us and sitting back on the couch. He's closer to me now, our legs almost touching. "I don't think he would have done something like this out of the blue. It's not exactly his style."

"We uh... he called me last night," I admit in a small voice.

The look Ash gives me, full of naked lust, lets me know he understands exactly what sort of phone call we had.

"He wanted me to... use a toy," I continue, voice barely audible even to my ears. "But I didn't have any."

Ash's brows raise in surprise.

"Not even one?" he asks, stunned.

What is with these men? Are women out there hoarding sex toys and I'm the only one crazy enough not to own one?

Making a mental note to check that with Jade, I shake my head.

Lips curving to a grin, Ash nods slowly. "So, he sent you a variety," he says, understanding. "For you to try. Smart."

He reaches into the box, plucking an item out of it.

It's the pair of wrist cuffs.

Ash runs his thumb over the leather for a moment before asking, "Have you ever been tied up before?"

I shake my head.

"Is it something you've ever thought about? Maybe even... fantasized about?"

God, yes.

I nod a little too quickly. I can't believe I'm admitting this to him. I've never admitted it to anyone.

Ash sets the cuffs next to the box with a grin and reaches in for another item.

This one I don't recognize. It's a thick strap of leather, with a long handle. Ash watches me closely as he holds it, assessing me.

"Do you know what this is?" he asks, voice low.

I shake my head.

"This is a riding crop," he says. He reaches out to take my hand, and I give it to him. He strokes the leather over my palm. Then, with a quick flick of his wrist, he snaps it. I cry out, more out of shock than pain, as the leather strikes my palm with a loud slap. The skin where it struck me tingles.

"Is that something you might like?" Ash asks, and the way his eyes move over my body, I know he doesn't want to use it on my palm.

I hesitate, a beat too long.

Nodding as if that's answer enough, Ash lets my hand drop, turning back to the box and putting the toy away.

"Wait!" I say, too quickly.

He stops, glancing over at me.

"I..." My heart is beating so fast, my body aching to know what he would do with the crop. "I... need time, I think. To work up to that. But I'm not... uninterested."

Something flares in Ash's eyes. He licks his lips, his breathing a little heavy as he nods. But he keeps the crop in the box.

"Thank you," Ash tells me. He leans over me, pushing my thighs open and lifting one leg onto the couch so he can get closer to me. "For being honest with me. And if you want to try that, *fuck*." He shudders when he exhales. "I could make it so good for you. You have no idea."

Oh God. I want it now. Ash's gaze burns into mine, and I want it, want to feel it. I want to know exactly what he'd do to me if I let him.

"Not tonight," he tells me.

My disappointment is short-lived when he reaches down and slides a hand over my shirt, cupping my breast. I gasp when he rolls his thumb down, catching my nipple between his fingers and giving it a light tug.

"I love that you want to try that," Ash says. "And I can't wait to show you all the fun we could have together. But let's keep things simple tonight, okay? Let's go slow."

I swallow, my mouth suddenly dry.

I feel like I've agreed to a game without knowing the rules, but Ash is already grinning, releasing my breast, and going back to the box. He pulls me closer as he does it, wrapping an arm around my back until I'm flush against his side.

His hand rubs up and down my back as he reaches into the box and pulls out a toy.

He holds it up to me, eyebrow raised.

It's a vibrator, the insertable kind, slim and slightly curved.

"Have you used one of these before?" he asks.

I nod.

The next one he brings out is bigger.

I shake my head immediately.

"Why?" he asks, sounding genuinely curious. "What's wrong with this one?"

"That's... too big," I tell him. But, the idea of it, of putting that inside me...

I clench, trying to hide the movement. But I'm pressed so hard against him, I'm sure he feels me wriggling against his hip.

"Too big?" he repeats, looking between the toy and me. "I saw you take three of Alec's fingers, Babygirl. This isn't that much bigger."

Isn't it? It looks huge, even in Ash's massive hands.

Before I can summon a response, Ash sets the toy on the table and takes my hand in his.

"This? This is much, much bigger," he says, pressing my palm against the bulge in his pants.

Oh my *god*.

I squeeze reflexively, and a shudder goes through him, his head tipping back with a groan. He's massive. I run my hand over the length, through the fabric of his pants, mouth dry with need.

It *is* bigger than the toy. Much bigger. I think back to Alec, the sheer size of him during our video call. Could I take that much? Would it even fit?

"Fuck, if you don't stop, I'm not going to be able to control myself," Ash groans, hips jerking forward under my touch.

I realize I've been stroking him this entire time, lost in thought, and I pull my hand back quickly.

"Sorry," I murmur.

"You don't ever have to be sorry about touching me," Ash assures me with a grin. "But let me return the favor."

Pivoting on the couch, Ash moves over me, pushing me down against the cushions with his body and lying down on top of me.

I feel so small underneath him, and I love it. His hands slide under the hem of my shirt, lifting it up and over my shoulders, pulling it off me.

"I'm not going to fuck you tonight," he says softly, against the skin of my neck, kissing down to my collarbone. "Alec would kill me for being with you first. But I really want to play with you. Can I?"

Alec. Hearing his name from Ash's mouth as he touches me summons a wave of guilt.

"Would... would he—" I start to ask. Ash's mouth closes over my nipple through the fabric of my bra, and the words disappear into a gasp.

"He won't be mad," Ash promises. The bra is gone a second later, tossed aside, and when his mouth returns with no fabric between him and my nipple, I arch into him with a breathy moan. "He bought these for you, remember? I'm just helping you play with them, that's all. No harm there, right?"

Somehow, that logic doesn't quite track, but I can't think rationally with the things his mouth is doing to me. It's even worse when he kisses down my stomach, licking and nibbling at my hip bones as he pulls off my pants.

"Fuck, you're so wet already, aren't you?" he says, kissing up my leg and to my center. He rolls his knuckles over the soaked front of my underwear, eliciting another moan from me. "I love these panties, Babygirl. You look so fucking hot right now."

At least today I'd been prepared. After my call with Alec, I'd wanted to feel sexy, even if no one saw, so I picked out a risqué black lace thong to wear. A huge step up from the panties Alec saw me in.

"But beautiful as these are, they have got to go," Ash tells me, lifting my hips up so he can pull my panties off, sliding them down my legs.

"Don't you dare pocket those," I tell him, breathless from his attention. "They were expensive, and they're *mine.*"

Ash chuckles, setting them aside.

"Anything you say, Babygirl." He grins. "I'll buy you a whole store of them if you want."

His knuckles roll over me again, this time without any fabric between us, and I moan, arching up for more contact.

"Do you trust me?" Ash asks, staring up from between my legs. His eyes are an ocean blue so bright I feel like I'm drowning in them.

Honestly? No, I don't trust him. I don't even know this man. But at this moment, I'm willing to say anything that will keep him touching me. I nod eagerly.

"Good," Ash smiles. He leans back to the table.

"Give me your hands," he says, holding up the cuffs. I whimper, trying to clench my legs together, but Ash is between them, holding them open. I hold my wrists out in front of me, strangely thrilled by the prospect.

He's done this before, I realize, watching how quickly he gets the cuffs open, and how deftly he clasps them around my wrists. He's done this *a lot* before.

"Put your arms above your head," Ash tells me. "And don't move them unless I tell you to."

I obey, trembling.

"I'm going to start slow, okay?" he tells me, reaching for the first vibrator, the smaller one. "But you tell me if I go too fast for you. Just say the word, and I'll cool it. Understand?"

I nod. He trails the toy down my body slowly, only flicking it on when he reaches my hips. I jump, shocked by the sound as it jolts to life, and Ash chuckles.

"Jumpy little thing, aren't you?" He laughs.

He slides the toy lower and lower, finally slipping it between my legs and—

"Oh!" I gasp, arching up as Ash touches the toy to my clit, the sensation almost verging on too much.

He leaves it there for a few seconds, sliding it up and down just a fraction, letting me get a feel for it. Then he moves it even lower, wetting it with my own arousal before slipping it inside me.

It slides in easily enough, and I sigh, relaxing back against the couch.

"How's that?" Ash asks, pumping it in and out of me slowly.

"That's good," I moan. "That's so good."

Ash grins. With his other hand, he reaches down, gripping himself through his pants.

"I'm glad you like it, Babygirl, but I think you can take more," he says. He pulls the toy out slowly with little warning, switching it off and setting it back on the table. I expect him to grab the other toy right away, but he doesn't. He takes off his shirt instead, then stands, hands going to his belt.

Seeing Alec through the video camera was a whole new experience for me, but it's nothing compared to having the real thing. When Ash steps out of his jeans, kneeling next to me on the couch, the air goes out of me.

He's gorgeous. Every part of him is so excruciatingly perfect and toned. I reach out to touch him unthinkingly, completely forgetting my hands are cuffed.

"If you move those hands again, I will spank your ass raw," Ash warns me. My whole body goes stiff at those words, a surprising flood of desire flowing through me. But I do what he says.

"I want to make sure you're wet enough to take it," Ash says, leaning over my body to kiss my thighs. His hips are up near my face, and his cock is so close I can see it twitch as he spreads me open, tongue flicking out to lick at my clit.

I gasp, almost forgetting to keep my arms above my head. I remember just in time, gripping the cushions beneath me to keep them in place.

"Fuck, I love the way you taste," Ash groans, lips closing around my clit. I believe him, too. I didn't think it was possible for Ash to get harder, but he does, his cock pulsing next to me.

He licks and sucks at me until I'm close to the edge, and then stops, pulling away and reaching back to the table for the bigger toy.

This one has a remote. Ash grips it in one hand as he positions the toy with the other, sliding it up and down over me until it's nice and wet. I tense when he pushes it against my entrance.

"Relax," Ash says, arms flexing as he holds it in place. "Take a deep breath for me and let it out slowly."

I do, inhaling for three full seconds, and then exhaling. As I do, the toy slides in.

I gasp, clenching around it. But it's not as bad as I thought it would be. It's...

It's wonderful.

"How does that feel?" Ash asks. His other hand clenches around the remote.

"It's good," I gasp, writhing. I clench around it again, desperate for him to move it, for him to fuck me with it.

"Good," Ash nods.

His fingers deftly flick the controls of the remote.

"Oh!" I cry out, shocked, as the toy comes to life. Not just a buzz, but a rhythm, a pulse, inside me.

"You did so well, taking that toy," Ash praises, fingers sliding over the buttons again. A new, stronger pulse starts. "Take your reward."

It's heaven. I writhe against the couch, incoherent. There's another sound, another vibration, and this one I almost recognize, like it's buried somewhere in the recesses of my mind.

The toy switches off suddenly. The other sound remains, and it's almost...

Ash leans down next to the couch, and I'm vaguely aware of him pulling something from our pile of clothing.

"Well, speak of the devil." He laughs. It's my phone, I realize. The sound is my phone vibrating with an incoming call. Ash waves it at me with a grin before answering.

"Hey, boss," he says cheerfully into the receiver. "You'll never guess where I am."

My eyes go wide with horror, unable to fully comprehend Ash answering my phone while I'm naked and bound on the couch next to him. I open my mouth to say something, anything, but before I can, Ashton taps my phone screen, sending the call to speakerphone.

"Ashton?" Alec's voice asks through the phone.

"Mm hm," he answers, winking at me. He sets the phone on the back of the couch, freeing up his hand to slide down my body.

Through the speaker, Alec huffs in irritation.

"I should have known you'd go and see her," he grumbles. "Is she there?"

"Oh, she's here," Ash answers pleasantly. "But she's a little tied up right now, sorry."

I scowl at him, and Ash just laughs.

The pause on the other end of the phone is just a beat too long.

"What the fuck is that supposed to mean, Ashton?" Alec's voice is low. Dangerous.

Fuck.

Ash flicks his thumb over my clit, completely unconcerned, and again my head empties of any thoughts not related to his touch.

"It *means* that she really, really appreciates the gifts you sent her," Ash says, no fear at all in his voice. "And we're having a lot of fun with them right now."

Alec swears, low and vicious, and there's a scuffle on the other end of the line. I hear him saying something in the background, but it's too muffled to make out.

More shuffling.

Then the sound of a door closing.

"Everything okay over there?" Ash asks, his voice full of innocent concern as he traces slow circles over my clit.

"Fine," Alec snaps. "I just needed to clear the room. We were just about to start a meeting here."

Ash chuckles. Smiling at me, he presses down on the remote in his hand, sending the toy roaring back to life. The sound I make in response is embarrassingly loud.

"You mother fu—" Alec snarls, hearing me cry out. "Show me. Now."

Still chuckling, Ash reaches for my phone, switching it into video mode.

Maybe I would object if I could think properly. But Ash's hand on the toy is pushing it slowly, so slowly, in and out as it works absolute magic inside me, and all my thoughts are lost to the sensation.

"See how good she is?" Ash purrs, angling the phone to give Alec a long shot of my body, ending where he's sliding the toy in and out of me.

I hear Alec swear on the other end of the line.

"She's close," Ash tells him. "Want to watch her come?"

Oh God. I grip the cushions under me. I didn't think I could get wetter, but Ash's words have me dripping, soaking the toy he's sliding into me.

"Such a good girl," Alec says breathlessly on the phone. "Fuck. If I was there, I'd..."

There's a knock, and I panic for a moment before realizing it's coming from the phone, not my own front door. There's a hushed conversation, muffled.

"I have to go," Alec says, sounding harried. "I can't postpone this meeting and I ... *fuck*."

"I'll take good care of her," Ash grins smugly. "You go back to your meeting. I got this."

"I hate you so fucking much right now, brother," he sighs. Ash laughs and hangs up, tossing my phone back on the floor.

"That was mean," I gasp.

Ash just shrugs.

"He'd do the same thing in my place," he explains, like that forgives it. Then he shifts, sliding closer on the couch, leaning his head down between my legs. He licks at me, one hand holding my thighs open, one hand moving the toy, and suddenly I can't find the energy to care if he was mean or not.

My fingers clench and unclench on the cushion.

"I want to touch you," I admit, practically begging.

Ash chuckles.

"You keep those hands right where they are," he murmurs, lips against my skin. But he moves a little closer, bringing his hips next to my face.

"Open your mouth for me," he says.

I do, moving forward to take the tip of him into my mouth. It's salty with precum, and I can only barely get him past my lips—but it's *incredible*. Just what I need right now. I groan around him, hips grinding against his tongue.

"Oh *fuck*," Ash swears. "That's it, Babygirl. Fuck, use your tongue, just like that."

I roll my tongue over his thick head, right on the edge...

Ash sucks at my clit, pounding the toy inside me, and I explode. His cock falls out of my mouth as I scream, legs shaking, rolling my hips in time with his attention. Ash groans, fucking me hard with the toy, wringing every drop of pleasure he can out of me.

The toy is gone a half-second later when I collapse, exhausted, against the couch. Ash tosses it aside, then moves up on the couch until he's kneeling over me, angling my head up.

"Open up for me, Babygirl," he says, gripping my hair roughly. "Let me have that pretty mouth."

He slides his cock between my lips, pushing it deep enough it hits the back of my throat.

"Fuck. *Fuck*," Ash groans. He holds me in place, dragging himself in and out of my mouth. "I'm so fucking close already."

I moan eagerly around him, letting him know how much I want it.

"You're going to swallow it," Ash tells me, grunting as he fucks my mouth. "Swallow every last drop I give you." He groans, pace picking up.

Holding me by my hair, he pushes himself in deep, so deep I can't breathe. Ash's body shakes, cock pulsing as he throws back his head and groans, spilling himself deep in my throat.

There's so much of it, hot salty liquid flooding my mouth, and just as I panic, needing to draw another breath, needing to swallow, he pulls out.

"Look at me," he commands. There's a dark fire in his eyes I haven't seen before when I do.

I stare into his eyes as I swallow.

"*Fuck,*" he gasps. He makes it sound like a prayer, somehow. "Open your mouth. Show me."

Eyes still locked on his, I open, sticking out my tongue to show him I did exactly what he asked. I swallowed it all.

Ash drops to the couch, crushing our lips together and swallowing my shocked gasp. No man has ever kissed me after...

"You're so perfect," he murmurs against my lips. "Fuck, Babygirl, you are so fucking perfect, aren't you?"

I feel it. In that moment, pressed against him with the taste of him fresh on my tongue, I feel perfect.

———

WHEN I WAKE UP THE NEXT MORNING, FEELING BONELESS and pleasantly sore, I can't stop smiling. Ash carried me to bed afterwards, dressing me in my favorite sleep shirt, tucking me in, and even kissing my forehead before saying goodnight.

But I hadn't noticed him bringing in my phone and certainly hadn't noticed him plugging it in to charge. It's such a small, insignificant gesture, but it makes me feel strangely cared for. Loved.

Venturing out into the living room after my morning shower, I notice even more signs of his thoughtfulness. He cleaned the toys from last night before placing everything back in the box.

He even unloaded the dishwasher.

It's a stark contrast to the morning after Chase and I had sex for the first time. Wanting to stay in bed and luxuriate in the aftermath of our night together, I'd asked him if he'd go out and get us both coffee. I'd wanted that small token of romance, a gesture to show he cared for me, wanted to please me. He'd refused. And even worse, he'd called me lazy for even asking. It was our first fight.

First, but definitely not the last.

After that experience, I'm not sure how to process Ash's thoughtfulness. No one has ever cared for me like this before.

I think I love it.

26

SYDNEY

"How many sex toys do you have?" I ask Jade, leaning my hip against the counter and watching her carefully write out a new café specials board in perfect, practiced calligraphy. The soft morning sun is brightening into early afternoon, and traffic to the café has finally hit its usual mid-morning lull.

"Tons," she answers, not looking up at me. *Lavender Bunny Macaroons*, she writes on the board. Then, after a moment of contemplation, she adds a little heart next to the words.

"And do you... use them often?" I ask her, genuinely curious. "Like... all of them?"

"You're going to need a *different* best friend to answer that question without a fat glass of wine in front of her," Jade tells me. "What happens between me and Lady Petunia is a complex business, thank you very much."

"Did..." I blink. "Did you really name your vagina Petunia?"

"*Lady* Petunia," Jade corrects me, crossing a *T* on the board with a flourish. "She's a classy bitch, and she deserves a proper title."

"You know, I can still never tell when you're joking or not," I tell her, shaking my head.

"Good." Jade smiles. "That's half the fun." Apparently satisfied with her creation, she sets the sign back in its usual place next to the register.

"Why do you want to know, anyway?" she asks, capping her marker and looking at me. "Did you spend some quality time last night getting acquainted with all those gifts Alec sent you?"

She wriggles her eyebrows suggestively, and I look away, blushing as I mutter "something like that."

"You can spare me the details," Jade says with a dismissive wave of her hand. "I'm just glad your own Lady Petunia is finally getting the attention she deserves."

I roll my eyes and turn away from her, facing the shop. And not for the first time, I find myself looking for one particular person at one particular table.

Sebastian.

He's been back here every day since the first morning he came in, always arriving less than ten minutes after I flip the closed sign to open and staying until we close for the night. Like clockwork.

At least Jade finds our new high-tipping customer amusing.

"Are you glaring at him again? Come on, Sydney, how can you be upset?" she asks me, leaning against the counter next to me and shaking her head. "Look at him. He's not bothering anyone. Just think of him like another piece of furniture."

She smiles at him, almost fondly. "He's like a plant we never have to water."

I hate to admit it, but she's right. Sebastian doesn't bother any of the other customers, and he always orders more than enough from the café to justify taking up a table all to himself. Aside from the revolving door of women who spend a little too long sitting at the tables across from him, trying to catch his eye, he draws very little attention to himself.

"He just..." I struggle to put it into words before finally giving up. Shrugging, I admit, "I just don't like him."

"Uh-huh. Sure, Syd. I'm sure *that's* the reason."

Jade saunters away with a knowing smile on her face. I'm not sure why she looks so smug, but even I can't unlock all of that woman's mysteries.

I let out a long, deep breath. I have a lengthy list of things that need doing in the bookshop, and I should get started sooner rather than later.

Shooting Sebastian one last suspicious look, I wander back into the bookshop to get started.

Work waits for no woman, and all that.

———

It's just over an hour later, and I'm busy at the back register, finishing up with a customer, when I hear the shouting.

"I don't know why the fuck I even bother coming here!" It's a man's voice, raised enough to carry over the store, reaching every corner of our shop. Loud and angry enough to draw attention from several other customers.

I shove a receipt into the book I'm ringing up and pass it to my waiting customer with a quick apology before abandoning my register and racing toward the front of the store.

"At least the Starbucks around the corner can get my fucking order right!" the man bellows.

I break into a jog, heart in my throat and fists already clenching. Jade doesn't need me to protect her. She's a grown woman, capable and independent and strong. She doesn't *need* me to protect her.

But I sure as hell will do it, anyway.

When I reach the front of the store, I spot the problem customer immediately. A balding, middle-aged man with a polo shirt stretched too tight over his stomach is waving his hands around, shouting at Jade.

My Jade.

With one glance at her face, I can tell Jade is already close to crying. Her eyes are a little too wet, and her bottom lip is quivering almost imperceptibly. Jade wasn't built for this sort of confrontation. For all her swagger, for all her confidence and strength, a raised voice is enough to strip her to her core.

"Sir? What's the problem here?" I ask, managing to make the words sound calm as I approach them. I move behind the café counter, placing myself so I'm standing between the irate customer and Jade.

"This, this...*whatever she is...*" he starts, waving his hand in Jade's direction, "doesn't even know how to make a decent Americano. She keeps telling me there's no *milk* in an Americano."

"That's probably because there *is* no milk in an Americano," I explain as diplomatically as possible. I keep my palms flat on the counter between us, scared I might slap the words right out of his mouth. "But we'd be happy to add some if you'd like."

His face turns red at the indignity of it all, at the unfathomable disrespect of being questioned, and he's so mad he's close to shaking.

"No milk in an Americano!" he shouts at me, throwing his arms up in the air in frustration. He stares around at the other customers, a *can you believe these idiots?* expression on his face. He doesn't seem to notice that none of the looks from them are friendly or sympathetic. They're uncomfortable, at best. Disgusted with him, at worst. "You're as stupid as she is!"

I take a deep breath, schooling myself *just a bit.* If it were just me that he was shouting at, I think my breathing exercises and mantras might work. I think I'd be able to calm down enough to talk to him sensibly.

But no one—*no one*—calls Jade stupid in front of me. No one makes her cry in front of me. And I won't let that go.

I want him to pay for that.

"You know what? Let's do this." I pull out my phone and bring up my search bar, leaning over the counter closer to him, and tapping the search into my phone. He instinctively leans closer, eyes tracking my hands as I type. "Why don't we Google it together?"

I'm entering my sickly saccharine form of sarcasm that comes before the dead-eyed rage brewing beneath my surface. I can tell this man is about to argue with me more, so I lower my voice until only he can hear me, twisting my phone around and showing him the search results.

"You see here, where the internet defines an Americano as *fucking* espresso and *fucking* water and *no fucking milk?*" I hiss at him. He takes a step back, jarred by the level of my anger.

But this is *nothing* compared to how angry I can really get.

He opens his mouth to speak, but I cut him off before he can utter a single word. "And before you try to argue again or threaten us or whatever bullshit you think you can say to me, let me assure you that I don't care who you are, why you're here, or if you ever come back to my store. I will literally jump over this counter and smash my phone into your face as many times as is necessary for this *very simple* information to make it to your *useless fucking brain.*"

He's so bewildered he's frozen in place.

"Don't you ever, *ever*, insult my friend again," I say, baring my teeth in a snarl. "Or it will be the last thing you ever do."

A tall specter appears behind the man, the sunlight coming

in from outside casting an odd halo around him. I shift back in surprise at the familiar figure as he places a long-fingered hand on the customer's shoulder.

"If your little tantrum is over, I think it's time for you to leave," Sebastian says to him in a quiet, menacing voice. "Now."

The sharp look in his eyes as he stares this man down sends a shiver down my spine and an unexpected surge of heat through my veins.

Honestly, his cold, angry intensity is kind of hot when it's not directed at me.

"Fuck you," the guy snaps, finally breaking out of his stupor and trying to shrug Sebastian's hand off his shoulder. "Piss off and mind your own business. This has nothing to do with you, so—"

It takes barely any movement at all. Sebastian's hand tightens, and a look of pure agony bursts over the man's face. I watch as Sebastian digs his thumb under the man's shoulder blade, hitting a sensitive bundle of nerves with enough accuracy it looks like this asshole might pass out.

"You should leave," Sebastian repeats in that same measured tone. His face is completely blank, the same cold, bored expression he always wears. "And if you ever come back here again, you'll be leaving in pieces."

And that's all it takes. The guy practically runs out the door after Sebastian lets him go, leaving his Americano behind on the counter, steam still rising from the cup.

Jade stares at Sebastian as though seeing him properly for the first time, her mouth open in shock. I'm sure I look just the same. Never in a thousand years would I have expected this. Without a word to either of us, without even glancing in our direction, he reaches out to take the man's drink, lifting and taking a sip.

He rolls it in his mouth.

"The man's an idiot," Sebastian declares, eyes flicking up to Jade, before setting the drink back on the counter. "This drink is perfect."

Jade's expression lifts, and she gives him a small, proud smile.

"Thanks. Really. I *did* have it handled," I say. I may hate him, but anyone that defends Jade deserves some recognition from me. "But thank y—"

"Forget it," he cuts me off in an indifferent tone and turns around to walk back to his table, dismissing me entirely.

Maybe he doesn't deserve anything from me after all. My anger rises again, threatening to break the surface for the second time today, but this time I'm able to quiet it. Pushing that rage down, I close my eyes and go through my breathing exercises.

One, two, three, four, five... I hold the air in my chest.

Six, seven, eight, nine, ten... I let it out slowly.

"Why do you do that?"

The voice jars me out of my routine. It's Sebastian, paused halfway to his table, staring back at me over his shoulder.

"Do *what*?" I snap.

"Swallow your anger like that." For once, he seems genuinely interested. Almost confused. "Pretend you don't feel it."

"I'm not *pretending*." The words come out harsher than I mean to, and I force myself to take another deep breath.

I am an ocean of calm.

"I won't let myself be a slave to my negative emotions," I tell him, reciting another mantra one of many, many therapists I went to following my parents' accident taught me. I have a journal full of them somewhere in my bedroom—lines and lines of positive affirmations about reclaiming the good and letting go of the bad. About refusing to let the darker, angrier side of me take over.

Sebastian considers me, eyes narrowed. Then, with a dismissive snort, he walks away.

———

"You should hire him for security," Jade tells me later, during the evening lull while she helps me restock books. I know without asking exactly who she's referring to.

"We couldn't afford him," I scoff. "I don't know what Alec is paying him, but I'm sure it's more than this place makes in a year. And let's not forget, he's an *asshole*. And, also, I hate him."

"He'd do it for free, I bet," Jade shrugs, ignoring the second half of my statement entirely. "Hell, he's doing it for free right now."

"You just like that he appreciates your drinks and pastries," I tease. Sebastian has been eating breakfast and lunch from the café every day this week and has had nothing but compliments for the food.

"I like a man with good taste, that's true," Jade agrees, nodding. "But I think it's your pastries he's really interested in, Syd. Not mine."

I scowl at her suggestive wink.

"I know you're coming off the high of being right about Alec, but can we please not forget the most important thing here? The whole 'he's an asshole' and 'I hate him' thing? He's done nothing but ignore me, cut me off, and belittle me," I remind her. "He's not interested in anything but insulting me, believe me."

Saying it aloud makes something twist unpleasantly in my stomach. It feels like a lie. He *is* interested in me; I just don't understand why. Or what his interest means.

I never catch him looking, but it's like I can feel Sebastian's eyes on me all day, all over the store. It's not a friendly feeling. It feels like he's constantly assessing me, judging me. Waiting for me to make some kind of mistake that he can use to tattle to Alec.

Still, it *was* nice to have him step in like that. Like he was looking out for us. And seeing him handle that man? Seeing that dangerous side of him?

It was strangely thrilling.

"Maybe you're interested in his pastries, too." Jade laughs, watching me blush.

27

SEBASTIAN

The scene replays in my head, over and over again.

I can't stop thinking about it. I stare at the laptop screen in front of me, watching my work pile up. There are accounts to shift through, books to cook, but I can't focus on anything but that moment. For the rest of the afternoon, I sit in front of my laptop, thinking of nothing else.

Nothing but Sydney, her face tight with exquisite rage, bristling with anger, saying something inaudible but obviously threatening to that waste of oxygen stuffed into cheap polyester. Sydney, looking like she was three seconds away from snapping and ending that man's life.

For a moment, her eyes were as dark and merciless as Viper's.

And then, just a few seconds later, it was gone. I watched her swallow down all that beautiful rage and push it back inside herself. Painting that disgusting, pseudo-calm façade on her face.

I fucking hate it.

And I can't stop thinking about it.

Ignoring my work, I spend a few hours digging deeper into Sydney's past. I find little beyond what I already knew. Her parents died in a car accident, but this time I pull the full hospital records and discover there was a girl in the backseat at the time who survived with minor injuries. Sydney Sinclair herself. Still, nothing suspicious about that. It might be a little traumatic, but everyone has some trauma in their past.

Doesn't make her special.

Hacking into her school records gave me a little more information. A perfect angel throughout college, and most of high school after her parents' death, just as I'd discovered previously. But *before* the accident? There were a *lot* of behavioral write-ups from back then. Counselor appointments and suspensions. Fights.

Her behavioral record doesn't sound anything like the Sydney I've been watching these last few days. They sound like the write-ups Ashton used to get, after they tried separating us. The first time he was adopted.

By the time they close their shop for the day, and I pack up my things to go, I'm a whirlwind of emotions. It's bad enough Alec has me on babysitting duty, bad enough that I'm spending every hour of the workday here in this cutesy little store keeping tabs on his little pet. But now she's in my head too, and I can't have that.

I need a release.

A few hours in the wet lab would do it. That would be enough to quiet this energy humming inside me and set me right. But with Viper sorting out a few contracting issues in Seneca, and no one currently high enough on our shit list to justify an unexpected visit from me, I'm left with only one other option. A last resort to let off some steam.

The private parking lot beneath the Second Circle hotel is nearly full when I pull my motorcycle into Sterling's reserved space. It's not a surprise to see it like this. Of all our business ventures, this has always been the most reliable source of income.

Nothing sells better than sex.

From the outside, the Second Circle is a five-star splendor. Rivaling any high-end hotel in the country, this place is the epitome of class, luxury, and impeccable service. The manager, Francesca, runs the Second Circle like a well-oiled machine, catering to anyone willing to shell out several thousand dollars a night for a lavish hotel room and treating them all like royalty.

There's truly nowhere better in all of Fortune City to rest your head for the night.

A select clientele know the Second Circle for more than its opulent rooms, perfect service, and world-class spa, though. Francesca handles that side of the business too, and she's one of the few employees on our payroll that Alec trusts without question.

He should. Francesca has never once given us reason to doubt her. And she has always been more than accommodating on days like today, when any of us needs a little extra attention. Days when I need to get out of my own head for a few hours.

"Master Sterling!" the concierge greets me when I enter the hotel lobby, beaming at me. It's not my last name—not my real last name, anyway. But we're a family, and Alec insists on the staff greeting us as such. "What a pleasure to see you! What can we help you with today?"

"I'll take this, Jonathan." Francesca's voice is cool and professional as she approaches. Her high heels click against the marble floor. She touches him on the arm gently. "Why don't you go to the kitchens and see about rustling me up a nice cup of tea, hm?"

"Of course!" Jonathan inclines his head, stepping back from his station. "With a splash of bourbon, maybe?"

Francesca's lips twitch. "Naturally."

As the eager young man bounds away, Francesca turns to give me her undivided attention. At sixty years old, most of her peers are enjoying their retirement, spending time with their children or grandchildren, learning to knit, hosting book clubs, and complaining about the weather.

While Francesca has made a name for herself as the most successful Madam in the region. Hell, maybe even the country.

I ran an extensive background check on her when she was hired for this role, but it wasn't necessary. Francesca has been an open book since we found her. Born into an even shittier situation than most of my brothers, she had to steal and fight for everything she ever earned. She started as a sex worker when women in this city were forced to work the corners and parking lots of cheap motels, hiding whenever a cop car drove by. And when she finally reached the top, she made it her mission to ensure no one else in her profession ever had to suffer the way she had.

Sex work is work. Hard work. But thanks to people like Francesca, and places like the Second Circle, it's far less dangerous than it once was.

When we first approached her with our plans for this brothel, she came back to us with a lengthy list of demands. And the first, most important rule for her was this: anyone working in her hotel had to be there of their own free will and would never be pressured to do anything they didn't feel comfortable doing.

It was the same rule we'd decided on amongst ourselves when we'd come up with the idea. A rule we refused to break.

"What can we do for you tonight, Mr. Sterling?" Francesca asks me, clasping her hands in front of her. The gemstones on her rings alone are worth more than most high-end houses. She wears luxury well.

"Is Vicky working tonight?" I ask, sliding my hands into my pockets. I don't need to specify why. And Francesca would never need to ask.

Francesca inclines her head ever so slightly. "I can inquire if she's available to see you. In the meantime, we have a few viewing rooms open, if you would enjoy that?"

I shake my head quickly. I don't want to watch tonight. I need something more. I need something to stop myself from thinking, to get me out of my own head.

"In that case," she waves a hand toward the elevators, "you're welcome to wait in your penthouse. I'm sure someone will be available to join you shortly."

———

THE PENTHOUSE SUITE OF THE SECOND CIRCLE IS BY FAR the most opulent of Alec's rooms throughout the city. A private elevator takes me up to the room, and without thinking, I find myself heading over to the bar, taking my gun out of its holster on my back, and setting it on the glass tabletop.

I don't enjoy drinking. Even when I'm dragged to Alec's stupid fucking charity events and business parties where the bottles of liquor cost more than most people's rent, drinking is a rarity for me.

I like my control. I don't often give it up willingly.

But I'm feeling unsettled enough tonight that I don't stop myself when I reach for a bottle of scotch and pour myself a good two fingers into a crystal glass. I swallow it without even tasting it, feeling it burn all the way down my throat.

Dull little Sydney has a dark side. It's all I can think about as I pour another shot and bring the glass to my lips. Maybe she's not such a perfect little angel after all. That little flash of anger, that spark of something more?

That was unexpected.

I've caught a few glimpses of it before. But this afternoon was something different. Not irritation, not anger.

Violence.

Sydney has a violent side.

The sound of the elevator doors opening makes me look over, just in time to see Vicky step into the room. She keeps her eyes on the plush crimson carpet at my feet, the picture of decorum.

A perfect submissive.

"Hello, sir," she greets me. There's an unmistakable eagerness to her voice. A breathless anticipation.

I swallow the rest of my drink and set my glass down on the bar top

Vicky has been my favorite girl here at the Second Circle for a little over a year. She knows exactly what I like, and how I like it. And the enthusiasm with which she engages in all the filthy things I make her do makes me think she might like it too.

Whether she does or not is irrelevant to me. I'm not here for her sake.

"Take off your clothes," I order, leaning back against the bar. I watch her closely as she complies.

Eyes still lowered, Vicky reaches behind her back to unzip her dress, gracefully shrugging it off her pale shoulders. It pools around her on the carpet, a puddle of expensive silk. The matching bra and panty set follows.

She keeps the thigh-high stockings and garters on. It's a nice touch. They look good on her.

I take my time drinking in the sight of her, completely exposed before me. She's flawless. Perfectly smooth, not a single hair or ounce of fat visible on the full length of her taut body. Before she started working for Francesca, Vicky was well on her way to becoming the next big runway sensation. In a few years, she could have been the next It Girl. But she turned down a modeling contract in Empire City to stay here after finding sex work suited her.

She's exactly what I need tonight. Vicky looks nothing at all like my brothers' little obsession. Her hair is dark and smooth as silk, her pale face delicate as a doll's. She's exactly what I need right now.

"Get on your knees," I say, rolling up the sleeves of my dress shirt slowly. Anticipation thrums through my body. "Crawl to me."

"Yes, sir."

There's a quiver of eagerness to her voice, a hint of excitement, like she needs this just as badly as I do. Maybe she does.

It can be just as satisfying sometimes to be the one giving up control to someone else. There's something cathartic about letting go and trusting someone else with your agency.

She sinks to her knees gracefully and crawls to me on all fours, stopping only when she reaches me. Then she sits back on her ankles, running her hands up the front of my pants and to my thighs.

Fuck, I need this. My breath hitches as her hand glides over my stiffening cock before she continues up to my belt. I'll make her suck me off for a while before I fuck her. I want to take my time with her tonight. I want it rough. I want her bent over the bed, facing away from me the way I like it best, screaming for it. Begging for it.

I feel a little tipsy already, the alcohol making its way quickly through my system.

Her fingers make quick work of my belt, and before she can unzip me, I reach out to grab her by the hair, pulling her head back and forcing her to look up at me. Her quick intake of breath is exquisite.

Fuck yes. This is exactly what I need right now. Her on her knees before me, her soft chestnut curls wrapped around my fist, my—

I drop Vicky's silky black hair and yank my hand away.

Soft chestnut curls.

Sydney. I was imagining Sydney's hair clenched between my fingers. Sydney, on her knees in front of me. Sydney, waiting patiently for me to use her.

"Is something wrong?" Vicky asks, staring up at me with big liquid eyes, framed with expertly applied black liner. And in that moment, she's perfect. So beautiful, and so perfect, and so willing.

But not what I want.

"We're done," I say suddenly, turning away from her. It's suddenly hard to catch my breath. I press both of my palms against the wood of the bar top, scared if I don't, I won't be able to stop them from shaking. "I need you to put your clothes back on and leave."

"But..." Vicky's voice quavers slightly as she speaks. "I didn't... Did I do something wrong? Sir?"

I can't answer her. I can't breathe.

I can't do this.

———

It's a terrible idea. A reckless, idiotic, dangerous idea.

But I do it anyway.

Less than two minutes of digging, and I have Sydney's address. It takes me another minute to fully comprehend what that address means.

You'd never guess from the front that her little bookshop has two duplexes hidden on the second floor. The building owner did a good job concealing the back with privacy bushes and trees.

A shame they didn't think about the height of the windows when they planted those trees. Didn't think about how the branches would offer a perfect, uninterrupted view straight into her bedroom.

Really, such a shame.

I'm not exactly comfortable, sitting on a thick branch with my back against the tree trunk. But I've put up with worse. The pain is almost comforting.

I glance at my watch. Barely 10 PM. Her bedroom light is on, but the room is empty for now.

My breath catches when she appears.

Her hair is wet from the shower, and she's wearing a comically large T-shirt, long enough to cover everything but so threadbare the fabric is almost transparent.

I'm suddenly aware of how hard I am. Vicky in nothing but her thigh highs had barely given me a reaction, but this?

I reach down to adjust myself.

Sydney towel dries her hair, plumping her curls, her movements practiced and unhurried. She disappears briefly to put the towel away, and when she returns, she has a book tucked under her arm and a glass of wine in her hand.

The bedroom light turns off, and a moment later, the soft glow of the lamp at her bedside flickers to life. Sydney crawls onto her bed, propping pillows up against the headboard. She settles down against them and opens her book, her legs tucked up next to her as she starts to read.

I... I simply watch her.

It's uneventful. Mundane. But not boring, not to me. I watch her gasp as she reads. Then giggle, the noise so soft I can't hear it. I can only imagine it, bright and joyous, like music. More than once, she closes the book and squeals, her feet kicking out against the covers like she can't stop herself. Uninhibited, private enjoyment.

I feel calm watching her. And after a while, I let myself smile.

28

ASHTON

It's past midnight by the time I hear the roar of Sebastian's motorcycle tearing up the driveway of our compound.

Finally.

There's an art to making protein smoothies that don't taste like compost mixed with human waste. An art I'm still perfecting. I love my sweets, and I love food, but sometimes you need to feed your body the right fuel to keep it running properly. I've just finished prepping all the leafy greens and measuring out just the right amounts of everything when the front door opens and Sebastian walks in.

"Hey, Doc!" I have to shout over the sound of the blender. Not that it matters. Sebastian doesn't answer. He just drops his helmet and laptop bag at the door and hangs up his jacket without so much as a *hey brother, how's it hanging?*

Rolling my eyes, I pour my smoothie into a fresh glass and rinse out the blender in the sink, leaving it for the cleaning staff. Not even sparing a glance in my direction, Sebastian walks to the fridge and opens it, grabbing himself a bottle of water.

I slide into one of the dining chairs, setting my smoothie down on the table in front of me. Our compound has a formal dining room—a massive one with a table big enough to seat at least twenty—but we've always eaten in the kitchen. The little wooden table set up here seats us all comfortably enough, and most of the time we eat on our own, anyway. Especially lately.

"I figured you'd come home right after the shop closed," I muse, looking at the clock. The second hand moves slowly around the face, inching the time closer to twelve thirty. "Where have you been all night?"

Sebastian pauses, the bottle of water almost at his lips.

"Francesca's," he says finally.

Ooooh. I grin. Good for him. About damn time he found someone to spend some time with.

"Well. Hope you had fun." I chuckle.

Sebastian doesn't answer.

"So…" My leg bounces under the table, and I rub my hands together, eager for any bit of news. "What's the report? How's our girl doing?"

Sebastian gives me a sideways glance. "Go there yourself if you want to know."

Yeah, okay, I should have figured he'd be a dick about it. When is he ever not?

"Yeah, I would if I had the time, believe me." I run a hand through my hair. "I don't know how Alec handles all of this stuff, you know? It's meeting after meeting after meeting, and that's just the Sterling Enterprise stuff. I had to go to two different clubs tonight, you know that? Anthony is making a fuss again, and—"

"What are your plans with her?"

I blink hard, a little surprised at the ice in his tone as Sebastian leans against the fridge and narrows his eyes at me.

"With Sydney?" I ask, trying to recalibrate to the sudden

turn in the conversation. "I mean… there's a carnival coming in a few weeks, I thought I could—"

"What are your *long-term plans* with her?" Sebastian interrupts. He threads the cap back onto his bottle of water, squeezing it a little too hard as he does so, the crinkle of plastic loud in the quiet of the kitchen. "What the fuck are we doing here, Ash? Why ask me to watch her?"

I let out an exasperated breath. "Look, I told you, I would do it if I had the time! But when Alec's gone, *someone* has to go to these stupid meetings. They don't even want me to say anything. Do you know how boring that is? I just have to sit there while they talk and talk and fucking talk!"

Sebastian glares at me.

"Once Alec is back, you can back off. And I can—"

"It's not going to work," Sebastian says. "What you're planning."

I hate this. Every fucking conversation with him is like having two different conversations at once. I run my hands over my face and let out a frustrated grunt.

"I'm not planning anything," I say through gritted teeth.

"When are you going to tell her about all of this?" he gestures around at the compound with his bottle of water when he says it. "When are you planning to tell her what we *do*? What we really do?"

"I haven't thought that far," I admit.

A muscle in his eye twitches. "Of course you haven't. You're lying to her. You get that, don't you? Maybe Sterling more than you." He pins me with a glare when he says it. "But you're both lying to her. And she will find out."

"*I'm* not lying to her!" I insist.

"You two can be so fucking stupid, you know that?" Sebastian shakes his head. "You think this is what she wants out of her life? You think this is what she's spent her life dreaming of?"

"We can ease her in slowly," I say, already forming the plan in my mind. "You know, bit by bit. And she doesn't have to know about all of it, right? She doesn't have—"

Sebastian stalks toward me and slams his water bottle down on the table, leaning over it to stare at me.

"We're not her happy ending, Ashton." He hesitates then, something flickering in his eyes, before he corrects himself. "*You're* not her happy ending. You think you can give her the things she really wants? What if she wants to get married?"

Oh Christ, that shouldn't get me hard, should it? But fuck it does.

"I could get married," I say, the words tumbling out of my mouth too quickly. I have to reach under the table to adjust myself, imagining it. Sydney in a white dress, Sydney with a ring around her finger, marking her as ours. Oh *fuck*. "You... you think she wants that?"

The look in my little brother's eyes could be pity. Or it could be disgust. It's hard to tell.

"This life? This would break her." He stares at me for a beat. "You get that, don't you? You get that she's too fragile for this?"

I shake my head quickly. "No. *No*."

"What are you going to do when Viper finds her?"

"Isn't that your job?" I ask, raising my voice. "Keeping him on a leash?"

There's no mistaking the pity in his eyes this time. "No one can hold his leash forever, brother. Not even me."

"You can be..." I stutter, stumbling over the fear and anger and just... general *shittiness* he's making me feel. "You can be such a *dick* sometimes, you know that?"

The insult rolls right off him, like always. He doesn't even blink.

"She's not made for this. For our world. The sooner you realize that, the better, Ashton," Sebastian says. He walks away then, leaving his bottle of water behind on the table. "And the sooner we can all go back to doing the shit that matters."

29

SYDNEY

Another day, another good morning text from Alec. Followed an hour later by one from Ashton.

And another day of feeling Sebastian's eyes on me while I work, watching me from the table he occupies each and every day.

At least there's a semblance of comfort in the routine of it all. The days have a familiar cadence, and I'm lost in the rhythm of it, setting out some of our newest shop merchandise near the front of the store, when the door chimes and a familiar older woman in a bright floral blouse enters.

"Hello, deary," she calls to me.

"Mrs. Cohen!" I greet the older woman with a smile. "What a pleasant surprise! Can I get you anything? I'm sure Jade has some of those little chocolate cookies you like so much."

I wave a hand toward the pastry case, but Dorothy just shakes her head.

"No, no, dear, I'm fine." She sighs and straightens her spine, drawing her shoulders back. "I'm afraid I'm not here with good news."

My chest tightens.

"Your son?" I ask, already fearing the worst. Dorothy's son went through chemotherapy a few years ago, beating back an aggressive form of cancer. He was lucky to survive it, and it's been a constant worry of hers that one day it will come back.

Dorothy's smile is a sweet relief.

"Oh no, he's fine. Better than fine, actually. They're adopting a baby!"

I clap my hands excitedly. "That's wonderful!"

So... where is the bad news?

"They want me to move out there, to help them," Dorothy says, lips folding into a frown. And I know. Before she even says it, I know why she's here, and my heart sinks like a stone. "I need to sell the property, dear. It's time."

I struggle to keep the smile on my face, but somehow manage it. I've spent a lot of time practicing, after all.

"I understand," I tell her, clasping my hands together in front of me to stop them from shaking. And I do understand, of course I do. Dorothy should be able to go live with her family, finally retire, and enjoy some money from everything she's built.

But at the same time, my mind is racing, my chest tight with dread.

One of the only reasons we've stayed in business is because of Mrs. Cohen. Sure, the rent for this place is only a little below the market rate, but if she sells?

A different business could make much, much higher profit in this location, I'm sure of it. And a more profitable business could pay a higher rent. Any new owner would be crazy not to take advantage of that. Would be crazy to extend our lease when they could charge so much more.

I'm suddenly sick with dread.

Whoever buys this building is sure to hike up the rent higher than we can reasonably afford to pay. And since my apartment upstairs is included in the rent, that would mean having to move into a new home as well. With things going the way they are, Jade and I are barely making a profit as it is...

Dorothy must see the worries written on my face, because she reaches out, taking my hand and giving it a comforting squeeze.

"I will do my best to sell to someone who *cares* about this property," she assures me. She stares into my eyes, sincerity etched in every line on her face. "Someone who wants to keep you as a tenant."

I shake my head, forcing myself to smile.

"You will do no such thing," I tell her, firmly. "You will sell to the highest bidder, no matter what, because you *deserve* that money, Mrs. Cohen. Your family deserves that money."

She shakes her head in protest, though, and I let myself cling to that tiny hope that she will find that perfect buyer. Someone who actually cares.

Because that small hope is all I have left to cling to.

―――――

Our conversation weighs on me for the rest of the afternoon. The worries and anxieties pile up in my mind until it's all I can think about. I know I should start researching other buildings we could move the business to, if it comes to that. Hell, I should start looking for apartments. Jade wouldn't hesitate to let me crash with her, but that's a temporary solution, at best.

I try to focus on my restocking, perched on the top rung of the step of the ladder I use to stock the higher shelves, but my head is full of static. Overwhelmed. All I want is to curl up on my couch and forget the world exists, if only for a few hours.

Which is probably why the universe decides to throw another hurdle my way.

"Hey, babe," a familiar voice says from behind me, smooth and casual. "Miss me?"

The voice alone sends a chill down my spine. I go still, frozen on the stepladder, my arm outstretched. I don't need to turn around to know who it is. My hand trembles as I finish placing one last book on the shelf.

Maybe a week ago, a small part of me was missing him. But not anymore. Now, just hearing his voice makes my stomach curdle.

"No, Chase," I say, anxiety settling into my throat and coloring my words. "I don't miss you."

He's too close when I glance down, so close that I'm forced to brush against his chest as I step down from the ladder.

It hits me, then, how far back we are in the store. This is the farthest section from the entrance, and there's no one else around. No one to step in if things get bad.

Knowing that makes my palms start to sweat.

I don't want to talk to him. I don't even want to look at him. But when I try to step around him to leave, Chase grabs my arm, pulling me back toward him.

"Come on, don't be like that," he chides, his voice dripping with feigned sweetness. "Jesus, Sydney, I just want to talk."

I manage to yank my arm out of his grip, but when I take a step back to distance myself from him, I find the wall of books at my back. Trapped.

It hurts where he grabbed me. I rub my arm, trying to shake off the ache, but my voice remains steady. "We don't have anything left to talk about."

I remember, belatedly, our conversation at the charity

banquet and how he'd wanted to return some of my things. I'd never contacted him to collect them. I'd never even bothered unblocking him from my phone.

Since that night with Alec and Ash, I haven't thought about him at all.

"If this is about my stuff, you can have the rest of my things shipped to my apartment," I say. "Or throw it all away for all I care. I haven't missed any of it since I left. I doubt I'll even notice it's gone."

I'm surprised at how easily I say it. I spent so many years submitting to his every whim that I forgot how to stand up for myself. I forgot I can speak up for more than just Jade's sake. But I remember now.

I finally remember what it's like to stand up for myself.

I can't help but feel like Alec and Ash have something to do with this. They make me feel like I'm enough. Like I don't have to play pretend all the time. God, even Sebastian seems to like me more when I stand up for myself.

Chase isn't as taken aback by my attitude as I expect him to be, though he does narrow his eyes, considering me.

"That's not what I want to talk about," he says, frustration simmering beneath his tone. He rakes a hand through his hair. "Could you just listen to me? Please?"

The pleading catches me off guard. And, as quickly as it came, my confidence waivers. Just like that, I revert right back to the people-pleasing version of myself.

Maybe it's okay that he's here. He doesn't seem angry. Doesn't seem like he's in one of his moods. Maybe I can just hear him out. Maybe if I just listen to him, he'll leave without a fuss.

My curiosity is piqued, and like always when he's in one of his sweeter moods, I find myself relaxing, just a bit.

"Fine. What is it, Chase?" I ask tentatively.

"Come on, you never call me by my name. Why don't you call me 'babe,' like you used to?" He smiles, the kind smile I remember, the one that used to make my heart flutter. The sweet smile I used to love. "You know I like it better when you call me babe."

"*Chase,* we broke up," I remind him. I rub my arm again, absently. "Please, just tell me what you want to say and go before Jade sees you and has a meltdown."

Just like that, his mood shifts, and his smile shifts to a scowl. "That girl always had her issues with me," he says. "It's not my fault she never liked me, you know. That's on *her*. It's not my fault she's always been a bitch."

I know the drill. I've heard this argument too many times. How Jade had never given him a chance. How a *real* friend wouldn't be so critical of my boyfriends. And even if she had given him a fair shot—even if she'd loved and adored him—how Jade wasn't someone I should spend time with, anyway.

Jade was a bad influence, according to Chase. According to Katie and Sarah, too, he'd told me.

I've heard it all before, for years. But I never really appreciated what utter bullshit it was until this moment.

Because, yeah, maybe Jade never gave him a real chance, never really warmed to him, but she was right about him in the end, wasn't she? He was every bit as bad as she thought he was.

Worse, even.

She'd kill you if she knew, I think. *She'd never let you live another day if she had any idea how awful you really were to me.*

"You're frowning," Chase admonishes me. "Don't frown, babe. You're so much prettier when you smile."

I ignore that. "Chase, I—"

"Look, it's over between Caroline and me. *We're* over." He reaches out to straighten the strap of my dress, and his fingers linger a beat too long on my shoulder. I have to fight the urge to flinch away from him.

"What do you mean you're over? What are you talking about?"

"I broke up with her," Chase says, all too casually. "It's *you*, okay? You're the love of my life, babe. My favorite person. I just needed time to...figure myself out." He says it all with absolute sincerity and a self-deprecating little shrug. "But deep down, I always knew it was going to be you. It was always going to be *us*."

He shifts closer to me, eyes locked on my lips, and this time I do flinch away. He doesn't seem to notice.

"You were made for me," Chase says. "Remember? We always said we were made for each other. That you're mine."

I've heard this all before. Every time he fucked up, every time he'd hurt me, he'd remind me of the way things used to be. When we first started dating, he said we were the luckiest two people on earth. Back then, it was all cute dates and handholding. Little nicknames and forehead kisses.

I thought my heart was safe with him. I thought *I* was safe with him.

And then I found out how wrong I was about all of it.

It didn't happen overnight. It happened slowly, piece by agonizing piece. Until every little thing I did would cause an argument. If I needed him too much, I was overbearing. If I didn't need him enough, I was punishing him. And the pure exhaustion of playing that game whittled me down into a person I didn't even recognize. Someone dull and lifeless.

For so long, my worst fear was losing him and the life I had built around him. But while trying so hard to keep him, I lost myself. And then, when that worst fear happened—when he left me, after making me promise a million times *I* would never leave *him*—I survived it.

No. More than that. I finally started to *thrive*. And now I'm finding myself again. Not the Sydney I forced myself to be to make him happy. Not the mask I made myself wear. The real, true me.

And losing her again is not an option.

I take a deep breath to steady my nerves. "I know what we said, Chase." I force myself to look him in the eyes when I say it, so he knows I mean it. "But that's not enough anymore. It's over. *We're* over."

He shakes his head, not listening to me. "I know I sabotaged everything. I do, babe. But you'll come around. I'll wait forever for you. I'll wait ten more lifetimes. I know I screwed up, but I'm ready to settle down. To go all in. To get married and have a life with you. Just like you always wanted."

Chase finishes his monologue with an eager smile, reaching out to take my hand in his.

I don't even try to stop him. I'm too stunned to do anything but blink. "I'm sorry...did you just...did you just try to propose to me?" My voice sounds as incredulous as I feel.

"Sure." Chase shrugs. "If that's what you need to move on, why not? Let's do it. Let's get married."

He says it with all the emotionality of someone ordering at a drive-through. *I'll have a burger with large fries, and oh hey, why don't we get married?*

There was a time in my life when I would have given anything for this moment. Where even this half-baked, shitty proposal would have made me the happiest woman in the world.

That time is behind me.

"This isn't going to work, Chase," I say, voice steady despite the nausea rising inside me. "You think you can just pick me back up after Caroline didn't work out? God... you knew how much I loved you and you used that against me. For *years*. I can't do this. I can't be that person anymore."

I shake my head in disgust, and suddenly the words are coming out of my mouth too fast, but I can't stop them. "I have more important things to deal with right now, like figuring out if our building being sold is going to financially ruin me. Like figuring out where I'm going to live! I can't... I can't do this with you right now. You need to go. I need you to leave."

I try to pull away from him, but he grips my hand even tighter, squeezing it so hard the bones grind against one another. He moves closer until he's pressed against me, his body flush against mine, and I shrink back against the books to escape him.

"Fine," Chase says. I recognize the anger in his voice burning under the surface. And I recognize that look in his eyes. I have the sudden urge to shout for Jade, to let her know I'm here. That I might be in danger. "If you want to be like that? I'll go."

He finally lets go of my hand, but instead of leaving, he lingers, reaching up to play with a loose curl hanging down my chest. His fingers lightly graze my nipple as he does it, and he pauses there, touching me through the fabric of my dress.

"Call me when you come to your senses, Sydney," he says. "We both know what we have. You know I love you. Will *always* love you."

I might throw up. I can't believe this is the man I was missing for months, the man I spent weeks crying over. All I ever wanted was to be enough for him. And here I am hearing everything I had hoped I'd hear... and I feel nothing but disgust.

I don't know when it changed, when I actually closed my heart to him for good, but I can confidently say that I feel nothing but contempt for him right now. I can see his manipulation from the outside so clearly now, and just like that, I'm free.

His touch is revolting, but I suppress the urge to react. To give him a reason to push things further. I keep my face stoically calm.

"Go home, Chase," I tell him, voice little more than a whisper.

"You need me, Sydney," Chase insists. The words sound more like a threat than a promise. "Don't ever forget that."

Finally, he steps back, giving me one last sickeningly sweet smile before he slips into the aisle of books and disappears. I release a shaky breath and try to calm down. My nerves are shot, and I'm so tightly wound, I want to scream. I can only hope that whatever karmic energy is hell bent on punishing me settles down now.

I don't think I can handle anything else today. I really don't.

And as if summoned by the very thought, a cold voice comes from the shadows.

"Lover's quarrel?" Sebastian asks.

30

SEBASTIAN

I KNEW SHE WAS HIDING SOMETHING.

Of course when Sydney's ex showed up—using the afternoon rush to sneak past the café without Jade noticing—I followed him. That's why I'm here, isn't it? To keep an eye on her. To keep her *safe*.

To figure her out.

Imagine my surprise at seeing her tucked away in a dark corner with her "ex" Chase Levine. Seems like they aren't as over as Alec thought.

I saw something in his eyes when he was looking at her, something like love. And she just stood there, letting him put his hands all over her. Letting his fingers toy with her.

From the angle I was watching them, I couldn't see her face, but she didn't pull away when he touched her, didn't rebuke any of his advances. She just stood there, frozen.

And isn't that curious? I'm starting to suspect she knew *exactly* who Alec and Ash were when she so innocently encountered them. Maybe the two of them are in this together. It makes sense now why she was so adamant Alec not terminate Chase's employment. Why she was so protective of a man she supposedly was no longer dating.

When he finally saunters away, I watch Sydney take a deep breath, closing her eyes and retreating into herself. Her face is perfectly blank.

"Lover's quarrel?" I ask, leaning against the bookshelf next to me. Sydney jumps, yelping in surprise.

"Jesus!" She gasps, pressing a hand to her chest. "Someone should put a bell on you, you know that?"

I ignore the irritated glare she shoots my way, my eyes fixed on Chase's retreating figure.

I want to cut that smug look right off his face.

"You know, it's funny," I muse in a cold voice. "I could have sworn my brothers were under the impression that you and Chase were *exes*. As in, no longer together."

Sydney bends down to straighten the books haphazardly stacked next to her stepladder. "We *are* exes," she says.

"Then what was he doing back here with you?" I ask.

Sydney tenses. "Nothing," she huffs. "He wasn't doing *anything*."

"It didn't look like *nothing* to me," I say. "Looked like he had his hands all over you. And you let him."

Tell me why your ex was really here, something inside begs. *Tell me I'm wrong. Tell me you want nothing to do with him. That you aren't leading my brothers on.*

Just say it.

Sydney straightens and glares at me, lips pressed in an angry, tight line. "You know what?" she says, pointing a finger at my chest. "I have enough shit to deal with today, and I don't owe you anything, least of all an explanation. Who the *hell* do you think you... you—"

She stutters and stops, her arm falling to her side. A look of uncertainty spreads over her face.

She's staring at my arms.

"Are those..." Sydney blinks slowly. "You have *tattoos?*"

Surprised, I glance down. The sleeves of my shirt are rolled up to the elbows, exposing my forearms and the ink covering them. I don't remember doing it, and that bothers me.

What bothers me more is the realization that I left my jacket back at the café table. That the gun at the base of my spine might be visible. An amateur move.

I'm getting sloppy lately.

"You have a problem with tattoos?" I ask, arching an eyebrow.

"No! No, I just..." Sydney hesitates, twisting her fingers together nervously, eyes locked on my arms as I uncross them, my forearms flexing. "I'm just surprised. You didn't strike me as the tattoo type. That's all."

Like you know anything about me, I think, but I roll the sleeves of my shirt back down, slowly covering them. Her eyes track the movement, her tongue darting out to wet her bottom lip.

"I don't think I've ever seen your arms before," Sydney continues, voice softer now. "I knew you had nice hands, but..."

She snaps her mouth shut, cheeks flushing crimson.

"Forget I just said that," she says.

"No, please, continue," I tell her sarcastically. "Tell me more about how you've been objectifying me." I wag my fingers at her. "And my hands."

"You're just... so prim and proper, I thought." She fluffs her hair and stares intently at my sleeves, but when she catches me watching her, she quickly looks away.

"What are you doing back here, anyway?" she asks, tucking an errant curl behind her ear and refusing to meet my eyes. "Don't you have a table you're usually glued to?"

Following your ex. That's what I was doing.

"I was looking for you," I say, instead. "I'd like a book recommendation."

"And I'd like you to fuck off." Sydney rolls her eyes dramatically. "But we don't always get what we want, now do we, *Seb*?"

I can't help it. A smile tugs at my lips, and despite myself, I feel my mouth curve up. A small, but noticeable grin.

Sydney doesn't miss it. Her eyes go straight to my mouth and widen.

"What is your childhood trauma?" she asks with a laugh, sounding more amused than angry. "How is it the first time I see you actually smile it's because I told you to fuck off?"

"You surprised me." It's harder than I would have thought to stop smiling at her. Harder than I expect to put my own carefully crafted mask back in place. "I like to be surprised."

She snorts, but her eyes soften slightly. "Considering how much of a crazy stalker you are, I can't imagine that happens a lot."

"It doesn't," I admit. The smile falls from my face. "Enjoy it. I sincerely doubt someone like you has the capacity to do it again."

The growing softness in her eyes vanishes, replaced with a cold anger I recognize all too well.

"You know what?" Sydney snaps. "I'm not sure what I did to make you hate me or whatever the hell it is you feel, but don't you think it would make both of our lives better if you *literally just fucking left?*" Scowling, she stoops down and grabs a book from the pile at her feet, and when she looks at the cover, a vindictive smile spreads across her face.

"Here's that book recommendation you wanted!" Sydney says in an overly cheery tone, striding forward and shoving the book hard against my chest. "Enjoy! Maybe this will improve your shitty attitude."

The Prince's Knife. I keep my expression blank as I stare down at the cover, recognizing it immediately. Alec has been trying to hide a copy of this same book on his desk, hoping we wouldn't notice.

Her point made, Sydney storms off with an irritated huff, heading back toward the bakery. I follow behind her, not ready to let this go.

"Jade, my love, can you add a copy of The Prince's Knife to Sebastian's bill?" she asks loudly.

I emerge from between an aisle of books just in time to catch Jade's confused frown.

"Okayyyy...um, sure," she says warily, glancing between us. She purses her lips, clearly unsure how to read the situation. "That's totally something you could have done yourself at the other register, but anything for you, Syd."

Jade waves me toward her. "Come on, Doc. I'll even make you a fresh cup of tea if you ask me nicely."

I don't want tea. And I don't want to be sidetracked. I pull a few bills from my wallet and set them on the counter, pushing them toward her.

"Here. That should cover it," I say. It better.

Jade's eyebrows lift, but I don't stick around to hear how much I'm grossly overpaying for a single book. My full attention is on Sydney, who's walking away, back toward the bookshop, ducking into another aisle.

"What other shit?" I call out after her, following her.

That stops her escape. She turns to frown at me, brow wrinkling in confusion. "What?"

"You said you had other shit you were dealing with," I remind her. "So tell me. What other shit?"

Exasperated, she rolls her eyes. "Can we please not pretend like you care, Seb? If Alec wants an update about me, tell him he can ask me himself."

She's clearly upset over something. Her conversation with Chase was short and didn't seem overly emotional, so ...did one of my brothers upset her?

Seems unlikely. Alec won't return from Empire City until later tonight, but the last time we spoke, he seemed fine. Busy, but fine. And Ash has been positively insufferable with his good mood. He won't shut up about her and how well things between the two of them are progressing.

"What if I'm the one that wants to know?" I press.

"And I'm sure you're asking with purely altruistic motivation, right?" She smirks when she says it, though. Then she sighs, reaching up to touch her hair nervously. "I'm stressed about money, okay? Happy?"

Huh.

"Must be hard to have invested everything in such a fragile business," I say.

From the way Sydney stiffens, her shoulders tightening, I know immediately it was the wrong thing to say.

I didn't say it to offend her. Independent bookstores aren't exactly a booming business—not in today's era of online shopping. Their store runs a profit, sure, but small businesses are risky, and a single mistake can be all it takes to ruin one.

I was trying to be empathetic. That's all.

"I've got it handled," Sydney says, fists clenching at her side. "My business is doing *fine*." Ah. A touchy subject there. I file that away with all the other information I'm learning about her.

"If money is the problem," I venture, "you could always ask my brothers. I'm sure if you need them to—"

"I don't *need* anyone," she cuts me off. "And what I absolutely don't *need* is a man stepping in to try to save me." She pauses, shutting her eyes for a moment to collect herself.

"Don't... don't tell Alec. Please, Seb. I don't want him involved. I can handle this on my own."

Fine. I shrug. "Then handle it."

She scowls at me one last time before storming away.

"Asshole..." she mutters under her breath, maybe thinking she was far enough away for me to not hear. Maybe not caring if I did.

My lips twitch up into another smile.

That's... interesting. So maybe she isn't after Alec's money, after all. As far as I can tell, she hasn't directly asked him for anything. This could be a ploy, of course, pretending that she doesn't want any help until he "finds out" and swoops in to save her. Considering how obsessed he is with her, he would do it, too. Hell, maybe she's expecting me to be the one to tell him, to defy her request out of spite. Then her hands are clean, and she still gets the money.

But I have no reason to tell Alec.

If money really *is* the problem, well... There's a way I can help with that, while still keeping Alec in the dark.

I pull my phone out of my pocket and type out a quick email to Ashton and his social media team. Maybe this is one problem we can solve without cash. Maybe Ash can fix this by doing what he does best.

Making someone look good.

31

SYDNEY

The Boss: Dinner? Tonight?

The text from Alec immediately puts a smile on my face, despite my foul mood. He's finally back in Fortune City tonight, and, apparently, eager to see me.

I don't get off work until late tonight.

The Boss: Late is fine.

I snort, setting my phone down. Instantly, it chimes again.

The Boss: I can take you out after you close for the night. Any time. My evening is all yours.

I'm almost tempted to say no. I'm exhausted. The stress of a new landlord and seeing Chase weighing on me more than I'd like to admit.

But...

My heart beats a little faster at the idea of having dinner with him. I guess I'm eager to see him, too.

> Fine. We close at eight.

The reply is instant.

> The Boss: I'll pick you up then.

We've only spoken a few times since our last video call—the one where Ash picked up. Even thinking about it makes me blush, heat rushing to my cheeks and... other places. For a while, I was worried Alec might be mad. Or, at the least, irritated with what we'd done together without him.

But if he is, it's not coming across in his messages. He sends me a text every day to wish me good morning, and another at night asking how my day was. If he's terse, it's no more than his usual communication seems to be.

And yet...

He wanted to take me out alone tonight.

I'm still not sure what this *thing* is between us. Between all three of us. And I'd like clarification before things get any more intense.

Just the thought has me rolling my eyes. Yeah, right. Like things aren't already *super intense.* Alec has to be the most intense man I've ever met. Followed closely by Ash.

Actually...

I look over at Sebastian, hunched over his laptop, typing away.

He might top them both, now that I'm getting to know him better. Sebastian feels like a rubber band, about to snap. He's so cold, so quiet, but underneath that mask is a rage I sometimes feel in myself.

His tattoos... Now that I know they're there, I spot them sometimes when his sleeves creep up. Stark dark lines against his skin. I hate that I've always had a thing for tattoos...

I find myself watching Sebastian a lot lately. The way he watches everything, without seeming to. The way he sits, the way he eats.

I catch the way he looks at me, sometimes, when he thinks I won't notice. Always assessing. I like to think I'm just doing to him what he's doing to me. If he can watch me, judge me, belittle me, then why can't I do the same thing to him?

A taste of his own medicine.

———

WHEN EIGHT FINALLY ROLLS AROUND AND I TURN OFF THE lights, waving goodbye to Jade and closing and locking the shop door behind me, Alec is already waiting.

I'd know the black town car idling in front of my shop was his, even if he weren't leaning against it watching me close up the shop. Cars like that aren't common in this part of the city.

Seeing him there waiting for me, I feel a little nervous. He's so gorgeous, in a suit that probably costs more than our store makes in a month. My little sundress feels incredibly childish in comparison.

But when he looks up at me, all those thoughts vanish.

Alec stares at me, taking me all in, from the top of my head to my feet in a way that makes my heart flutter.

When his eyes finally reach mine, I go molten under the heat of it.

"I missed you," he tells me in a husky voice.

I give him a shy smile, trying not to think about the last time he saw me... tied up on my couch, with his best friend playing me like a fine instrument.

"I've missed you, too," I manage to say.

He opens the door of the town car, helping to guide me inside, and climbs in after me.

The interior is just as nice as the outside. Soft, supple leather seats with plenty of room. The cabin is partitioned, separating us from the driver and giving us privacy. I wonder if this is the same car that drove me home from the banquet. The moment the door shuts behind Alec, we take off, pulling smoothly away from the curb.

"Where are we going?" I ask, trying not to sound too eager.

Alec stretches his arm on the seat behind me, moving against me until our thighs are touching. Even that little bit of contact with him is enough to make my blood heat.

"You'll see," he says, smiling cryptically.

Fine. I can be patient.

"How was your work trip?" I ask instead. He places his hand casually on my knee. The sundress I'm wearing today, freshly rescued from the back of my closet, is bright yellow with a floral pattern and buttons up the front. It's a little short, ending just above the knee, leaving my legs bare. His palm is warm against my skin, his touch electric.

"Productive," he tells me, after considering the question. "Though some meetings were less productive than others."

His eyes sparkle when he says it, and it takes me a second to remember.

Oh. Right. He was in a meeting when he'd called me that night, probably had only wanted to say goodnight during a brief respite in his day.

"I, uh..." I glance away, blushing. "I hope you weren't mad."

Alec stares down at me, lips pulling down into a slight frown.

"Mad?" he asks, sounding genuinely confused. "Why would I be mad?"

"I mean..." I hedge. He can't be serious, can he? "That Ash and I were..." I clear my throat, unsure of what to say.

"I bought you those toys for you to enjoy yourself," Alec says, voice gruff. "And for you to explore what you might like. So my question is, did you enjoy yourself?"

I swallow and nod.

His hand moves a little higher up my leg.

"And did you learn anything from Ashton about what you might like?"

My legs press together as I remember the riding crop. The wrist cuffs.

I nod again, biting my lip with a smile.

"Good," Alec says in a voice like a purr. "And for the record, I will never be mad at you for what you might do with him."

"Why not?" I ask in a small voice.

"He's my brother," he tells me, as though it's as simple as that. "Not biologically, but... we grew up together. We're close. And my brothers mean everything to me. We run our business together, we live together, we... share things."

"What kind of things?" I ask, feeling a little lightheaded.

"Everything," he answers. The way he says it makes it sound like the answer is obvious.

I don't mind sharing, his voice echoes in my memory.

The car slides to a stop, putting an end to the conversation.

"Ah," Alec leans back, taking his hand from my knee. The air is shockingly cold against my skin where his hand was resting. "Looks like we're here."

The door opens from the outside, and Alec slides out, offering a hand to help me exit.

"Thanks, Earl," Alec says.

The man inclines his head. He's an older gentleman, maybe in his seventies, with kind eyes.

"I'm Sydney," I say as I hold out my hand to shake his. "It's nice to meet you."

Earl looks up at Alec, as if waiting for permission, before reaching out to grasp my hand with both of his.

"It's lovely to meet you as well, Sydney," he says with a twinkle in his eyes. With that, he turns to head back to the driver's side.

There's something about him that feels familiar, like I've heard his voice before. I shake it off and turn back to Alec, finally registering the scene in front of me.

I stare up at the tall building, slightly shocked by the lights, the colors.

"It's a casino," I say, surprised.

"It is," Alec says, sounding amused. He rests his hand on the small of my back, escorting me forward. "It's my casino, in fact. The largest in Fortune City."

Sterling Silver, the name reads, in bright neon lights.

All my years living here, and I've never actually been inside. I've seen a few of the other smaller casinos, but never been here, in the city's most spectacular one. I find them fascinating, but I'm not exactly a gambler. I prefer to keep the small amount of money I have exactly where I can see it.

We're greeted by smiling, happy faces as we make our way inside. Every employee seems to notice Alec's arrival, falling all over themselves to welcome him. It's a little overwhelming. That, and the sounds, the sights. The front doors open to the main casino floor—a massive room of slot machines, and card tables, and flashing lights and noises. There's so much to see my eyes can't seem to focus on any one thing.

"Did you know Vincent Laurent has a restaurant here?" Alec asks, steering me gracefully away from the lights and toward the edges of the room.

"Vincent Laurent?" I ask, in shock. "The celebrity chef?"

Alec nods. "The same, yes."

Wow. Even I know Chef Laurent. Though, truthfully, I only really recognize him from his TV show on the Food Channel. Still, I know enough to be impressed.

A sudden realization hits me. I glance over at Alec, looking glamorous and rich in a bespoke gray suit, and then down at myself.

In my flowery sundress. That I bought on sale. Long enough ago that I don't even remember the year.

"Alec," I protest, stopping. "I can't go to a restaurant like that looking like... like this."

"What's wrong with the way you look?" Alec asks, bemused.

"I'm not dressed to go to a fancy restaurant," I insist.

Chuckling, he adds a little pressure to the hand on my back, urging me forward.

"Don't worry," he says. "We're not dining in the restaurant tonight. Though..." He leans down as we walk, murmuring in my ear. "I, personally, love what you're wearing, Sydney."

The way he says it, in such a dark velvety voice, makes it sound wonderfully dirty. I tremble against him as he straightens.

"We're dining privately," he informs me, leading me toward a series of elevators.

There's even an attendant here, I notice, and she leaps forward to call the elevator for us.

"Let me guess," I smirk when the doors open and he ushers us inside, slipping the attendant a tip. "The penthouse?"

Alec smiles.

"Of course," he says. "Where else?"

THE PENTHOUSE IS SPECTACULAR AND EVEN BIGGER THAN my apartment. It seems to take up the entire top floor of the casino, with massive windows revealing a stunning view of the city below us.

It's also occupied.

"Welcome! Welcome," a voice greets us once the elevator doors open and Alec uses a key code to let us inside.

A plump, graying gentleman in a crisp, white smock ushers us inside, gesturing us forward and toward an intimate candle-set table.

My mouth gapes open as I recognize him.

It's Vincent Laurent.

"Vincent," Alec greets him warmly, taking his hand with both of his and shaking it. "Thank you for doing this."

"It's my pleasure!" the exuberant man insists, waving Alec's words away. "Ah! And this must be her! Ah, elle est très belle!"

I blink in surprise as he steps forward to take my hand. He lifts it to his lips and kisses the air directly above my knuckles.

"Oh! Thank you," I murmur.

"Please, please, sit! Sit! I am so happy to be cooking for you this evening!"

He pulls a chair out, motioning for me to sit down.

I do, blushing. Alec sits as well, looking pleased.

"What, uh... what are you making for us?" I ask.

"That's up to you, darling," Alec says softly.

I shake my head, smiling. "I don't understand."

"Whatever the lady desires," Vincent says, bowing at the waist. "I will cook. This I will do."

Whatever I desire?

The words conjure a thousand dishes, each more intricate than the last. I could ask for lobster. Filet mignon. Hell, I could probably ask for ortolan, and he would make it happen.

Alec would make it happen.

But... what would make *me* happy? What do I want?

Alec and Vincent are watching me expectantly, and I take a deep, calming breath and count to ten.

"A cheeseburger," I decide, sounding more decisive than I feel. "I'd like a cheeseburger. With bacon, please."

I look between Alec and Vincent, expecting to see disappointment, maybe even irritation, at such a banal request. Instead, the chef smiles widely, displaying small white teeth.

"That sounds wonderful," Alec says. "Make that two. And fries?"

I nod eagerly.

"Put an egg on mine, as well," Alec says. He glances at me, raising an eyebrow.

"Not on mine, thank you," I smile. Eating a burger on a date is going to be messy enough as it is. I don't want to add a runny yolk into the mix.

"Très magnifique," Vincent says, clapping his hands together. "I shall make for you the best cheeseburger with bacon that you have ever had, d'accord?"

With one last shake of Alec's hand, and another polite kiss near mine, he's gone, the elevator doors dinging as they shut behind him.

"I hope you're not disappointed to be eating burgers," I tell Alec. "It feels almost like a waste, with such a great chef, but..." I give him a little smile. "It's my comfort food, and I've been craving one *all* day."

"I don't mind at all," Alec assures me. "I love a good burger."

"It's just not exactly, you know, fine dining."

Alec smirks in answer. "There's nothing special about fine dining. In life, there is food you enjoy and food you don't. And tonight, I want us to have food we will enjoy. It's that simple."

I grin back at him.

Everything feels so easy with Alec. I forget that when I'm alone with my thoughts in the bookstore, obsessing over everything and getting caught up in my own thoughts.

"What did you mean in the car?" I ask, running my fingers over the tablecloth. It's fine linen. Probably a higher thread count than my sheets. "About... sharing. With your brothers."

Alec watches me closely, measuring my reaction.

"My brothers and I..." He pauses, as though choosing his wording carefully. "We're a package deal."

My insides twist unpleasantly.

"So, if I'm with one of you, I have to be... with all of you?" I ask.

Alec shakes his head.

"Not in the way you mean," he says. "But you need to recognize that they're a big part of my life. An inescapable part. We run our business together. We live together. We're not often apart. I'm not saying I'm expecting you to fuck them, darling."

His voice holds an edge that almost makes me feel bad for asking. "But..." he continues. "You have to accept that if you're in my life, they will be in your life as well."

"And do I get to choose?" I ask. "To what... extent, they're in my life?"

Slowly, Alec nods.

"And if I decide one thing, and then change my mind?" I press. "What happens then?"

"You mean, if you decide to sleep with Ashton," Alec says, leaning forward and putting his elbows on the table. "And then decide you no longer want to have a relationship with him?"

I nod, a little surprised he understood the question beneath my question.

"You are free to do so," Alec says. I release my breath,

shoulders untensing. "But that would be a conversation you would have to have with him. Not with me."

"Okay," I say.

Alec takes my hand in his.

"I'm glad you're asking this," he tells me. "I want you to know. To not be surprised. I want you to be comfortable with me, Sydney."

"Does he... does he expect to sleep with me, too?" I ask nervously. "To share me with the rest of you?"

"Ashton?" Alec frowns. "I think he's made his intentions quite clear, Sydney. Yes. I imagine he's very eager to have that sort of relationship with you."

I shake my head quickly.

"Sebastian," I clarify. I know he hates me, but if this is how these guys operate... if they are used to sharing? Would he expect to sleep with me just by default? Is that why he keeps hanging around the cafe? Is that why he hates me so much, because I've made no move to welcome him into my bed? "Does *Sebastian* expect to sleep with me?"

Looking surprised, Alec shakes his head slowly. "No. Sebastian... I don't think he's expecting that. He may want to. And he can be hard to read, even for me. But expect it? No. You can ask him if you'd like."

I laugh, shaking my head.

"I could never just ask him something like that. He's too intense. He's... like bottled lightning. Or like a snake, all coiled and waiting, ready to strike." I describe, still laughing a bit. "And I'd say we're safely in the mutual hatred zone. He can't stand me."

"I very much doubt that's true," Alec counters, looking away from me. "But you're not wrong in that characterization of him. He can be... intense when he needs to be."

The ding of the elevator is all the warning we get before Vincent Laurent comes back in, a team of waiters at his heels. Quickly, the waiters fill our table with food, placing a massive pile of fries between us along with a collection of dipping sauces and two heavenly-looking burgers. Someone places a cloth napkin on my lap, and to my surprise, a sommelier appears, pouring a small dribble of wine so dark it's crimson into a glass and handing it to me.

"For you, this evening, I have picked a robust red," he explains, eyes on me. "To compliment the meat of your burger. If Madam approves?"

A little unsure of what exactly to do, I raise the glass to my lips and drink the small portion of wine down in one sip.

It's earthy. Strong.

"It's great," I tell him honestly. "Thank you."

The words are barely out of my mouth before he takes the glass again, filling it this time, and pouring another for Alec. He leaves the bottle on the table, bowing his head to both of us. Then, as quickly as they arrived, the crowd is gone, the doors shutting heavily behind them.

"Wow," I mutter. "A girl could get used to that." Alec chuckles, picking up his burger.

After just one bite, I know, beyond any doubt, that Vincent Laurent is a genius. It's the best burger I've ever had in my life. Even the fries are sensational, and since none of the dips are labeled, we have fun guessing what they all are before trying them.

I'm halfway through my burger when I work up the courage to ask another question that's been plaguing me.

"What about Viper?"

Alec freezes, his hand reaching for his wine glass. It's such a small reaction, only a fraction of a second's pause, but I catch it.

"Who told you about Viper?" he asks, voice a little too flat.

"Sebastian," I tell him, and I know from the slight tick in his jaw that I've thrown the doctor right to the lions. "But I don't think he meant to. It slipped out."

"I see," Alec says, taking a sip of his wine.

When he doesn't continue, I press the issue.

"Where does Viper fit into all of this?" I ask. "You've never even brought him around to the shop to meet me."

"Viper is... complicated," Alec says, swirling his wine. He won't meet my eyes. "He's out of town right now, taking care of something for us. But I'm sure you'll meet him when he gets back."

"Complicated how?" I press.

Alec laughs, shaking his head.

"Has anyone ever told you that you're like a dog with a bone?" he asks.

"A few," I answer, truthfully. Jade certainly has. And just like her, somehow Alec makes it sound like a compliment, not a complaint.

"It's not a bad thing, believe me," Alec assures me. "But tonight, I'd rather not talk about Viper."

"I thought you didn't want me to be surprised," I accuse.

If I'm annoying him, he doesn't show it.

"We can prepare you for meeting Viper," Alec insists. "Another time, please."

Fine. But only because this burger is so delicious, I don't want to waste any more time talking when I could be eating it.

When I finish—setting my napkin on the table and leaning back with a contented sigh—Alec pulls my chair around the table, closer to him. He plucks one last fry from the pile, dipping it in something we're both confident is a garlic aioli, before popping it into his mouth and settling back in his chair, cuddling closer to me.

"How do you usually relax after work?" he asks, wiping the salt from his fingers with a napkin. "Do you like to watch TV?"

I do. I like reality TV, mostly, letting the inane chatter fill the silence as I unwind after a long day. Turning my brain off and just letting myself relax.

"We could watch something together. Maybe a movie, if you would like?" He gestures vaguely toward a room, hidden somewhere deep in his penthouse suite. "I have a TV room up here. We could order anything you'd like to watch."

I shake my head, grinning.

"I'd like to just sit with you," I tell him. "If that's okay?"

Alec smiles. "That's more than okay, Red," he tells me. He shifts, once again sitting so close that his leg presses against mine.

"Red?" I ask, tilting my head to look at him.

The corners of his mouth twitch. "You were wearing red the first time I saw you."

"At my store?" I purse my lips, trying to remember what outfit I was wearing the first time I saw him. I don't own a lot of clothing that's red.

Alec makes a noncommittal sound in his throat, and stretches across the chair behind me, pulling me closer to him.

Leaning against him, I release a long breath and let myself relax. My eyes close, and I breathe in the smell of his cologne.

It's not a surprise at all when I feel Alec's hand settle on my knee again.

"You like touching, don't you?" I ask, smiling, eyes still closed.

"Sometimes," Alec admits, sounding almost embarrassed. "I enjoy touching *you*. I like it so much I feel like I'm addicted to it. I don't think I can stop."

"I don't mind," I say.

His hand moves up further, thumb stroking the skin on my inner thigh.

"I loved our video chat, darling, truly I did, but nothing, *nothing*, compares to this. To feeling your skin against mine."

His hand moves higher.

I sigh again, relaxing even more against him, letting my legs part a little. A tacit invitation for him to go further.

Alec shifts next to me, moving closer, and I feel his lips hovering over my own before he speaks.

"I'd like to kiss you, Sydney. May I?"

I open my eyes, wanting to see him when I answer. His eyes are dark and beautiful.

"Yes. Please," I tell him.

Alec almost groans in relief, closing the gap between us and capturing my mouth with his. His hand slides all the way up my thigh, gripping me by the hip and rolling me until I'm suddenly on his lap, straddling him.

"I've wanted to do this all night." Alec breaks the kiss to growl. Then he pulls me to him again, tongue tangling with mine, pulling me hard against him.

I place my hands against his chest and sink into the kiss. Under me, I can feel him hardening, straining against the fabric of his slacks.

Screw going slow. What the hell was I even thinking when I'd wanted that?

I shift my hips against him, moaning into his mouth at the sensation. There's too much clothing between us, and I want—no, I *need*—to feel him.

Alec seems to agree.

"I need to see you," Alec murmurs, kissing down to my neck. Gripping my hips, he rocks hard against me, pulling a gasp from me. "All of you."

His hands make quick work of the buttons on my dress,

pulling it from my shoulders and letting it fall away. I pull at his shirt, and he doesn't even bother undoing any buttons before he drags it from his waist and rips it over his head.

"Look at you," he growls, trailing a hand down my chest and stomach. "You're so beautiful, you know that?"

I don't bother fighting back the smile that creeps over my face. I've never done well with compliments. It's not so much a self-esteem thing as much as just...awkwardness. But I love the way he and Ash look at me, the way they call me beautiful.

He pulls me back in for another searing kiss, his hand sliding up my back as he does so and unclasping my bra. I let it fall off my shoulders and down to the floor.

"Stop me if I'm moving too fast," Alec murmurs against my lips. "You can tell me if you want me to stop."

I don't. I've never wanted anything more in my life.

"Fuck me, Alec. Please," I plead. "I need to feel you."

He breaks our kiss with a groan, rolling his hips underneath me. He's practically panting when he pulls away from me enough to stare into my eyes.

"Wrap your legs around me, darling," he orders, standing as he says it. Startled, I do, wrapping my arms around his neck too, a little scared he'll drop me.

But Alec carries me effortlessly to a bedroom, like I weigh nothing at all, coming to his knees on the mattress before laying me down gently on top of it.

"I promised myself I'd be gentle," he tells me, voice rough. "For our first time together, I fucking promised myself I would be gentle with you."

His hands are on his pants, practically shredding them as he pulls them off and tosses them aside.

I moan when he kneels between my legs, his hard cock even more beautiful in real life. I reach out to touch it, stroking it. It's so thick my fingers barely touch.

Alec's hips buck under my touch, and he growls, low and primal.

"Feel how hard you make me, Sydney? I don't think I can keep that promise." The words almost sound like an apology. His stare bores into me.

But it feels inevitable at this point. And I want it. I want him to ruin me.

"Then don't be gentle," I whisper.

He holds my gaze for a beat, chest rising and falling with his breath.

And then, faster than I can react, his hand is around my neck.

I give a small, shocked gasp, my hands coming up instinctively to wrap around his wrist. The gesture is pointless. The muscles in Alec's arm are hard as stone, pinning me effortlessly to the bed, and there's not a chance in hell I'd be able to move him even if I wanted to. He doesn't even notice my hands gripping him, his full attention on my lower body as he rips my underwear off with his other hand and tosses them aside. I can't move, pinned to the bed by him, and suddenly his fingers are there, rubbing down my slit, and making me moan.

"You're so fucking wet, aren't you?" he growls, sliding a single finger inside me and tightening his grip on my throat.

Holy. *Fuck.*

This shouldn't be such a turn-on. I shouldn't be enjoying this. This is dirty. This is violent. This is dangerous.

This is... *so fucking hot.*

I let his wrist go, hands falling to the side to grip the sheets as he thrusts another finger inside me.

"I need to be inside you," he says, fingers pumping into me. "But you need to come for me first, sweetheart. You're going to take every inch of me, and it'll be so much easier if you come..."

I'm already almost there, pleasure coiling inside me, when he adds another finger.

"So fucking tight," he says, fucking me relentlessly with his hand. He grips my throat a little harder, and I moan, head lolling back.

"You like this, don't you?" he asks, flexing his hand and making me gasp. The fingers wrapped around my neck press dangerously hard against my pulse. Inside me, his other fingers curl, hitting that perfect spot. "You like it a little rough, don't you, darling?"

It's more of a shock to me than it is to him, but he's right.

I love it.

Why do I love this?

"Because you're mine." Alec somehow answers my silent question while fucking me faster, harder. I cry out, my body shaking, wanting to move, but he's holding me so completely still against the bed. I feel powerless under his grip. Helpless. And I love it. "This pussy? This is mine. So be a good girl and come for me, so I can finally take it."

Holy shit.

It doesn't take much more than a few more thrusts, and I'm coming undone, screaming as I break, my pussy convulsing over his fingers.

"That's it, darling, give it to me. Get that pussy ready for me."

I feel like I'm breaking, every muscle in my body tightening. When it finally dies down, I relax in waves, riding his fingers, until I collapse back against the bed, gasping for breath.

When Alec's fingers leave me, I briefly mourn the wonderful sensation of being filled by him, but a moment later, he climbs on top of me, and something thicker presses against my entrance.

He enters me slowly at first, one hand at my throat and the other under my thigh, pinning me open for him.

But even slow, it's too much. I almost hyperventilate, panicked that I can't do it. With a snarl, Alec leans forward, clasping his mouth over mine, tongue savaging my mouth, and —in one hard thrust—he pushes all the way inside me.

I try to scream, but it's swallowed by his mouth, and then he's moving, pulling out inch by delicious inch only to slam into me again.

"Fuck," he moans, throwing his head back to swear. He releases my neck, but only to grab my wrists, pinning them above me on the bed. My unpinned leg wraps around his waist as he fucks me.

His fingers were nothing compared to this. The toys were nothing compared to this.

There's nothing in the world that even comes close to how incredible Alec feels, his cock filling me more than I've ever known, his hips rolling against me with every thrust.

His tempo picks up, and my leg pulls him to me tighter, needing him closer.

"That's it, darling, take me," he grunts. "Take every fucking inch you need. Fuck, you're close again already, aren't you? I can feel you gripping me, feel you wanting more. Take it. It's all for you."

I struggle against his hold on my wrists, wanting to touch him, wanting to wrap my arms around him.

"Such a good girl," he tells me. "You take me so fucking well, darling. Show me how much you love it. I need to feel you come apart on my cock."

I can't. I've never come like this before, not once, not with anyone. But the way he's moving his hips, the way he rubs against me each time our bodies connect...

The orgasm hits me so hard I almost break his hold on me, my body arching and bucking with the force of it.

Alec swears, fucking me harder, harder than I even thought possible, gripping me with enough force I'm sure to bruise, and then he's following me, shouting my name as he buries himself inside me.

I feel each pulse of his cock as he comes, filling me up. And I ride that high with him, chasing the last of my own pleasure as we spiral down together.

32

SEBASTIAN

Something is different about Sydney today.

I watch her closely, obsessively, trying to figure out *what it is*. Trying to figure out what's wrong with her.

It's irritating that my brothers' little obsession seems to be rubbing off on me. She's so completely wrong for any of us, for our lifestyle. So fucking fragile. Alec and Ashton have found themselves a little glass doll and think they can play with her all they want without breaking her.

Still...

There are flashes of something more, and that's what I can't seem to tear my eyes away from. Brief moments, here and there, of something darker. And every time I think I'm kidding myself, I see something that makes me think that maybe—just maybe—she's not as fragile as I originally thought.

And today, there's something different about Sydney.

There's a stiffness in the way she moves around the shop this morning, a hesitation before picking up a box that hasn't been there before today. I devour her from afar, feasting on all her little movements.

Is she sick? I tap my fingers on the table and consider it. I haven't spent enough time with her to track her full cycle yet. Maybe it's cramps?

It's not until she brings my lunch over, our odd little routine that I've come to rely on, that I get my answer.

I glance over when she sets the plate on my table, opening my mouth to thank her, when I spot her wrist.

I don't even think. I reach out to grab her arm automatically, ignoring her quick intake of breath as I pull it closer, twisting it in the light.

Her wrist shows signs of bruising. Dull red and purple marks mottled around her delicate little wrist bones.

"Do you mind, asshole?" Sydney snaps, trying to yank herself out of my grasp. I don't let go.

It's an easy pattern to recognize when you've seen it before. You can make out where his fingers dug into her.

"Sterling?" I ask, voice devoid of emotion, inspecting them, admiring his work. I'm well aware they had a date last night. And he didn't come back to the compound afterward. It's safe to assume they finally fucked.

Maybe now his obsession with her will finally ease. Maybe now they'll move on, and we can go back to the way things were. Go back to focusing on what matters. Like a potential dead man coming back to life.

My eyes slide up to her face, noting the blush on her cheeks. She nods quickly, just once.

Her pulse is rapid under my grip. Before I let go, I slide my thumb over her wrist, gently skimming it over the bruises he left there. Her skin is so smooth, so delicate. I'm not surprised she marks so easily.

I let her wrist drop and nudge the chair next to me with my foot.

"Sit," I order.

She hesitates but does it, sinking into the chair without a word of protest.

Such a good girl, I think, swallowing the words before they slip out from between my lips. My mind flashes back to the Second Circle. To my fantasies about her. Fantasies I can't seem to let go of.

I move my chair closer to her, leaning forward and gently brushing her hair off her shoulders.

"What do you think you're doing?" she asks suspiciously, as I run my finger under her chin, tilting her head up and to the side.

"Looking for any other injuries," I tell her, inspecting her neck. "Like any medical professional would."

There are two, but they're minor, barely even noticeable. One is likely a suck mark, a red aberration just below her right ear. The other is a barely discernible scratch, probably from a fingernail.

This close to her, it's impossible not to notice when she swallows.

"You know he likes to...?" She stops before finishing the question, biting her lip.

Fingertips still holding her chin, I raise my eyes to meet her gaze, letting her see the answer there.

Do I know Alec well enough to know he'd want to wrap his hands around her pretty little throat while he fucked her? To know he'd get off on holding her down, feeling her pulse race under his fingers?

"I know," I tell her.

She swallows harder this time and looks away.

I keep a med kit in my laptop bag, just a small one for emergencies. In our line of work, there are a lot of emergencies. I reluctantly let go of her face, reaching into my bag to pull out a small tube of antiseptic ointment.

It's probably unnecessary for such a superficial wound, but I apply a thin coat to the scratch, anyway.

"Is there anywhere else I need to look?" I ask, screwing the cap back on the ointment and sliding it back into my med kit. "Any other injuries?"

Her eyes go wide.

"Of course not," she tells me tersely, like she can't imagine there'd be anywhere else he could possibly have left a mark.

Me? I can list a thousand.

Like her pretty little ankles, if Alec had gotten out his ropes and tied her up. Bondage has always been something he's favored with the women he brings home.

Like the muscles in her jaw if he'd used a ball gag, forcing that perfect little mouth of hers to open uncomfortably wide.

Or the soft, golden skin on her back if Ashton had been involved. I've seen the damage he likes to do with his whips. The way he likes to mark his women.

I don't even bother thinking about all the ways Viper would hurt her.

I don't say any of these, of course. Her question is more than enough to assure me she isn't injured anywhere else, in any way that matters.

"Do you have a bathtub in your apartment?" I ask her. I already know the answer. But I wait for her nod before I type a quick note to myself on my phone, setting an alert to remind me to stop by the pharmacy when I leave. "I'll pick up some Epsom salt for you. Add a quarter of a cup to your bathwater tonight. That will help with any lingering... soreness."

She shoots me a quizzical look, but the way she subtly clenches her legs together, shifting on her chair, confirms exactly what soreness she's dealing with. And explains the slight hesitation in the way she's been moving.

I wish I'd been there to see it. To watch him take her. The

bruising on her wrists and neck tells me he wasn't gentle. Did she like it rough? Did she beg him to fuck her harder? Faster? Did he spend hours playing with her, getting her ready to take him, working her until she was dripping wet and needy? Or did he make her take it hard, holding her down and forcing it in, inch by inch?

I don't realize I'm frozen, lost in my own thoughts, still holding my phone, until Sydney speaks.

"Earth to Sebastian?" she says, waving her hand in front of my face. She wets her bottom lip with the tip of her tongue when I look at her. "Why are you helping me?"

The phone in my hand springs to life, the vibration from an incoming call cutting her off.

One glance at the screen, and I feel my stomach drop.

"I have to take this," I say, the words coming out too fast. I stand, knocking my chair back an inch in the process. To anyone else, it would be a normal, almost natural movement.

For me, it's a full-blown meltdown.

I let the phone continue to ring until I'm far enough from the table that I know she won't overhear, ducking into the literary fiction section of her store. Only then do I accept the call.

"What's wrong?" I ask immediately.

There's a long pause on the other end, followed by a smooth exhale, almost like a sigh. I can picture exactly how Viper looks in this moment, cigarette dangling from his mouth as he exhales smoke, phone pressed between his ear and shoulder. He likes to keep his hands free.

"Why would something be wrong, Doc?" he asks.

If he hears the panic in my voice, he betrays nothing. I listen for the soft tap of him ashing his cigarette.

"I wasn't expecting to hear from you until Thursday," I remind him. Viper never calls early unless there's a problem.

The laugh starts low and builds until it's almost manic.

"It *is* Thursday," Viper tells me, almost deliriously happy at my mistake.

I frown, pulling my phone from my ear to check the date and see he's right.

Fuck.

"Distracted, Doc?" he asks. I can hear his smile in the beat of silence. "Feeling antsy without me?"

I hate that he can read me. Hate that no matter how perfect my mask is, Viper can see right through it. And I hate, *hate*, that I have no read on him whatsoever right now.

"It's been a long week," I tell him truthfully.

Another laugh, another long exhale of smoke.

"I'm done here," he says, finally. "Tell Sterling the contracts are signed. I'll be coming back tomorrow."

I nod, even though he can't see me.

"Great. I'll meet you at—"

The line clicks. He ended the call.

Fuck.

Fuck.

I'm already dialing Alec's number, heart racing.

Viper is going to find out about their obsession with Sydney eventually. But we need to do everything possible to keep him far away from her for as long as we can.

Because the three of us? We're dangerous.

But Viper?

Viper is fucking psychotic.

33

Alec is standing with his back to the room when I enter his office, staring out the window at the city skyline. It's a spectacular view, probably one of the best in the city. A view of everything that's ours. Of everything he's worked so hard to achieve.

Every one of Alec's rooms scattered around the city has a view like this. Like he can't help but admire the empire he's built, no matter where he is.

"What's up? You said it was an emergency?" I plop myself down on his couch, lying back and stretching my legs out. My morning workout kicked my ass today, and I'm feeling it from my feet to my face.

"Doc just called," Alec says. "Viper is finished up in Seneca. He's coming home."

At first, I'm relieved. Seneca is a tiny little thing, barely even a city, just a few hours south of where our territory ends in Empire City. But it has taken months of work to push out the old guard there and expand our little empire. And every time we came close, something would come up that inevitably sent us back to square one. Viper's work there is the culmination of something we've all been pushing toward for a long time, a final rinse with bleach to wash the slate clean.

If Viper is on his way home, that means everything went according to plan, which isn't exactly a surprise. Viper might be insane, but he's the best at what he does.

Hell, he might be the best *because* he is insane.

My relief is short-lived, though, as the full weight of what Viper returning means crashes down on me.

Viper doesn't know about Sydney.

I love my brothers, I really do, all three of them, but Viper never learned to play nice with others, and it has caused… problems in the past. It's one of the reasons Alec has never really dated, not seriously anyway. We don't know what he'd do with a stranger in the house, especially a woman.

"How long do you think we have until he finds out about her?" I ask, not even bothering to hide the panic in my voice.

Alec shrugs, his back still to me.

"A few days?" he answers. "A week if we're lucky. And when are we ever lucky?"

He's right. We can't rely on luck to help us out here. Empires aren't built on luck. They're built on blood and sweat and more dead bodies than I'd care to remember.

I sit up, feet planted back on the ground. I need to feel grounded, need to feel the world under me, steadying me.

"You're awful fucking calm, considering," I accuse, eyes narrowing. Alec is tense, sure, but that's nothing new. He doesn't look as panicked as he should be. He looks like he's doing his fucking taxes.

Me? My leg is bouncing up and down, the muscles twitching in my shoulder, telling me to *move* to *fight*. I couldn't calm down even if I wanted to.

When Alec just shrugs, finally turning his back on the view and settling into his desk chair, it hits me.

I grin.

"You fucked her, didn't you?" He doesn't deny it, and I bark a quick laugh. "Holy shit, you did. You fucking dog."

Alec exhales loudly.

"How was she?" I ask, leaning forward eagerly.

I won't pretend I haven't been thinking about it, almost to the point of obsession. The night of the banquet was incredible, but our night together, one-on-one? Fucking *outstanding*. And I can't wait for a repeat. I can't wait for *more*.

"She was..." Alec drums his fingers on his desk, considering. "She was *exquisite*."

I groan, my dick kicking into high gear just thinking about it.

Exquisite.

Yeah, that describes our girl perfectly, doesn't it?

She'd been so timid, so naïve, looking at all those toys Alec bought for her. Such an innocent little thing. And I'd been patient, hadn't pushed her too far—hell, I'd practically been a saint, when all I'd wanted to do was roll her over and show her exactly how I liked it best.

I was being so fucking patient.

But the second she'd slipped that little mouth of hers around the head of my cock, all that restraint had gone right out the window. I'd thought we would have a fun night just for her, a night that was all about her pleasure and figuring out what she enjoyed.

And I'd ended the night fucking her mouth so hard I could come again just thinking about it.

I hadn't mentioned that part to Alec, of course. We'd both agreed to be gentle with her, introduce these things slowly, over time. You don't want to scare off an exquisite little thing like Sydney by pulling out the nipple clamps too soon.

But she'd loved my hands in her hair, loved me forcing my cock down her throat. I could see it in her eyes, could feel it in the way her body reacted.

She was going to *love* all the things I wanted to do to her.

I'm rubbing myself through the fabric of my pants, lost in the memory, when Alec sighs in irritation.

"Keep your dick in your fucking pants, Ashton," he snaps. "I'm sick of paying to have the couches cleaned."

I shoot him a grin, but I stop, leaning back on the couch and stretching my arms out on either side of me.

"She's fair game now, right?" I ask, not looking at Alec to confirm. "You broke the seal. She's ours now."

Alec glares at me.

"She's *mine*," he snaps, tapping his desk. I just grin back at him. "I made it *very clear* to her that she can draw whatever line in the sand she needs to with the rest of you. Including you."

I just shrug.

"I don't mind wining and dining her," I tell him, waving his concerns away. In fact, the moment I say it, it hits me just how much I'd love it. I'd love taking her out, showing her the night of her life, almost as much as I'd love making her come. I *want* her to want it. To want *me*.

I want to be good to her, to take care of her.

Fuck, we've barely spent any time with her and I'm already all in.

"I think I'm in love with her," I admit, grinning up at the ceiling. Alec just snorts dismissively.

"You can wine and dine her all you want," he warns. "But if she tells you no, that's that. You'll have to accept it, brother."

I laugh.

Of course I will.

But she's not going to tell me no.

With a little time and patience, I know I can have Sydney however I want. And I want her begging for it, hands tied behind her back, covered in whip marks and our cum.

Groaning, I grip myself through my pants again.

"Focus. We need a plan for how to deal with Viper," Alec says, pulling us back on track.

Right. I let go again, reluctantly.

"A distraction," I say. The frenetic bounce of my leg is back. "If we keep him occupied, put him on another mission right away, we can buy more time. Prepare her for it." Prepare her for *him*.

Alec nods.

"I was thinking the same thing. And I have just the man in mind."

Before he can expand on that thought, there are three quick raps on the door. It opens before Alec can tell him to enter, and Seb strolls in.

He nods a greeting at Alec, before his eyes shift to me. He immediately glances down at the erection straining the front of my pants and rolls his eyes.

But he doesn't call me an idiot. And he doesn't curl his lip in disgust.

In fact, my little brother seems like he's in an unusually good mood, and I immediately start forming theories before I spot a copy of *The Prince's Knife* sticking out of his bag. My eyes widen and eyebrows quirk a bit when I glance back up at him.

Holy shit. He's fallen just as hard, and he has no idea.

Poor guy. He doesn't have a chance with her.

I'll admit, I skimmed a lot of the book. It was all a bit too complicated for me. I liked the sex scenes, though. Read those a bunch. Even filed away some of the juicier tidbits to try later. But I've never been much of a reader; that's always been Doc's thing.

"I just told Ash about Viper. Thanks for the heads up on that," Alec tells him.

I hop up from the couch, ready to head out when Alec fixes me with a pointed look.

"I guess we're not done here?" I ask, sitting back down. "What's up, boss? More psychos to worry about other than Viper?" I joke. It may not be in writing, but breaking the tension and keeping things light around here might as well be my number one responsibility. Between all these morose motherfuckers, it feels like a funeral home half the time.

Except Alec's frown deepens.

"Shit, really?" I press. "More psychos?"

"I wanted you both to hear this." Alec pauses, like he's struggling to continue. Considering his job has always been to share bad news and assign the worst tasks, and he has never struggled to do so, the hesitation is starting to freak me out.

"Rip off the band-aid, you're killing me," I urge.

"When I was in Empire City, the team shared some surveillance pictures with me." Alec's eyes flick over to Sebastian, his gaze laced with concern. "Annika is back."

With that one name, it feels like all the air has been sucked out of the room. My eyes fix on Seb as he stiffens, shoulders tensing. He stares out the window behind Alec's desk, his fingers tapping rapidly against his leg.

Fuck.

"I think she's the one behind all of this," Alec continues, speaking more to Sebastian than me. "She knows more about Dante's organization than anyone. And she has her own score to settle with us."

Sebastian shakes his head. His jaw is clenched so tight, I'm worried he might crack a molar. "No. No, that doesn't make sense. It wouldn't be her."

Alec looks to me, then back to Seb. "I know you want to believe—"

"'*He* said his name was Dante,'" Sebastian interrupts with a snap.

When Alec and I only glance at one another, not speaking, he continues. "That's what Giovanni said to Viper. We all heard the recording. '*He said his name was Dante.*' Not she. Giovanni dealt with a man."

Alec's face is unreadable.

"No one else on your list came up on any of our security footage," Alec says. He reaches into a drawer and pulls out a glossy 8.5x11 photo, tossing it onto the surface of the desk for Sebastian to see. "Only her. Only Annika."

Sebastian is quiet as he stares down at the image. Unnaturally still.

"I know what you want to believe, Doc," Alec says with a heavy sigh. "But if she—"

"She's looking at the camera," Sebastian says.

Alec frowns as Sebastian steps forward and taps the photograph. "She's looking directly into the camera."

"What does that—"

"It means she knows where the camera is," Sebastian stresses, finger pressing hard against the image as he stares Alec down. "And if she knows where the camera is, why the hell would she let herself be seen by it *unless she wanted us to see it.*"

I glance between the two of them, baffled as to where he's going with this.

But what he's saying clearly makes Alec reconsider. His brows knit together, and he looks at the photograph as if just seeing it for the first time.

"Annika isn't behind this," Sebastian insists, tapping the image of her face.

I look from him to Alec, frowning. "Then who the fuck is?"

"I don't know, I need to think. I —" An alarm sounds from Sebastian's phone, and he swears as he fishes it from his pocket and silences it.

"I have to go, I have to..." Sebastian stops. Tightening his jaw, he slides his phone back into his pocket. "I have somewhere else I need to be tonight."

"I need your attention on this," Alec reminds him as he turns to leave. "Your full attention, Doc."

Sebastian pauses at the door, his back to us and face hidden when he answers.

"Where else would it be?"

34

SEBASTIAN

The sun is a violent shade of orange as it sets over the back of the Book Boutique and Bakery. I glance at the time on my phone. Nearly 8 PM, which means Sydney will be locking up soon, shutting the store down and heading back here, to her apartment.

I've been watching her come home almost every night since my impromptu visit a few days ago. But this will be the first night I'll let her see me.

Maybe I'll stay and watch her after I drop off her package tonight. Once Viper gets back, it's going to be harder to get the chance, harder to break away to watch her sleep without someone noticing.

And Sydney is so beautiful when she sleeps.

The paper bag I'm holding is surprisingly heavy, and I switch it to my other hand for a few minutes, leaning back against my motorcycle. The pharmacy I visited had two different brands of Epsom salt, the one I'm used to buying for Ashton for muscle aches, and one that was scented. Lavender.

I bought them both, just in case. I'm curious which one she'll use tonight. Lavender, I imagine.

Like clockwork at just past 8 PM, Sydney rounds the corner of the building, making her way to the little staircase that leads up to her door, curls bouncing as she walks. Her front door opens directly to the outside. It's a security nightmare. Anyone could break in with just one door separating her from the cruel, uncaring world out here.

I shift the bag in my hand and prepare to step forward out of the shadows where I've parked my bike. I'll only stay a little while, after I hand the bag off to her, maybe an hour or two at most, I promise myself. That's it.

I need to break this habit.

Before I can step into the fading light and get her attention, though, someone else rounds the corner after her. Someone I instantly recognize.

The paper bag crinkles loudly as I clench my fist.

Motherfucker.

Chase Levine calls out to Sydney as he rushes toward her, snaring her attention. From the instant she turns and recognizes him, it's clear she doesn't want to see him.

I couldn't see her face when I was watching them last time, but I can see it now. She doesn't look happy to see Chase at all. Doesn't rush forward to greet him.

She looks horrified.

"Chase?" Sydney asks, immediately taking a step away from him and crossing her arms over her chest. "What are you doing here?"

I hold perfectly still, half in shadow, watching. Neither of them has seen me yet. Neither one of them is even aware I'm here.

"I've been calling you," Chase says, sounding annoyed.

"Nonstop. You haven't unblocked my number yet, have you? I told you to unblock it. But you never fucking listen to me, do you?"

He takes a step toward her, but she holds her ground, shaking her head.

"I'm not going to do that," she says. "I meant what I said. We don't have anything to talk about anymore. Please just go, Chase, I—"

"What do you want from me, Sydney? I already told you I made a mistake!" He's speaking over her, and it's obvious to me this isn't a conversation at all. It's a monologue. "Caroline and I are done, okay? It's over. I just want to go back to what we had. To *us*."

This time, when he steps forward, Sydney does take a step backward, away from him.

"There is no *us*," she says, firmly. I'm strangely proud of the steel in her voice, the way it doesn't waver at all. That's my girl, the one I keep seeing glimpses of. The one she tries to hide away. Sydney holds her back straight as she glares at him. "You made sure of that."

"It was one mistake," Chase says, throwing his hands up in the air. "You're being unreasonable, babe..."

"No," Sydney snaps. "Not *one* mistake. You did it *multiple times*. You only got *caught* once. And then you *left me for her*."

Something in his face twists. Darkens.

"Is that why you think it's okay to be fucking around with other men?" Chase asks.

Sydney blinks, clearly taken by surprise at the sharp turn in his attitude.

So am I, in fact. But I shouldn't be.

I've known a hundred men like Chase before. That petty anger creeping into his voice, the clenching fists. The way he's standing over her, trying to intimidate her. He's not a tough guy. He's just a weak little man, needing to make her feel small.

Weak men like him break so easily with the right tools.

"First Mason fucking Sterling," Chase says, raising his voice. "Don't think I've forgotten how you were rubbing your little date with him in my face at that bullshit charity thing. And then that fucking blond?"

"What?" Sydney asks, sounding genuinely perplexed.

"The fucking... *model,* or whatever I saw leaving your apartment a few nights ago." Chase shakes his head, disgusted.

Ashton. It had to be. Had he really been so pussy-whipped he hadn't noticed someone watching him that night?

Fucking amateur.

"What were you doing watching my apartment?" Sydney asks. She takes another step away, fear starting to show on her face.

"I told you, I've been trying to talk to you." Chase spits the words at her. "But you're too busy whoring yourself to every man in town to even notice that I'm the only one who cares about you."

"Leave," Sydney snaps. Her arms uncross, and her hands grip into tight fists at her side. I want to bathe in her anger right now. "Leave right now. You don't get to speak to me like that. Not anymore. Leave, or I'm calling the police."

"If you would just fucking *listen to me—*"

He reaches out to grab her, and she twists away from him so violently she stumbles and almost falls.

The instant he touches her, I move.

I'm going to tell him to leave. I'm going to remind him that they're finished, that he fucked up, and she's moved on. I'm going to tell him just how hard Sterling and Ashton made her come the night of the banquet, how he could never hope to give her a modicum of the pleasure they gave her that night.

I don't.

When they both turn toward me, startled by my sudden appearance, I catch the look of fear in Sydney's eyes. Her panic.

Panic at seeing him. Panic at having him touch her.

And I don't say anything at all.

I pivot and punch him right in the face.

35

I ALWAYS KNEW CHASE WAS A COWARD.

But watching him cry on the ground, hands cradling his broken and bloody nose, I realize I never knew just how much of a coward he really was.

"Who the fuck are you?" Chase whines, staring up at Sebastian.

Sebastian looks like a dark, avenging god standing there in the fading light, staring down at my ex as he cowers on the ground.

"I'm your worst fucking nightmare if you don't leave right now," Sebastian answers. He's impossibly calm as he stands between Chase and me, the blood on his swelling knuckles the only indication of what he's just done.

"You *punched me.*" Chase takes his hand away from his nose and stares at the splash of red there in disbelief. "That's... that's fucking assault!"

"It is," Sebastian agrees with a nod.

Chase sputters. "I could have you arrested!"

"You could try. But I promise you, if you go to the police,

they won't do a thing about it." There's a cold surety in Sebastian's voice as he says it. "I doubt they'll even take your statement. But go ahead. Try it."

"Fuck you," Chase snarls, getting shakily to his feet.

"She told you to leave," Sebastian says, taking a calm step toward him. Chase scrambles back, holding one hand out as though to ward him off. "You should listen to her before this gets a lot worse."

Chase looks at me, his eyes pleading.

"Go," I tell him, making my voice as firm as I can. "And don't come back again, Chase. I mean it. We're done."

I almost expect him to put up a fight. To show Sebastian that same anger he so easily unleashed on me, time and time again. But that's not how cowards act.

"We're not done," Chase mutters, shooting me one last furious look before he turns to leave. "Not by a long shot."

I stare daggers at him as he walks away. It's not until he's gone and out of sight that I can finally breathe again. I count to ten. I try to think happy thoughts. I try to remember my therapy mantras.

I can't think of any. Not today.

"Did he hurt you?" Sebastian asks, turning toward me. There's an intensity in his eyes I've never seen before.

Hurt me? Even where he'd grabbed me, it hadn't hurt. Just ... surprised me. But I'd been worried, for a moment. Reminded of the times he had...

I shake my head.

Sebastian nods slowly. "Good. That's good." A drop of blood falls from his split knuckles onto the pavement. He doesn't even seem to notice.

"We should get some ice on that," I tell him, taking him by the other hand and tugging him toward my place. "Come on."

He's pliant as I drag him up the stairs and to my apartment

door. But he stops in the doorway, frozen, after I unlock it and let myself inside.

Sebastian stares at the threshold like he can't bring himself to cross it.

"Are you a vampire or something?" I ask, smirking. "Do you really need an invitation to come in?"

"No. No, I just..." He stares around at my place but doesn't move. You'd think I was asking him to commit a mortal sin, just by inviting him inside.

I shake my head, making my way toward the kitchen. "Jesus, come in, you freak. Stop being so weird about it."

He takes a long breath and finally steps inside, closing the door behind him.

"I don't know if vampires need permission to use the furniture," I call out to him as I open up my freezer door. "But you should sit down."

I don't own any ice packs, and whatever ice I have is buried beneath several months' worth of frozen dinners. I pluck a freezer-burned package of peas out of the mess of ice cream and microwave meals, and wrap it in a paper towel, hoping it will be better than nothing.

"Has he done this before?" Sebastian asks when I come back into the living room. His eyes are piercing as he watches me from the couch. "Followed you home?"

"No, never. I haven't even seen him since he came by the café." It feels strange talking about it. "And before that, not since the charity banquet."

I sit down next to him, taking his injured hand and holding the bag of frozen vegetables against his knuckles. When my leg touches his, he flinches, going tense.

"Does it hurt?" I ask.

Sebastian shakes his head.

"I barely feel it," he says. He won't look at me. His eyes are glued on the wall, the fingers of his left hand tapping ceaselessly against the couch.

There's a brown paper bag on the floor between his legs.

"What's in the bag?" I ask, frowning at it.

Sebastian's eyes flick to it and then to mine so quickly I almost miss it.

"Epsom salt," he says softly. "For your pain."

Oh.

After he'd taken that phone call earlier, I'd forgotten all about him promising to get me some. It's a nice gesture. Strangely kind, coming from him.

"Thanks," I say quietly after a moment.

Silence descends between the two of us. It should feel awkward. I'm basically holding his hand, even if it is just to keep the bag of peas in place. But it feels... comforting. Nice.

"I can't believe you did that," I tell him after a while, chuckling as I say it. "You just... *punched* him. Out of nowhere!"

"He deserved it," Sebastian says.

"For touching me?" I ask. When his only answer is to give me a scathing look over the rim of his glasses, I laugh. "Wow, you guys really are crazy, you know that?"

Sebastian's head tips back against the couch, and to my shock, he laughs too, a huge smile forming on his face.

"You really have no idea, Sydney," he says, shaking his head and grinning.

I'm so stunned, it takes me a moment to process what is happening. But when I do, I let out an animalistic squeal, scrambling closer to him to see it more clearly.

The smile on his face vanishes.

"Oh no, don't hide it! I saw it!" I say excitedly. "That was a smile. And a *laugh*!"

"I didn't smile," Sebastian lies.

"Bullshit," I say. "You can't lie to me. And I already texted everyone to let them know. Your reputation will never recover."

I let out an exaggerated gasp when he smiles again. Not a little smirk. Not the faintest twitch of his lips. A full, uninhibited smile that curves up both sides of his face.

"I knew it!" My laugh is a little too loud, bordering on manic. I scramble over him, climbing over his leg to grin down at him. "Oh my god, ladies and gentlemen, he's not a robot! Wait until I tell *everyone.*"

"Sydney." Sebastian's voice is a warning. Something flickers over his face. An emotion I don't recognize.

His uninjured hand flexes on the couch next to me. For a wild moment, I think he might touch me.

And I suddenly realize what I'm doing. Where I am. With my leg thrown over his, I'm practically sitting in his lap.

We're close enough to kiss.

"Sorry," I mumble, scrambling away from him. My cheeks are burning hot, my heart beating so fast I'm almost dizzy from it.

Sebastian is so still next to me, I'm not sure if he's breathing. He doesn't look at me. The quickly thawing bag of peas has fallen to the ground. I clear my throat awkwardly, and pick it back up, taking his injured hand again and laying the bag over his knuckles.

He really does have gorgeous hands. I try my best not to notice.

Sebastian is quiet for a long time before he speaks again.

"Are you really okay?" he asks. When he turns to look at me, his face is just as blank as always. "You can be honest with me."

"Yeah, I'm okay. Thank you for... for intervening," I say. "I wasn't sure what he was going to do, and... I'm glad you were there."

"He said he was trying to reach you," Sebastian says, fingers of his uninjured hand drumming nervously against the couch.

I blow out a long breath.

"Jade blocked his number on my phone," I tell him. "So he probably has been. It's not like I would know. I'm not interested in hearing any of his shitty apologies anymore."

"Sterling will want to file a restraining order," Sebastian says. "I can get the paperwork started, but if you have any—"

I tense, accidentally squeezing Sebastian's injured hand. He turns to frown at me but makes no other complaint. He doesn't even wince.

"Don't tell Alec," I plead. "Please, Seb."

Sebastian watches me closely, eyes narrowing behind his glasses.

I wait for him to ask me why, and truthfully, I'm not sure what to tell him. But if just hearing that I had an ex was enough for Alec to buy his company and threaten to fire him, what would he do if he thought I had one stalking me? One that would, maybe, try to hurt me?

To my surprise, Sebastian agrees.

"Okay," he says. "I won't tell him."

My heart skips.

"Really? You'll keep this between just the two of us?"

He nods, slowly. "On one condition."

"Sure, anything," I tell him.

"If he does anything like this again, I need you to call me. No matter what time it is, no matter what you think I'm doing, I want to know. Immediately, Sydney. Can you do that?"

I nod.

"Where's your phone?" he asks.

I reach into my pocket and hand it over.

He takes it with his left hand, fingers flying over the screen as he unlocks it.

"How did you know my passcode?" I ask.

"It's the same as the bathroom code in your shop," Sebastian answers, sounding almost amused that I would ask. "It wasn't hard to guess."

He pulls up the contacts and enters his information, sending a text to the new number. A second later, a phone buzzes in his pocket.

"I mean it, Sydney," he says, handing my phone back to me. The look in his icy blue eyes is so intense, so fixated on me, it makes me feel a little lightheaded. "You call me, day or night, okay?"

"And you'll break his nose again?" I joke.

Sebastian's eyelid twitches.

"Something like that," he says.

36

SYDNEY

Kids are fun. I really do mean that.

But I'd be lying if I said watching four kids systematically dismantle our children's section—pulling nearly every book out of the cubbies and upending two different toy displays—didn't make me just a little relieved that I don't have any of my own.

The dad who brought them in had been sincerely apologetic for their behavior, rushing along behind them to clean up as best he could. And he *had* bought each of his kids a book and a toy, more than making up for the chaos they'd brought to our store for the twenty minutes they'd been there.

It's still a relief when they finally leave.

I've just finished restoring the children's section to its former condition when my phone buzzes. I fish it out of my pocket and feel an instant tightening in my chest when I see Katie's name flashing on the display. Shit.

I'm not sure I have the energy to deal with her right now. I debate just ignoring it and letting it go to voicemail, but I need to make more of an effort with my other friends. Unless I really do plan on running off to the woods with Jade, leaving humanity behind like we always joked, I probably shouldn't just ignore everyone else in my life.

I've had a lot of time to think about my friendships since running into the group at the club all those weeks ago. To think about why it's been so hard to maintain that friendship group. Jade has always been more than just a friend—she's been my only family for a long time now. When everyone else has come and gone, she's been my constant.

I've always had to try so hard to fit in with everyone besides her. It feels like I'm constantly wearing a mask, trying to be the person I want them to see me as. Maybe it's how I grew up, never having a settled childhood. Feeling like one mistake will take everything from me again. I love my friends, but there's always been an undercurrent of not feeling fully accepted by them. Not feeling like they really know the real me.

I've known Jade since I was a kid, but I only met Katie and her group of friends when I was in college. And they never really made me feel like I could be myself, never really felt safe the way I suspect real friends should. I'll never forget how many jokes they made over the years about my English degree being a waste of money. And despite everyone's best efforts to get along, they never really "got" Jade, with her crazy hair and piercings. They certainly never thought us opening a shop together was a good idea, making veiled passive-aggressive comments thinly disguised as concern about how difficult it was to succeed with a small business.

The only thing in my life they ever seemed to approve of was Chase. And we all know how *that* turned out.

The phone in my hand continues to vibrate, and against my better judgment, I answer with a hesitant, "Hello?"

"Oh my god, Sydney! I'm so, so glad you picked up!" Katie's voice is so cheerful and loud through the speaker that it leaves my ears ringing.

"Hey, yeah, of course!" I force out, trying to match her chipper tone. "What's up, Katie?"

"So! We're having a little get together at my place tomorrow. A barbecue, just like we used to do, and we'd just all love to have you *actually* join us this time."

I wince at the accusation behind her words, holding the phone between my shoulder and my ear so I can keep shelving the last of the books while she talks. Maybe I shouldn't have picked up, after all.

"Please, Sydney? We *never* get to see you anymore," she adds before I can even form a response.

"Um. Sure. I'd love to go to your barbecue," I lie. Right now, I'd rather shave my head and go running down the city streets naked and covered in syrup than attend one of their get-togethers. "But Saturday is our busiest day. I can't ask Jade to cover the shop all on her own, that's not fair to her."

She would do it, of course, without hesitation. And I have no doubt she'd handle it just fine. But why should I make her do it, just to go to some barbecue they suddenly *insist* I attend last-minute? They usually plan these things weeks in advance.

Why are they only inviting me *now*?

"Then just close the shop for a few hours," Katie suggests, and I have to gnash my teeth together to keep from snapping at her. "It's not like you have that many customers, anyway. I doubt anyone would even notice."

We have *plenty* of customers, I want to scream. Even now, on a weekday morning, we're practically full.

Though, that is a little unusual, isn't it? In fact... now that I'm thinking about it, we have been a lot busier lately. I make a mental note to take stock of our inventory sooner than usual this month, to make sure we're not running low on any of our popular items.

"I can't just close the shop whenever I feel like it," I

explain. "This is my business. It's my responsibility, and I'm committed to it."

She sighs dramatically, and I shrink back into myself. Amazing how she can make a long-suffering sigh convey so much disappointment and frustration. But then again, Katie always was the little leader of our group, always able to bend everyone to her will. Knowing that all of us will just fall in line.

"If you don't want to see us"—she sniffs—"I wish you would just *say so*. You don't need to make up all these excuses."

Guilt pools in my belly.

"I *do* want to see you," I lie again. It feels like lies are coming a lot easier to me lately. "It's just..."

"Then you'll be here! 12:30 tomorrow, okay? And don't worry, Chase isn't coming. He's out of town on some work thing."

Her tone makes it clear that any more arguing is pointless. And while it is a relief knowing there's no risk of running into my ex again, I can't help but feel like I was just manipulated into agreeing to something I don't want to do.

Gritting my teeth, I force myself to ask, "Do you want me to bring anything?" I barely listen as she rattles off her answer.

I'm in a foul mood when she finally hangs up.

I wonder what Jade would say if I asked her to block Katie's number, too. Maybe I should do it. Cut them all off, completely.

Letting out a long breath, I straighten, brushing dust from my legs as I stand up.

When a hand unexpectedly slides over my back and hooks around me, I panic. For one terrifying moment, I think it must be Chase again.

But when I look up and see those soft blue eyes and warm smile, I relax, all thoughts of Chase and Katie and the rest of them vanishing in an instant.

"Good morning, Babygirl." Ash grins at me. He leans down to plant a kiss on my cheek. "How's this beautiful day treating you?"

I open my mouth to answer, another lie forming on my lips as I prepare to tell him how great I'm doing. But before I can, Ash pulls a single red rose from behind his back and presents it to me.

I laugh, a little shocked by the gesture, but more thrilled than anything. I love roses. There's something just so inherently romantic about them. I take it from him and tuck it under my nose and inhale, savoring the sweet floral scent.

Some florists buy their roses from growers who prioritize beauty over scent—preferring the picturesque look of a rose in full bloom to one that has the distinctive smell. But to me there's something special about the smell of a rose.

And this one? Wherever Ash bought it from, it smells *perfect*.

"God, you're beautiful," Ash adds, watching me. He raises his phone, wriggling it at me. "May I?"

I wave him off, laughing, but Ashton quickly snaps a photo of me.

"Look at you!" he says, grinning. He pulls me close again, showing me the photo on his phone screen. And, I suppose, I look nice. My smile is genuine, and the rose is stunning.

I look like a woman in love.

Blushing, I look away from the image of my face on the screen, twirling the stem absentmindedly between my fingers.

"*Ouch!*" I suck a sharp breath through my teeth, almost dropping the flower.

A thorn. I stare down at the bright red droplet of blood forming on the pad of my thumb. The stem is covered in them.

"Don't they normally remove the thorns before they sell

them?" I ask Ash. I stick the wound in my mouth, sucking away the blood.

"Yeah, sometimes," Ash says with a shrug, sounding unconcerned. "I guess they forgot with this one."

"I guess," I say, unsure. I handle the rose more cautiously now, careful of all those tiny barbs.

"It's a weird practice, don't you think?" Ash comments, scratching the back of his head and watching me a little too closely. "Taking off the thorns, I mean. Maybe it's just me, but..."

"But?" I press.

"I don't know. Maybe the danger is part of what makes them so beautiful." He grins. "Maybe to really appreciate them, you need to endure a little pain. Don't you think?"

I laugh, rolling my eyes at him.

"That's certainly poetic," I tell him.

His answering smile is contagious, and despite the pain in my thumb, I can't help but smile back at him.

"Well, you sure are in a good mood, aren't you?" I tease.

"Of course I am," he says. "Because I'm going to ask you on a date. And you're going to say yes."

"Oh, I am, am I?" I say, a playful lilt to my voice.

He nods enthusiastically. "You are. It's destiny. We're meant to be."

I laugh, giving him a little shove to push him back from me. There's no world where I'm strong enough to move him, but he steps back anyway, giving me space.

"And what sort of date did you have in mind?"

"Lunch? Tomorrow?" He's so excited, I almost say yes without thinking. But...

Crap.

I shake my head sadly, watching his smile wilt.

"Sorry, Ash, my friends are hosting this stupid event tomorrow." I sigh. "They literally *just* called to invite me."

Ash's waning smile turns into a frown. "They just called? To invite you to an event that's happening tomorrow? That's a bit short notice, isn't it?"

"Yeah, things have been a bit...strained," I tell him. I let him follow me to the front of the store, where Jade is making a latte. I grab an empty mug from the counter and set my rose inside. The stem has so many thorns, it's a miracle I only pricked myself once. "I'm trying to fix things with them. Which is why I *really* do need to go."

"Okay, so... tomorrow's a no-go," Ash concedes, perking right back up. "Maybe... Monday, instead? We could get dinner after you finish work?"

I smile.

"Sure. Dinner on Monday sounds great," I tell him. "Maybe takeout again?"

Jade is watching us, her eyebrow raised as she looks between Ash and me.

"Takeout *again*, huh?" she asks, smirking.

Double crap.

I haven't exactly been keeping Jade abreast of this whole... situation.

"Jade, can you do me a massive favor?" I ask, putting on my best begging face. It's nothing compared to the sad kitten eyes she's capable of, but I do my best.

"Sure, anything," Jade says, barely appreciating how well I can plead. She deftly pours milk over the espresso and passes the cup to a waiting customer.

"I need you to cover for me tomorrow afternoon, for a few hours," I say.

"Alec taking you out again?" she asks, glancing at Ash as though ready to measure his reaction.

Ashton answers for me.

"Nah, he took her out a few nights ago," he says, all smiles and confidence. "Now it's my turn."

I shoot him a look.

"It's Katie," I tell Jade. "She's having another barbecue, or something, and totally guilt-tripped me into going."

"Ah," Jade sighs. "Katie's back, huh? Can't live with her, can't change your entire identity and pretend you never met her. But sure, no problem. I'm sure the silent doctor and I can hold down the fort on our own."

I laugh, but when I look over at Sebastian's table, I'm surprised to find it empty. For the first time since he started showing up, he's nowhere in sight.

"Wait... where is Seb?" I ask Ash, frowning.

Something flickers in his eyes before he answers, so fast I could almost convince myself I hadn't seen it.

"Helping Alec with a work project," he tells me, a little too quickly. "Nothing important."

Ash spends the next hour trailing me around the store, chatting and flirting and helping me while I take stock of our inventory. I flirt back—it's easy with him—but it doesn't quell the apprehension I feel slowly growing in my gut.

Because, whatever his reasons, I'm pretty sure Ash just lied to me.

37

Viper is in the lab cleaning his tools when I finally track him down.

He's humming to himself while he works, deftly unpacking his case and laying his instruments out on the metal table, where they glisten under the bright lights.

Well, most of them do.

A few are so coated in dried, darkened blood they don't reflect the light at all.

"Hey, Doc," Viper greets me, not looking up. It's not intuition or some preternatural acuity that has him correctly guessing it's me when I enter our little sanctum.

I'm the only other one who comes down here. This isn't a place for people like Alec and Ashton. This isn't a part of our business they like to look too closely at.

"How'd it go?" I ask Viper, keeping my voice neutral and unconcerned as I lean against the tiled wall.

"It went." Viper grins. One by one, his instruments go into a white gallon bucket, which he carries to the industrial sink. "Seneca is ours."

"No issues?"

"Nothing I couldn't handle." Viper chuckles. He hums to himself as he opens a jug of hacmoscrub, an enzymatic cleaner made for dissolving blood, and scoops some into the bucket. Hot water comes next, and after they soak, he'll spend the next hour or so carefully scrubbing every one of his tools clean.

Viper may be crazy, but at least he follows my rules for a clean and orderly torture.

"Sterling has another job for you," I say, keeping my face blank and tone even. Practiced. "But it's an easy one."

I hope I'm imagining the almost imperceptible way Viper tenses. I must be, because his tone is completely unchanged as he asks, "Oh? What job?"

"Anthony Reicher," I tell him, giving no other information.

Anthony has been a pain in our side for months, a mid-level thug constantly needling us with small acts of disobedience. But he's so low on our radar that he's been little more than a nuisance, a small ignorable annoyance we haven't bothered to deal with.

And just this morning, someone sent Anthony a whisper through back channels that it was time to up and run. He's had a long head start to buy us time.

A perfect distraction.

Viper laughs.

"What did Anthony finally do to piss off the big man enough to get me involved?"

I shrug, even though Viper can't see it. The movement is casual, unconcerned. It's the shrug of someone with nothing to hide, no secrets to keep. It's perfect.

"Don't know," I lie. "But Sterling wants him gone. As soon as possible."

Bait.

That's what Alec wants. He wants to buy a little more time

to ease Sydney into our world. He sees her as too breakable right now, too fragile, to handle Viper, just as I had. But...

I've seen it. Little flashes of what lies beneath her innocent exterior. She's not as weak as she pretends to be, not as pure of heart, no matter how much she wants to think she is.

"Consider it done," Viper tells me, reaching into the near-boiling water to pull out one of his tools and start his cleaning. I turn, moving toward the exit, when Viper adds, "You can tell the boss I'm giving it my full, undivided attention."

His laughter follows me out and into the hall.

38

THE NEXT MORNING I WAKE UP WANTING NOTHING MORE than to cancel.

I don't want to go to another of these barbecues. Katie and her husband throw a few of them every summer, inviting our gang from college, their friends and acquaintances from work, and all their favorite neighbors from their ritzy neighborhood. I used to think I enjoyed them. It was a chance to work on perfecting that persona I'd curated so carefully over the years. I would laugh at the right times and chat with the right people, I'd stand quietly beaming up at Chase once he started joining in.

Those parties were a way to prove I wasn't a dark, twisted person. I was perfect. Sweet.

Maybe that's why I feel so stressed about going now. I feel like I'm becoming something new, maybe not the angry girl I was when I was younger, but maybe not that perfectly curated version of myself, either. I don't have the energy for that version of me anymore, I realize.

But this newer version of me is so fresh, I'm not sure how to act. How to *be*.

And even worse, this will be the first barbecue I'm attending without Chase. The first one I've been invited to since we broke up.

Sure, my friends were bad back then, constantly nagging me about when we'd be getting married and if we were planning to have kids. But at least my relationship with Chase was something they approved of.

Not like every other decision I've made.

This is part of the reason I've been avoiding them. Why I haven't bothered to reach out to them much or tried to stay in touch.

As I shower and get dressed, I wonder if it's possible to fake something serious enough that Katie would let me off the hook and insist I stay home. I could call up right now and say I've come down with a serious case of something infectious and awful, forcing me to stay locked in my apartment indefinitely. Something stomach-related and disgusting.

Would she believe it?

I know without giving it serious consideration that it's a lost cause. I have to face my demons sometime, and today those demons will be living in an affluent suburb and dressed in a novelty food-themed apron. How fun.

And so, at twenty past twelve, I slap a smile on my face, straighten my back, and push open the gate to Katie's backyard, two massive boxes of Jade's best pastries in my arms, ready to grit my teeth and get through this.

But the backyard is empty.

I look around, confused, a sinking feeling forming in my stomach. Where are the long plastic picnic tables they always set out, one for food and one for seating? Where are all the other guests?

Where is the barbecue?

I hesitate, considering turning around and just leaving, when the sliding glass door opens, and Katie pokes her head out of the house.

"In here, Sydney," she says, waving me over.

Something is wrong here. I can just feel it, my intuition sending an uncomfortable prickle down the back of my neck and over my spine.

But I swallow my apprehension, telling myself it's all in my head, as I follow Katie inside.

Right into my nightmare.

The boxes of pastries I'm carrying almost slip from my arms before Katie can take them, as I stare in horror around their living room. At *who* is in their living room.

There's Katie's husband, Lance, looking annoyed and uncomfortable, seated on the couch with Sarah. And next to them...

Is Chase.

"Hi, babe," Chase greets me, smiling. There's a white medical strip over his broken nose, and a dark purple bruise under both eyes.

My stomach sinks.

"What is this?" I ask, voice sharp. "Katie... what's going on?"

"Okay, don't get hysterical," Katie says, setting the boxes down and holding her hands out in a placating gesture. "Think of this like..." She waves her hands in the air, searching for the right word. "An intervention."

My miscellaneous friends nod in agreement from around the room.

I think I might throw up.

"Why would I need an intervention?" I ask. I'm trying to keep my voice down, trying to stay calm, but I can hear the raw anger in my words. I feel a deep rage brewing inside of me.

My relaxation mantras aren't going to fix this.

Hell, all the mantras in the world wouldn't do the trick right now.

"We're worried, that's all," Sarah says, sitting forward to rest her elbows on her legs. She skipped a few trips to her hair stylist, I notice. Her roots are starting to show, a dull brown contrast to her usual golden blonde. "Chase came to us the other day to talk about you, about how you're doing, and some of the things he told us... well, they have us worried about you."

I glare at Chase, my hands tightening into fists at my side.

"And what did Chase tell you?" I grind out with a scowl, the perfectly manicured mask I've cultivated over years finally slipping. We've never fought in public before. I've never been anything but the perfect, quiet girlfriend in front of these people.

They have no idea what I can really be like when I need to be.

"The truth. Like how you're going to lose the bookstore," Chase says, with a shrug. Like it's no big deal. Like the end of my business and everything I've worked for is just casual fodder for the gossip mill.

My heart pounds in my chest. "I'm going to... *what?*"

"We know Mrs. Cohen is selling the property." Katie sighs dramatically after she says it. "Chase called her, okay? And you can't actually think whoever buys that building will see your store as a good investment, can you? I know that old bat has a soft spot for you, but things will change when someone new buys it."

I had been thinking something similar, had even put off telling Jade the bad news because of my own fears, but the moment the words come out of someone else's mouth, I realize how stupid it sounds.

Our store *does* run a profit. It always has. Even when other shops around us have shut down, we've kept standing. And things have been picking up lately.

Hell, we're doing *well* now. Not barely making ends meet, not fighting to make a profit. We're doing *well*.

And we've never once been late on our rent. We've never once paid a penny less than we owed.

Any new owner would be lucky to have us as tenants.

"Why wouldn't they see us as a good investment?" I challenge. And, this time, I believe it.

Chase just shakes his head.

"I warned you when you and Jade started this *venture* that it was risky," Chase says. "Running a business is a lot of work. And even people who know what they're doing don't always succeed."

The implication behind his words, of course, being that I'm not one of those people. That I don't know what I'm doing.

I am not an ocean of calm anymore.

I am a goddamn *raging storm*.

Fuck this.

"My store is fine," I snap, eyes narrowing at the group in front of me. "And you," I point at Chase, accusingly, "you know *nothing* about it. This is my business. My store. You need to stay the hell out of it."

Katie exchanges a look with Chase. On the couch, Sarah shifts uncomfortably.

"Woah, calm down, Syd," she says, holding her hands out defensively. "This isn't like you."

"It's not just the store, either," Katie says in a tone so clearly meant to be soft and reasonable. "We know that Chase made a mistake when he...had his little indiscretion. But he is so remorseful! He's just been beside himself, and he came to us to help us talk some sense into you. We all spent so much time together, and we know how much you two love each other. Don't let one mistake undo so much work. He said he's tried apologizing, and he's just here to win you back."

On the couch, Chase smiles benevolently at me. *Aren't I such a good guy?*

"Can't you see how romantic this is, Sydney?" Katie continues. "He knows losing you was the worst thing he could have ever done. And he's just trying to fix it. He's sorry!"

It occurs to me then that Katie is doing more apologizing for Chase than he ever did for himself.

I knew they were all still close, but I never expected they would ambush me like this. This isn't...this isn't normal. When I don't immediately respond, when I just stare at them all dumbfounded, Sarah picks up where Katie left off.

"Chase says you've been entertaining a lot of dates lately," she offers gently.

"Entertaining?" My laugh sounds insane, even to me. "What is that supposed to mean, *entertaining*? Are we in some kind of eighteenth-century novel? If you want to say I'm whoring myself out, just say it instead of implying it."

Katie and Sarah both flinch at the crassness of my tone and words. Predictable as fuck.

"They're thugs!" Chase snaps. He stands from the couch and steps forward to grab my shoulders. And I realize then how it must look to them all. Like he cares. Like he's worried and wants to protect me. But the whole time he's gripping me so tight it hurts. "They're dangerous, babe. One of them *attacked me*."

I shake him off, unable to stand him touching me. The laugh that escapes me is sharp and cruel. It doesn't sound anything like the perfected version of myself these people know. The group must think so, too. Katie takes a step back, while everyone else won't even meet my eyes from sheer discomfort at the entire orchestrated situation.

"Oh, sure," I say, throwing my hands up in the air. "Sure, if that's the way you want to tell it, have at it. Tell me, Chase, *babe*, tell me more about how *they* are the dangerous ones."

Chase's eyes darken, the implication behind my words clear. "I don't know what you mean," he says in a low voice.

I grin, wide and angry. "Really? Maybe I should *explain* exactly what I mean, then. Maybe I should tell them exactly what kind of person you really are."

I see the flicker of fear in his eyes, then. The panic that I might out him.

And *I love it.*

"You're not making any sense, babe," he deflects, while confusion scatters through the group. "And you're acting hysterical."

I don't bother responding. I just stare him down, the buried fury of the last decade finally breaking free through my eyes. It's oh so satisfying when he breaks eye contact first.

How many times? How many times did I cover up the bruises he left on me before coming to one of Katie's events? I lost track over the years.

But I'm done covering up the ways he's hurt me.

"It's not enough that you're ... entertaining so many men," Katie says, trying to regain some control of the situation. "But dangerous men? Really, Sydney?"

"Just say *fucking*," I snap, exasperated. "We all know that's what you're implying. Why not just *say it*?"

The group looks genuinely shocked.

"And it's none of your business, any of you, who I might be fucking," I add, shaking my head. "I could fuck my way through this whole city, and it still wouldn't be any of your damn business."

"Sydney!" Katie shrieks. "What is with this language? What's happened to you?"

"Blow it out your ass," I snap.

"See?" Chase motions toward me but speaks to the room like I'm not even here. "Do you see what she's like now? How she's been acting? It's like she's gone crazy!"

"You've been acting up since you and Chase had your little disagreement, and it's time to put an end to it." Katie manages to say the words, but she doesn't sound so sure of herself now. There's a waver in her voice, a hint of uncertainty in what this new, vulgar Sydney might do. How she might act.

"Dude, we get it, like, Chase made a mistake," Lance admits, finally piping up from the couch. "But you guys belong together. You've always been such a perfect couple. Just put him out of his misery and take him back already."

The words are so ridiculous, I honestly don't understand them at first. It takes me a minute to rewind the dialogue in my head and comprehend the words he just said to me.

"You can't be serious. Now you're concerned? Where was this concern when he left me for his mistress? And you all were happy as can be to welcome her into the group?" I laugh. "Now you have an opinion on my life? What are you, my parents? Because they're dead, and I want your opinion about as much as I'd like to dig them up and ask for theirs." The words come out caustic as acid, and I'm almost shaking with the rage coursing through my body.

"Sydney." Katie reaches for me, and I jerk away violently. "Chase is a good man. And he makes a decent living. When your shop closes—"

"My shop isn't going to close," I insist. But no one is listening. They've never really listened to me, have they?

"—you'll be grateful to have someone like him to take care of you. Not just emotionally, either," she continues, as though I hadn't interrupted at all. "But financially!"

Standing close to the couch, Chase just nods along.

"No," I say, shaking my head. "No. That is not happening."

"He made some mistakes, sure, but—"

"He cheated on me," I say, looking around at everyone. No one will look at me, now, their eyes glued to the floor, lips tight. "And not just once, almost the entire time we were together. Did any of you know about that before calling it a...mistake or a disagreement? Before you dragged me here?"

They did, I realize, when the silence goes on and on. When none of them will meet my eyes. They knew. The whole time.

And somehow that makes everything so, so much worse.

"Men make mistakes," Lance says slowly. Like Chase scratched my car, not like he slammed his dick repeatedly into another woman. "And he really is sorry. Doesn't that count for something?"

"I'm willing to move on from this, babe," Chase says. "I'm willing to forget about this time apart. Forget the stuff you did with all those other guys, too." He says this last part like he's doing me a huge favor. Forgiving my crimes.

I'm stunned, rooted to the spot as he takes a step toward me, holding his arms open like we're going to hug.

"You had your fun. But it's over now. It's time to come home. So, why don't we—"

I don't have Sebastian's strength, and I never learned how to properly throw a punch.

But I have an excellent backhand, thanks to years of tennis.

Chase's head whips back when I slap him, the sound of my hand against his cheek so loud it echoes in the silence of the house.

No one moves.

"If I ever see you again," I tell him, hissing the words between clenched teeth. "I won't stop what they'll do to you."

I don't say another word. I don't even take back the boxes of pastries, though I should. They never deserved Jade's kindness, and they sure as hell don't deserve her baking.

I just turn around, and leave, slamming the glass door behind me and storming toward the street. I'm shaking so hard it takes me three tries to pull my phone out of my pocket, fumbling with it over and over until I finally unlock it and make the call.

Sebastian picks up on the first ring.

"Sydney?" he asks, immediately. "What's wrong?"

"Chase," I snap, rage oozing out of every pore.

Traffic is loud around me, whipping past me as I walk to my car. But even with all the noise, I hear his quick intake of breath.

"I'm on my way. Tell me where you are."

39

SEBASTIAN

I RUN EVERY RED LIGHT IN THE CITY, MY MOTORCYCLE dodging between traffic at a dangerously high speed.

It still doesn't feel fast enough.

Their shop is closed when I get there, the lights in the cafe dimmed, an inauspicious sight in the middle of a Saturday afternoon. But I spot Jade at the counter and knock hard on the window, and her eyes perk up when she sees me.

"Where is she?" I ask when she unlocks the door and ushers me inside. "Is she okay?"

"She's in the stockroom in the back," Jade says, shaking her head. "And *no*. She's not okay. She's—"

I hear a crash from the back of the store, and don't bother staying to hear the rest. I bolt, my long legs carrying me quickly through the store and to their backroom, where—

I duck, and the book flying through the air toward me misses by mere inches before it crashes into the wall.

"Stupid mother*fucker!*" Sydney yells, picking up another book and throwing it full strength against the back wall. It hits with a loud crash and drops.

Sydney is pacing, shoulders tight with fury, and she's—

She's—

She's *fucking resplendent.*

I stand there, stunned, as she picks up another book and throws it. This is not the timid, breakable girl I've seen these last few weeks. This is not the shy, naïve little mouse I thought she was. She's a storm of rage and violence.

I've never seen anything so beautiful in my entire life.

"What happened?" I ask.

My voice snaps her out of her pacing, and she turns toward me, eyes blazing. It takes everything in me not to kiss her.

Because this woman? This goddess?

She could survive us.

All of us.

"I walked into a fucking *set up*, is what happened," Sydney snarls, picking up another book. "My friends invited me to a luncheon, but it was just... just a trap! Just an excuse for Chase to corner me and call me a whore in front of everyone."

My jaw clenches. Next time I see him, I'm taking his tongue for that.

"And *then*." She throws her arms up, still clutching the book. "*Then* he has the nerve to say he's willing *to take me back.* Like... like *I'm* the one who did something wrong!"

"And tell the good doc what you did then," Jade says from the stockroom door. I glance back to see her grinning, leaning against the frame.

"I slapped him," Sydney says breathlessly. Her free hand clenches and unclenches rhythmically. "I looked right in his stupid face and—"

I clear the few steps between us in a heartbeat, taking her face in my hands. Sydney stops, shocked, as I stare down at her in wonder.

"I'm so proud of you," I murmur, running my thumb over the curve of her cheekbone. "So fucking proud."

She blinks. Then the book she's clutching falls to the ground with a dull thud, and her hands come up to cover mine, our fingers lacing.

"I wanted to hurt him," she admits to me in a small voice. "I... I wanted to kill him."

My grip on her tightens.

More than anything, I want to give this vengeful goddess the world. I want to give her Chase's severed head and lay it right at her feet.

"Say the word," I whisper to her. My eyes drop to her lips. Full and red and made to be kissed. Fuck, I want to know what it feels like to kiss those lips. "Say the word, and he's a dead man, love."

In the doorway, Jade clears her throat.

Reluctantly, I let my hands drop away from her.

"As fun as premeditated murder sounds," Jade says, giving me a leveled look. "What Sydney needs right now is a restraining order against that prick."

I force myself to nod in agreement. Sure. We can do this the hard way. The legal way.

"Let me handle that," I tell them. "I'll have the papers drawn up tonight. I know a few judges who can fast-track it. You won't have to do a thing."

Sydney's cheeks are flushed when she gives me a shy smile.

"Well, *I* need some hot chocolate," Jade announces. "Any for you?"

Sydney nods, but I shake my head. I have other places I'm needed right now.

"I'll leave you two lovebirds to it then." Jade gives me a shit-stirring smile and saunters back to the front of the store.

"Thank you," Sydney tells me. She hugs her arms around

herself, self-consciously. "For not telling Alec, I mean. And for being there when I needed you."

She's retreating, pushing that anger back inside, building up a sweet mask around it.

"Always," I promise her. I watch that vicious queen slip away from me piece by piece.

I'd give anything to have her back.

40

SYDNEY

"Spill," Jade says, setting a mug of hot chocolate down in front of me.

Now that I've calmed down and cleaned up the books from my little tantrum, there's no reason we can't open the store back up. But for now, I'm enjoying this moment, just me and Jade alone in our shop. Our private little sanctuary from the world.

"Spill what?" I ask, knowing full well what she means. I take a sip of my hot chocolate and watch her with a smile.

"Oh, you know *damn well* what." She laughs. "Sydney... come *on*. I'm just supposed to ignore the three gorgeous men that you've suddenly collected? You honestly think I'm emotionally strong enough to resist that?"

"It's really only two," I tell her. Jade scoffs.

"And you're kidding yourself if you think that," she says. "I *saw* the way he looked at you back there. Christ, if I hadn't been there, he probably would have bent you over that table, ripped off your clothes and—"

"Jade!" I gasp, laughing in shock.

"I'm serious, Sydney! You owe me details! What is going on with you? With them?"

I smile, trying to find the words to sum up what's happening. It's been such a whirlwind, with Alec and Ash and—

Instantly, I'm back in Katie's house, listening to them talk about me. About the men I'm "entertaining." My stomach clenches.

"What just happened?" Jade asks, reaching out and touching my hand gently. "You were all smiles, and then your face just... dropped."

I take a deep breath.

I am an ocean of calm.

I am not a slave to my negative emotions.

"It's something Chase was saying this afternoon," I admit, when I finally calm myself enough to speak. "About all the men I've been seeing. And you know... he's right. My god, Jade, I'm basically dating two men at once, and—"

"Hey," Jade snaps. "Don't do that. That dickhole doesn't get to make you feel bad about this. He doesn't get to take this away from you."

"But... shouldn't I feel bad about it? I'm doing *exactly* what he's accused me of, and—"

"Stop that. Right now." Jade sets her mug down hard enough on the counter that her cocoa splashes over the rim. "There is *nothing* wrong with what you're doing. Are you having fun?"

I think about it and nod.

"And you're all consenting adults? Capable of making your own choices?"

A tiny grin tugs at my lips and, again, I nod.

"Then who the *fuck* is he to say it's wrong or try to make you feel bad about it?" Jade jabs her finger at my chest. "*No one*, that's who. He doesn't get to make you feel guilty about something that isn't hurting *anyone*."

"You're way too okay with all of this," I laugh.

Jade rolls her eyes. "I just think people should be happy, Syd. That's all."

"You don't think there's anything wrong with me... dating two different men?"

"Three," Jade corrects automatically. "And no. Not if it makes you feel good. And not if they treat you well."

"It's... actually four, maybe," I admit, biting my lip.

Jade's eyes go wide, a startled laugh bursting from her.

"Alec said... well, he has three brothers. Found family, not like they're actually related, I don't think. And they share... things."

"And he's, what, pressuring you to be shared by all four?" Jade asks, voice a little tense. I can feel her mood shift.

I shake my head.

"Not pressuring me, no. He said the choice of how I choose to... interact with all of them is totally up to me." Jade relaxes, nodding. "But I've only met the three of them, so..."

Jade's smile comes back with full force.

"So, there's *potentially* another brother who, *potentially*, you might want to fuck the living daylights out of, right?"

"Yes, exactly," I say, straight-faced, taking a sip of cocoa.

Jade howls with laughter.

"Oh, Syd," Jade says. "Can I just say how much I love this for you? I know you've always been reserved, at least as long as I've known you. But the last few years have been on another level. You withdrew so much when you started seeing Chase, and I *missed this*. I missed *you*."

Grinning, Jade reaches out to take my hand. I let her, squeezing hers tight.

"So did I," I admit.

"I love you, Syd," Jade tells me. "Forever and always."

"To the moon and back," I promise.

41

SYDNEY

That Sunday is our busiest day yet.

And I finally find out why.

I'm carrying a box of new books out from the back when two customers grab my attention. I don't mind the interruption at all. I'm never too busy to help the people who come to our shop.

"Excuse me?" the woman asks me in a gentle voice. She's young, probably late teens. "Can you tell us where the Staff Picks display is? We can't find it."

The question momentarily throws me. The Staff Picks are just a fun thing I started doing about a year after we opened, to fill an empty corner of the shop. It's not exactly something we advertise or expect customers to ask for.

"Uh, sure, of course. Follow me." I take them to the back of the store, where the display is kept, and show it to them, feeling like a game show hostess as I gesture toward it with a one-armed flourish.

"Awesome!" the woman says, grinning. And then, to my surprise, she raises her phone and snaps a quick picture of it.

Her thumbs move quickly across her keyboard as she lowers her phone, typing faster than I've ever seen someone type on a screen before. "This is great content, thank you!"

Huh. *Weird.*

I watch her a moment longer, eyes narrowed in suspicion, as she and her friend each pick a few books from the display, chatting excitedly to one another, before I turn to go.

"Oh!" the girl calls after me. 'I *love* your bookstapix account, by the way!"

My... what?

Abandoning my box of books behind the front counter, I ease up next to Jade.

"Do you know who or what a bookstapix is?" I ask her.

She nods, scooping up a chocolate croissant from the bakery case and depositing it on a plate for a customer. There's a long line today, snaking around the shop and almost out the door.

"Yeah," Jade tells me. "It's like a social media app for bibliophiles. Some stores use it for advertising."

"Do... do we have one?" I ask, feeling stupid.

Jade gives me a long look, pausing her work.

"Not unless you set it up," she says. "You know social media isn't my thing. I can barely handle having a dating app."

As she takes the next customer's order, I pull out my phone, quickly finding and downloading the app. As soon as I've made a profile and linked it to my email, I type *Book Boutique and Bakery* into the search bar.

And sure enough...

"We do have one," I say, stunned. "But... I never set this up. I didn't even know this app existed."

I scroll through the posts on our profile. Yep. That's *my* store. Some of the shots even look professional. There are only a handful of posts, each within the last week, but when I click on mentions…

We're everywhere.

I scroll through hundreds of posts, each one tagging our shop.

"OMG! I can't get enough of the #bunnycookies at the Book Boutique and Bakery! Everyone in Fortune City, get your tails down here and try this place! Hop to it!"

There are several pictures of our Staff Picks display, some even showing it empty at the end of the day, with crying emojis peppering the photo.

"Okay, but if you didn't set this up," Jade says slowly. "Then… who did?"

Alec, I think instantly.

Or…

"Ashton," I say aloud. Who better to set this up than Mason Alexander Sterling's chief marketing officer, after all? I flick my thumbs over the screen, going back to the official *Book Boutique and Bakery* bookstapix profile, and sure enough, there's a picture I instantly recognize.

It's me. Holding a single red rose. The caption underneath advertises our wide range of romance novels.

I want to be angry, I really do. Ashton didn't ask me, didn't run any of this by me or get my permission, but…

I look around at the crowd of people waiting to try Jade's delicious baked creations. The recipes she spent months perfecting when we were teens. I look at the people chatting and laughing in the bookstore, some of them even wearing our merchandise. I realize, for the first time, that there's not a single seat in the store that isn't occupied.

And I don't feel angry. Or even upset.

Because it's everything I've ever wanted. And Ashton—handsome, thoughtful, kind Ashton—gave that to me.

Ashton: I'll pick you up at close, babygirl.

I read the text from Ash again and grin. I must have read it twenty times already since he sent it earlier today.

Honestly, with everything that's been going on, and with how busy we've been, I'd almost forgotten I'd agreed to this date. But I'm glad I did.

It's almost time to close up, and even though I'm tired, and even though the stress of Dorothy selling this place is hanging over me like a dark cloud, tonight at least I feel satisfied. Happy.

I look around at my little shop—the business that Jade and I built from the ground up with nothing but sheer determination and love—and feel a moment of pure, blissful contentment. I never thought I could have this. A simple life with simple pleasures, a best friend who accepts me inside and out, my own little business. I've worked so long to leave the past behind, and it finally feels like all the pieces are shifting into place.

And I want to fight for that. I want to keep it.

I want to keep them, too, I realize. Ashton and Alec.

After years of feeling unsupported in my career and business choices, years of refusing to second-guess myself because everyone around me, except for Jade, was second-guessing me, I finally feel... supported.

And I think I might be falling in love. With both of them.

Is that insane? Some part of me is screaming, *Yes! You can't be in love with two men at the same time!* But...

I've never felt this way before. Alec treats me like I'm a princess. And the way he touches me... reveres me, I've never felt the way I do with him, not ever.

And then Ashton?

He's like a best friend. Everything feels so easy, so light with him.

So what if he didn't run the account by me? The fact that he cared enough about my store to try to help means the world to me. He went out of his way to support me, and knowing he did that for me fills my heart with a warmth I can only describe as love.

As I slide my phone back into my pocket, I hear a loud bark of laughter from just outside the store. I smile. I'd recognize that laughter anywhere.

Sure enough, when I make my way up to the front where Jade is closing out our registers for the night, I spot them through our store's window. All three of them.

Alec is leaning against the back of his town car, looking as collected and dreamy as always. He must have come straight from the office, and he looks absolutely sinful in his dark suit. I watch for a moment, just drinking in the sight of him.

Next to him, standing with one hand on the largest motor-cycle I've ever seen, is Sebastian. Unaware I'm watching them, Sebastian says something inaudible to Alec, who shakes his head, looking amused. Sebastian's face remains as cold and blank as always.

Not always, a voice inside my head purrs.

Not when he'd touched you back in the stockroom. Not when he took your face in his hands and looked at you like you were his whole world. Like he'd kill for you.

I quickly tear my eyes away from him, feeling uncomfortably warm. And standing next to Sebastian, laughing...

Is Ashton. Looking every bit as handsome and perfect as I remember.

"There she is!" Ashton grins as I open the front door to our shop, giving him a small wave. His entire face lights up as he sees me, and it makes my stomach feel like it's full of butterflies. "Our beautiful girl!"

"Hello, Red." Alec straightens to greet me as I approach, pulling me against his chest to give me a kiss on the cheek. His hands linger on me as I step back.

"Are you coming with us tonight?" I ask. After that kiss, after smelling his cologne and feeling his hands on me, I'm almost hoping he says yes.

"Fuck that," Ashton says with a laugh at the same time Alec answers, "Sadly no."

"Tonight is *my* night," Ashton tells me, pulling me away from Alec and kissing my other cheek. "And I'm not sharing with anyone."

His grin is devilish as he stares down at me. "I have the perfect night planned for us," Ash assures me. "I made reservations for us at The Blue Sea. They do things with shrimp you would not *believe*. You're going to love it."

Slimy nausea floods my stomach, and it's an effort to force a smile. Still leaning against his motorcycle, Sebastian adjusts his cuffs, muttering something under his breath.

"What's your problem?" Ashton asks, turning toward him.

"No problem," Sebastian says, shrugging a shoulder. "No problem at all."

Ashton snorts and folds his arms over his chest. "Yeah, right. Come on, spit it out, Doc. Let's hear it."

Sebastian gives him a long look over the rim of his glasses. "She *hates* shrimp," he tells Ash. Then he picks up his helmet. "And you'd think you would bother to learn that simple little fact about your *date* before you picked the worst possible restaurant to take her to."

I don't have time to question how Sebastian knows that before Ashton turns back to me, his face falling.

"Wait… is that true?" he asks, sounding devastated. "I had no idea."

"Of course you didn't," Sebastian counters.

"Well, shrimp isn't my favorite," I say, giving him a small smile. A half-truth. Frankly, the entire idea of them is so disgusting, I'm not sure I could eat a meal of shrimp with a gun to my head. They are bugs that live in the ocean, and no one can convince me otherwise. "But that's okay. I'm sure they'll have something I'll enjoy."

"Nope, no, not happening." Ashton shakes his head. "We'll just go somewhere else! Easy fix!"

I open my mouth to argue more, ready to insist it's fine, but then I realize he actually means it. There's no hidden hostility to his words, no passive-aggressive tone. No irritation that he made reservations for nothing.

"There must be *thousands* of restaurants in this city." Ashton laughs. "Why would we go to one you wouldn't enjoy?"

And it's so normal, the way he says it. So obvious. Why would we?

My heart soars. Perfect. Ashton really is the perfect man.

"I'll grab my car and—"

"Actually—" I interrupt, feeling suddenly daring. Suddenly bold. "I could use your help with something inside. Before we go."

I can feel the blood flooding my cheeks as I say it, like it's so obvious. And maybe it is. Alec's lips twitch slightly, and Sebastian glances at me, quirking an eyebrow.

Only Ashton seems oblivious.

"Yeah, of course!" He grins. "Whatever you need. Tonight, I'm all yours."

I manage a quick goodbye to the other two, blushing even harder when Alec kisses me and murmurs "have fun, darling" in a voice that makes it very clear he knows what I'm planning.

Sebastian refuses to meet my eye, slipping on his helmet and taking off on his bike without a word.

I usher Ashton into the shop, flipping the open sign to closed, and shooing Jade outside. She snickers as she leaves, waving to me over her shoulder.

Am I really doing this? I engage the deadbolt, heart pounding.

I've never been good at initiating sex. Chase seemed almost disgusted the few times I tried. He liked the hunt, liked to think he cajoled me into it. A woman who wanted it unprompted was just too easy.

But Ashton isn't Chase. I swallow hard, suddenly nervous.

"So, what do you need help with?" Ashton's voice is chipper as he follows me deeper into the store. "You need some boxes moved, or—?"

The moment we're far enough away from the windows that I hope we can't be seen, I push him against the nearest bookshelf, shift forward until I'm standing on the tips of my toes, and kiss him.

There's no hesitation. The moment our lips touch, Ashton gives a single grunt of surprise and then kisses me back, threading his hand into my hair and pulling me closer so he can slip his leg between my thighs and press my body tightly against his. He kisses me greedily, groaning as he opens his mouth to let my tongue slide over his.

"*Oh*," he murmurs when I finally break away to catch my breath. "So this is what you wanted help with."

There's no derision in his voice, no disgust. He sounds excited. When I nibble a line down his jaw and to his neck he groans loudly, sliding his hands down my back to grip my ass.

I'm going to do this, I think wildly, reaching my hands under his shirt to feel the hard plane of his muscles. *Oh God,* his muscles. How many times have I fantasized about touching him? Feeling him under my fingers? I run my hands over his chest and abs, over each impossibly perfect inch of him.

More. I need more.

Ash swears low and in his throat when I finally reach for his belt, my fingers fumbling with the metal and—

My stomach growls loudly, the sound cutting through the haze of lust between the two of us like a knife.

"Sorry," I mumble, mortified, still fumbling with his belt. "Ignore that, I'm—"

Ash takes my hands in his, pulling them away from his pants.

"You're *hungry*," he says, grinning.

"I'm hungry for more than just food," I tell him with a half-smile.

"Nope," Ash says. He lets go of my hands and starts to do his belt back up. "Trust me. It's no good fucking on an empty stomach. Not when your body needs fuel."

"But—"

Ash interrupts me by pulling me in for another searing kiss, parting my lips with his tongue and stealing every thought from my brain.

"Let me take care of you, Babygirl," he whispers against my lips. "*Please.*"

My stomach growls again, almost angrily this time.

"I am pretty hungry," I admit sheepishly.

"I know the perfect place," Ashton says. "Do you like Mexican food?"

———

THIRTY MINUTES LATER, WE'RE SEATED AT A PLASTIC outdoor table in front of a food truck, surrounded by an ungodly amount of food. When Ashton told the cook we wanted two of everything, I thought he'd been joking. But...

"You have to try this one," Ashton says, handing me another compostable plate with a pile of carne asada tacos. "At least one bite. This has got to be the best one so far."

I've tried at least four different dishes Ashton swears have been the best, but I take the plate from him without complaint and have a bite of the small taco, moaning as the rich flavors hit my tongue.

I'll admit it—Mexican food has always been my favorite, hands down. And with Fortune City so close to the border, I can be a bit of a snob about what's authentic and what's not.

This food truck Ashton brought us to? It might be the best Mexican street food I've had in years.

By the time we've finished off everything (with Ashton eating at least four times what I could manage), I'm pleasantly full and more than content. I feel happy. Happier than I have been in years.

"There's an amazing ice cream place just down the street," Ashton tells me after he clears away the empty plates from our table. "What's your favorite flavor?"

I can't help but laugh. Of course Ashton still has room for dessert after devouring what had to be at least ten pounds of food. The man must have a black hole for a stomach.

"I'd never say no to chocolate," I tell him with a smile.

"Great choice." Ashton grins back. "You stay right here, Babygirl, and I'll be back before you know it."

It's no surprise when several women—and even a few men—turn to watch Ashton as he walks away. I feel a strange sense of pride knowing I'm the one he's choosing to spend his night with. I'm the one he's dating.

I watch him as he disappears around the corner, smiling at him and admiring the view.

"So what's his name?"

I jerk back, startled, as Chase slides into the seat across from me—the seat Ashton just vacated. The bruising on his face looks even worse today. He looks like something out of a horror movie.

"What the hell are you doing here?" I hiss at him, my chest tightening.

"I think I at least deserve to know his name, don't you?" Chase's lip curls in an angry sneer as he says it. "So tell me. What's the name of the man you're whoring yourself out for now?"

"How dare you," I seethe, the fury in my voice rising.

"How dare I?" Chase places his palms flat on the table, leaning toward me, and I flinch back reflexively. "How dare *you*? You think your little stunt at Katie's was cute? Slapping me like that?"

"I think it's better than you deserve."

"Careful, Sydney," Chase says in a low voice. "No one likes an angry woman."

It's a phrase he's thrown in my face since our first big fight. A phrase that's never failed to make me do what I'm told.

"I saw you, you know," Chase says, smirking as I back down. "You and Mr. Movie Star, back in your shop. Didn't take you long to shove your hand down his pants, did it?"

My heart stutters in my chest. *He saw us. He was watching me.*

"Are you following me?" I ask. I can't keep the tremor of fear out of my voice when I say it.

Chase's smile is anything but friendly. "Maybe I am. Maybe I'm not. Guess you'll find out."

"I'm getting a restraining order," I tell him, my voice hardening. "I'm sick of this, Chase. I want you out of my life for good."

"And you think a little piece of paper is going to stop me?" he taunts, leaning closer. I feel untethered, lost, as he forces himself into my personal space. "I'm done playing nice, Sydney."

"You were never nice, Chase," I say. "Not to me."

Rage flickers in his eyes. And the way he smiles then chills me to my core.

"You're going to regret fucking with me," Chase promises.

Fear. Acidic, dizzying fear sweeps through me, and—

"They had three different types of chocolate," Ashton says, his voice light and carefree as he approaches, cradling three bowls of ice cream in his arms. "Chocolate fudge, rocky road, and something called death by chocolate. I wasn't sure which one you'd like best, so I got all three for us to share, and—"

Ashton stops, looking up from his armful of dessert to notice Chase sitting across from me, and his smile falters.

"Oh! Hey, who's this?" He sets the bowls down on the table with effortless grace, not missing a beat.

Who is this? I look from Chase to Ashton, and I'm struck by the differences between the two of them. Not just their size—Chase works out, but he's never come close to looking like Ash—but everything about them.

Ash is kind. Ash supports me. Cherishes me. Maybe even loves me.

And it's so obvious to me now that Chase was never capable of any of that.

"He's nobody," I say, my voice firm and unwavering. I stare Chase straight in the eye as I say it, meaning every word. "Nobody at all."

A flash of anger crosses Chase's face before he smothers it. He stands abruptly, his chair scraping loudly against the concrete.

"We'll see about that," he tells me, staring me down.

Something shifts in Ashton at those words, and his body goes taut. Until now, he and Sebastian were nothing alike in my mind. Smiling, warm-hearted Ash, who wears his heart on his sleeve and every emotion clear on his face. The mirror opposite of cold, unreadable Sebastian.

But the anger that creeps into Ash's bright blue eyes is so familiar to me, it's suddenly impossible not to see the resemblance between the two of them. That icy rage that's ever present in Sebastian's gaze fills Ashton's as he stares down at Chase.

"Is this guy bothering you, Babygirl?" Ashton asks, his voice low and deadly.

Chase doesn't even glance at him. He's too focused on me, disgust etched into his face.

"Babygirl?" Chase mocks, his lip curling.

"Go," Ashton says, taking a step forward. His voice drops, and there's a menace in his stance I've never seen before. "Walk away."

"Fine. I'm gone." Giving Ash one dismissive glare, Chase shrugs his shoulders and walks away, his hands shoved deep into his pockets.

"Huh," Ashton mutters, his gaze following Chase, brow knit in confusion. "Kind of a weird guy, right?"

He settles into the seat Chase just vacated, shifting his concern and focus to me.

"Did he do something to upset you?" Ash asks, frowning. "Is everything okay?"

I pull the bowl of rocky road toward me, picking up the little plastic spoon sticking out of the heaping scoop and taking a big bite.

"Everything is perfect," I tell him. And in that moment,

with a bright smile blooming over Ashton's face and the taste of chocolate on my tongue, it is.

"Here." I scoop some ice cream onto the spoon and hold it out for him. "You *have* to try this one."

42

SYDNEY

PERFECT. THE NEXT DAY, THE FEELING CONTINUES, making everything look and feel brighter. Everything is *perfect*.

Thirty minutes after the best ice cream of my life, Ashton walked me home. I'd been nervous as we approached my door, not sure how to go about inviting him in, or asking him to stay the night...

Not even sure if I *wanted* him to stay the night. My run-in with Chase had left a sour taste in my mouth and a panicked flutter in my belly. I didn't feel as adventurous, suddenly. Didn't feel as comfortable coming on to him or having a man in my bed.

But at my door, Ashton had done nothing but give me a sweet, toe-curling kiss that tasted like chocolate before wishing me a good night and walking away. He didn't push. He didn't pressure me. He just... left. Like he sensed my hesitation without me saying anything, and understood.

It feels too good to be true. *They* feel too good to be true.

I woke up to a text from Alec the next morning. Not

jealous or demanding answers about what happened on my date with Ashton—no, Alec simply asked when I was free next, so he could take me out again.

I can't keep the smile off my face all day. I'm grinning like an idiot all day at work.

Even with the increase in customers, the usual post-lunch lull arrives, and the crowd begins to thin. I help Jade clean up, surprised at how empty the bakery case is—wiped clean by wave after wave of customers eager for her tasty treats—and then take a much-needed coffee break.

When I'm caffeinated and energized, I finally finish the restocking I started yesterday. A new Stephanie Kong thriller just came out, and I'm pleased I thought ahead and ordered extra copies of her earlier works. Every time she comes out with a new bestseller, her old work just flies off the shelf.

I feel happier than I have in years as I step out the side entrance of the building into the alley. It's a creepy, unsettling place, weirdly thin because the buildings on this block are built too close together, and even in the daylight, it's always a little dark here, but it keeps the trash and recycling bins out of sight, so who am I to complain?

There's someone out there leaning against the building next door, smoking, when I drag a pile of broken-down cardboard boxes outside. I don't mind if people use the alley, so long as they aren't bothering anyone, and this man certainly isn't.

He's a massive thing, though. Almost as big as Ashton, which is saying something. I nod politely to him as I pass, but he doesn't return the gesture. He just watches me, tilting his head to the side like I'm a puzzle he's trying to solve.

He's not unattractive. In fact, he's rather sexy, even with the scar above his eye and his short, buzzed hair. He looks wild. Feral.

But I don't give him much thought as I open the recycling bin and toss my boxes inside.

After a few seconds, I'm not even thinking about him at all.

Not until he grabs me, shoving me hard against the brick wall of the alley, and puts a knife to my throat.

43

VIPER

I'm not upset that my brothers lied to me.

But isn't it so *interesting* that they tried?

Anthony has been a low-level pain in Alec's ass for over a year now, and there's no reason at all he'd suddenly jump to the front of the queue and need my attention. No reason at all unless the *reason* was to keep me occupied.

So very interesting.

It took me a day to find Anthony. And even less time than that to break him and dispose of the body.

Now Anthony is at the bottom of the Fortune City River, weighed down with concrete, and I have all the time in the world to find out why my brothers wanted me *occupied*.

The answer is a surprise. She's not what I expected to find.

For all his paranoia and perception, Sebastian is an easy mark to follow. When you think you're untouchable, you let yourself relax, let your guard down. Doc should know better than that, but it's okay. Maybe this is just what he needs to learn that little lesson.

No one's untouchable.

Not Alec. Not Sebastian.

And not the woman they tried to keep from me.

"So very interesting," I murmur, pressing her against the brick wall of the alley with my body. She trembles like a rabbit as she stares up at me, eyes blown wide with fear.

I take a moment to appreciate how she looks, with her soft brown curls and her big brown eyes. She wants to run, run far away, my little rabbit, but she's frozen in place, trapped in her fear. Frozen at the sight of a predator.

"What do they see in you, little rabbit?" I ask, pressing the blade of my knife against her neck. Not enough to cut her, oh no. But she flinches away as if it hurts.

She doesn't know real pain. Not yet.

The rabbit doesn't answer me, so I drag the knife tip up to her chin, forcing her head up. She's pretty, so very pretty, but who gives a shit about pretty?

She's soft.

I run my other hand up her leg and grab her hip, gripping hard enough to make her cry out. So very soft.

I want to touch more of her. I need to touch more.

I flick my knife closed, sliding it back in my pocket for now, and run my other hand up her leg. She's wearing a flowy little dress, a modest cut to the knee, and it offers so little resistance when I slip my hand under there, up the smooth skin of her outer thigh.

She's tense under my touch, soft, scared little thing. Her body goes stiff, muscles rigid, and I'm distracted enough by her soft skin that I don't notice the danger in it. Not until she shifts her weight to one foot and slams her knee between my legs with all her strength.

For a few seconds, all I can see are stars. The pain is electric. It knocks the air right out of me, my body curling over itself as I dry heave.

So many stars.

Our little rabbit takes advantage of the moment, scrambling away, but the second the initial wave of pain passes, I erupt with laughter.

The rabbit has claws.

Oh, what *fun*.

It gets even better. Groaning, I straighten back up, reaching down to grip myself and make sure everything is still there, and I notice our rabbit isn't running back to the safety of her warren, or out of the alley to get help.

No. She runs to a pile of trashed furniture abandoned in the alley and grabs a broken table leg, brandishing it at me like a baseball bat.

"Don't come any closer," she warns. She gives the piece of debris a test swing, threatening me with it.

Fuck. This time, I'm not gripping myself to check for damage at all. I stroke myself through the fabric of my jeans as I walk forward, letting her see me do it. Her eyes dart down to watch me, face going tense. She raises her makeshift weapon higher, ready to strike.

It takes nothing more than a flick of my wrist to yank it out of her hands. I toss it away, down the alley, watching her face fall as it clatters over the pavement. Maybe I should have let her hit me with it. It's nothing more than cheap plywood, probably wouldn't have left a bruise, and it would have shown her exactly how pointless it is to fight me.

Now, she's terrified.

"I see it now," I console her, still laughing. She backs up until she hits the brick wall, and I'm right there with her, pressing her hard against it, feeling her body tense against mine.

Hands on the backs of her thighs, I lift her up, spreading her wide enough to fit myself right up against her. I don't want her to run, not again. And I want her to feel what her little outburst did to me.

I roll my hips, pressing my hard cock into her center. She trembles so deliciously against me.

She's not going anywhere, not when I have her pinned between me and the wall. I reach my hand up to cup her face, staring into those soft brown eyes.

"I see what they see," I tell her, running my thumb over her sweet, red lips. I expect to see a smear of lipstick, but that's all her. All that plump, delicious color.

I groan, bending down to take her bottom lip between my teeth. She makes the most wonderful sounds as I bite down.

When I let go, there's a nice juicy red drop of blood sliding down her chin, and that's so much better than any smeared lipstick.

Her breathing is fast and erratic, heart pounding in her chest. She's scared, sure, there's no question about that.

But one look in her eyes, at those dark liquid pupils, and I know she's feeling something much sweeter than just fear.

I roll my hips again, and the little whimper she gives me in answer is sweet enough to almost make me come.

"What...what do you want from me?" she asks, trembling.

I laugh, hard enough my shoulders and chest shake with it. What do I want? *What do I want?*

I press her harder against the wall, ducking my head so I can nuzzle into the soft, vulnerable skin of her neck.

"*Everything,*" I hiss.

The sound she makes in response could be from either pleasure or fear. It doesn't matter. It's all the same to me.

Fuck, her skin is so soft. I bite down on her neck, wanting to taste her blood, wanting to know what her fear tastes like on my tongue.

Sebastian's voice is loud as a gunshot in the quiet of the alley.

"Let her go," he says, an undercurrent of barely controlled rage in his voice.

Tasting her will have to wait. I sigh, deflating against her body.

I glance over my shoulder, and there he is, my little brother. I'm not surprised he caught me, not surprised he's upset. The only surprise is the gun clenched in his hands, pointed at the ground.

I can count on one hand the number of times I've seen Sebastian draw his gun.

Turning back to our rabbit, I see she's looking at him, her eyes flickering between the two of us.

"Of course he's watching. Doc loves to watch," I tell her. I don't like the way she's looking at him, like she expects to be saved. Gripping her jaw, I turn her back to me, so I have her full attention again. "Has he told you that yet?"

She blinks those big brown eyes at me and doesn't answer. I don't think she's understood a single word I've said. But that's okay. There's plenty of time to make her understand.

Such a pretty little rabbit.

I run my thumb up to her lips, collecting that drop of blood and sliding it into her mouth. She shudders, trying to yank her head back.

But just for a second, I feel her tongue slip over the pad of my thumb, tasting that blood.

"That's it," I tell her, pressing my hips harder against her. Her mouth parts in a little gasp. "Tell me how it tastes, little rabbit."

The sound of Sebastian flipping off the safety switch on his gun is an unexpected shock.

My shoulders tense.

I can count on just one finger the number of times Sebastian has shot someone. That's the only time he's ever needed to.

"Last warning, Viper," Sebastian tells me, meeting my gaze without a hint of fear when I turn to glare at him. "Let her go."

I drop my thumb from her lips just in time to see her mouth the word *Viper*, her face going pale.

So, our little rabbit knows who I am. That's very interesting.

Almost as interesting as the gun Sebastian has pointed at me, ready to fire.

It would kill him to have to shoot me. That more than anything is the reason I let go, stepping back and letting our rabbit drop to the ground.

The second her feet are back on land, she bolts straight for the door she came out of, not even sparing Sebastian a glance as she runs inside.

Run, little rabbit, run.

I don't mind a little chase. And I'm going to have so much fun with this one when I get her down in our wet lab to play.

44

My hand shakes as I lower my gun.

It's subtle, just a tremor. But it's a crack in my mask I don't expect. A sign of just how lost I've become.

Viper stares after Sydney for several long seconds after the door closes behind her, a wistful smile on his face. I've seen that look before, that obsession. But never when looking at a woman.

We're absolutely fucked.

"You shouldn't have tried to keep her from me, Doc," Viper says, shaking his head. "You know better than that."

He finally turns to look at me, and his eyes go straight to my gun, still clutched tight in my hand. When he steps forward to take it from me, I give it up with no resistance at all.

I don't know what to expect when he palms it. You can never predict what Viper is going to do. Maybe he'll just shoot me straight in the head for interrupting his fun. Maybe he'll end me right now.

But all Viper does is engage the safety and hand the gun back to me.

"Don't point it at someone unless you're ready to shoot them," he reminds me, eyes dark.

That's the problem, though. I was ready.

I hold his stare, refusing to back down, and wonder if he can see it in my eyes. I wonder if he knows how close I came to killing him.

"Sterling will kill you if you hurt her," I tell him, taking my gun from him and sliding back into its spot at the small of my back. "He likes her, Viper. *Ashton* likes her."

I don't need to tell Viper how I feel about our Sydney. He can see it written all over my face.

"Of course, you all like her, brother," Viper says, grinning. He puts a hand on my shoulder, giving it a comforting squeeze. "She's so, so pretty."

His smile is a thing of nightmares.

"Just imagine how pretty she'll be when she breaks," he says.

His laughter is haunting, and it stays with me long after he's left.

———

Sydney isn't in the café when I go to find her. She's not in the shop anywhere I look.

The stockroom is the last place I check, and I know I've found her when I find it locked.

I don't even bother knocking. The thin metal card I keep in my wallet is all I need to pick the lock open and let myself inside.

Sydney doesn't look surprised when I enter, shutting the door behind me and reengaging the lock.

She looks terrified.

Arms wrapped around herself, cowered against the table,

she watches me approach with fear in her eyes. There's a smear of blood on her mouth, and a mark on her neck that looks like a bite. I stare at it, gritting my teeth and hoping Viper had the good sense not to break the skin there.

The human mouth has over 500 different species of bacteria. I make a quick mental note of exactly which antibiotics I'll need to get for her.

"*That* was Viper?" Sydney asks, voice unsteady.

I nod, stepping toward her. She doesn't flinch away from me, not yet. I take that as a good sign. She held her own against him. She didn't even scream.

All good signs.

"He's a maniac," Sydney breathes, holding herself tighter. "He's... he's *dangerous*."

The way she says it, the way she spits out the word *dangerous* like it's the single most disgusting thing a person can be hits me surprisingly hard. I feel my mask crack, just a little.

"He is," I try to tell her, keeping my voice gentle. Easy, like I'm talking to a frightened animal. "But he's loyal. He's good at what he does. He's our brother, and—"

She laughs, and there's an edge of cruelty to it. "Loyal? He's a fucking maniac! He—he should be locked up!"

The mask cracks even more as my hands clench at my side.

"He *was* locked up," I say in a low voice. Sydney's eyes jump to mine as I take another step closer to her. "That's *why* he's like this. Because of what *being locked up* did to him."

Where is my vengeful goddess? Where is my queen of wrath and darkness? The woman who was willing to kill?

I don't see her anywhere in Sydney's face right now. I see a frightened woman. I see a doll made of glass, so easily broken.

"And of course he's dangerous," I say, my voice a little too dark, a little too real. Sydney tries to move away from me, but she's already right up against the table, and there's nowhere else for her to go as I close the distance between us. She holds a hand out to my chest to stop me coming closer, and I grab her wrist, squeezing it tight.

"We're *all* dangerous," I tell her. Because I need her to understand this, I need her *to get it.* I need her to finally fucking see it. "Me. Viper. Alec." I chuckle as she winces, tugging in vain to pull her arm out of my grip. "Even *Ashton*, with all his pretty smiles. We're dangerous men, Sydney."

She shakes her head quickly from side to side, like she refuses to believe it. Like she can't believe it.

"You should be thanking Viper, you know," I tell her. "He's the only one of us who's actually been honest with you about who we are." I laugh, sounding a little manic even to my own ears. "Hell, he probably couldn't lie to you if he *tried*."

I can feel her pulse rapid as a trapped hummingbird against my hand, and I know I should stop.

But that fierce woman is in there.

I know she is.

And this version of her just *won't fucking understand*.

"You know what I think? I think you *like* that we're dangerous," I say. I press closer until we're chest to chest, pressed against one another. This is the closest I've ever been to her, and my body immediately responds, blood filling my cock until I'm so hard it hurts. "I think you're a little dangerous, too, Sydney."

"No." She shakes her head violently. "I'm *not*."

"Stop pretending," I snarl. "You fucking love it. You love *us*. When Ashton and Sterling took you to their room and spread you out on that bed, you knew exactly what they were. They gave you just a taste of what they could do for you, and you loved every second of it."

"How..." Sydney's pupils are wide enough to eclipse the brown in her eyes as she stares up at me. "How do you know that?"

I'm so fucking tired of wearing this mask.

"Because I was watching you," I confess without an ounce of regret. My cock is rock hard, digging into her, as I finally, *finally*, let the mask fall away completely for her. Let her see *me*. "Because I was watching the whole fucking thing, from start to finish, Sydney. Everything they did to you." I lean down, pressing my lips to her ear as I hiss, "And I fucking loved it."

There's a fine line between fear and arousal. Sydney's pupils are blown wide, her breathing and pulse erratic. But her cheeks are flushed, her lips are a deep, rich red, and when I press against her harder, pushing her back against the edge of the table, her legs clench together, desperate for friction.

I've spent years learning to analyze the subtle expressions of people.

I know when a woman is aroused.

"I loved watching you," I tell her. I drop her wrist, sliding my hand into her hair instead, gripping it to bend her neck back and force her to look up at me. To see the truth in my eyes. "I loved watching them spread you open to feast on you. I loved how wet your pussy was for them, how much you wanted it. You would have taken them both if they'd offered it, wouldn't you? Given them any hole they asked for."

She doesn't answer.

"Our perfect, filthy girl," I say, twisting her hair in my hands.

I'm close enough to see the exact moment when her gaze hardens. There's a flare of something dark in her eyes when she looks away.

There she is.

"Let's play a game," I say, kicking her legs open and reaching down, under her skirt. "Tell me you don't love this, and I'll stop. Tell me you're not soaking wet right now, dripping down your thighs, and I'll leave right now. And never come back."

It takes no effort at all to lift her to the table and spread her legs wide. My hand hovers at her hip, fingers playing with the hem of her panties.

Sydney's lip twitches, and her eyes flick to mine, but she says nothing. She glares at me with those beautiful, dark eyes, completely silent.

"That's all you have to do, Sydney," I promise her, stroking my fingers over her skin. "Tell me you don't want this. Tell me I'm wrong, that you don't belong to us, that you want me to stop..."

My fingertips dip under the fabric, just a fraction, and she sucks in a breath.

"Or don't say anything. And let me find out for myself how wet you are."

Sydney's eyes narrow at me.

But she doesn't say a word.

"That's what I thought," I sneer, yanking that tiny piece of fabric aside and sliding my fingers over her, searching for the truth.

She's *soaked*.

I groan, running my fingers through her slick heat. She feels like silk. She's so soft, so wet, and so *perfect*.

"I knew it," I say. "Fuck, you were made for us, weren't you, Sydney?"

Sydney gasps as I touch her, hips rising to meet my fingers. But I hear it. Soft, and almost inaudible.

"Yes," Sydney whispers, grinding against my hand.

"Our filthy girl," I say, fingers sliding over her until I find that hard bundle of nerves. She moans, arching when I circle it.

My fingers move faster and faster, enraptured by the sounds she makes, by every single movement. In every twitch, every gasp, she tells me wordlessly exactly what she wants and how she wants it.

She's a work of art. Exquisite.

When her legs start to shake, trembling on either side of me, I know she's close. But I'm not ready to stop, not yet. Not after wanting to touch her for so long.

I pull my hand away, ignoring her cry of protest, and drop to my knees, pulling her to the edge of the table. I need to taste her.

Pushing her legs open even further, I shove her panties to the side and slide my tongue inside her. It's better than I could have ever imagined. Better than watching Ashton and Sterling with her. She tastes like salted honey. She tastes like every sin I've ever wanted to commit.

She reaches for me, burying her hands in my hair to pull me closer, and I groan in encouragement, sucking and licking at every perfect part of her.

"Don't stop," Sydney gasps, rocking against me. "Please, oh God, Sebastian... don't stop."

When I look up from between her legs, she's watching me, lips parted, panting. I hold her gaze as I slip a finger inside her, feeling her buck.

That bundle of nerves is even better on my tongue, and I lap at it greedily while I fuck my finger in and out of her. Her thighs clench around me, trembling.

"Look at me," I demand, moving my hand faster. I let my lips graze against her when I say it. "This is mine. All this pleasure?" I curl my finger as I say it. "This is *mine*. Look at me, filthy girl. I need to see it when I make you come."

The second my tongue finds her again, she comes undone, throwing her head back in a soundless scream. Her entire body shakes, thighs squeezing me tight as she rides my face, chasing every ounce of pleasure I'm willing to give her.

I let her take it.

45

SYDNEY

With just a single finger and the tip of his tongue, Sebastian shatters my entire world.

Something terrible shifts inside of me. And when I finally come back down, collapsing back against the table, knocking several books to the ground, I know nothing will be the same.

And that terrifies me.

I think Sebastian knows it, too.

He pulls himself to his feet, staring down at me. I'm horrified by how wet his face is, his lips glistening in the low light of the stock room, covered in evidence of my body's betrayal.

As the final bit of pleasure eases from me, everything else comes crashing down. I feel unbound, untethered from reality.

Sebastian leans over my body, sliding his finger over my lips.

"Lick it clean," he orders.

Wordlessly, I obey. I suck the finger into my mouth, tasting myself on it.

Tasting every terrible, dirty thing he said to me.

Tasting what started in the alley when Viper touched me. Tasting a truth I desperately want to escape.

Because he's right.

I'd loved it. All of it.

What is wrong with me?

The sob shudders through me before I can stop it, and before I know what's happening I'm crying, eyes screwed shut, curling in on myself. All these years, I pushed myself into this tiny box of what I thought I needed to be, and within weeks, these men completely unraveled all my work.

Sebastian snatches his hand away like I burned him, taking a quick step back. When he reaches for me again, his touch is soft. So gentle and soft.

"Sydney?" he asks, wiping the tears from my face. "You're okay, love. I've got you. Talk to me. What's wrong, what—?"

"Go," I tell him, through the sobs. "Please, just… just *go*, Sebastian."

He hesitates, not sure what to do. For once his face is an open book, all his emotions laid bare. And I hate him a little for it, for finally showing some vulnerability.

"Sydney, I…"

"Leave!" I sob.

"Okay," he says gently, taking another step back and holding up his hands as if in surrender. He looks destroyed. "If… if that's what you want me to do. I'll… I'll go."

He waits, like he's expecting an answer.

I don't give him one.

For a long time after he leaves, I just lie there, curled on my side on the table, trying to understand what sort of monster they've unleashed into the world.

46

ASHTON

"W E'RE ALREADY HEARING CHATTER THAT ANTHONY ISN'T reachable," Alec says, tapping the arm of his chair. "Which means either Viper already found him or he's so hidden that—"

The door to his office swings open with enough force it hits the wall, knocking a photo off its nail and to the ground. I sit up straight on the couch, and Alec's hand instantly goes to his gun, as Sebastian rushes in.

He's a mess. Hair mussed, clothes disheveled.

And... my nostrils flare. He smells like sex.

"I fucked up," he tells us, voice high with panic.

I register the split second of shock on Alec's face at seeing our brother like this before he locks it down, his jaw tightening. His face is all business when Sebastian finally looks at him.

"What happened?" Alec demands, voice cold.

Sebastian paces, hands moving constantly as he stalks around the room. This isn't like him, this isn't like our cold, collected brother. This is what he was like when we were kids. A nervous ball of energy, unable to keep himself still. This is the Sebastian I remember from before the orphanage.

"Viper found her," he tells us. His fingers twitch, hands clenching and unclenching nervously.

A lead weight drops into my stomach at those words. *No. No, no, no.*

"Is she okay?" Alec asks, leaning forward over his desk.

Sebastian's answering laugh is devoid of any humor. He shakes his head.

"She was," he says, and he's not even trying to hide the pain in his voice. "He scared her, but ... she was fine. Shaken, but he didn't... he didn't hurt her. Not badly. She was *fine*."

"So, what happened?" I demand.

"*I* hurt her," Sebastian spits out, turning on me. "I touched her. And, and she let me, I swear she let me, Ash, but afterward... after..."

"Hey." I stand up and hold out my hand, forcing him to stop his pacing. "Stop. Take a breath and explain."

"I think I pushed her too far," he says, words coming too quickly. "She started crying. *Fuck*, Ash, *she cried* afterward." He stares down at his hands like he's never seen them before. "It was too much, it must have been too much for her. First Chase, then Viper, and then me..."

"What do you mean Chase?" Alec growls. "How does her ex fit into this?"

"Fuck. I just...I keep fucking up!" Seb forces the words out, running his hands through his hair and pulling at the roots. "She asked me not to tell you. I was keeping her safe, I swear."

"She asked you not to tell us *what*?" Alec's voice is heavy with barely controlled rage.

"He...he showed up a few days ago. To the shop. He... fuck...he went to her apartment. He scared her."

My vision goes red. I don't think I've ever felt pure rage like this before. I like to be the one who doesn't take things too seriously, but the idea of someone frightening her?

I need him to pay for that.

I make eye contact with Alec, and he's barely breathing, teeth clenched.

Sebastian keeps talking. "He's been following her, threatening her…"

Following her. A man … following her.

"What does he look like?" I ask, my voice sounding like it's a million miles away, like I'm in space or some shit. I've never seen him, I realize. Like always, I passed the buck, made Seb handle his termination paperwork.

It takes a second for Sebastian to pull up the image on his phone and show me. And there he is.

The man from my date with Sydney.

He's nobody.

The cold calm I usually feel when I'm in the arena enters me, slowing my heart rate and grounding me.

I'm ready to fight.

"Fix this," Alec snaps.

When I look up, he's not looking at Sebastian.

He's looking at me.

"She trusts you, Ashton," Alec says. "You need to be the one to fix this. She thinks you're safe."

Sebastian laughs, and it's a cold, broken sound.

"Not anymore," he says, a crazed look in his eyes. "She knows what we are now. I don't think she'll trust any of us, not even you."

I glance at Alec, noting the tension in his face. The fear. When he looks at me, he doesn't look so sure this time.

"I can do it," I say, with a confidence I don't entirely feel. Alec doesn't look like he believes me. "I can fix this."

Because I have to do it. Because I don't know if we can go back to not having her.

My hand flexes. And I know just where to start.

47

ASHTON

Smoking is a disgusting habit. But that doesn't stop me from lighting up my fifth cigarette in a row, taking a deep lungful of carcinogens and tar as I lean against the side of an office building in the middle of downtown and wait.

My trainer would kill me if he knew I was smoking again. He'd use it as an excuse to punish me, to push me even harder than he usually does. But right now, I can't bring myself to give a single fuck.

I exhale a cloud of smoke and watch it curl around me, dancing on the light breeze. My leg bounces incessantly, my muscles twitching. I'm sick of waiting here. All I want to do is talk to Sydney. I want to hear her side and figure out what the fuck happened. I want to start fixing it.

But I need to do this first.

The thought of Sydney's ex scaring her like that has me seething. I spent a lot of my life angry, but this is different. There's something so potent about the rage simmering under my skin right now. It makes me want to destroy something.

He frightened her. And Sydney... Sydney kept it from us.

That breaks my fucking heart.

I get that she wants to handle everything on her own. She's used to it, I bet. And she's too goddamn kind-hearted for her own good. That's why she didn't want us to interfere with Chase's job—because she's sweet. She's *good.*

I want her to stay good. I can be a monster for her. I can be the awful thing that keeps her good.

Because this? I can't let this go unpunished. I take a deep breath to steady my racing heart, anger and anxiety swirling together inside my chest.

My phone vibrates in my pocket and I slide it out to read the message.

Alec: Come back to the compound. I'll handle things with Sydney.

Fucking control freak. I can handle this. I know I can handle this. I just need to talk to her, that's all.

I'm putting my phone away when I spot him, my body going instantly still. Chase. That stupid motherfucker.

I watch him through narrowed eyes as he leaves his office building, heading straight for the alley where I'm standing. My hands tighten into fists reflexively at the sight of him. He has no idea what's coming.

We should have had him fired. We should have bankrupted him, evicted him, left him bleeding in a gutter.

We should have handled him before he became a problem.

He's oblivious, walking toward me like he owns the world. He doesn't even see me yet. Motherfucker should really know better than to walk through sketchy alleys all on his own. You never know who might be waiting in the shadows.

"Chase?" I ask when he's close enough, tossing my cigarette to the ground. Not for verification, but just because I want him to know that *I* know.

He looks up, frowning when he sees me. Like he can't quite place where he recognizes me from. "Yeah?"

My fist connects with his already broken nose with a sickening crunch so loud it echoes around the alley. Chase stumbles backwards, confused, barely able to react, barely able to make a sound. Before he can fully regain his balance, I slam my fist into his kidney.

He coughs violently, his body jerking with the force, but he still doesn't crumple. He's tougher than I expected. I've faced guys in the ring who wouldn't be standing after those swings.

"What the fuck do you want?" Chase manages to shout at me, spitting blood—and what looks like a tooth— onto the ground next to my feet.

I duck down to meet his eyes, grinning when I see the flicker of recognition there—the understanding of who I am and why I'm here. And then the moment passes, and there's nothing in his eyes but fear.

"You're one of *them*," he spits the words at me, straightening. "I don't know what that bitch told you, but she's *my* fiancée, and I—"

I don't let him finish. I can't. I launch myself at him, tackling him to the ground with all the fury I've been holding in.

How fucking *dare he*? How dare he imply that she lied? That she's *his*?

She's mine.

Chase flails, throwing wild punches, but they're nothing to me, even when he manages to land a few. I was born for this. Trained for this. My blows land with precision—each one harder than the last, overwhelming all his attempts to defend himself, smashing his body into the ground with each hit.

Only when he stops trying to fight back and goes limp do I stop.

But I'm not finished yet.

I grab him by the collar, pulling him close. "If you ever go near Sydney again, if you ever even *think* about her, you will regret it. Do you understand me?"

Chase nods weakly, his eyes swollen shut, his face battered.

I stand up and take a step back, taking in the wreckage I've made of him. A better man would leave it at that. Would walk away, the fight over.

But I'm not a good man.

I kick him once, hard, in the ribs, and then finish the job with another kick to his head.

With my rage finally satiated, I gaze down at his unconscious, barely recognizable figure, and a grim smile curls on my lips.

48

SYDNEY

When I remember the night my parents died, my most vivid memory is the rain.

And the rage.

It was storming that evening, and the rain was so heavy it was almost impossible to see through the windshield, even with the wipers going at full speed. And the storm just kept growing, kept getting worse.

I was so angry. I remember clenching my fists so tight my fingernails bit into my palms. I remember wanting something bad to happen.

"I hate you," I told them.

And I'd meant it.

After the funeral, I spent years bouncing from therapist to therapist, trying to dull the sharp edges of that memory. Years of trauma processing and desensitization that only left me feeling sick and raw. Years of mantras, of breathing exercises, of mindfulness training.

But therapy only works if you're willing to let it work. If you face your trauma and learn to let it go.

I don't want to let it go. Even now, when I let the memory wash over me, I want it to hurt. I *need* it to hurt.

I need to remember what happens when I let myself be that person.

I stare at my reflection in the mirror over my bathroom sink and let that memory hurt me. A monster stares back, her bottom lip still swollen from Viper's bite. I drag my tongue over the wound.

Nobody likes an angry woman, Chase's voice mocks me as I stare down the monster in my mirror.

Then Sebastian's. *I think you're a little dangerous, too.*

And I am. I know that I am. I'm dangerous. I'm a murderer. I'm the reason my parents are dead.

Next to the sink, my phone flashes with another message from Ashton. The twelfth so far. I've lost count of the number of missed calls.

Ashton: Are you okay?

Ashton: Please pick up, babygirl. I need to
know you're okay.

And I want to. I want to pick up my phone and talk to him. I want to invite him over and eat his stupid takeout and let him comfort me. I want him to make me laugh. I want him to tell me that everything is okay.

But it's not.

Because today a stranger held a knife to my throat and—even knowing I should be scared and disgusted and furious with him—I'd wanted him. Every single touch had lit a fire under my skin, and some disgusting part of me wanted him to strip me naked and take me against that alley wall where anyone could have seen.

Everything isn't okay because Sebastian was right. I let

these men into my life, and I knew deep down that they weren't good or safe or *nice*. From the first moment I'd met him, I'd known Alec was dangerous. And it hadn't stopped me.

I won't let Ashton tell me everything is okay. I'm not sure it will ever be okay again.

Another message lights up my phone screen.

Ashton: Please, babygirl. Just talk to me.

What a pretty rose, all covered in thorns.

I swipe the notification away.

When I first met Ashton, I thought he looked like a model. His movie-star face and perfect body. His bright, easy laugh.

We're all dangerous, Sebastian's voice reminds me. *Even Ashton, with all his pretty smiles.*

I see the truth now. He's pretty, sure, but Ashton isn't built like a model at all, is he? He's built like a fighter. All those delicious muscles I'd loved running my hands over and feeling beneath my fingers. They're not for vanity. They're not there to look good.

They're for causing pain.

My hands are fisted so tight at my side that they hurt, my knuckles aching from the force of it. I stare at myself in the mirror, stare at the angry woman I tried to bury years ago, and I hate her. I hate her so much I want to scream.

But I know if I start screaming now, I might never stop.

I can't remember any of my mantras. I can't remember any of my breathing exercises. My breaths are coming too fast, my heart is beating too fast, and I can't think, I can't breathe, I can't move, I can't—

The mirror above my sink shatters into a thousand dangerous pieces when I slam my fist into it, fracturing my image and sending shards cascading to the floor.

Regret hits me before the pain does. Horrified, I twist my hand around to see the damage. There's blood, hot and bright red, on my knuckles, but there's not as much as I'd feared.

The mirror, on the other hand…

Shit. *Shit.* There are pieces of it everywhere, all over my bathroom counter and on the floor. Dangerous, sharp pieces.

I swear, furious and ashamed, as I rinse my bleeding hand in the sink. I'm lucky. It's not so bad, not really. I'll need to bandage it and apply some antiseptic cream. But first, I need to grab a broom and clean up the glass. I need—

The knock on my front door is so loud I jump, my heart leaping into my throat. It's followed a few seconds later by another knock, louder this time. Gingerly, I wrap a clean washcloth around my hand and carefully step over the shards, out of the bathroom. I shut the door behind me, hiding the damage.

I know without opening my front door that it's one of them. I'm not surprised they've come to check on me. My only surprise when I peer out through the peephole is that it's not Ashton on the other side of the door.

It's Alec.

He's a mess. His dark hair is disheveled like he's been running his hands through it. He looks frantic, standing there, waiting for me to answer the door. For a moment, I let myself see him—really see him. Not just Mr. Tall, Dark, and Handsome. Not just the man who waltzed with me at a charity banquet.

Mason Alexander Sterling. A businessman who never let anything stand in his way. A man with presence. A man to be feared.

A man who is dangerous.

I keep my injured hand behind my back as I open the door, hiding it.

"Hi," I say in a small voice.

He doesn't return the greeting. Alec's gaze goes to my swollen lip almost instantly.

"What happened?" he asks, eyes locked on the bite. His voice is sharp.

I manage to force a laugh. "Well, I met Viper."

Alec doesn't laugh. He doesn't even smile. He moves closer to me, reaching out to graze my bottom lip with the pad of his thumb. His touch is too gentle to hurt.

"Did he hurt you?" His voice is softer now. He cups my chin gently, like I'm something precious.

I give a small shake of my head. "No. No, not... not really. He scared me, but..."

I swallow hard and go quiet, pulling away from Alec's touch. Because what could I possibly tell him?

He scared me, but I'd liked it. He'd scared me, but I'd wanted more. He'd scared me, but I'd been so wet, so desperate for what he could give me, I would have gladly let him do whatever he wanted to me.

I look away before Alec can see those thoughts in my eyes.

"And Sebastian?" Alec asks. "Did he hurt you?"

That question jars me, surprising me.

"Sebastian?" I repeat, sure I misheard him. "No. Why?"

Alec gives me a long, searching look. "He seemed to think he did, darling. He says you were... upset."

Right. I shift a little on my feet. Of course he'd said something to them. About how we...

"So he told you what happened, then?" I wrap my arms around myself, staring at a patch of rust on my stairs' railing. Staring at anything but him. "After Viper?"

"A little," Alec says. "But I need to hear your side of it. Did he..." He pauses like he can't bring himself to say it. "Darling, if he touched you without your permission—"

I do look at him, then, and I hold my hand out to stop him before he says anything more.

"He had my consent, Alec." My voice is steady, and I hope he can hear the surety in it. I'd wanted it. Wanted *him*. Wanted every dirty thing Sebastian did to me.

Needed it, in a way that scared me.

"What happened to your hand?" Alec asks.

I look down at the cloth wrapped around my knuckles. The dull throb of pain echoes my pulse, aching with every beat of my heart.

"I cut it on some glass," I tell him, delicately peeling the washcloth away. There's a patch of blood, a deep red against the clean white of the terry cloth. But there are really only two small cuts, across my knuckles. I flex my fingers, savoring the hurt. A fresh spot of blood wells to the surface.

Alec takes my hand in his, staring down at the wounds. Then he brings it to his lips and presses a soft kiss just above my knuckles.

A man used to the sight of blood. Unafraid of it.

"He scared you," Alec murmurs, lips against my skin.

He did more than scare me. That's the problem.

"You told me Viper was *complicated*," I accuse him. But I don't pull my hand away. "He's not complicated. He's..."

A monster, I almost say.

Like you, that voice in my head coos.

I keep those thoughts to myself. "Were you ever really planning to introduce him to me? Or was that a lie?" I ask.

There's a flash of something in his eyes before he answers.

"I'd never lie to you." His voice is husky when he says it, and his fingers caress mine, carefully avoiding the cuts on my knuckles.

"I don't believe you, Alec," I admit.

Hurt. That's the emotion that flashes in his eyes this time.

"Can we go somewhere to talk?" Alec asks.

"We're talking now," I answer, taking my hand back.

"Sydney." Alec pins me with a look. "I don't want to have this conversation here. Please."

It's the desperation in his eyes that gets me. Like he's afraid I'll say no. That I'll close the door and leave him here, pleading on my doorstep.

I trace the wound on my lip with my tongue one more time. "Fine. Just... let me get my things."

It takes me a few minutes to pull my phone out of the bits of broken mirror without cutting myself more. On my way out the door, I grab my purse and shove my phone and keys inside.

His town car is parked around the side of my building, the headlights bright in the fading evening light. Alec guides me toward it after I lock up, his hand a comforting presence on the small of my back as he opens the car door to let me inside. When he climbs in next to me, I half expect him to cuddle up to me, like he always does. But he hesitates, his body stiff. When he finally settles against the seat, he leaves a few inches of space between us.

We're both quiet as the car pulls away from the curb and glides down the street.

"Where are we going?" I ask, finally.

There's a beat of silence before Alec answers. "My apartment."

I trace the stitching on the leather seat between us with my finger, staring at the cuts on my hand. The bleeding has stopped. "Another penthouse?" I ask. The words are meant to be teasing, but they come out flat.

Alec's expression flickers. "Yes and no." He exhales loudly, running a hand over his face. "I'm taking you to *my* apartment, Sydney. The one place my brothers don't know about. The one place that's all mine."

My fingers still on the seat.

"He told me he saw us, you know." I tell Alec. "After the banquet. Sebastian told me he was watching us." I stare at him, trying to read his expression. "Did you know?"

Alec squeezes his eyes shut. He looks tired. Crushed. And he won't look at me.

"I suspected," he admits. "When Ashton wanted you on the bed, I assumed that was the reason. But no. I didn't know, not for sure."

"How was he watching?" I ask. "Were there cameras in the room?" Oh God. My stomach sinks. "Do you... do you have a recording of me? Of us?"

Alec shakes his head quickly from side to side. "No, darling. No."

"Then *how?*"

He does look at me then, and his eyes look so tired.

"Two-way glass," he tells me. "There's a room behind the mirror."

The mirror. I blush remembering it. Remembering how Ashton positioned me, legs spread wide before my reflection. Like he was showing me off.

"We should have told you," Alec says, regret heavy in his voice.

I don't look at him. I don't answer him.

They should have told me. It's vile that they didn't, vile that they let me be seen like that by someone who was a stranger to me.

But the thought of Sebastian behind that mirror, watching me? The thought of him touching himself, staring at me?

I must be broken. There must be something so deeply wrong with me that I like that idea. That it thrills me to know it happened.

The rest of the ride is short and quiet. I can't seem to bring myself to say anything more. When we pull up in front of a high-rise building on the outskirts of downtown a few minutes later, I know without being told that we've reached our destination. The building design is modern and expensive, and it's exactly the sort of place I imagine Alec living.

Earl opens the doors for us once the car rolls to a stop. He gives me a small smile and a friendly nod in greeting when I climb out of the car.

I'm nervous, I realize, as the building's doorman ushers us inside and calls the elevator to the top floor for us. Nervous about being alone with Alec. Nervous about this conversation.

Our ride to the top floor is spent in painful silence.

When the doors open again and Alec exits, I follow, wiping my sweaty palms on the fabric of my dress as I tail him down the hallway. We finally slow and come to a stop in front of a corner apartment.

Alec pauses after he unlocks his apartment door, one hand on the doorknob, the other pressed against the wood. He lets out a long breath.

"You're the first person I've ever brought here," he says. And before I can process that, he opens the door.

49

ALEC

I've shown Sydney luxury. I've shown her opulence. Up until now, I've shown her the very best of what my empire has to offer, in the hopes of winning her heart.

Tonight, I intend to show her something else. Tonight, I want to show her the real me.

I wish I'd cleaned the place better. But I wasn't lying when I'd told Sydney that she was the first person I'd ever brought here. No one else steps foot inside this room—not my brothers, not our security force, not even the team of cleaners who take care of our compound.

I watch Sydney closely as she sets down her bag and moves through my apartment. It's large, but still little more than a studio. She starts in the kitchen—a kitchenette, really—just inside the doorway, pausing by the sink. Her fingers brush over the empty coffee cup I left there, waiting to be washed. A newspaper from last month sits next to it, unread. My kitchen table is covered in documents and contracts, pieces of work I've brought home with me over the years.

For the first time in a very long time, I'm not sure I'm

making the right decision. Maybe I should have trusted Ashton to handle this and waited for him to talk to her first. She's calm around him. Relaxed. Maybe I should have stayed away and let my brother fix this.

But I couldn't. If someone is going to set this right, I need it to be me. And if she decides this is too much, if she decides my *brothers* are too much?

I need to be the one she chooses.

My bedroom is little more than a queen-sized bed, just beyond the kitchenette. When Sydney reaches it, her fingers trail over the dark gray bedspread before her attention shifts to the windows.

The curtains are drawn and thick enough to keep out any light. I've been told the view here is as breathtaking as any of my penthouses, but I wouldn't know. I've never seen it. I keep the curtains closed, always.

This is where I come when I need to be alone. When I don't want to be reminded of the legacy I've built with blood and sweat and terror.

"What do you think?" I ask. I want her to like it. Simple and bare as it is, I need her to like it.

"It's not what I expected," Sydney answers. She runs her fingers over the curtain. For a moment, it looks like she might open them, and my heart skips a beat in my chest. But then her hand falls, and the curtains remain closed.

There's still blood, dried and flaking, on her knuckles. I don't believe for a second she cut herself on some glass.

Maybe she fought back against Viper. It's my fault that no one warned her what a terrible idea that would be.

"It's nice," she says, giving me a small smile. A smile so at odds with the blood on her hands. "Your other rooms are so, I don't know. Expensive?" She gives a self-conscious laugh. "I guess I expected gold paint, and a flat screen TV. But this is nice. Simple."

It warms something in my chest to hear her say it. I don't tell her this "simple" studio would sell for more than half a million dollars, if I ever got rid of it.

"I'm glad you like it," I say. "This place is important to me. I come here when I need to be alone."

Sydney's soft lips purse. "Does that happen often?"

I lean against the wall by the door and consider how to answer. "More and more lately," I say. "I love my brothers, I do. But you know now how... overwhelming, they can be. Sometimes I need my own space. Away from them. From that life."

A small line forms between Sydney's brows. "Sounds lonely," she says.

"It is," I admit. "But I've been lonely for a very long time, darling. Longer than I can remember. And I don't think I realized how lonely I truly was until I met you."

She tenses at those words, shifting under the weight of them. The distance between us is suffocating me. I want to hold her. I want to touch her.

I need her in a way that I've never needed anything before.

I force myself to look away before I'm too tempted. Sydney doesn't need that from me right now. What she needs is her space. She needs time to process.

If you hold something precious too tightly, you're liable to break it.

After a long pause, Sydney finally speaks. "You wanted to talk, Alec. So... talk."

Where do I even fucking begin? I take a deep, steadying breath. "I care about you, Sydney. Deeply. And I—"

"Maybe I should talk instead," Sydney interrupts. Her eyes burn when they meet mine. "Because right now, I'm not sure I trust you, Alec. Or anything you say to me. Not when you keep lying to me."

"No." I shake my head, vehemently denying it. "I have never lied to you, Sydney. Not once. Not ever."

"You have," she insists. "Lies of omission are *still* lies, Alec. And you've been lying since the first day we met. About your name. About who you are. Lying to me about your brothers."

"Darling—"

"I want the truth, Alec," Sydney says in a hard voice. "I want your full honesty, with no more lies. If you can't give that to me, if you can't *promise* me that, then what we have together? It's not going to work."

I hold her gaze and know she means it.

"I only wanted to protect you," I say, hoping she can hear the truth in my voice. "I didn't want to scare you away, before..."

Before I could convince you to love me, I almost say.

Sydney shakes her head, jaw tight. "You don't get to make those choices for me. You don't get to lie to me and pretend you know best."

You would have left, I want to argue. *If you knew everything, you never would have stayed.* But I don't say that to her. I hold my hands up, palms out, in defeat.

"No more lies," I promise. "Whatever you want to know, darling, it's yours."

"Why did you keep Viper from me?" she asks.

There are so many reasons, many of them stained in blood. But if she wants the truth, here is as good a place to start as any.

"I didn't want to scare you," I tell her. "And I ... I didn't want him to hurt you."

It's an effort not to look at the wound on her lip as I say it. At the cuts on her hand.

"Because he hurts people?" Sydney asks. "Because he's dangerous?"

I nod.

"Sebastian told me you're all dangerous." Her voice drops as she says it, her gaze falling to the carpet. She wraps her arms around herself in a defensive hug, clutching her elbows. "All of you."

It's not until she looks up at me, expectant, that I realize it's a question.

"Anyone can be dangerous under the right circumstances," I say carefully.

"That's not—" Sydney shakes her head angrily. "*Honesty*, Alec! For once, just be honest with me!"

I'm going to lose her. My heart feels like it's gripped in a vise as that realization sets in. I might have already lost her.

"We are." My voice is so soft even I barely hear it. "Sebastian told you the truth."

She swallows hard.

"Do you hurt people?" she asks.

"Sydney—"

She cuts me off with a fierce glare. "Yes or no, Alec. Have you ever killed someone?"

I don't answer right away. I want to lie. I want to twist the truth until it's more palatable. Something I think she can handle. But I promised her.

Slowly, oh so slowly, I nod.

"Yes." The words are heavy. Weighed down by years of difficult choices. "I've killed people."

Maybe honesty is just as damning as deception. Sydney flinches at my words, hugging herself tighter, and I think this is it—this is how I lose her. This is how I break the most precious thing in my life.

But staring at her now, at the blood on her knuckles, I can't help but remember the first time I saw her, my woman in red. How my first impression of her was so wrong. Sydney is not the meek, breakable thing she pretends to be.

I'm not the only one here who's lying.

"Does that bother you?" I ask, straightening from the wall and moving closer to her.

"Yes!" She hisses the word when she says it, gripping herself tighter. "Of course that bothers me!"

I step closer. She's angry. So angry.

But it's not all directed at me. And under that anger... is *guilt.*

There are marks on her arms from where she's holding herself, the flesh around her fingers white with the force of it. And there's a flicker of emotion in her eyes I recognize.

When I'm close enough to touch her, I reach out to cup her face. She doesn't flinch.

"You wanted honesty, Sydney," I murmur. "Do me the courtesy of granting me the same. Does it really bother you?"

Sydney blinks.

"I..." Her gaze drops.

"Honesty, Red." I remind her, my thumb tracing her cheek.

"It should!" The words burst out of her. She takes a gasping breath. "It has to, doesn't it? It has to bother me. Because... because it makes you evil. People who hurt others, they... they're evil."

But she's not arguing with me. She's arguing with herself.

"I don't want that sort of violence in my life, Alec," Sydney tells me, shaking her head. "I promised myself that—"

She stops, snapping her mouth closed.

"What did you promise yourself, darling?" I ask.

"I promised myself I wouldn't be that person." She won't

look at me when she says it. "That I wouldn't be that violent person anymore."

When she finally meets my gaze, her eyes are devastatingly sad.

"I'm the reason my parents are dead. Did you know that?" she asks. "If I hadn't gotten in yet another fight at school. If they hadn't been forced to come pick me up. If I hadn't decided to scream at them in the car, tell them I *hate* them? They would still be alive. But I couldn't keep from escalating an already bad situation because of this...rage I have inside me. And it cost me *everything*."

I open my mouth to argue. "Sweetheart—"

"If you say it wasn't my fault, I will leave right now, and you will never see me again," Sydney warns.

I close my mouth and say nothing. But her pain is a palpable thing between us, tugging at my heart.

She pauses to take a breath. "I promised myself that I would never be that person again. And then Chase... with Chase, I could finally prove that I wasn't that person anymore. I could *fit* with someone. And even when things got bad with him, I *proved* that I had control over my anger. That I didn't have to fight back."

"Sydney, I—" My thumb strokes her cheek again, but Sydney jerks away from me. She takes a few steps away, putting distance between us, and turning her back on me.

"And you think you can just ask me if it *bothers me?* Does it bother me that you've killed people? Hurt people?" She shakes her head. "I don't want this violence in my life. And I've worked so hard to move past it. And now... now you've ruined it, you know that? You and your fucking brothers. *You've ruined it.*"

Her shoulders shake when she says it. I want more than

anything to hold her. To comfort her. I reach out for her without thinking, but stop myself, letting my hand fall to my side.

Instead, I stand there and watch as she curls in over herself, whispering so softly I almost don't hear it. "Bad things happen when I get angry, Alec."

"Bad things happen when I get angry, too," I tell her.

She doesn't say anything to that. Just hugs herself tighter.

"I don't want to lose you, darling." That's another lie. I don't know if I can stand losing her. I don't know if I could survive it. "If this is too much for you... it can be just the two of us. If that's what you need, we can do that. If my brothers are the problem, if Viper is too much—"

She flinches at the mention of his name, and my heart shatters. For the first time in my life, I hate my brothers just a little. I hate that they might be the reason she leaves me.

"Please," I plead. "I can't lose you."

But it's happening already. She's retreating, curling in over herself, her arms wrapped around herself so tight she's sure to bruise.

I take a panicked step closer, desperate to be near her. "I know he scared you. But we can keep him away. We can—"

"That's not—" Sydney shakes her head. "Him scaring me wasn't the problem, Alec."

Of course not. It's so much worse than that. He *hurt* her. He showed her how violent we really are, the darkest side of all of us. Made her relive some sort of fucked up trauma she has with her own anger. "I can send him away," I promise, reaching for her. "You'll never have to see him again."

"Alec—"

"We can keep him away from you. Sebastian knows how to handle him. We can—"

"I liked it!" she cries out, turning back toward me. "I liked it, okay?"

She doesn't look at me when she says it, staring at the ground next to me instead, and I let my hands fall back to my sides in shock.

Sydney takes a hysterical breath, more like a sob. There are tears in her eyes, and when she blinks, they spill out and over her cheeks. "He put a knife..." She stops and swallows hard. "He *bit* me, Alec, and I ... I liked it."

My heart beats hard in my chest. Once. Twice. Thrice. Three full heartbeats before I realize what she's really saying. Before I understand.

"You liked it," I say softly. "You... you wanted him."

Sydney takes a quick step back and turns away from me, distancing herself.

No. I surge forward into her space, taking her face in my hands, needing her to look at me.

It's not just me. It's not just me she's fallen for.

"You don't want me to keep him from you, do you, Red?" My voice is raspy. Hungry. "Any of them?"

Sydney shakes her head, still refusing to meet my eyes. "I know it makes me sick, but—"

"You have no idea, do you?" My voice is thick with awe when I say it. "You have no idea what a wonderful creature you are?" I trace my finger over her cheek, gathering the tears there, marveling at this beautiful queen before me. Made for us.

She looks at me then, and her eyes are so beautiful, sparkling with tears.

"You can have it," I promise her, brushing her tears away when they fall. "All of us. And we'll give you everything. We will give you the fucking world if you ask for it."

My brothers have always been a part of me. The best and the worst parts. And this beautiful woman?

She wants all of it.

"I could make you a queen," I promise her, meaning every word.

She draws in a quick breath, staring at me in shock.

"Why?" she breathes. "Why me?"

There are so many reasons. Everything I learn about her leaves me wanting more.

"When did you know?" I ask her. "When did you know you wanted to open your own store?"

Sydney's so shocked by the question, she almost laughs. She blinks a few times, considering.

"Way back in high school. After my parents died, I... I spent a lot of time at Jade's," she says. Her lips quirk up into the ghost of a smile. "I'd just hang out and read, and she ... she would bake things for us. I think it started as a joke. Our little shop, just for the two of us. But then... the more we talked about it, the more it became real."

Another tear slides down her cheek, and this time, I duck my head down to kiss it away, tasting her salt on my tongue.

"And you made it happen," I say, lips against her skin.

"It wasn't easy," Sydney whispers. Her gaze is distant as she remembers it. "And it took all of my savings, everything I had left over from my inheritance. But... we did it. I did it."

I know all of this, of course. I know from Sebastian's research how long she spent planning it, how many business electives she took during her degree. I know the name of the bank manager who granted them their first business loan.

I know how hard she worked to build an empire of her own.

My beautiful queen.

"You want to know why I care about you, Sydney?" I ask her.

Slowly, she nods.

"Because you're smart. Angry. Ambitious. Because you had

a dream and you made it happen." I thread my fingers through her hair while I say it. "You remind me of me, do you know that?"

Speechless, Sydney shakes her head.

"For a while, I think I mistook my fascination with wanting to save you. Protect you," I admit.

"And now?" she asks.

"Now I think you're something that I've been missing. Something I want in my life more than I've wanted anything." I stare down at her, willing her to see the truth in my face. "I can't stop thinking about you. Wondering what you're doing. Wondering what you're thinking. You've consumed me, heart, body, and soul. I'm yours."

She wants to believe me. I can see it in her eyes. She wants this, all of this.

And all she needs to do is take it.

"I care about you too much to let you run away from who you are. To let you run away from *us*." My fingers flex in her hair, just enough to tilt her face toward me. "I'm addicted to you. Your dark and your light."

She swallows, and something in her eyes shifts. She's so close. So close to being mine.

To being ours.

"So what will you do, Red?" I ask. "Will you run away from us, knowing we'll chase you?"

And I will. I'll chase her to the ends of the Earth if I have to.

"I'm so tired of running," Sydney whispers. Her body relaxes as she says it. She blinks, and a fresh tear slides down her face as she reaches up to grab the back of my neck, fingers playing with my hair.

"Tell me what you need. Anything. And it's yours." I promise her.

I watch her consider it. Watch as she weighs the dark and the light.

"You," Sydney answers, finally. "I need you."

And then she pulls my mouth down to hers and claims me with an earth-shattering kiss.

50

I'm so sick of pretending. Sick of running from what I want. From who I am.

Alec's kiss tastes like everything I've ever denied myself. His fingers flex in my hair when he deepens our kiss, his tongue rolling over mine.

He moans when he lifts me, hands firm and hard where they grip my legs, as he carries me to his bed.

God, he's so beautiful. I stare at him in awe when he breaks our kiss, losing myself in his dark eyes. Alec lowers me on top of his bedspread, body dominating mine as he crawls on top of me, before kissing me again, his tongue savaging my mouth.

But when he presses too hard against my swollen lip and I flinch, everything changes.

Alec stills, his lips hovering over mine, his body lifting just a fraction, so he's no longer pressing me hard against the mattress. The next kiss is hesitant. Sweet and soft.

Far too soft.

He's holding back. I grip his shoulders tighter, pulling him against me, but the lips that press against my neck are barely a whisper against my skin. His hands are so gentle as they glide over my ribs, barely touching the fabric of my dress.

Like he's scared of hurting me. Scared of frightening me away, even now.

"Stop," I whisper.

Those hands stop moving. Alec's dark eyes find mine. He waits patiently, his face unreadable.

"I... I want it like before," I say, wriggling against the mattress. "I want it rough."

Alec is perfectly still as he considers me, muscles tense.

"Are you sure, Sydney?" he asks.

When I nod, something like victory flashes in his eyes. He shifts, spreading his knees a little further on the bedspread. Then his mouth is on mine, his tongue is slipping between my lips, and the hand that grips my ribs is anything but gentle.

I gasp when he bites down, teeth sharp against my bottom lip, and it's not just the pain, and it's not just the sensation that has me arching up against him, hips grinding into his body. It's the memory of Viper doing this same thing, the memory of him pressing a blood-covered thumb against my tongue.

"More!" I gasp as Alec moves down my jaw, licking and biting at the sensitive skin of my neck.

His hands are rough now, clawing at me, gripping me. There's a sound of tearing fabric as he grabs my dress and pulls.

"Is this what you want?" Alec's voice is a dark rasp as he tears my shredded dress off me, tossing it aside. My bra is next, practically torn from my body.

"I want *you*, Alec," I pant. "I want—"

I gasp as he bends down and takes my nipple in his mouth, his teeth rough against my flesh. I reach down to grab his hair, tugging at it as he bites down again. It hurts, a sharp jolt of pain.

And I love it.

"Roll over, darling," Alec says, releasing my nipple. When I don't comply fast enough, lost in a haze of sensation, Alec lets out a sound like a growl and grabs me by my hips, flipping me onto my stomach.

Oh fuck.

"Look at you," Alec says. There's awe in his voice as he says it, like he's admiring a work of art. He runs his hand down the small of my back and grabs my ass, fingers digging into my flesh. "Perfection."

His hand moves to the nape of my neck, and he grips it, pinning me to the mattress with one hand as he pulls my underwear off.

"You want it rough, darling?" Alec asks in a gruff voice, letting go of my neck. "You want *me?*"

I gasp at the sound of him removing his belt. Alec moves until he's straddling my back, one knee on either side of my hips, and grabs my hand.

In a practiced movement, Alec loops the belt over my wrist, then grabs my other hand and does the same, tightening the leather until it almost hurts.

He presses my bound wrists against the mattress above my head, threading the belt through his bed frame and securing it in place with a hard yank. Then he leans down until his lips brush the back of my neck.

"You look so good like this. Tied up for me to use."

I moan, writhing against the mattress. A moment later, I feel his hand snake down my back, over the curve of my ass, dipping between my thighs.

With one hand on my neck, holding me in place, he slips his fingers into me.

My scream is muffled by the bed as he fucks me hard with his fingers.

"Who do you belong to, darling?" Alec asks. There's a dark edge to his voice that makes me tremble.

I can't think. I can't move. My world has narrowed to the wonderfully dirty things his fingers are doing to me.

"Answer me, Sydney."

"You," I gasp. I raise my hips as far as I can off the mattress, gasping every time his fingers enter me.

"Are you *mine*, Sydney?" His voice is rough. "Or *ours?*"

His fingers thrust hard inside of me. The words tumble out of my mouth without thought, without reason.

"All of yours!" I gasp.

And I mean it.

I want all of them. Alec, my dark prince. Ashton, my sweet friend. Sebastian, my vicious protector.

Maybe even Viper.

I don't even think when I say it, don't even consider that it might not be what he wants to hear. But Alec groans his approval, his fingers thrusting into me harder.

"That's right, darling. You're all ours."

God, I'm so close. I pull against the belt holding my wrists and arch against the mattress, wanting more.

With a cruel laugh, Alec pulls his fingers from me, depriving me of my release. He shifts further down the bed, moving until he's between my legs. Then he presses those same fingers into my mouth, forcing them as far in as he can get them.

"That's our fucking girl," he says. The deliciously thick head of his cock presses against my entrance, rubbing against me, before he forces himself inside.

It's impossible to scream around the fingers invading my mouth. The noises I make are garbled and warped as he starts to fuck me.

"You were made for us, darling," Alec grunts. His pace is fast and rough and exactly what I want from him. He slams into me, words punctuated by his hard thrusts.

"All." Thrust. "Fucking." Thrust. "Four." Thrust. "Of us."

Light explodes behind my eyes as I come, my body arching against Alec's as my muscles go almost painfully tense. With a guttural curse, he follows me, burying himself entirely inside me and filling me with his release.

I should be mortified. When Alec pulls his fingers from my mouth, a trail of drool follows, and I notice that I've drooled a small spot on his sheets. My makeup must be a mess, my mascara smeared over my face.

I can't seem to bring myself to care as I pant for breath, every nerve in my body fuzzy and satisfied.

"Are you okay?" Alec's voice is breathless. But his hands are unfathomably gentle as he carefully undoes the belt still wrapped around my wrists. He leans over my back, cock still buried inside of me, and softly kisses the inside of each wrist.

I nod, head heavy against the bedsheets.

"Use your words, darling. I need to hear it."

"I'm okay," I mumble.

Alec grunts in acknowledgement. He pulls out of me slowly, inch by inch, before sliding off me.

"Stay right here," Alec tells me. "I'm getting you some water."

This time, apparently, I don't need to answer out loud. The mattress dips and rises as Alec rolls off the bed.

I feel like I'm floating. With a soft groan, I roll over onto my back. I'm sore all over. My lips, my hand, my wrists. Lower, I feel stretched from his cock. But the pain feels oddly pleasant.

I *like* it, I realize.

Alec returns with a glass of water, lifting my head up off the bed so he can hold it for me while I drink.

"That's it, that's my girl," he murmurs, as I swallow. "You did so well. I'm so proud of you."

My God, this man. The praise makes me arch against the

mattress, wanting even more, and Alec's lips twitch into a smile as he takes the glass from me and sets it on the bedside table.

"Come here," Alec says as he lies down next to me. He pulls me toward him until my head is resting on his shoulder, our limbs intertwined. We lay there like that, curled up together, content. Happy.

"Stay the night with me," Alec says, tracing his finger down the curve of my back. "Please."

I lift my head to look at him. He looks vulnerable after he says it. Like I'll break his heart if I leave. Like he needs this. Needs me.

My lips curve into a small smile, and I nod. "Okay. I can stay."

"Earl can drive you home early tomorrow," he tells me. His hand goes to my thigh then, pinning me open. His fingers dip between my legs and gather up the cum that has dripped out of me. I gasp when he uses his fingers to push all of it back inside.

"I want you to keep this in you," Alec says, pushing his fingers in even deeper. "I want to spend all day at work tomorrow knowing I'm still inside you."

My pussy throbs at the words, clenching around his fingers, and I lick my lips before I nod.

With a satisfied grunt, Alec removes his fingers and reaches over me to grab my panties, sliding them back over my legs and onto my body. I reach for my dress to cover myself, before remembering it's ruined. When I hold it up, the front is torn nearly in half.

Unwearable.

"You don't happen to have a shirt I could wear to bed, do you?" I ask coyly. "Since you destroyed my clothes?"

Alec doesn't even do me the courtesy of looking ashamed. He chuckles, taking the ruined dress from my hands and tossing it aside. "The closet over there," he gestures toward the back of the room, farthest from the door. "Take anything you'd like."

I feel his eyes on me as I slip off the bed and walk to the door. Devouring me.

I shouldn't be surprised that the closet is a walk-in. Rows of suits and dress shirts line the walls, carefully hung on wooden hangers. I run my hands over the sleeves, luxuriating in the feel of the fabrics, before settling on a soft white dress shirt with a starched collar.

He said I could take anything, right?

The shirt goes almost to my knees when I put it on, and after I've buttoned it, I turn to leave.

But...

I wiggle my bare toes against the hardwood floor. Surely, *anything* also extends to a pair of socks, right?

A small dresser sits in the back of the closet, nestled beneath a row of meticulously arranged ties. Something tells me Alec is the sort of man to own cashmere socks, and I'm not passing up the opportunity to wear a pair.

I step forward and open the top drawer, admiring the detailing on the ornate brass handles. To my surprise, inside I don't find socks or underwear or any clothing at all.

What I find are documents.

I move to close it, but the photograph on top of the stack of papers immediately catches my eye. Four adolescent boys stare back at me from the dark of the drawer, and though I instantly recognize Ash's wide, white grin, it takes me a moment to realize the dark-skinned, brooding boy his arm is flung around is Alec.

I lift the photo carefully out of the dresser, only touching the edges to avoid getting fingerprints on the glossy surface.

Alec couldn't be more than fourteen in this photo, arms crossed, face defiant as he stares at the camera. He looks so angry, and for a moment, I feel an intimate connection with this angry boy.

Photos of me from this age look the same.

Beside him, Ashton grins without a care in the world. But... no. When I look closer, even though the image is blurry and old, I can see a faint bruise darkening one eye. And his smile is strained. Just a little too tight.

Ashton's other arm is around another boy, short and lanky, and it's the glasses I recognize first. In all those years, Sebastian never changed the style of glasses he wears.

Unlike his brothers, Sebastian stares at the ground, not the camera, his hands shoved awkwardly in his pockets. He's younger than they are, maybe twelve, and yet to hit the growth spurt that will end with him being taller than either of them. He looks unfinished.

And sad. So very sad.

There's one final boy in the photo, shuffled off to the side, like he can't stand to be touched.

The scar above Viper's eye is more pronounced in the photograph than it is now. It cuts through his eyebrow and part of his forehead, healed but not yet faded. And he's painfully thin. There's no sign of the terrifyingly large man I met for those brief moments in this young boy.

Viper isn't staring at the ground, or even at the camera. His eyes are focused on something else, out of frame, his face carefully blank.

Above them all, a sign.

Fortune City Orphanage for Wayward Boys.

My heart clenches. I remember this place from the news. It burned down five years ago, though luckily no one was inside at the time. The building had been abandoned, after a new orphanage had been built. Funded by the Sterling Children's Foundation.

No wonder they're so close. No wonder they love each other like brothers. They grew up together. They probably had no one else but the four of them.

It makes me love them all a little more. Four boys with no families who made their own.

Smiling and a little misty-eyed, I set the photograph on the top of the dresser and look into the drawer at the next one.

They're older now, Alec and Ashton. Men, not boys. This one is a Polaroid, with white lining the edges and bottom, and this time Alec is smiling at the camera. The anger from his youth is there but dulled. He looks happy.

The woman squeezed between Alec and Ash—the woman Ashton is kissing on the cheek—looks happy, too.

A wave of jealousy threatens to rise inside of me, and I fight to push it down.

She's beautiful. Skin so pale it's milk white, with sharp gray eyes and high cheekbones. She looks like a model. It occurs to me that she could be one.

She isn't smiling at the camera. But there's a hint of a smile at the corners of her mouth, and her eyes are bright and happy.

I have no right to feel jealous of her. He told me, didn't he? Or at least implied it. He and Ashton have shared before. This must have been one of their girlfriends.

I reach into the drawer to lift this one out and get a closer look, but something slides off the photograph and falls to the floor as I do, clattering against the wood at my feet. Curious, I bend down and pick it up.

It's a golden ring, too large to belong to a woman.

A wedding ring.

I stare at it between my fingers, not comprehending what I've found. It's only when I go to put them both back in the drawer that I see it. The document the photo was hiding.

It's a wedding certificate.

My stomach drops.

Mason Alexander Sterling and Annika Basso.

"Did you get lost?" Alec's amused voice startles me.

I turn, catching the flicker of surprise when he sees the ring in my hand.

"Sorry," I laugh, though it comes out hollow. "I was looking for socks, and found some photos and I—"

There's something strange in his expression as he watches me. His face goes blank. Guarded.

I set the ring back in the drawer, my gaze lingering on the names. Mason Alexander Sterling and Annika Basso.

"I didn't realize you were married before," I say looking back at the woman in the Polaroid. I give the photo a soft smile. "She's beautiful."

Alec doesn't say anything.

"When did you divorce?" I ask.

It takes him so long to answer I almost repeat the question.

"We didn't," he says.

There's a sharp note of pain in his voice when he says it, and for a moment, my heart breaks for him. He's so young to be a widower. I look up to offer my condolences and stop.

Yes, there's pain in Alec's face, but there's so much more there.

Fear.

The truth hits me like a punch to the gut.

"You're still married," I whisper.

The room tilts. My hand clenches without me realizing, crushing the photo in my fist.

All at once, the pieces come together in my mind, and I realize just how stupid I've been.

Of course he's married. How did I not see it before? The hotel rooms. The secrecy. Dining together away from the public, away from prying eyes. This is why I've never seen his home, isn't it? The one he shares with all his brothers?

I'm not Alec's girlfriend at all.

I'm his mistress.

"Tell me I'm wrong." My voice is weak and fragile as glass. "Tell me I'm wrong, Alec."

He flinches.

"It's complicated," he says.

Rage. Hot, blinding rage fills me.

"It's not *complicated!*" I shout at him. "Tell me! Are you married?"

There's a long beat of silence before he answers.

"Yes."

He says more, trying to explain, trying to justify it, but I can't hear him. There's a ringing in my ears, and my breaths are too loud. My pulse is thundering in my skull.

I drop the photograph and shove past him, out of the closet.

"Sydney, you don't understand," Alec swears, reaching for me. "It's not what you think. Wait, I—"

"Don't fucking touch me!" I shriek, jerking away.

Alec freezes, arm still outstretched.

My things, where are my things? I'm going to be sick. I'm going to scream.

"Please, let me explain," he pleads.

"There's no explaining this." My hands shake as I grab my purse. The door—where's the damn door?

I tug on the door twice before realizing it's locked. As I fumble with the deadbolt, Alec steps closer.

"Darling, I—"

My whole body goes cold.

"Don't you dare call me that. I'm not your darling," I say in a voice that doesn't sound like my own. I turn to meet his gaze, hate in my eyes. "And don't you ever contact me again."

I yank the door open, and he moves forward as if to stop me.

"If you follow me, I will scream," I warn, voice deadly calm. "Let's see you explain to your shareholders why you have a woman in your apartment. A woman who isn't *your wife*."

Alec's eyes darken.

"You wouldn't," he says.

The laugh that escapes me is almost inhuman. I sound like a monster. "You have no idea what I would do, *Mason*. Or what I'm capable of."

And then I leave him there, slamming the door behind me.

51

SYDNEY

I'm so stupid.

My vision is blurry from the tears in my eyes, and even after I scrub my face with the sleeve of Alec's dress shirt, I can't seem to clear it.

So, so stupid. I knew it. I knew from the start that it was too good to be true. I knew something was off.

It's not until I reach the first floor and see the look of shock on the doorman's face that I realize how I must look. Makeup ruined, my bag clasped against my chest, wearing nothing but a man's dress shirt.

"Ma'am?" the doorman says uncertainly. "Do you need assistance?"

I don't answer him. I can't. I race outside, clutching my bag and letting the door shut behind me.

What am I even doing? Where am I going? It's late, too late to be outside wearing nothing but a shirt, to be trapped in a part of the city I'm not familiar with, to be—

"Miss Sinclair?"

I look up, startled by the voice. Earl is sitting on the bumper of Alec's town car, reading a book.

He looks from me to the door of Alec's building and back again before sliding off the car and slipping the book into his pocket.

"Do you need to get out of here?" he asks.

Yes. I do. I need to be anywhere but here. But when he moves toward the back of the car to open the door for me, I hesitate.

"I don't want to get you in trouble with—" I stop, a fresh wave of pain cresting over me. I can't even say his name. I can't even think it.

Earl gives me an assessing look. "Miss Sinclair, I doubt very much I would get in trouble for giving you a ride. But if I were to leave you in this state without offering to drive you home?" He chuckles. "Mr. Sterling would probably kill me for that."

He might, I think. He's killed before.

"Thank you," I say, tugging nervously on the sleeve of Alec's dress shirt. "Sorry to inconvenience you."

"It's not a bother at all." Earl gives me a kind smile as he holds the door open for me. "There's tissues under the cushion in the middle seat—you just need to give it a lift. And I have bottled water up front if you need some."

I shake my head. "Thank you, but... I just want to go home."

"I can do that for you, ma'am."

When I slide into the back seat, pulling the shirt down as far as I can to cover myself, Earl looks away to give me my privacy.

Then the door closes, and I'm trapped in the backseat with nothing but my pain and the ghost of Alec's voice.

I could make you a queen.

He could, too. Alec has the money and power to give a girl

anything she could ever ask for. Anything I could ever dream of.

You already have a queen, I think furiously, wiping my face on my sleeve. *You should be giving her the world, not me...*

I'm such an idiot. And I knew. From the very first day, I knew I should have been more careful, should have been cautious with him. With them. It was all too good to be true.

Now I'm nothing but another home-wrecker.

My phone rings, loud and impatient in my purse, and I jump, startled by the noise. I pull it out, noticing for the first time how much I'm shaking. My fingers are trembling.

When I look at the caller ID, I'm shocked enough by the caller listed there that I can't bring myself to answer. The call rings out. My phone goes dark, but then it rings again immediately, the same name displayed on the screen.

This time I answer.

"Katie?" I ask, apprehension thick, answering on speaker phone. I don't think my hands are steady enough to hold it right now.

"Hey," she says. She sounds tired. Hesitant.

There's a long beat of silence.

"Why are you calling me?" I ask. My voice is surprisingly steady. As if my heart hadn't just been ripped out of my chest. "If you're trying to apologize for that horrible set up, spare me. I can't believe you would put me in that position—"

"I'm not calling about that," Katie says quickly. "Look, things got out of hand, whatever, I get it. But that's not..." There's a pause while she takes a shuddering breath. "Chase is in the hospital, Sydney. Someone nearly beat him to death today. He's not doing well. You need to come down here."

I don't process the words right away, my mind skipping over them. "He's... what?" I finally manage to say. "Wait, what happened?"

"I have no idea!" Katie's voice is shrill as it echoes in the car. "He was on his way home from work and...someone just jumped him, I guess? He was unconscious when he was brought in, so we don't know all the details yet." I can tell she's near tears, her voice frantic and close to breaking.

How the hell did that happen? Chase works in a relatively safe part of town. He's never been super flashy with his money or the way he dresses. For a moment—just one fleeting moment—I feel the urge to go to him. Like I should rush to the hospital to be by his side.

And then another thought snares me, tight as a noose. I don't actually care what happened to him. I don't actually care that he's hurt.

After all the pain he caused me? I'm almost happy to hear it.

I stare at the reflection of myself in the car's dark, tinted windows, lights blurring behind my image as we drive through the city. This will irrevocably break my friendship with Katie. With Sarah, with all of them, really. There will be no going back after this.

But after everything I've been through with Chase, I can't be his support system anymore. I can't even wish him well.

I want him to suffer, I realize.

"I'm not coming," I say with renewed strength in my voice. The reflection of me doesn't seem to move as I say it. She just stares back at me, face a cold, calm mask.

"Excuse me, what did you just say?" Katie asks. She sounds horrified. Like I just blasphemed in the most disgusting, vile way possible.

"He's not a part of my life anymore, Katie. I don't want him to be. Call his parents. Go there yourself, have Lance hold his hand and look after him for a while. But I'm *not* going to go see him."

All I hear is a disbelieving huff followed by a quick intake of breath, as if she's about to start arguing. But I don't need to hear it. I reach down and end the call.

With that, I realize I'm ready to shut the door on Chase, Katie, Sarah, the whole group...and most importantly, that version of myself.

She's gone. I left her behind on the floor of my bathroom, splintered into a thousand pieces, with no hope of being put back together.

Now it's up to me to figure out who I actually am.

52

DANTE

There's a stillness that hangs in the air before a storm. A nervous quiet, like nature itself is holding its breath.

I live for that moment. The anticipation of ruin.

I lean back against the scratchy fabric of the waiting-room chair and feel that anticipation brewing, heralding the coming storm. A storm that has been building for years.

Two photos sit on the table before me, one clipped from a newspaper several years past and one from the recent style section of a magazine.

The pictures show the same woman.

I pick up the newspaper clipping, giving it my full attention.

She's younger, in this one, standing in front of a cheap folding table that's piled high with sugary treats. She smiles at the camera a little awkwardly. Almost like she's shy.

She's flanked by two people. A pretty Asian woman on her right, with bright colored hair and a big, toothy grin. And a man on her left, his arm looped possessively around her waist,

The caption reads: **Local business owners Jade and**

Sydney—pictured with her significant other, Chase —join many others in celebrating the success of Fortune City School District's annual bake sale.

I run my finger over her name, my fingers smudging the ink. Sydney.

The next picture is my favorite.

Her hair is longer. It's a candid pic, and the photographer captured her mid-laugh. She looks beautiful. Elegant.

But I'm not looking at her, I'm looking at the man she's pictured dancing with.

Mason Alexander Sterling.

The pain in my leg flares to an inferno as I stare at his image.

I haven't seen him in years. Not since the bastard tried to walk away from my organization, taking three of my best assets with him. Not since one of them tried to kill me.

I barely made it out alive that night. And while I was gone, they took everything. My organization. My money. My power. My life's work, blown to pieces by two gunshots.

They took *everything.* And it took years for me to crawl my way back up from the bottom and finally take back what's mine.

They think they've won. They think they've buried me, left me and my business behind them. But you don't leave my organization. There's no retirement plan, no escape. You're in it until you die.

The day Mason Sterling and his so-called brothers took off, he signed his death warrant. But he's been untouchable. Too powerful for me to take down, even with the weight of my organization building behind me. And he's never had a weakness, other than his fucking brothers. Never had something I could exploit.

Until now.

Mason Sterling and friend, the caption reads, **at last evening's Sterling Charity Banquet**.

Friend.

The photographer who captured this image was good. Real good. They had a real talent for capturing the emotions behind the picture.

With Mason's fingers gently touching her arm, his head tilted toward Sydney as they waltz across the dance floor, it's impossible to miss the look in his eyes.

Mason Sterling is a man in love.

And I can't wait to take it away from him.

I toss the magazine back onto the table and lean further back in my chair. My back twinges as I settle in, the pain flaring in my leg again. I ignore it.

A voice cuts through the quiet of the empty room. Patient visiting hours ended hours ago. "He's awake."

I glance across the room to Annika, standing rigid by the hospital room door. My Annika, the spitting image of her mother.

The newspaper clipping is still lying on my thigh, and I tap it, fingernail sharp against the figure standing next to Sterling's woman. The woman with bright hair.

"Find this one," I order.

She doesn't answer when she takes the clipping from me, eyes scanning the woman in the image. But I know she'll obey. Loyal until the very end, my Annika.

It hurts to stand. Everything hurts now. I lean heavily on my cane as I rise, letting the worst of the pain pass before I head to the hospital room.

The man laid out in the hospital bed is barely conscious. His face is still swollen from the beating, his skin mottled with angry purple and red bruises. I've seen his file, and I know that isn't even the worst of it. He has three broken ribs, and a partially ruptured spleen that almost killed him.

But most importantly, he has a grudge. One I can use.

"Good evening, Mr. Levine." I approach his bedside with smooth, deliberate steps, despite the pain. You learn to keep up the appearances. You learn to let the pain fuel you from the inside out.

Chase's head lulls against the pillow as he looks toward me. His eyes narrow suspiciously. "Do I know you?"

"No. But you will." I smile at him. "I have a proposition for you. One I think you'll quite like."

THE END

WANT MORE?

Sydney's story will continue in Dangerous Thoughts, Fortune City Mafia book two

If you enjoy dark fantasy, be sure to check out The Broken Blade trilogy, starting with The Queen's Blade

For release announcements, sneak peeks, and bonus content visit our website at evelyn-ward.com and follow us on social media:

instagram.com/evelynwardbooks

tiktok.com/@evelyn.ward.books

amazon.com/stores/Evelyn-Ward/author/B0D932HHG9

facebook.com/328082750395931

ABOUT THE AUTHOR (...S)

We're sorry to tell you, dear reader, that Evelyn Ward does not exist.

The real authors of this book are two best friends. As always, we will call them M and K.

K is a resident of New York City where she works in advertising. Her hobbies include reading and making men cry in bars.
M is a resident of Seattle where she works doing something confusing and science-y. Her hobbies include writing and getting tattoos.